HARVEST OF RUIN

ARTHUR MONGELLI

SEVERED PRESS
HOBART TASMANIA

HARVEST OF RUIN

ISBN: 978-1-925597-48-6

For my wonderful wife, Brenda, without whom, this book would never have been written. And for Freyja, my darling daughter, may the light of my eternal love always shelter you.

"Life, although it may only be an accumulation of anguish, is dear to me, and I will defend it."
-*Mary Shelley*

"Denn, die Todten reiten Schnell. (For the dead travel fast.)"
-*Bram Stoker*

HARVEST OF RUIN

Chicago, Illinois, Early 21st century

"Why would it be dangerous? We're talking about a number of substances that have all been approved for use in foods."

"But has the appropriate effort been put into looking at the effects these substances have in combination? I mean, it's not as if we are talking about one or two things here, it's not sugar and flour, you know, not like making a cake. We are talking about cattle that have been pumped with growth hormones and antibiotics, and now we are going to change their feed to introduce wheat and corn. Grains that have been genetically altered to grow larger and faster, all while being infused with pesticides and who knows whatever else they do to it."

"Look. The bottom line here is that the FDA says it's okay. It will cut overhead by nearly fifteen percent. You know how much that means to our bottom line?"

"I still think we need to evaluate it further. You know as well as I do that the FDA is a political machine. Just think about the potential for lawsuits if something were to happen."

"As I said earlier, the Board's decision is final: we are making the shift to genetically improved corn in the feed. It's the responsibility of the FDA to regulate this stuff. If they say it's okay to use and it suits our purpose, we use it. Listen, Phillip, I know that your concerns are coming from a good place, I do. But you are the COO of one of the biggest commercial meat packers in the country. We just can't afford – our clients can't afford – the prices of non-GMO feed. We cannot survive without the contracts we have; we can't risk them shifting to our competitors. Dissent is a dangerous thing here, Phil, and we need a united front to instill confidence in the shareholders. I suggest you drop this now, before I have to speak with the Board about it."

Tim DeMott clicked the key into the off position as Laura, his wife, unbuckled their toddler in the back seat. As the engine sputtered and chunked to a stop, Tim stepped out into the chill air of autumn. He stretched broadly before moving to the rear of the car to unload the stroller and diaper bag from the trunk. Little Luna was fast asleep. She normally did not wake well; thankfully, she was in good temperament today as Laura jostled her awake, pulling the little girl out into the overcast October air. The little girl had just celebrated her second birthday a few weeks prior. Laura plopped the wriggling, stretching girl into the awaiting stroller, and with Tim locking the car via key, the three started moving down the promenade that led to the bridge.

The DeMotts had spent the last two days camping at Riverview campsites and hiking around Lake Minnewaska. It was a trip they had planned to do every year for their anniversary, although they skipped the prior year since Luna was too small. It was a nice reset for them as a couple. They both had stressful jobs that required them to be on-call, both overnight as well as on weekends. Taking vacations was the only break they had to reconnect with one another. It was for this very reason that they chose to vacation in an area where there was no cell phone reception, so their employers couldn't get in touch with them, even if they wanted to. Although it was unusually cold for this time of year and Luna's nose had consistently been running, the three had a wonderful time camping. Tim and Laura held hands, sharing the duty of pushing the stroller as they walked along the promenade towards the water.

Passing underneath a banner indicating that today was the Fourth Annual Green/Ecology Festival, they proceeded past a series of small crowds gathered around a variety of vendor booths distributing pamphlets. Displays of composting, sawdust toilets, and alternative energies were being showcased; one even had a twelve-foot-tall windmill setup, powering their booth. It was the kind of thing that they normally would be into checking out; today, however, they were purpose driven to get across the walkway and back without a Luna-meltdown, so they edged around the crowds. The earth to either side of the walkway began to fall away as they continued along, eventually dropping off completely. A hundred feet below them, they could see railroad tracks that ran along the river and the Hudson River itself, wide and powerful as it swept southwards towards New York City and the Atlantic beyond. The view was dizzying, and although the wind was brisk and neither of them was fond of heights, the scenery was too wonderful not to continue across. Joggers passed in their garishly colored attire, as well as cyclists and people out walking their dogs. There was even a unicyclist swerving around. Tim's heart plummeted and was certain the man atop was going to strike the handrail and plummet over the side to his death, but as inept as he seemed on the thing, he avoided that fate.

Their daughter had been asking, "What's that?" from her seat in the stroller ever since they came clear of the trees and over the top of the river. All they could see was a little hand with a pointing finger waving about. They had reconnected as a family and ignored their surroundings for the most part, enjoying each other completely. Tim and Laura held hands and had their arms around one another, something they hadn't done much of since Luna was born.

About halfway across the span, they stopped for a rest on some molded concrete benches and made sure that Luna was doing okay. Tim was breathing heavily, as he had put on some weight over the past few years. Quitting cigarettes hadn't helped for sure, and as many times as he vowed to take off the weight, it never came to fruition. He blamed the stress of the job and Laura for fixing his plates too big, but knew deep down that he needed to get off his ass more often. Laura took Luna out of the stroller, changed her diaper, and offered a breast for some milk. Laura was slender, even after childbirth, though she could eat like an ox. She was eyeballing him as he breathed.

"I'm okay," he said, steadying himself so she didn't hear him panting the words out.

"Well, let's get going then. I'd like to get off the bridge and get to lunch sometime today, old man," she replied with a wink and a smile.

They buckled Luna back into the stroller and Tim took control of it, figuring that he could rest a bit here and there while "showing" Luna some boats and such. Laura threw the dirty diaper in the bottom of the stroller and they continued on. Laura rooted around in her massive purse and slotted quarters into a telescope. They took turns looking at the few scattered boats cruising about below, even hoisting Luna, who wriggled and fussed, to have a look. About three-quarters of the way across the span, the river ended beneath them. Many ribbons of railroad tracks lay under the bridge on this side of the river followed by industrial areas. Giant fuel tanks spotted the ground below, as well as storage yards filled with metal and timbers. Tim had been somewhat of an urban explorer in his early twenties, and looking to the crowd below, he thought that it was rare to see so many people gathered in such rarely used areas.

"Are they racing?" he asked Laura.

"Huh?" Laura asked in return.

"Down below, looks like a footrace of some kind."

Laura joined him near the railing, both oblivious to the change in noises on the bridge. Sirens wailed in the distance and a far-off scream pierced the strange hush that suddenly came from the city side of the bridge ahead.

"Weird," she remarked, looking below. "If it's a race, there aren't any markers."

Tim shrugged, and after watching for a moment longer, continued walking. They were on the last leg of the trip before heading back to the car. His stomach was rumbling, and he started thinking about an omelet with hash browns and biscuits from Cracker Barrel. The industrial area below them gave way to buildings and the city proper began to unfold all around them. Tim always thought it must be strange for all the people that lived around the walkway to have people looking into their apartments and homes. As nice as it was to have a new purpose for the decaying railroad bridge, he assumed it was a curse for those who lived near it. Telephone timbers held green vinyl mesh across backyards on the left side of the walkway, some attempt at privacy from the thousands who pass by.

Luna started fussing, stopping their progress as Laura stepped in front of the stroller to attend to her, again changing her diaper.

"She shit," Laura announced.

Tim silently celebrated not having to change her. Being well-trained eight years into marriage, he quickly asked, "Want me to change her?"

"No, I got it," Laura huffed.

Tim leaned lightly on the handle of the stroller, only half-watching as his wife changed their daughter and a peace came over him. He smiled, as much as he despised his job, as much as the rest of life could suck, with arguments, bills and all the other stressful nonsense that entered into it, he felt a sense of contentment. He was truly happy with his life. Laura had finished changing Luna and wrapped the diaper up, first looking at Tim, then past him. After a moment, Tim noticed her lack of movement and looked directly at her. He saw a face splayed on her that he had never seen before, somewhere between confusion, panic, and disgust.

"Laur?" he asked quizzically.

She snapped from her reverie and grabbed the stroller. She started running towards the Poughkeepsie side with the stroller bouncing along precariously behind her. Tim, still tired and now confused, stood there with his hands splayed out. *What the fuck?* he thought.

"Tim, fucking run!" Laura screamed, her voice shrill with panic.

His first thought as he stepped forward was that the bridge was collapsing. He had a nervousness about bridges from his childhood, his fear of heights coupled with the fact that he hadn't learned to swim until he was nearly a teenager had ingrained a natural fear of bridges into him. He heard the sounds of sneakers slapping the concrete behind him and felt the breeze of something swinging past his arm. His sphincter clenched, spurring him into a white-knuckled-fist-clenching run to catch up with his family. He had no idea what was happening, and once the footsteps behind him grew distant, he finally took the opportunity to glance back. His mind reeled at what he was seeing; he couldn't believe it, and his mind refused to accept it.

Tim thought it was a terrible prank at first, seeing a zombie shambling towards him. Someone was either filming a prank show or a low-budget movie, he was sure of it. He glanced around briefly looking for a cameraman or a TV host with a microphone. The thought was dashed from his mind when the thing veered at a jogger wearing Oakley sunglasses and spandex shorts. The zombie sank its teeth deep into the man's chest. Tim knew it was not a prank. No special effects could recreate that sickening tearing of flesh and tissue. His stomach lurched and his heart sank in fear. The thing dragged the jogger, screaming, down to the concrete of the walkway. Another zombie joined the first, dropping onto all fours and starting to feast as Tim stood transfixed. The jogger fought briefly, as the two things came atop him, biting at his hands and fingers as he tried to fend them off. Tim was frozen in fear, and most likely wouldn't have intervened anyways, not with his family present and at risk.

Tim stood stock-still as the first undead sunk its mouth around the throat of the man, his final scream warbled, sounding weirdly in the morning air as the airway got pinched briefly. Then the head ripped free of the jogger, tearing out a chunk of flesh, silencing the man altogether. Gooseflesh crept up his spine as he stood, frozen, petrified. Laura grabbed him by the arm and started desperately pulling him away. It was only then that he realized she was screaming at him. He shook his head vigorously, clearing it, finally ripping his eyes from the scene in front of him. All hope faded as he looked down the bridge, back towards where their car was parked.

Scattered about the walkway were a half dozen or more of the things feasting on the remains of cyclists, pedestrians and even a Chihuahua being eaten like a corn on the cob. Tim stopped, his heart felt like it was on the verge of bursting through his chest. It took him a moment to digest his surroundings, to digest that there was a horde of flesh-eating undead separating them from their car, on the edge of a city they were unfamiliar with. A city that, Tim could now tell, would not be a refuge if they traveled the remainder of the walkway into. The sound of sirens and the smell of fire coming from ahead were good indicators that the city was experiencing some difficulties as well. A smattering of gunfire that sounded from different parts of the city told Tim that their best bet for safety lay on the other side of the bridge, in their car. Laura had stopped a few feet ahead of him and he could hear her mumbling, "Fuck, fuck, fuck" under her labored breathing.

"The car," Tim growled at her "We have to move now. Ditch the stroller and follow me closely."

He hated the idea of dragging his family back across the bridge, past those things, but he felt in his bones that it was a necessity. Laura began to protest, and half-turning, he could see that she was terrified.

"Laura!" he said, settling a stern gaze on her.

Laura just looked at him with her sad, concerned eyes.

"Move!" he shouted, knowing that his tone would make her angry, and that anger would get her moving.

Without waiting to see her reaction, Tim moved off, skirting widely around the two undead things as they gorged on the flesh of the hapless jogger. Tim glanced back to see Laura following behind, afraid that she would lose her nerve to run past the gruesome scene. Her eyes were tearing but angry, and her jaw was set in determination as she followed just a few steps behind, clutching Luna against her chest. He slowed his pace so they were aside one another and they continued along at a slow jog. Tim's breathing came in labored gasps and sucking heaves.

Against his better judgment, he advanced on the next undead they came upon. The thing was busily eating the innards of a cyclist, and paid him no attention as he edged in close. The thing was so intent on devouring the coils of intestines it pulled through a rough-edged wound on the stomach of the shirtless man that Tim stood within arm's reach without drawing its attention. He eased his hand in slowly then lunged, grabbing the seat of the ten-speed that lay pinned beneath the body of the cyclist. With a sharp jerk, he yanked it free, jostling the undead in the process of gorging. The zombie's head snapped around with gore streaming from its open maw. It lunged at Tim, surprisingly quick. Tim held the ten-speed by the seat and handlebars and used it as a shield to keep the thing from him. The thing nestled in between the wheels, its chest pushing against the sprocket pushing towards him, arms reaching around the bike. Tim shoved it backwards towards the bridge railing. As he shoved, the back of the thing's foot caught on the dead cyclist's leg, and it tumbled backwards into a heap. His face twisted in rage and disgust, Tim began stomping on the thing's skull over and over and over until it had completely stopped moving.

Laura appeared on the verge of shock when he finally turned from his gruesome task, his lip curled in disgust.

"Get on the back of the bike!" he screamed at her, releasing the rest of his pent-up tension.

All around them, chaos was breaking out, an inhuman-sounding roar split the air from behind them. Tim and Laura froze, turning towards the source. From the Poughkeepsie side of the bridge, a large gathering of people were approaching them, maybe twelve in all. At the front was a man, or what had once been a man, its face contorted in rage, its shirt hung limply in rags from one shoulder. The thing locked its gaze on the two of them and began running headlong towards them. Its speed was tremendous, closing half of the thousand feet that lay between them in mere seconds.

"Fuck," Tim uttered, not even intending to speak the word.

"Go, go, go," Laura repeated, slapping at his back with her free hand as she and Luna waited on him to mount the bike.

Tim leapt onto the bicycle, spinning the pedal to near its apex to get a good start as Laura, holding Luna, climbed behind him, occupying the seat. He hazarded a look back at the fast thing as he stepped heavily downward to get the bike moving. The enraged thing was within fifty yards, and Tim could clearly see that the thing was not living, nor was it corpse-like, like the others. For some reason, this thing was really, terrifyingly fast. He was unable to tear his eyes from it as it closed the gap. He watched as things seemed to move in slow motion. The elevator from the waterfront park below climbed up the last few feet to the walkway. The enraged thing veered immediately as the doors opened and disappeared inside. The sounds of multiple people screaming inside snapped his attention away from the scene and got him focused on their own plight.

Tim awkwardly pedaled the thing up to speed, using his bulk to force the pedals down each time they rose at him. Looking down, he could see the tires flattening underneath their combined weight, roughly four hundred pounds on a bike meant for a two-hundred-pound man. He held out hope for the tires and redoubled his pedaling as they were approaching the next undead on the bridge, this one was busily gnawing on the wrist of an elderly gentleman whose cane hung limply from his dead hand. The thing barely turned to look in their direction when they passed it, so intent it was on its current meal. A slight relief came over Tim at that moment. *We will make it,* he thought. *As long as the things are still eating, and no more of those fast ones come.*

They weaved across the bridge numerous times to avoid the undead feeding on their victims; on two occasions, the undead stood and began to lumber along after them. Fortunately, the things were slow and they were quickly outpaced, even by the heavily encumbered bicycle. At the point where the river met the rocks below, before the railroad tracks, hope sank for Tim. Ahead of them, nothing but carnage met his gaze, just a couple hundred yards in the distance. The festival area where the booths and bathrooms were located was a sea of gore and shifting, shuffling movement; there would be no riding through that heaving mass of blood, gore, and teeth. He stopped pedaling the bicycle about a hundred and fifty feet short of the melee ahead and dismounted as he quickly came to a stop. Laura's face began to show her appreciation of the scene ahead, and Tim grabbed her arm to snap her attention away from the scene.

*

The buzzer from the emergency room downstairs dragged Linda Henson's concentration from her paperwork. She dropped the ballpoint pen on the medical supply catalog and rose from her desk to determine the cause of the alarm. Since her arrival in Donner five years prior, as the sole medical practitioner in town, the bulk of her emergency work was from fistfights at the Oasis or injuries from the occasional farm accident. The Oasis was the town's only bar, and as anywhere else, when alcohol was involved, it was a regular source of violence-related injuries. She looked at her watch and saw that it was only half-past three in the afternoon, definitely not late enough for a bar fight; she assumed a car accident or a work-related accident. Coming out of her office, she turned right, pushing through a perpendicular doorway. Her feet squeaked noisily on the polished linoleum floor as she rushed down the flight of stairs. She emerged into the triage area, dousing her hands with hand sanitizer from the automated dispenser. She vigorously rubbed the gel into her hands and looked across the staging area of the ER. Seeing Betty's nurse's whites moving within, Linda moved towards the first emergency bay. The curtain was wide open, and Betty was busy getting the heart monitor in place.

"What is it, Betty?" she asked, coming to the side of an unconscious and pale, sweaty boy.

"Wilmer's youngest...Ed," the woman cast back to her as she re-positioned the boy's head and slid the side gate up on the triage bed.

"How does he present, Betty?" Linda cast back, a bit sharply.

"Food poisoning maybe?" Betty responded. "One-oh-three fever, sweats, high BP...unresponsive."

Linda moved to the side of the bed and pressed on the boy's hand before releasing.

"What makes you say food poisoning?"

"His friends say they ate at Taco Bell in Steamboat Springs before heading back to town. He was fine prior but got really ill on the ride back."

"When was this?"

"Just now. They brought him straight in when they got into town."

"Ninety minutes at most..." Laura trailed off, doubting it was food poisoning.

She dismissed influenza, as the boy was asymptomatic aside from the fever. She could see out of the corner of her eye that Betty had stopped prepping the bay and was waiting for her response.

"Get a PICC line in him and get him on a saline drip," Linda said as she checked for pupillary contraction. Linda set about her routine that had been ingrained in her since med school, moving from checking vitals to checking for wounds. Once her preliminary evaluation was done and she was satisfied the boy was stable, she went to reception where she knew Betty would be.

"Get some ice packs ready in case he hits one-oh-four, Betty. He doesn't present anything more serious than a bug. Run a tox-screen and a blood panel please; in the meantime, just keep an eye on him. I've got to get that order in by the end of the day so I'll be in my office."

"You got it, doc," Betty said with a lilt in her voice and a shit-eating smile.

Bitch, Linda thought as she climbed the stairs. Betty didn't like Linda; she had made that obvious from the moment Linda walked into town. She didn't like that Linda had found funding and turned the two-exam room clinic attached to Dr. Skinner's house into the 'monstrous' healthcare facility. Betty's idea of a 'monstrous' facility was a twelve-bed hospital clinic with a nursing care wing. The closest nursing home before Heartland opened was a two-hour drive, and most of the residents of Donner were grateful to be able to retire near their families and the farmland they'd worked their whole lives. Mostly though, Linda surmised, Betty didn't like taking orders from a woman, especially not a young, pretty one. Linda had done her best, pandering to Betty and catering to her wishes and needs, but secretly, she despised the woman for making the transition so difficult for her.

Linda had just gotten off the phone with the Masune salesperson and looked at the clock. *17:15,* she thought. *Time to check on the boy and call it a night.* She made her way to the bottom of the stairs when she heard a loud beeping noise coming from the nurse's station. The station was rarely used for more than a coffee station due to the low volume of patients that came through the clinic. Immediately after recognizing the beeping sound, a crash sounded, followed by a scream. She hurtled down the last five stairs, fingering the emergency call button on her cell phone as she ran, just in case. Coming into the triage area, she could hear the sounds of a struggle coming from the bay the boy was in. Linda started jogging towards it.

"You okay?" she called as she ran.

"Get the Posey cuffs," came Betty's strained voice, referring to the heavy leather restraints rather than the fabric ones usually employed to restrain volatile patients to a bed. The leather cuffs were only used in severe combative cases, usually mental health or drug-related cases. Linda had used them twice prior, both times during her residency at St.

Francis' Medical Center in Colorado Springs. Since initially ordering the cuffs on arrival at Donner, she had never needed to use them. She ran to the supply room next to the nurse's station. A tense moment of rifling and digging later, and she came out with the brand new pair of the leather cuffs. She ran to the bed, and from this angle, she got a better picture of what was going on. Betty and Stuart, one of the other R.N.s, were wrestling violently with the teen atop the gurney. As she came to their aid, Kelly, a third nurse, came sliding into the triage area, throwing her purse and coat to the side to jump into the fray. Stuart grunted.

"Ow, fuck!" he yelled hoarsely. "Someone get his head, bastard's biting me!"

Kelly, still looking for a place to squeeze in and help, moved to the head, placing her palms on the kid's cheeks. Linda pried the teenager's hand from the back of Stuart's bleeding neck and threw her whole body weight on the arm, still it flailed about. The hand turned and was clawing at hers as she fought to ease the cuff around his wrist. She finally managed to get the cuff on and affix it to the bed before crawling over his chest to help Betty on the other side of the gurney. Stuart lay across the kid's knees, using his body weight to keep him from kicking while he assessed the wound on his bleeding tricep.

Kelly screamed, scaring the wits out of Linda. She knew her entire back was exposed if Kelly lost her grip. She flinched from the shrill yell and just barely avoided getting bit by the kid as he sat bolt upright. Only this wasn't the same handsome young man that had come in a few hours earlier. Linda cringed as she pushed off and away from the bed. The teenager's pallor was ashen and burst blood vessels spider-webbed across his face. His eyes were milky, looking as if they had somehow cataracted in the past four hours. Rage contorted his mouth into something vile-looking, and his jaws snapped at them. Linda could see Kelly holding her bloody thumb in the background. *No more fucking around with this one,* Linda thought, sliding off the gurney and moving around to the head of the bed. She pulled the pillowcase off a pillow that had gotten knocked to the floor in the struggle and threw it around the teen's head, covering his face. She struggled and pulled down on it from both sides, hanging under the bed. The thing fought against her stubbornly, as Stuart and Betty finished securing his hands, feet, and finally, his chest to the bed.

Finally, when they announced that his limbs were secured, Linda released her hold on the pillowcase. The thing that was the teenager a few hours before struggled furiously to get out, flipping the entire bed on its side. Once they got it back onto its wheels, they secured the bed to the wall and Linda instructed Betty to call Sheriff Daltry while she tended to

Stuart and Kelly's injuries. The teenager-turned-thing struggled and snarled, violently thrashing about atop the bed in order to get at them. Eventually, worried that the boy would get loose of the restraints, they moved out of the room and turned the lights off, hoping it would calm him. It didn't.

"The sheriff is on his way," Betty said, moving to help with Kelly's thumb.

"What is that beeping? Can you please turn it off, Betty?" Linda asked.

"That's the alarm on the heart-rate monitor," Betty said with superiority dripping from her voice as she moved to silence the alarm.

"I don't care what it is, just turn it off," Linda said sharply, more than she intended.

Betty walked into the darkened triage area and flipped on the lights. She came back a minute later with a strange look on her face.

"What's up, Betty?" Linda asked, forcing herself into an even tone.

"The heart monitor is still hooked up to him," Betty said.

*

The late fall winds blew in from the north, and Tar pulled his collar close to the sides of his face, hunching his shoulders to shield himself from it. He was attending the funeral out of respect for the young man's grandfather who had got him out of some trouble with the law some years ago. There were maybe twenty people gathered around the coffin, paying final respects to the boy who was only a week from his seventeenth birthday. The young man was the latest in a string of tragedies the people of Donner, Colorado had suffered.

The town of Donner was a small grid of five blocks intersected by five cross streets. The main thoroughfare consisted of Elsie's Diner, Grace Methodist Chapel, a post office, Otter Creek Savings Bank, Bernard's General Store, and a McDonald's. A large municipal building and Heartland Health facility sat on Route 10 just outside the grid heading east towards Fort Collins. The Municipal building housed the sheriff's office and jail, the fire department, the mayor's office, planning department, and town court. The streets that bisected the main business district were comprised of homes and offices, apartment houses, a K-12 school, parking lots, and a park that connected the municipal building to the east side of downtown.

Over the past few days, both the young and elderly alike were falling victim to the same illness that had been all over the papers and news the day previous. The scale of this tragedy was unlike anything that had ever struck the town before. Donner was a small town nestled in the heart of the Rockies, ninety miles northwest of Boulder. Prior to this week, the largest tragedy that had befallen the town was a drunken accident that claimed the life of four, ten years past.

Just three days prior, Tar had been driving down Route 10 headed home from an afternoon spent fly-fishing. For the most part, he had spent the day drinking Busch while standing in waders in the Michigan River, hoping to catch a trout worth eating. It was a slightly buzzed state that kept him from digesting the scenario that lay before him as he passed by Elsie's on his way home. He'd heard that there had been an incident the day prior at Heartland, but he had blown the story off as drama from Betty up at the clinic, who relished in the kind of gossip that tore at the fabric of the small town.

He cruised down Route 10, just over the bridge when he saw Mabel Thomas crawling up from the culvert on the side of the road. She was barefoot and had her apron on. Her boy, Ralphie, appeared a moment later, his face covered in blood. Tar slid the truck into park and stepped out of the vehicle, shifting his pistol in its holster back where it sat comfortably on his hip. He was an old timer and never went anywhere without his gun, a common occurrence in the area. A farmer or farmhand never knew when a bear, coyote, wolf, fox, or even a lame steer might need dispatching. Aside from the off-chance situations, isolated up in the mountains, it was better to be safe than sorry. Tar moved around the front of his Silverado, walking slowly towards Mabel when Ralphie let out an ear-splitting scream and dove, tackling his mother to the ground. Tar waded in, kicking the boy in the side to dislodge him from the woman.

"Ralph, goddamn it, that's your mother," he grunted out as the toe of his western boot connected firmly with the boy's ribcage.

Mabel was screaming unintelligibly at this point, crawling away towards the diner. Tar looked back just in time to see Ralphie lunging at him. The boy's features were screwed up in a fit of rage, and his mouth leaned hungrily in on Tar's midsection. The experience of a handful of barroom brawls as a younger man served him well as he swung a short right cross, his heavy, bony fist connecting solidly with the boy's ear. To his surprise, although the boy was redirected by the blow, Ralphie grabbed hold of his button-down shirt, spinning him about and pulling him down atop him. The boy was very strong and fully fueled up. Tar pinned him down by the throat and struck him with a blow to the side of the jaw that should've ended it. Ralphie ignored the punch and clawed at Tar's arms and neck. Slowly, the reality set in on Tar as the boy struggled to bite the hand that held his throat. Ralphie's eyes seemed off; but, between the slight inebriation and the failing light, he couldn't be sure why. His muscles ached beneath the strain of fighting the strapping young man. His early onset arthritis sapped the strength from the hand around the boy's neck. Unsure of how to proceed, Tar struck the boy once more and rolled away. He came up, spinning to one knee with his .38 caliber pistol drawn, aimed center-mass on the boy. Ralphie didn't flinch; he just came roaring in. Tar pulled the trigger, opening a hole the size of a dime where the boy's heart had been. The boy kept coming, and Tar barely had time to scramble out of his reach, ducking to avoid the swipe of his hand. Ralphie roared past, narrowly missing Tar as he shifted away. Tar spun, pulling the trigger again, this time aiming about a foot above the apple-sized hole in the center of his back. Ralphie was buried three days later on the other side of the cemetery.

Sheriff Daltry had held him overnight and contemplated charging him with the young man's death, but after a visit to Mabel's farm showed him the half-eaten corpse of Ralphie's wife, he let it go. Over the course of the coming days, the McDonald's had locked its doors. All fourteen of the teenagers it employed had been interred at the cemetery. It had been the only available work available in town that wasn't farm labor. Now that they were all dead, there was no one left to run it other than Big Eddie, the owner. Big Eddie was a hotshot rancher with over two hundred head of cattle he tended to. Eddie chained the doors shut; not only were all his employees dead, but the majority of his clientele. Most of the adults in town liked what they referred to as 'real food,' not what most viewed as 'frozen shit.'

Tar waited patiently for the pastor to finish the service before he came forward to pay his respects. He approached Bob and Sally, Steven's parents, and took Sally's hand in his. There were no words to speak; nothing would make the loss easier to bear. After a moment, Tar touched her shoulder and stepped over to shake Bob's hand.

"Thanks for coming, Tar," Bob said with a deep breath. "Thanks, y'know, for everything."

"No need, Tim, we take care of our own," Tar replied, referring to Tim's inability to pay for the plot in the cemetery Tar owned. "You take care of the missus now. We'll catch up in a few weeks."

Bob clapped him on the shoulder, and Tar walked to his truck breathing a sigh of relief; he hated being around emotional people. His own wife had died a few years earlier of Lymph cancer and his son nearly a decade before that from a drug overdose. He had a hard time being sympathetic without reliving his own losses, and he refused to get emotional in front of others. He grew up hard and raised his family hard, realizing his own mistakes too late to seek forgiveness. He slid the key in his 1982 Silverado and she fired right up; there was a meeting he needed to attend at Elsie's in an hour and he was hungry. He steered the gold-trimmed red Silverado out of the cemetery and towards the town proper to get a bite to eat before business.

Tar eased the truck into the angled parking spots in front of Elsie's and slid the shifter into park. He pushed the truck door open with his foot; sliding out of the seat into the chill air. He rubbed his rabbit's foot absently as he put his key in his pocket. He picked up his western hat from the passenger's side of the seat and, donning it, stepped purposefully towards Elsie's.

*

Will awoke, mildly hungover from the night before, with his retro alarm clock/radio blaring out the news. He'd purchased the thing after falling asleep on his iPhone on too many drunken nights only to oversleep the next morning. He was trying desperately to graduate on time, but his partying schedule often got in the way of his school schedule.

Dominic Terea, reporting from Krakau, Poland. I'm standing at a barricade hastily erected by the Polish military and they are letting none through. Early reports are sketchy at best, and we cannot confirm whether or not the quarantine is due to a terrorist attack. We are receiving multiple reports of numerous attackers on the streets of Krakau. Reports are coming in from surrounding communities as well. We will continue to update as information comes in...

Will listened with little interest in the NPR news report blaring across the room. He swung his legs free of the mattress he slept on and rubbed the sleep from his eyes as he sat up. He took two Aleve with the aid of a glass of water from his nightstand and sat unmoving on the edge of his bed. He nearly fell back asleep before he groggily forced himself to stand. He walked across the room to the alarm and switched it off, seeing the time was 8:04. He grabbed his pants and shirt from the night before, pulling them on before slipping his naked feet into his vintage Brooks running shoes. Will wasn't a hipster, but he felt the need to adopt certain bits of fashion in order to fit in among his peers. In his first few weeks in New York, he'd been called a 'tourist' numerous times. He hurried to the bathroom, making his hair neat, then intentionally messy in a way that made sense to him while brushing his teeth.

Ten minutes later, he pulled the heavy, steel-reinforced apartment door shut behind him, leaving for his nine o'clock Readings in Western Civilization class. He bit open the artisanal granola bar someone had left at his apartment a few weeks prior, looking at the label and laughing to himself. He tried to imagine what his father and uncles would say about a nine-dollar granola bar. Will was a transplant from Wisconsin, coming to New York for college, but mainly for the escape from the endless farmland and the people that he associated with it.

Three blocks away, Will pushed through the turnstile as he swiped his MetroCard through the reader. He walked out onto the open-air platform, finding an open seat to wait for his train. He flipped through the songs on his phone for a bit before settling on an early album by Trucktighters. The second song on the album had just started when the train pulled in, its windows covered in heavy graffiti. Will stood and moved up to the yellow-ridged plate and waited for the doors to open. After an eternal pause, the doors slid apart and out flooded a throng of people screaming and clawing over one another. Taking a hesitant step into the now-empty train, the woman standing next to him shot a nervous look at him. The train car was empty as he stepped aboard, only noting as he begun to swing his bag off his shoulder the pool of crimson liquid coming from the rear of the train-car where the handicapped seats are. Will assumed it was some sort of hydraulic fluid, but his Midwest curiosity overcame that bit of urban flight common in many long-time city-dwellers.

He crept ahead, towards the expanding pool, peering hesitantly around the side of the seats to see a shabbily dressed man crouched over an elderly black woman. The man was slowly pulling the woman's innards through a gaping hole in her stomach towards his mouth. Her bloody tweed jacket was torn open, its buttons scattered about the floor around her. Will's stomach lurched and his mouth hung open in silent horror. In the recesses of his mind, he could hear his iPhone clattering loudly on the floor of the car. *My fucking screen better not have broken,* came a thought from a dark corner of his mind as the cannibal lowered a length of intestine and turned to face him. The man's face was ashen, and his skin seemed to be slacking off his skull. His face was riddled with lesions, and his eyes were milky like his grandmother's had been before she passed. Will felt his bladder release, and somewhere in the recesses of his mind, he knew he had to run. His mind was on the verge of shutting down on him as he fought the revulsion of the scene, his heart pounding through his chest. He stood paralyzed. Will's horror built to a crescendo which snapped as he felt a cold hand clutch around his bare ankle. Looking down, he could see that the thing had crawled to him, traversing the few feet between them while his mind had drifted away.

The paralysis finally broke, and Will spun, scooping up his iPhone from the steel step-plate as he turned to run. He broke the cannibal's grip on his ankle with the twist he needed to come about and fled towards the platform stairs, hurdling the turnstile without hesitation. He ran down the stairs and out onto the street. His body shuddered, convulsing him as he came to the bottom steps and out of the subway station. He furtively glanced behind him as he slowed to a quick walk, trying to compose himself. People were milling about, trying to hail cabs, waiting at the bus stop or otherwise going about their mornings. The smell of coffee and exhaust mingled equally in the air. He remembered his iPhone in his hand and dialed 911 as he ducked into a coffee shop to get out of the street noise.

All circuits are currently busy, came immediately back to him through the receiver. *Fuck,* he thought, rushing up to the counter, pushing his way past the queue, interrupting the flustered clerk who was reading back someone's order.

"Call 911 right now; there was a murder on the L," Will demanded.

The clerk looked surprised for a moment then reached over and picked up a circa 1985 wall-mounted phone, covered in faded, hand-worn stickers. She dialed, holding her hand over her other ear as she eyed Will up and down out of the corner of her eye.

"All the circuits are busy," she said to him, hanging up the phone with finality before looking around Will to the customer she had been helping. "Soy milk macchiato and a cranberry scone?"

Will tried again on his cell with the same result as he walked out of the coffee shop back onto the street. *Someone else will have called,* he reassured himself, remembering the panicked crowd fleeing the train car. The fear he felt in fleeing from the thing on the subway was replaced by the knowledge that if he is late one more time to Western Civ, he'll drop a letter point off his final grade. Will remembered that he had a change of clothing in his backpack, so there was no need for him to run home and change. In the distance, he could hear the roar of a crowd that reminded him of New Year's Eve three years prior, his first one in New York, and the last one he went to Times Square for. *Odd,* he thought as he walked to the curb to try to hail a cab. *It's too early for a ball game.* Since he couldn't think of anything else that would have that many people causing that much noise, especially this early in the morning, he pushed the thought from his head. It took him three cabs and about five minutes to find one that would take him to Manhattan; one cabbie didn't want to leave the borough, another just shook his head no and drove off before Will could climb in.

"Washington Square Park," he said through the heavy Plexiglas divider.

The cabby glanced briefly in the rearview mirror at him, assessing his appearance and likelihood of being paid before he gave a slight nod. Will tried one last time to call 911 as the cab pulled into the street with the same result as before. The overly soft seats and the bouncy shocks on New York cabs, adjusted for the pothole minefield they traveled daily, always made him feel seasick at first. When they got within a few blocks of the Brooklyn Bridge, traffic became snarled. Will waited in the cab, watching the meter tally up for about five more minutes before his need to get to class overrode his patience. He paid the cabby six dollars for the fare and a dollar tip figuring he could walk the bridge quicker, and hopefully hail a cab on the other side. He trotted up to the pedestrian footpath; coming around the corner, throngs of people were pouring from the bridge. He was untangling his earbuds to listen to some tunes on his walk when one passerby looked at him and said, "You're outta your freaking mind, kid, it's fucking bananas over there."

Will would have stopped to ask him what he was talking about, but the press of the crowd hurried the man along, leaving him standing like a rock in a stream, the only person, seemingly, headed into Manhattan. *Quite the opposite from the usual weekday morning*, he thought. Still unnerved about the aftermath of the murder he'd seen just a short while ago, but more so driven by the need to not have to call home and explain to his father why he needed an extra semester at NYU. Panic welled in at the thought of his father having to take loans out for another thirty thousand dollars because he couldn't make it to class on time. He finished untangling the wires and flipped his iPhone to listen to some old Sigh, a metal band he had an affinity for. Sticking to the railing on the right, he couldn't recall ever seeing this many people walking the bridge. Glancing below the footbridge, he saw that traffic on the lanes below was snarled in a standstill in both directions.

About halfway across the bridge, he came upon the reason for the stalled Manhattan-bound traffic. All the cars across all lanes were exiting from Manhattan, meeting the Manhattan-bound cars head on. The only thing he could hear above his iPhone was the incessant honking, as only New Yorkers in dead-stopped traffic know how to do. He paused about three-quarters of the way across the bridge, catching his breath against the railing. He pulled the earbuds out, and as his breathing slowed, he began to notice strange sounds and sights looming in the distance. The sounds were riotous, people screaming, glass breaking, shouted commands, and gunfire all echoed through the glass and steel valleys ahead. One thing that he didn't notice until that moment that suddenly struck him, above all else, was the absence of all air traffic. Planes and helicopters could be seen above the streets of New York at all times of the day or night. *Terrorist attack!* screamed Will's inner panic.

Smoke was rising from a few places in the distance; 9/11 was the only thing he could think of. He hesitated for a few moments, taking in the scene, unsure whether to continue on to his class or return to his apartment. He pressed the internet button on his phone to try and see if there was any information on whatever was going on; after a moment, he was greeted with a notification that a connection to the network could not be established. A pit formed in his stomach, growing equal in size and concern to the one about his tardiness. *I'll find a cop and see what the hell is going on,* he thought and continued on, nervously, towards Manhattan. At the end of the bridge, a couple hundred yards distant, he could see some hastily thrown together barricades with what looked like a handful of frantic cops rushing around trying to establish some order. The crowd rushing out of Manhattan trickled off as the cops secured the end of the bridge.

Will called out to the officers when he was about twenty feet behind them, and two of them wheeled about with guns drawn. Something about the look in their eyes troubled Will; it seemed as if they were touched with a bit of insanity.

"Get the fuck out of here, kid," yelled one of the cops holding a shotgun who appeared to be in charge.

"What the hell is going on? There was a murder on the L about 30 minutes ago," he yelled back, slowing.

"Well, there's a shit-load more of that downtown; now get the fuck on the other side of the bridge," he replied, using his head to indicate Will should return to Brooklyn.

Considering his options momentarily, Will considered the protection, in the form of guns, that the cops offered and, instead of listening, moved to help move the barricades to block off the footpath.

"Kid, I said get lost," the man repeated, but there wasn't much heart in the command, so Will settled in.

The people that turned in their direction were hastily turned around by the shouts and brandished weapons of the policemen. After about ten minutes, they had hastily put together sawhorses, forming a 'V' across the footpath with the cops at the bottleneck.

"What the hell is going on?" Will cautiously asked again.

"What's your name, kid?" asked the one in charge.

"Will," he replied.

"Well, Will, I'm Decker, and well, basically..." Decker continued, "we have no fuckin' clue what's goin' on. The hospitals are choked to capacity, they're setting up triage in the parking garages. Everywhere you go, these assholes are running, stumbling around like murdering drunks. We got a call in from the lieutenant to shut down the bridges.

Our squad cars are parked across the roadway below, but between the hospitals needing back-up and the streets running fuckin bananas, it's just us poor fuckin slobs to lock down the bridge."

As Decker finished his blunt recap, riotous screams broke out just below them.

For the first time since approaching the cops, Will looked over the walkway, past the cars gridlocked on the road below and onto the streets of the city. What he saw chilled him through. Mobs of people ran amok, smashing windows and looting, cars burned in the streets in the distance, sounds of women screaming for reasons he'd rather not think of, and through this scene of chaos, a few pedestrians caught his eye. He watched as a pair of them, their odd gait caught his eye as they shambled through the street, slowly but purposefully headed towards a small crowd gathered outside of an electronics store. Will wasn't sure why his eye was ensnared by them, but there was something wrong with them. He had just seen through the haze of his recent memory and correlated them with the thing on the train this morning when they first reached the throng of people.

The guy in the matching velour suit didn't even notice as it crept up on him, so intent he was on trying to make it within reach of something to grab. His first inkling that something was wrong was when the teeth of the thing ripped a chunk out of his shoulder. Will could hear the scream rise a second or two later, then the crowd around the man erupted into a mass of frenzied action. The cops, too, were enthralled by the scene in the near distance, until one of the cops, a young Hispanic man, was snapped out of the reverie by the sound of approaching footsteps.

"Fuck," he yelled and swung around, drawing his gun.

The others snapped out of their stupor and reacted as well. Turning to face the entrance of the bridge, Will saw a crowd of fifty or so people cautiously approaching the barricade. They had gotten to within twenty feet of the flustered officers before they were noticed. Thugs, businessmen, women, children, and construction workers all stood together before them. They stood stock-still when the same Latino cop raised his gun and the others followed suit. Decker quietly told the officers to "get ready."

Decker stood tall, shotgun across his folded arms and spoke clearly and loudly so the crowd before them would all hear.

"Brooklyn is closed. Go back the way you came and find someplace secure to hold out. The National Guard got called in about an hour ago; come nightfall, they'll shoot to kill anyone caught on the streets by order of the mayor."

One of the crowd came to the front and crossed his arms across his puffed-up chest and replied.

"A'ight, we'll go back. Shit is all fucked up in the city, and if things get worse out here, man, we will be back." To emphasize the point, he lifted the front of his shirt so that they could see the black handle of a handgun poking out of his waistband.

The gathered throng milled about for a couple minutes, seemingly deciding where to head, before slowly moving off the walkway and back into the city proper. Will fished his cell phone out of his pocket and began to dial home to check on his family when Decker interrupted.

"Don't bother, kid, you remember 9/11?"

"Yeah?" responded Will

"You ain't getting through to no one until this mess settles itself out."

Will looked quizzically at him, and Decker looking exasperated replied

"You know how many people are calling 911? The cops, firemen, ATF, FBI, CIA, their relatives in and out of the city, not to mention the assholes trying to get food delivered right now?" He paused. "All circuits are busy and they'll stay that way until this shit-storm is all done and over with."

About 15 minutes later, the first zombie staggered his way toward the barricade. Dressed neatly in an expensive business suit, it looked ready to sit at the head of a boardroom meeting. Only the blood spilling down the left side of its shirt from where it once had an ear, but now was just a ragged, bloody hole in the side of its head, marred the picture of urban success. Decker, without hesitation, raised his pistol to shoulder level, looked down the barrel, and fired off a round into the center of the zombie's forehead. Will's jaw dropped in shock; he wasn't sure what he expected them to do…cuff the thing, use a taser on it, but he sure as hell didn't expect to see an unceremonious execution. He recalled the scene this morning on the L train, and the scene that happened on the streets below, and for the first time in three years, he missed home.

As the hours ticked, the chaotic sounds of sirens and screaming from the streets below had begun to die off into isolated screams and short bursts of gunfire. It was a very subtle shift over the course of the morning, but Will was sure by noontime that more of the creatures could be seen shambling about the streets than normal people. For probably the twentieth time since Will had stationed himself with the cops, Decker moved back off the line and grabbed his radio off his shoulder

"Decker to base, Brooklyn Bridge remains secure, any updates?"

"Hold position, Decker; will get back to you ASAP, getting new info right now," came the garbled response.

The other officers looked anxiously at Decker as four more of the dead things turned down the walkway towards them.

"Fuck me!" mumbled Decker. "We're gonna run out of ammo sooner rather than later."

Will barely heard the last part as Decker walked past him back to the barricades.

"Call your shots and go for the kill, guys; we're gonna need to try to save our ammo. I got the one in the yellow shirt," Decker called

An officer Will heard referred to as Hernandez, called for the short one. Down the line, the cops called their intended target out one after another. Decker fired, followed by the rest, their guns popping off in rapid succession. Their training served them well and their aim was true. Five corpses now lay about on the walkway, crumpled into final rest.

"Decker," squawked the radio.

"Decker here; what's the status?" he replied

"Decker, the National Guard has arrived. They are about to enter the city from the GWB. They set up base on the bridge itself. They have requested that all current tactical positions be held until they can ensure quarantine and restore order, do you copy?"

"…Yeah, copy. Any chance of sending over some more bullets for us?"

"All units are engaged," squawked the dispatch, followed by a long pause before continuing. "There was a SWAT team sent over to Canal Street about two hours ago. We lost radio contact with them shortly after and they haven't checked in. If you are desperate for ammo, you could send a man over. If you find them, they should be able to help you out."

"Thanks," Decker replied, his voice dripping with venom and sarcasm.

"Let's get a count on bullets so we know where we stand, guys," Decker directed his men. "O'Malley, go check out that SWAT van and see if you can get some sandwiches and coffee." He smirked at the man.

At this point, and Will had been thinking about it all morning as he watched the events unfold, he wanted out of the city. He didn't want to go back to Brooklyn, as that just trapped him on Long Island. He needed to be out of the city. For the first time since he had come to New York four years earlier, Will longed for home. Not in the homesick way, but he longed for the solitude, the open spaces, and mostly, the clean air. His sudden need to see the city fading fast behind him overtook him. He ran up to O'Malley who had just hopped the barricade and was moving off towards the city.

"I'll tag along; think we can get a car?"

"We may be able to get one, but I'm guessing traffic is too fucked to make it worthwhile. You know how to use one of these?" O'Malley said, pulling and tossing a revolver at him from his ankle holster.

Will juggled the gun for a moment.

"Yeah, I can use it."

"Well, don't," O'Malley tossed him a quick re-loader and said, "unless I need you to and make sure, no matter what, that you don't accidentally shoot me in the back."

*

"Morning, Tar," he heard a voice call out from the bench in front of Elsie's where Clyde and Dave sat smoking. They sat with their legs stretched out, ample bellies overhanging ancient-looking rodeo belt buckles.

"Dave…Clyde," responded Tar, hand reaching up to touch the brim of his hat.

"Say, you think Lydia is gonna be about today? Donny borrowed my tiller last summer and I'd like to get it back," Clyde said, pausing Tar in mid-stride.

Lydia lived down the road from Tar; she had lost her husband, Donny, and son, his father's namesake, to the sickness two days earlier.

"Lydia is a good woman, Clyde; she is suffering real bad right now." Tar stared into Clyde's eyes for a few seconds, hoping to impress on him the need to leave the woman the hell alone. "Come springtime, I'll get the tiller back for you. On my word."

Without speaking another word, Tar continued past, taking his hat off as he swung the screen door that led into Elsie's open. He stepped into the vestibule and hung his hat and coat on the hooks to the left of the door before stepping into the restaurant proper and sidling up to the counter.

"Steak and eggs and coffee, Darla," he said as he sat.

Darla winked at him and walked to the kitchen window while scribbling on her pad. She hung the ticket with his order on a tack-board inside it. Darla knew what Tar was having as soon as she saw his hat moving across the front windows towards the door. She had been waiting tables at Elsie's since she was a teenager and Tar's breakfast only varied when they ran out of steak, or more rarely, eggs.

"No newspaper today?" Tar grumbled in Darla's direction.

"Truck hasn't been through since Tuesday. Got Monday's paper over there if you want," Darla replied, setting his coffee and a fresh pitcher of cream in front of him.

Tar glanced in the direction of the paper on the counter. It was the Denver Post with the headline 'Deadly Bug.' He had read the article two days prior; it offered no answers, no information, nothing but fear.

Tar grunted in response, "Any news on that thing?" pointing towards her iPad lying under the milk fridge on the counter.

"Internet's out; must be the weather affecting the Wi-Fi," she responded absently while marrying glass bottles of ketchup on the counter next to him.

Tar grunted and sat drinking his coffee, staring at nothing. A few minutes later, the kitchen bell jingled and Tar looked over, nodding at the man who stood there.

"Morning, Stan."

"Now, how'd I know that steak was for you?" Stan responded, smiling at him.

Stan was the owner of Elsie's, having inherited it from his mother when she became a resident of Heartland Healthcare up the road.

"Don't know if you saw it yet this morning, but the cable is out," Stan added a moment later before he turned to tend to the eggs cooking on the flat-top behind him.

Tar honestly couldn't care if the cable was out, and half the time, the newspaper didn't come under normal circumstances, but now, with the illness affecting his little slice of heaven, he wanted some updates on what was going on in the world at large. A blast of chilly air hit him on the side of his neck and he turned to see Dr. Henson walk through the doors with a stack of papers under one arm and a copy box under the other. She looked up at Tar pleadingly as she struggled to keep everything aloft. Tar jumped up and rushed over to help.

"Morning, doc," he said, taking the box from her and walking it to the table she led him to. "What's the good word?"

Dr. Henson was an outsider. She had graduated from UC Denver and moved to Donner five years earlier after Doc Skinner died, to take up his practice. What a beautiful, smart woman was doing moving to the middle of nowhere had always piqued his curiosity. She lived alone and had no visitors that he had heard about in the time she was here. He never had occasion to ask her, and generally left others to themselves as far as that kind of thing mattered. Whatever her deal, Tar couldn't care less, but small towns thrived on each other's business, and Donner was no different.

About twenty other townspeople filtered in gradually over the next thirty minutes. By the time Dr. Henson was ready to start the discussion, Tar had finished with his meal and was dabbing the corners of his mouth with a napkin. He spun around on his stool and leaned with his palms on his knees to take in the meeting.

"Thank you all for coming. I know it's been a devastating number of days," Linda began, "Between the deaths and...well, what's been happening after. I know we've all been running short on sleep."

People around the room nodded. Someone near the back called up.

"Have you heard from the government?"

"Yes, Erwin, is it?" She paused, receiving a nod from the man before continuing. "I spoke to someone at the CDC two days ago. They are testing some anti-viral concoctions at the moment and hope to have something by the end of the month."

"Month? What the fuck is that going to do for us?" Larry Helter bellowed, standing up angrily. "Twenty-three deaths in half-a-week; we'll all be dead and buried before a month is out."

The door swung open and Sheriff Daltry stepped in, taking his hat and brown sheriff's jacket off before nodding to the room.

Larry calmed immediately on seeing the sheriff, not wanting to spend another night in jail.

"Please. Continue, Doctor," Daltry said, leaning against a counter stool two seats down from Tar, facing the room.

"I just finished saying that the CDC was hopeful to have something by next month. They don't know much more than we do at this time. Though, the doctor I spoke with concurs that whatever the things are, the things that come back after the infected person dies are," Linda stammered over the words, "they lack emotion or intellect. They are basically nothing more than basic motor function wrapped by hunger and rage."

She said this last part looking directly at Larry, then with a quick nod to Tar continued.

"They show no signs of consciousness, memory, cognitive function, and should not be held in the same regard as the people they were in life. She also said to stay put. The situations in Boulder and Denver are deteriorating rapidly. Our relative isolation up here is most likely the main reason that we aren't in a more dire situation."

The room was silent, all of them unsure of how this affected their lives; at the very least, it meant that there was no help coming.

"You think that's why we didn't get the news the last couple days?" Darla asked quietly from behind the counter.

"It's possible, Darla. As of now, all we know is that the main mechanism for transmittal of the virus is through fluid contact, primarily bites. We suspect that the fast ones are the primary infected, but still don't have enough data to determine what differentiates the fast from the slow. We still have no leads as to what is causing their infection. The

CDC has no further information for us on this, but the federal and state governments are primarily focused on containing population centers at the moment."

Sheriff Daltry stood up and clapped his hands loudly, breaking the tension in the air as all present digested the update.

"Okay, deputies for the day! I need some volunteers to spread word to the surrounding homesteaders and ranchers. Step forward, please."

Five people approached the sheriff, and he proceeded to dispense instructions to where they should go when Dr. Henson cut in

"Sheriff, please, can your guys get a census of who is out there as well as ages?"

Daltry looked around and the five men nodded.

"Also, Sheriff, make sure they are armed, please. There may be infected out on the farms and roads."

"You heard the lady," Daltry smirked as he said. "Also, tell everyone to reach us by shortwave radio. I'll be on 7700 kilohertz."

The entire meeting, Tar had a butterfly in his stomach; something wasn't sitting right with him about this whole thing. When the meeting died down into small conversations, Tar gathered his hat and coat and walked out of the diner. The chill air burned in his lungs as he lit a cigarette and walked across the street to Bernard's general provisions and deli. He lingered outside for a moment to finish his cigarette before going in. He bought all the 12-gauge shotgun shells, 9mm bullets, .38 caliber, and 5.56mm rounds that Bernard had in stock. He then strode back to his truck carrying the Budweiser case that Bernard had packed the boxes of shells into, got in his truck, and drove home.

When he got home, Tar did something he couldn't ever remember doing before; he went room to room and locked all the doors and windows. In Donner, crime was nonexistent. There was the occasional punk kid here and there, but by and large, it was the definition of 'community.' He called his dog, Captain, a border collie, over and roughed up his head before the two walked to the barn out back together to gather up his lumber. Two hours later, Tar had dragged his substantial supply of planks as well as most of his tools into the back pantry of the house. He figured that if the town got overrun, he might not have time to do it later. Even if it amounted to nothing, having it there reassured him that if it did get bleak, he would be prepared at least to fortify his house. Exhausted from the labor, he showered and lay down for a nap; age was taking its toll on him.

*

"Laur, get over here," Tim beckoned to her from the railing to the left.

The drop from here to the ground below was only about 30 feet; more than enough to break an ankle, but there was some structural framework that Tim thought could be scaled to the bottom. He knew that he would have had no problem with it in his teens and twenties, but now, nearing forty and carrying a toddler as well, he wasn't so confident. The absence of other choices forced the situation at hand, and he scrambled over the railing. He stood on the outside of the railing and gestured to Laura to hand him their daughter. Laura reeled at the height as she approached the railing, but handed Luna to him. Despite her own misgivings, she also swung her long legs over the rail and waited as Tim started his descent.

Tim wasn't particularly a strong man; although not weak, he knew how to use his body, even with his balance being a bit off due to the added weight. He climbed downward rapidly. The black paint flaked off the steel lattice, crumbling into his palm with every handhold. He awkwardly had to press Luna into his chest and hook a couple fingers around the steel with every other handhold. It only took him about thirty seconds or so to climb down, but in that time, he was pretty sure that he had successfully crushed his daughter he was clutching her to his chest so tightly. Laura was not as graceful as Tim; her figure, although thin, was not graced with great coordination, so it took her a few minutes to climb down with a couple near falls and many fearful looks to her husband and child below. In the eternity that Tim stood at the bottom waiting on Laura, he paced about and eventually relieved himself against the concrete footing of the bridge. Luna fussed a little, looking up and reaching for her mother, making Tim anxious that she would cry out and alert the undead to their presence. He looked nervously around for more of the things before he turned his focus onto the remaining quarter-mile they had to get to the car. He figured they could remain under the cover of the woods until they got to the parking lot, but was afraid of what they would find once they got there.

Once Laura hit the ground, Tim hurriedly gave Luna to her and ushered her under the bridge, crossing to the other side. When they reached the open air, they had a clear view of the walkway as it curved back towards the right, heading along the final straightaway to the parking lot. The undead things milled about on the footpath in a varied array of completion. Some were missing limbs, while others appeared gnawed to the bone in certain areas. Some of the undead were gorging on the bodies of pedestrians, and others appeared to stare off into the distance, shambling around aimlessly. When Tim was reasonably sure that they could make it safely from under the bridge to the cover of the woods ahead, he ushered his family painfully through a bramble thicket into a copse of birch trees. He pulled on Laura's sleeve, bringing them to a stop here to look back and see if they were spotted. After taking a minute to examine the dead above and to the left, he was assured, for the moment, that they were undetected. They picked their way cautiously through the trees as quietly as they possibly could with the heavy blanket of dry fall leaves underfoot. Tim kept them within sight of the walkway on their distant left. After about twenty minutes, he could make out the shape of a dumpster ahead on the left; he hoped it was the same one he had noted on the way in. Once again, he stopped their progress and met Laura's gaze before quietly saying:

"Parking lot…going to get a look; stay here."

"Please don't leave us alone, Tim," she replied quietly, her eyes pleading with him.

In that moment, without even considering it, he began to think of his wife and child as baggage of a sort. Precious cargo, as it were, but baggage nonetheless. He needed them to be safe, quiet, and to follow his directions, nothing else. In this particular moment, he needed speed, the ability to run and not worry about them. He paused for a good thirty seconds, examining the area around his family for movement. He put his finger to his lips and pointed to Luna, and crouching, he moved off towards the wintergreen dumpster with a giant green and yellow WM emblazoned on the side. He scrambled to within twenty feet of the dumpster and came to a halt to try and get a good feel for the area. Those things were definitely in the lot; he heard a scream and a car door slam, followed by a great deal of shuffling and shifting of feet. Quickly, assuming the things would be drawn to the sound of the door, he skittered up to the dumpster. He intentionally put his back against it so he could check on Laura and Luna. Panic began to set in; *Where the fuck are they?* His eyes scanned furtively where he thought he had left them.

Laura saw Tim move to the dumpster and turn. She saw the look of sheer terror on his face as his head snapped around, scanning the area for them. To reassure him, she raised her hand a bit and waved. He caught sight of the movement and visibly relaxed; he had been looking well off to the right of where they were. No sooner had his knot of a sphincter loosened than one of those things passed him on the left side of the dumpster. Shirtless and looking as if it were burned badly, half its face and chest a mix of bone and gore. Its one arm raised straight forward, limp at the wrist, the thing moved slowly but inexorably towards where his wife and daughter had just waved to him. A low breathless moan issued from it as it shambled past a few feet from him. His blood ran cold in his veins as he gathered his feet under him, knowing he had to act, when another one, followed shortly after by a third, ambled around the side of the dumpster. Tim felt that terrible adrenaline kick in, a cold pit in his stomach. He thought momentarily about grabbing their attention and running to the car, but dashed that away; that was his doubt and fear trying to prod him to safety rather than confronting his fears head on. He dared a quick glance around the dumpster to see what else might be coming.

In the parking lot, he could see between twenty and thirty of the things gathered around a car slamming and clawing at it. The car that the undead were so interested in was three spots away from their station wagon.

No time for plans now, Tim. Move! he thought. *Go!* he screamed internally after he still hadn't moved. Spurred on by his inner voice, he spotted and grabbed a length of broken signpost that lay a few yards from the right side of the dumpster, at the edge of the pavement. He stood fully erect and started off at a jog to catch the things heading towards his wife and child. The four-foot-long piece of rusted post sat awkwardly in his hands; hands he could hardly feel anymore, as he was no longer in full control. His consciousness clouded a bit as it had done during all of the few times he had gotten into physical altercations in his life. The adrenaline took hold, and the knot in his stomach seemed to lessen as did his periphery, he saw his own arms come over the top of his head and the galvanized steel pole come smashing down atop the first thing's head. He felt the violent reverberation when steel met bone but managed to keep his grip on the awkwardly shaped weapon. The thing crumpled to the earth and leaves at his feet. Unthinkingly, he swung the pole sideways at the next one within reach only to have it thud heavily into the bole of a tree.

The pole bounced free of the trunk and continued on its course, connecting with the creature on the side of its neck. The impact with the tree left the blow with virtually no force left in it, and the undead turned, its mouth opening and its milky eyes blank. A moan escaped from its throat as it lunged, with surprising speed, towards him. He jumped back, throwing his arms up to shield himself from the thing and tripped over the corpse of the creature he had just disposed of. He landed heavily on his back, the force of the surprise impact blowing the air from his lungs. The dead thing descended down onto him. He pulled his legs in quickly without thought and launched a double kick at it, catching it heavily in the center of its chest. The force of his kick met with the equal force of what was once a beefy man, falling towards him. The two forces negated each other, ending with the thing laying atop Tim's feet with his legs extended upwards into the air. Tim shifted his weight and tipped the thing over sideways, toppling it to the earth and tree roots to the side of him. He sprang to his feet, scooped up the steel pole, and clubbed the thing in the head three times in rapid succession, dashing its skull into mush.

Laura, Luna, NO! he screamed internally, realizing that one more thing was still headed towards them. So absorbed in his own battle, he had no idea of time or space or whether the thing had reached them. It seemed that more than enough time had passed for the thing to stumble over to them; only the adrenaline surging through him kept the despair at bay. He scanned the area, eyes settling on the dumpster to realign his bearings and turned to see the thing still moving forward, so very close to them. Laura was on her feet, holding Luna and moving away from the thing that lurched towards her. Tim took in the scene in a flash and then ran headlong, dropping the pole when it got stuck briefly on a tree branch. He hadn't run so hard since he was a teenager running from the police when they came upon him and a bunch of kids partying on the railroad tracks. Unthinkingly, he hurled himself as hard as he could, shoulder first, into the thing's back when he got within reach of it. He landed heavily on top of it; its head twisted sideways, mouth snapping towards his stomach, barely three inches away. Quickly, he sat up, keeping his hands on its shoulders and sitting on its hips. Laura stopped running and started coming back towards her husband.

"Find me a good-sized rock, Laur, please...quickly," he hissed through clenched teeth as the thing thrashed and writhed, struggling beneath him.

Laura started kicking at the fall leaves hoping to unearth a rock. Precious moments slipped past and the adrenaline began to ebb from Tim's muscles. The thing's hips spun underneath his crotch and its right shoulder started to lift from the ground. Desperate, using the last of his strength, Tim hitched himself forward. Now straddling the thing's ribcage, he wove his hands through the thing's greasy, gore-speckled hair and started smashing its face into the ground. Over and over he struck; long after the thing ceased its struggle, Tim's hands rose and fell, the wet thudding of the impact sounding through the woods. He finally returned to the moment; looking around, he saw Laura with Luna collected into her chest, Luna's soft cries quieted quickly with a breast. Tim's hands were slick with blood and brain matter, a few scattered flecks of bone shone brightly in contrast with the black and crimson gore. He tried to wipe them off as best he could on leaves, shuddering violently as the leaves stuck to him before he scrubbed them off.

*

Will and O'Malley made a wide berth around the corpses of the zombies that the cops had killed on the walkway. Coming onto street level, they were met with an eerie silence, unheard of in lower Manhattan at mid-day. The only noises audible were the distant sounds of gunfire echoing loudly off the buildings and sirens, mingled with the car and building alarms going off. Traffic was gridlocked up to the entrance of the bridge, below and all around them. O'Malley started uptown towards Chinatown with Will at his heels. They walked the center line of the street, pinned in by rows of disabled cars on either side of them. They hoped that their distance from the buildings and sidewalks would give them a bit of warning if anything approached.

The walk through Chinatown was tense, Will anticipated the dead things to come out of every shadow, every alley and doorway. The streets were barren; cars with doors ajar littered about the street, accident scenes left unattended, with smoke drifting lazily into the air from ruptured radiators. Screams, muffled by the brick of the buildings, came down to them from the windows of apartments above. On a handful of occasions, they were able to catch glimpses of people or the things huddled in dim alleyways or store-front alcoves. Will liked to think they were shooting dice instead of what he feared they were doing. Corpses lay out in the open, half-devoured, covered in blood and gore. Were it not for the figures they caught a glimpse of, or an arm hanging out from an opened car door here or there, the eerie silence at street level made it seem almost as if everyone had just vanished. The spooky calm followed them for blocks and the tension built as they moved uptown.

The scene changed drastically upon arriving at the intersection with Canal St. The cross-town winds kept the noise of the scene ahead from reaching them until they were only a block away. A jack-knifed bus was stalled into the wall of the building on the southwest corner, keeping them from viewing the intersection. Once they edged around the tail of the bus, they were confronted by a scene of absolute carnage. Where previous blocks had seemed abandoned, here, from east to west, screams echoed loudly down the glass and steel canyon and the shuffling dead filled the streets. The wind hit them from the east, bringing with it the low sounds of almost inaudible moaning. Half-devoured corpses littered the street, the roadway slick with their blood. One corpse, seated in a BMW, had its upper torso pulled through the driver's side window, flesh hung in ribbons where the jagged glass of the broken window had rent it from its body. Its face was skinless, and its eyes bulged in the horror of death. Will reeled, the world spinning around him, and he would have collapsed right there were it not for the sound of a gun firing very near to them.

He snapped his head back to reality to find O'Malley firing his pistol. Will tracked the aim of the barrel of the gun across the flesh-littered street to a crowd of the undead things, headed purposefully towards the two of them. They shambled, crawled, clawed past one another in a slow-motion frenzy. Will turned to run, only to find himself face to face with one of the undead things as it lunged towards him. He tried to dodge to the side, but his momentum carried his shoulder into that of the zombie's, spinning it around and down on top of him as he landed on his back on the damp pavement. He struggled to pull a leg up and out from under the ghoulish creature which was attempting to sink its teeth into his thigh. Through panic and furtive jerking movements alone, he was able to keep the thing's hungry mouth at bay long enough to get his leg out. He threw the free leg up high and planted it on the thing's shoulder, shoving with all his strength, half-pushing the zombie, half-sliding himself away. The sound of gunfire continued throughout his struggle, the breathless moaning sounds that issued from the things mingled with the wind, then the gunfire stopped. The hollow clatter of metal hitting the ground was followed by the slit-click sound of a clip being loaded into a pistol, the gunfire resumed. He scrambled around to get to his feet only to find at least three sets of feet within inches of his hands planted on the gore-covered ground. Blood splattered loafers on one, New Balance on another, and Timberland boots on the third.

The moment lasted an eternity, then the spell broke, and he threw himself forwards like a runner coming off the starting blocks, hoping to shoulder through the undead. He hit the thing with the New Balance sneakers like a linebacker against a preschooler, his momentum carrying him for many feet past the trio. Fingernails scraped his neck as he tripped over a squishy corpse lying on the street in between two yellow cabs. He landed heavily on his chest and lay sprawled and senseless for a moment, before quickly jumping back to his feet. He clambered to the roof of one of the cabs, just ahead of the pursuing dead, and briefly surveyed the scene around him. Behind, the trio of zombies was in pursuit of him; beyond them was O'Malley, reloading once again. The man seemed completely oblivious to the fact that the thinned crowd of thirty or so zombies were no further than ten feet from him. He saw the first undead that he had collided with had turned back and was reaching for O'Malley.

"O'Malley!" he screamed over the incessant moaning. "Behind you!"

O'Malley looked up, his face showed surprise at seeing Will fifty feet west of him and on the roof of a cab. He spun, his reloaded pistol extended out before him. His pistol hand struck the lurching dead in the side as he wheeled around and the thing leaned in for a bite. O'Malley came across with a right hook and caught the dead thing squarely on the cheek.

"Mother fucker!" O'Malley screamed, his anger taking over.

Will watched as the cop rode the thing to the ground and smashed its face into the pavement.

"O'Malley, get up! Get the fuck out of there!" Will yelled, seeing the rest of the thinned horde of undead closing the last few feet, arms extended and jaws gaping hungrily.

O'Malley was lost in his rage at that moment. He hooked his thumb under the jaw of the zombie and mushed its face into the ground, pistol-whipping the thing repeatedly until gore came out of its eye sockets. Will watched in slow motion as the crowd of a dozen or so undead converged on O'Malley. Will's screams to him fell on deaf ears. He saw the revelation of horror and dread clearly on the man's face when the first of the crowd grabbed him by the collar of his shirt. He struggled for a moment in an attempt to break free, but the heavy stitching of his uniform kept him from pulling away as more and more hands caught hold of him. The officer's gun fired off three more times as he was dragged to the pavement by the mob. The dying screams of the officer rose to an eerily high pitch before a gurgling groan issued from the pile of tearing dead. Then all was silent but for the sounds of ripping flesh and moaning dead.

Will realized that he was absolutely alone in the street.

*

Linda wasn't very big on popular culture, though she had seen bits of zombie shows and movies here and there in her college days. She absolutely refused to refer to these reanimates as zombies; her scientific nature refused it, no matter how much her superstitious side screamed at her. Unfortunately, she was the only person in Donner with any kind of experience in dealing with infectious disease research. Even though she had a handful of registered nurses and a nurse practitioner under her in the clinic, her responsibilities left her little to no time to look into the cause and effects of the disease after the first few days.

Word had gotten out fast in the small town that there was something deadly going around, so people started avoiding close contact with one another. What were once warm handshakes or hugs among neighbors in town, quickly became brusque waves or a simple tip of the hat. After the first case, the Murphy boy, everyone started paying closer attention to the national news reports. They spoke of the illness in Denver, and CNN had round the clock coverage of Washington D.C, which was under quarantine. By the following morning, one after the other, the townspeople started making their way through the doors into the ER, as well as the few remaining residents coming down from the nursing home upstairs. People were coming in with fall colds, paranoid that they had the bug and wanting to head it off, as if that were possible.

Linda had been putting in 18 to 20 hour days since that first death, either in the triage area or on the phone with the Colorado Department of Public Health and Environment or the CDC in Atlanta when she could get someone on the phone. Those first days, she had a few hours where she could try to combat the bacterial infection herself. She had worked with the Colorado Department of Public Health and Environment for two years prior to moving to Donner and was affiliated with the CDC. The CDPHE was used to dealing with intermittent cases of Bubonic plague that cropped up occasionally around lower Colorado and wasn't much help, but it was nice to bounce ideas off her old colleagues.

Stuart and Kelly, the wounded nurses, were in isolated intensive care beds, having steadily degraded in condition since they were bitten. Their battles against the bug seemed to be coming near their tragic end. After that struggle with the Murphy boy, those who suffered symptoms of infection were monitored closely and restrained as their vitals started fading. In each case, the deceased reanimated to similar results. She felt terrible about their impending fates and tried desperately to get a lead on a treatment. Samuel Mekins, an infectious disease specialist that she knew from the CDPHE, mentioned a conversation he had with a colleague in the CDC detailing some specific similarities the bacteria had with MRSA, although obviously more aggressive. She attempted treatment on Stuart and Kelly with massive doses of meropenem, piperacillin, and tazobactam and found that, although it delayed toxicity and death by a day or two, it was only delaying the inevitable. The patients showed no marked improvement. When death was imminent, their beds were moved into the empty lockdown wing for psych patients, so that their post-mortem struggles might go unnoticed by those still living.

Sitting across from her desk at the moment was Sheriff Daltry, on his fourth visit since the Murphy boy came in, although this was the first visit she had requested.

"Thanks for coming, Sheriff; I know you are busy these days."

"No problem, Linda. What is it?"

"I wanted to talk to you about my contacts at the CDPHE."

"Over in Denver? They find something out?"

"Unfortunately not, in fact, they are trapped in their lab, and the dead are everywhere on the streets."

"You mean it's that widespread?"

Linda nodded soberly at the man.

"Fuck!" he said, again drawing a nod.

"I didn't want to raise the alarm at the meeting earlier, but I thought you should know that darker times might be looming ahead."

Daltry stood and started pacing the small office.

"Right, well, we can only do what we have control over. We need to put any of those…things you have floating about down for good."

"Sheriff, they can tell us more while they are still moving."

"Dr. Henson, these things are too damn dangerous to have floating around," he argued vociferously. "They are not people anymore, you said it yourself at the meeting."

"I know that, Sheriff!" she sneered back at him. "But if I can find time, maybe, just maybe, we can find out what's causing the infection. It would be silly not to study them at the very least. Every little bit we learn can be crucial to combating it."

"They're killing and infecting people, Linda; we can't risk them in our midst. It'd be one thing if you were keeping the slow ones around; those ones aren't nearly as dangerous. Those fast ones, they're death on wheels."

Daltry paused, eyeing Linda who stood defiantly with a fire in her eyes and her arms crossed, before continuing.

"It was one thing when the cases were only here at the clinic, Linda. Those things are out on the streets now. They are actively roaming the streets and attacking the people of this town."

This had been an ongoing argument between the two of them since after the second patient had turned. Daltry had been present for that, and Linda had to wrestle the gun from his hand as he tried to end it immediately. She knew they were dead, at least as far as their vital signs were concerned. She knew that they weren't the same people, but all the same, her medical curiosity took hold and she couldn't resist studying them. If the stories were true about what was happening in the rest of the world, any information they could gather from the primary infected could help come up with a solution.

"We are in agreement, the CDC, CDPHE and I, that the slow ones are not what we need," she stated. "We think the fast ones, or some section of them, are the primary infected; those are the ones that could be key in figuring this whole mess out."

"What do we need from these things Linda? Nothing. Nothing, but for them to stop moving and act the way they are supposed to: dead. They are predators, Linda, and damn dangerous ones," he blurted out.

"Answers, Daltry, answers. Mainly, what is causing this? We know how to kill them, what we need to know is 'how?' and 'why?' The rest of the world may be falling apart at the seams and that makes sense, as cities are hotspots in any infectious illness. What we need to know is why are we, an isolated community, still even now continuing to experience new infections? It could give us a solution to infection, a way to avoid it," Linda added. "We are learning some things. We have already reached a near-certain conclusion that post-mortem time of re-animation is the determining factor in whether one of them is a fast or a slow one. Whether or not rigor mortis has set in seems to be the deciding factor, so now we need to work on the other factors, the mechanism for infection, the cause, and a cure, if there is one."

Daltry calmed himself before proceeding.

"Linda, if that is what we need, then let's save one or two of them and put the rest down. The last thing we need is twenty of the rabid things, all of which are trying to break free, living in the middle of town," he said, his voice almost pleading with her.

"I need multiple specimens to examine, Daltry; any one could be an aberration. A proper study needs to be done," she continued.

Daltry had already given up on the argument, as he had on the few other occasions he had encountered the young doctor. He felt he had been exceptionally patient with her, seeing as he was a man that was used to being obeyed, in his home and in his uniform. He shook his head in disgust that the woman couldn't see the risks her 'research' was putting them all in. He decided in that moment, that if there were one more incident, he was going to put every one of the damn things to rest, and Henson would see the inside of a cell if she tried to stop him again.

Linda breathed a sigh of relief as she watched the sheriff retreat from her office. She knew it was only a matter of time before he put his foot down, so she needed to secure as much information from the infected as possible before he swept through. She wanted desperately to move one of the things to another area of the facility, to hide it for study for when he did finally come through to kill them. Linda was smart enough to know her limitations; she knew she couldn't do it alone and knew that no one else would keep the secret. Instead, she put in more hours to collect more data.

*

Tim rose from atop the corpse, scraping the gore off his hands with dry fallen leaves. He heard a commotion behind and spun about to get a view of the parking lot. His eyes focused just in time to see the car that was parked a couple spots down from theirs, surrounded by the things, lurch to life. It reversed through the mob that had gathered around it. Bodies flung off of the rear bumper, one crumpling to the ground only to get bounced over by the tires. The Honda reversed with the wheel cut and came to a violent stop, connecting solidly with the curb in front of where the dumpster sat. The reverse lights dimmed, and the wheels skipped on the gore that coated them for a moment before catching hold and propelling the car forward. The engine raced, and the car hurtled, at speed, into the horde that moved to follow it. Above the din of the engine and the moans, Tim could hear the distinctive sound of glass breaking. The car did not slow as it reached the end of the lot; rather than veering left towards the exit, it hopped a curb and careened down an embankment into the woods below the lot. The mob of undead the car had plowed through ambled, crawled, and shuffled after in pursuit.

Tim grabbed Laura by the hand, and the two started running to the dumpster, Luna in her mother's arms. As they reached the dumpster and ducked behind it, Tim crouched over top of his family protectively, edging around both sides of it to make sure they wouldn't be snuck up on. He caught Laura's eye.

"When I say move, you need to move, okay?"

No response.

"Dammit, Laura, I know, I'm scared shitless too, but if we don't get to the car, then what?" he queried. He could see the tears welling in her eyes. "We are going to be okay, I promise, now get ready and try to make sure Luna is quiet, okay?"

"'Kay," Luna responded, lifting her cherubic face from her mother's bosom.

When the last of the horde disappeared down the embankment, Tim scurried around to the front of the dumpster and scanned the lot quickly. A couple of the things that had been run down by the car still thrashed about on the blacktop, legs or spine incapable of allowing them to walk. Those were the only undead he could see in close proximity to their car. His hand shot into his pocket and came out quickly with the carabiner clip of keys. Once the keys were quieted in his grip, he looked down to them and put his thumb on the unlock button. He cast one more look to Laura and Luna, Laura the sight of abject panic, Luna calmly nursing, oblivious to the immediate danger.

"Now," Tim said, making sure she was moving before turning away.

Laura clutched to the sleeve of his shirt as he came clear of the cover of the woods and dumpster. Suddenly, he felt just how alone he was right now; alone and needing to protect not only his wife, but their child against whatever was going on. He felt the edges of his sanity start to peel back and panic started to creep in and take over, as they moved into the open. He shook his head quickly, as if physically shaking the fear off, and moved quickly across the lot to the car, taking a very wide berth around the disabled dead things struggling to move.

Everything seemed to move in slow motion as they raced across the lot, like they were running at the bottom of the ocean with weighted boots on. The feeling passed as soon as he double-hit the unlock button to open all the doors. The car chirped twice and the headlights flashed. All of a sudden, everything was moving too fast for his liking. Looking around quickly as he opened the rear driver's side door, he could see dozens of the thing's heads turn towards them from further up the walkway. He ushered Laura and Luna in, closing the door quickly before opening the driver's door and slipping into the seat. He pulled the door shut, and at the same time, he rammed the key home in the ignition. *Please, please, please,* he spoke as a silent prayer as he twisted the key in the ignition. They had never had a problem with the car before, but now would be the time of nightmares for the car not to start. The car fired up without hesitation, and Tim threw it in reverse, backing up just enough to be able to cut the wheel and pull out. Behind them, Tim could see in the rear-view mirror, a small gathering of undead were making their way towards the car.

As the slate-gray station wagon crept out of the lot and onto the side road that led to Route 9W, Tim started crying. They were not tears of joy nor fear, they were tears of relief and rage; the pent-up emotions of his family being in such dread peril. The drive back towards 9W on the side road was peaceful and both wondered, hoped, in fact, that it was an isolated incident. Although Tim composed himself by the time they reached it, their hopes were dashed when they reached the intersection at 9W. To the right, they could see a mob of the undead things attacking people at a gas station, and across the highway at a Sunoco station, a vehicle burned. Cars were stopped randomly, good Samaritans most likely that had stopped to help apparently injured, bloody people only to be ripped apart when their doors opened.

Tim ignored the traffic light, pausing just long enough to be sure no one was barreling north before steering across the intersection. As they turned, heading south to start their hour-long trek home, Tim grasped the dial and tried to find something on the radio. The emergency broadcast alert came blaring through the speakers, shattering the silence of the car, but no information followed it. They listened for many minutes before switching stations. After two full sweeps through both radio bands, he finally gave up, with nothing but static coming through the speakers at them. He thought briefly about putting some music on but thought twice of it, preferring the silence to sort his thoughts and feelings out about everything they had just been through, and what it portended for the immediate future. Laura tried calling her sister, but got only got a recording stating that *all circuits are currently busy* before hanging up on her. She tried five more times with the same result before giving up and closing the phone.

They drove on in silence with Tim mentally dissecting the situation. *Was home safe? If not, what then?* There were no answers he could come up with, none. All they could do was to try and get home; once there, they could see how secure it was and make the decision then whether to hole up at there or abandon it for somewhere else. *New Hampshire?* he thought, where his parents lived…it certainly was more rural, more locals with guns. He steered the car around all manner of traffic, abandoned and broken-down cars littered the rural highway sporadically. The undead things feasted on bodies here and there, usually still seatbelted inside the vehicles, sometimes in the middle of a lane of traffic. Most of the things tracked their movement as they passed by, some got up to try and intercept the car. Tim swerved skillfully around these, not wanting to damage their means of transportation. Some of the fast ones took up chase after them but quickly fell back, out of sight, behind them.

Laura sat in the backseat of the Dodge as they barreled down Route 9W. Her hands were shaking uncontrollably with the adrenaline and panic of the race across the bridge. She had to force herself to relax, her hands balled into knots, her fingertips digging painfully into her palms. *I just want to wake up, I just want to wake up!* she chanted to herself. Luna was crying plaintively and clawing at the front of her shirt, trying to pull her mother's breast out to feed. Laura was so used to the child's need for the comforting smell and feel of her breast that the only time she seemed to notice anymore was when her daughter pinched or bit her nipple. She absently pushed down the front of her blouse and gave her daughter the comfort that only she could.

The act of nursing her daughter had a calming effect on her own frayed nerves, as if reminding her of her purpose. Laura hardly noticed as Tim swerved around the monsters and vehicles around them, though she ensured the doors were locked numerous times. Her mind drifted back to the narrow escape on the bridge and the horror of those things devouring people. Her anxiety began to rise anew at the thought of the events, and she tried her hardest to force the thoughts from her head. Just as she began to compose herself, her head leaning against the window, she spotted a handful of the things staggering up the northbound lanes. She started to panic thinking of her mother and sister, and again, fished her phone out to get in touch with them. Scrolling through her contacts, she tried one then the other, both times receiving the same 'all circuits are busy' announcement.

"Tim! We have to go check on my sister and mom! I can't get through to them!" she called up to her husband, her voice filled with panic and dread.

"Take it easy, Laur," he replied, noncommittally.

She could feel him dismissing her need to make sure her family was safe, as if it were a slap in the face. The panic began to morph into anger. As she was getting ready to start screaming at Tim, Luna bit down on her nipple, sending a sobering jolt of agony through her.

"Ow!' she screamed loudly, as she yanked her breast back from Luna.

Thus the trip south went, both of them on the edge of hysteria. After a bit over thirty minutes of driving, they turned to merge onto westbound I-84. For most of the ride south Tim had been worried that I-84 might be gridlocked with people from both north and south looking to hit an interstate and head west to rural Pennsylvania or east to Connecticut. There was nothing, however, not even a state trooper in one of the many hiding spots along the wide median. The only thing Tim saw that represented any kind of emergency was occurring was seeing military Humvees atop many of the bridges that spanned overtop the highway, but there were no visible signs of occupants. Having driven fifteen miles on a deserted highway almost made them think that none of it was true, that it had been some sort of hallucination; had someone spiked their coffee with something? Were they having some fantastic delusion that was a symptom of mental illness, or were they just asleep, dreaming the whole scenario?

"Is this real, Tim?" Laura asked weakly, her thoughts in a similar vein as his.

"I hope not, sweetie," he answered honestly

*

The trio of dead coming after Will had reached the back of the cab he stood atop. The sound of their hands slapping and slamming onto the trunk, scrabbling for a handhold, snapped his attention off the gruesome scene of the undead rending and tearing savagely at O'Malley's flesh with their teeth and hands. Failing to find a way atop the cab, the dead came around both sides of the car, their hands reaching for him. He remembered the pistol in his waistband and pulled it out, leveling it at the undead wearing loafers. He pushed the safety off and squeezed the trigger, sending a deafening blast through the canyon-like streets, the zombie crumpled to the ground with a neat, clean hole through the bridge of its nose. As the report of the pistol echoed deafeningly off the buildings, Will was a bit shocked at the heavy recoil on the little gun. He recovered his aim and dispatched the other two with two well-placed shots. In his periphery, he could see a few undead that had been edged out of the feeding frenzy on O'Malley turn towards him and start advancing. Will desperately looked for a place to go. He had nine bullets left, three in the gun and six in the quick reloader.

Looking west, Will could see the reflection of police lights flashing off the windows of buildings a couple blocks down. There were dozens of undead milling about in that direction. Will hesitated as he examined his options, before deciding to continue on. Eastward, past the crowd devouring his former companion, were a few small clusters of dead things headed towards the scene of carnage. North of him was Centre Street past the mob, and to the northwest was Lafayette, neither of which Will was able to see down due to his position. To the south, his sight was blocked by the bus and the crowd of undead, and southwest was Lafayette, which he was also unable to see down. The undead ahead were spaced out a bit, and although he despised the idea, he figured he could run through if he needed to. Panic clutched at his heart as he realized how alone and exposed he was on the streets of the city. He wished he had never left the barricade. Although, as soon as he thought it, he realized that even with the relative safety of half-dozen armed men that the barricade was a very precarious position to be in. It wouldn't take more than a few dozen of the undead coming at the barricade at once and it would be overrun. Not to mention the crowds of living that wouldn't be turned back when they got desperate enough. Will wondered if their fate had already been sorted as he slid off the cab and began picking his way through the street westward.

A vast quantity of bodies lay scattered on the street, laying about, piled three high in places. To avoid them, Will spent more time walking on the hoods and roofs of cars than he did with his feet on the ground. Although it was slow moving, to him it seemed to be the safest way to travel. The undead, for as far as he could tell, would not, or could not, climb over or under the vehicles, so while they tried to stagger through the maze of cars, he would glide over the top of the mess of snarled traffic. All the while he moved, the wind and the incessant moan assailed him. The scene was chaotic, with blood-curdling screams coming from within buildings and down alleyways, gunshots in all directions and distances. Numerous bodies fell from above as he moved, though he couldn't tell if they were suicides or simply undead that staggered off rooftops or through windows. The scattered pockets of living people he had seen were running for whatever safety they could find. Some ran into storefronts, buildings, or even ducking into vacant cars. A few others were doing much the same as Will, all looking as frantic and as terrified as he felt. The undead that came after him soon lost interest, moving away in search of other prey as he put distance between them.

In the areas where he was forced to walk on the streets and sidewalks, either due to a lack of vehicles or where too many undead lurked, he had to wind his way around cars, corpses, and scattered debris that littered across his path. He took great pains to be silent and stay as far away from any of the straggling undead milling about. Traffic was a mess as he moved near Canal Street which led directly to the Holland Tunnel. Cars were snarled all about the road, doors ajar on some, motors still running, corpses or undead were confined within other vehicles. Hearing heavy gunfire from the direction of the tunnel, Will hurried on past Canal Street. Although the sound of gunfire was encouraging, meaning that there were people, he chose to continue on further north. He was concerned and didn't want to be mistaken as one of the undead by whoever was shooting. He also had dire suspicions as to how many of the undead would be drawn to the noise. The thought alone of the masses of dead sent a shudder up his spine and got him moving uptown a little faster.

The things must have some sense about them, Will thought absently, noticing that any time he got within twenty feet or so of one, it would spin about to give chase. When he reached the intersection of Lafayette, he looked south to see a gas main had ruptured a block south, flames were jetting high into the air; cars and a building near it were engulfed by the inferno as well. He ruled out going north on Lafayette, wanting to stay as far away from mid-town as possible. He had already made up his mind to try to cross the Hudson and get out of the city, and even though he was so close to the Holland, he didn't like the sounds he heard from that direction. He sighed deeply, wanting nothing more than ever to be clear of the damned city, before turning north and heading towards the Lincoln Tunnel. If the Lincoln didn't pan out, he would continue on to the GWB, where the police radio said the National Guard had set up base. More than anything else he wished for as he picked his way from car to car, Will wished he was back in Wisconsin.

As the streets grew more crowded with the shifting, shuffling dead and the shadows started to lengthen, Will started to think about finding a safe spot to hole up for the night. He was torn as to whether he should concentrate on that or on getting out of the city; it felt like he needed to completely focus on one or the other. A few blocks later, he decided that he would make for the tunnel, but if a safe place opened up to him along the way, he would duck in immediately. The idea of trying to go into a strange building where those things could be around every dim corner in the hopes of finding something suitably safe and defensible terrified him more than continuing on the streets. At least out in the open, he could see danger at a distance and try to avoid it, and if he couldn't, there was room to run. He hoped that he could make his way out of the city by nightfall. He had no interest in walking the streets where the dead were hidden by the veil of darkness.

The steady flood of panic and adrenaline that kept him moving also heightened his paranoia; in response, he looked around nervously and often. It was slow moving, picking his way through the streets. In the next few blocks, the sidewalks loomed heavily with undead, and darkened windows and doorways promised sure death to him. He was too unnerved to stray close to them, preferring the winding path through traffic rather than risking an ambush. The further west he moved, the more snarled the traffic became, with both uptown and downtown traffic merging together in an attempt to reach the tunnel. Intersections were the slowest areas to traverse, so densely packed with cars he often couldn't see the ground. The sounds of gunfire seemed to have petered out over the past few blocks, but Will hardly noticed, the blood was pounding so heavily in his ears that he couldn't hear much else.

In his peripheral vision, he could see what he thought were people looking out of windows on the upper stories of the buildings he passed; almost every time he would look, the faces would pull back out of sight, leaving only the sight of draperies closing behind them. The sky was beginning to dim when he came to the intersection with Church Street. Will was nervous about what he would find at the tunnel. More cops with a barricade to turn him away? Or worse, no cops, and a walk through the gloomy tunnel at sunset. He knew he had a scant couple hours of light left to find a way out of the city or a safe place to hide. The sound of footsteps pounding the pavement nearby shook him from his reverie. About halfway down the block ahead of him, five people were running headlong toward a storefront, a bespectacled man holding the gates open for them and beckoning.

Will could just make out his words and started moving towards the storefront himself.

"Hurry, they're everywhere, get inside!" the man pleaded with a heavy Spanish accent.

When the five runners got within feet of the gate, the man's face fell; he blanched and tried to pull the halves of the gate closed. Too late he realized that the five running headlong down the street weren't survivors in need of help. From Will's vantage point, perched atop a black Lincoln Town Car, he froze and watched as the five leapt on the man and began devouring him. He could hear numerous shrieks and shouts coming from inside the shop, and three of the five zombie's heads jerked up in their direction. In unison, they lunged inside the store in pursuit of the others, leaving just the two to finish their meal on the sidewalk. Will froze, his blood running cold at the sheer speed of the things. Every one of the undead he had encountered to this point had the gait of an arthritic old man. *These ones,* Will thought, *would give Usain Bolt a run for his money.* He slid off the roof of the car as quietly as possible and crouched to where he could see the two devouring the good Samaritan through the windows of the Town Car.

Thoroughly panicked and stricken with fear at the realistic possibility that he might have a foot race with these fast zombies if they became aware of his presence, he waited a couple minutes to compose himself and consider his options. He was barely able to achieve a cohesive thought with the sound of the blood pumping in his ears and his heart doing its best to pound through his ribcage. At length, he decided his best course would be to continue on and try to sneak past the building, moving up the block on the opposite sidewalk. The police lights he had been approaching were only a block or two away, and he was desperate to see if anyone was there to help.

He crept silently around the front of the Lincoln and headed for the north side of the road, hoping he hadn't been spotted by them. He clutched the revolver tightly in his right hand, crouch-walking alongside the cars parked against the curb. He stayed as far from the buildings as possible while using the parked cars for some cover. He had never felt more alert in his life, his heart was pounding so fast it seemed like a blur. He struggled to hear past the wind and the moaning for sounds of pursuit. Blind to the happenings on the south side of the street, his eyes were wide with fear as he got to the spot that he assumed was directly across from the most recent attack. He leaned around the front of a yellow cab minivan to hazard a look. He had to raise his head slightly to see over the traffic, and finally, the storefront came into view. The sidewalk was barren, deserted but for the bloody, mangled corpse staining the concrete with the fluids that drained from its many wounds. He looked desperately around for the fast undead before coming to the conclusion that they had joined the others inside, looking for a fresh game.

The tension of the past few minutes broke something in him, he stood and started running headlong up the street. He couldn't help himself; his muscles were taut and his blood pumped with epinephrine. He saw the opportunity to get past the awful fast things and took it. He ran as fast as his legs would carry him down the sidewalk. After about ten seconds of running, a SWAT van came into view parked in front of an MTA bus, its swirling emergency lights flashed off the windows and polished metal of the cars around it. He was very aware at the slapping sounds his Brooks shoes were making as he strode towards the van. He veered out into the road in between two cabs, making a beeline for the van. So intent on reaching his goal, he didn't see the undead, the fast thing, bolt out of the back seat of the cab behind him, gore pouring from its mouth. Ten paces later, roughly a hundred feet from the van, Will became aware of footfalls slapping the pavement aside from his own. He gritted his teeth in fear and panic and pushed himself to run faster. He ran on, pushing with all of his might, waiting, in breathless anticipation, for the thing's hand to take hold of the back of his hood.

*

It was the day after Bob Jr.'s funeral when Tar awoke abruptly on his couch. Looking outside, he could see it was late afternoon, the slate gray of the sky was a few shades darker than when he had laid down. He guessed he had been out for about ninety minutes. The sound of the air-raid siren going off cut through his thoughts. Confused, he shook his head to clear the cobwebs and rub the sleep from his eyes with the heels of his palms. Swinging his legs off the couch, he pulled on his cowboy boots and patted his thick gray mustache down. He walked to the front of the house and fetched his hat, gun belt, and coat from the vestibule. He couldn't for the life of him think of a reason that the alarm would be blaring other than an emergency of some sort.

A short drive later, he steered the Silverado into the parking lot of the municipal building where the alarm had just ceased its bleating. He scanned the people gathered in front of the building as he nosed the truck into a parking space. As he stepped out into the blustery fall air, he reached behind the seat and pulled out his gunbelt, expertly swinging the strap end around him and catching it before he buckled it in place. After ensuring that the reach to the handle was comfortable, he strode towards the court entrance where he could see the sheriff and a couple townsfolk were gathered.

"It's gonna take some time for some of the ranchers to get here, Sheriff," Tar said as he strode to within earshot of the group.

"Linda, why don't you get started here. We can tell the rest as they arrive, or let the information spread itself via the usual channels," Daltry said with a smirk, referring to the gossipy nature of some of the townspeople.

Linda stepped forwards confidently, almost expecting a confrontation. She scanned the gathering of eight people and cleared her throat before starting.

"Gentlemen, ladies, it is my opinion that we need to start thinking about shutting the town off completely. The folks I'm in communication with the Centers for Disease Control in Atlanta have stopped answering their phones, and frankly, things were pretty grim leading up to that. My colleagues at the CDPHE are also having…difficulties, to put it mildly. They are shut in their labs, as the streets outside the facility are unsafe."

Daltry, who had steadily been growing redder throughout Linda's opening, finally cut in.

"Dammit, Linda, we can't go shutting the town off, you should've talked to me about that when we spoke earlier. We can't go starting a panic here."

"I think it is time to panic, Sheriff. The people of the town have a right to know what little information we do have. It can be their decision what to do with it."

"You are overstepping your bounds here, Linda."

"You've seen them, Sheriff! You were the one telling me they were too dangerous to keep around just yesterday, or did you forget that?"

Daltry stumbled over the words that were forming in his mouth at that undeniable statement. Linda took a moment to breathe and calm herself before continuing her clinical evaluation of the situation.

"There very well may be good explanations for why we can't get in touch with the CDC. But the CDPHE is right down the road in Denver, and their situation is dire. At the very least, we need to establish a curfew and advise that all people should be armed and travel accompanied whenever possible."

Tar's head reeled with the gravity of the discussion; having just woken from a nap he wasn't prepared to deal with such a grave conversation. Daltry was trying to interrupt Linda again as Tar spoke up.

"Linda," he said in his early morning gravelly voice, drawing all eyes. "You're sure about this?"

"Now hold—" Daltry started before Tar shut him down with a look that could've wilted the grass beneath their feet.

Tar turned his gaze back to the woman who nodded before speaking.

"No, I'm not sure, Tar. The only thing I am sure of is that it is a risk we cannot take. We've seen these things and what they can do, even the slow ones. There could be thousands, if not tens of thousands of them right down the road in Denver. I think that there are some steps we need to start thinking about for our security."

Tar rubbed his mustache and thought about it briefly before looking back to Daltry

"You got your panties in in a knot about something, Daltry, but what if she's right? The suggestions she is making sure make a lot of sense to me, and they cost us nothing if she is wrong."

"We risk panicking the whole town for nothing."

"Sheriff, I don't know where you've been the past few days, but the dead are getting up and attacking people. Everybody already is in a panic."

As the conversation wound its way into the minutiae, Linda drifted back towards her bicycle to return to the clinic and check on things. As she stood the bicycle upright and swung her leg over the crossbar, she was startled by a voice.

"Doc, let me bend your ear for a minute, please."

Tar was standing three feet off to the side with his hands on his hips, looking squarely at her.

"Sure, Tar, what is it?"

"The sheriff is a stubborn old git. He may or may not follow your lead on this. I want you to be straight with me, as a doctor who went to school and knows about these type of things, what do you think and feel about this thing, whatever it is?"

Linda took a breath to steady and collect herself.

"If the CDC is gone, then it's unlikely we will find a cure other than what comes out of that," she said, pointing at the pistol resting in the holster on his hip.

*

Keeping their Dodge at a steady seventy-five miles an hour, it took a bit under fifteen more minutes on the abandoned roadway before Tim and Laura reached the exit for I-86. 86 is an east-west highway, but this far south in the state, it runs more north and south. As they crested the rise and rounded the final bend before the exit, all the hopes that they had been dreaming were dashed. Before them lay nothing but carnage, sprawled across four lanes of the highway. It looked as if a barricade had been hastily set up across all the lanes of the highway as well as the median dividing them. There were two military Deuce and a Halfs, one across the lanes eastbound, and the other in the westbound lanes. Four Humvees with roof-mounted heavy machine guns sat astride the Deuces, completing the blockade. Beyond the barricades lay the tangled, smoking wrecks of dozens of cars, little remained of them, as a fire had swept through, leaving nothing but burned-out hulks. Amidst all of the wreckage shifted a mass of shuffling, smoking forms. Tim quickly moved his eyes past the shapes, not wanting to bring the amorphous mass into focus. He slowed, stopping the car on the shoulder about a half-mile away from the barricade and slid the shifter into park. Above them, on the overpass, Tim could see the distinctive shape of yet more military vehicles.

The barricade and vehicles were situated on the near side of the overpass, meaning, that in order to get onto I-86, they would need to navigate around or through the barricade and through the tangled mess of dead traffic beyond it. If they were able to pick their way through the underpass, they then would be able to exit onto I-86 east, bringing them southwards towards their home in Sugar Loaf. To the right side of the highway, Tim could see the huge earthen embankment, the top rimmed by a guardrail, beyond which lay a shopping mall. To the left of the highway was a small boggy area; beyond that lay a fenced-in field that led up to some medical buildings. He scanned the edges of the barricade for any way around, but from the distance of a half-mile away, he couldn't be certain of anything.

"We have a decision to make, Laur," he said, catching her eyes in the rear-view mirror.

"We either need to go through that," he continued, nodding towards the wreckage and shifting forms, "and maybe we get through, maybe not…maybe we can get a weapon from one of the vehicles, I dunno. Or we have to turn around and try another way."

"I don't know, Tim, please don't ask me," Laura responded. He could plainly see that the stress of the situation was getting to her.

Laura was prone to panic in normal life situations, so he knew she was in pure hell at the moment. His fingers started absently drumming on the steering wheel as he pondered the choice without her input. He really wanted to see about getting a weapon from the army vehicles. In the rest of their normal lives previous, they had always viewed guns as a danger, laying around where a kid could pick them up and have a terrible accident. They were vegetarians and did not hunt for obvious reasons, but now the idea of having a gun, at this terrible moment in time, seemed an absolute necessity. He didn't want to leave his family in the car, nor would he ask Laura get out to go with him, not that she would entertain that as an option. As he sat preoccupied with his thoughts, his phone started vibrating in his pocket. Startled, it took a moment for him to realize what was happening. He plunged his hand into his pocket, producing his flip phone. Looking at the face of it, he could see that his best friend, Bjorn, was calling. He flipped it open and put it to his ear and as nonchalantly as he was able to, he said:

"Hey buddy, you guys decide to join us on the walkway?" A moment of silence followed.

"Only you, Tim... only you would joke with this shit going down. You guys okay?" Bjorn said, his raspy voice uttered between drags off his cigarette.

"Well, that all depends on your definition of 'Okay'," Tim said. "We are trapped on 84 right now with a barricade and a bunch of cars, and those...things between us and the on-ramp to get us back down towards home."

"Fuck," Bjorn said. "I was hoping to meet up with you. Me and Lilly and the kids stopped by Lowes so I could pick up some new drop cloths...and...well, we are kinda in a pickle here."

Tim could hear Bjorn's voice with an edge of panic to it, something he had never heard before. Bjorn was a calm and thoughtful man; he carefully considered every word he spoke and rarely got angry.

"You guys hiding?" Tim queried.

"Yeah, Lilly was changing Liam in the bathroom while I was paying at the register when the shit hit the fan here. A bunch of those dead things came in and started tearing people apart...Fuck man, it was intense. I froze for a minute and started to go over to help a lady that was getting attacked, but then the thing's head snapped up and half its face was fucking gone. When it looked at me, I grabbed Sophie and we ran into the bathroom where Lilly was. We barricaded the door as best as possible, but they are out there." Bjorn's voice quivered as he recounted his tale. "It's quiet out there now, and I'd be tempted to check it out, but I can't risk the family. Kinda fucked at the moment. One of the things was in here and bit Lilly on her arm. We got the bleeding to stop, but she isn't looking too hot."

Tim took a moment to digest what Bjorn had told him. Bjorn had been his best and only friend for the last 20 years, since Bjorn's divorce from his first wife. The two of them were like brothers who didn't fight. Tim wondered for a moment about the significance of the bite; his superstitious nature immediately went to the obvious conclusion before the skeptic in him pushed the thought far off.

"You guys hold tight. I'm gonna go and try to get some weapons. Don't hang up...we may not be able to reconnect if we do," he called back to his friend and handed the phone to Laura.

"Talk to Lilly if you want. I'll be back as soon as possible, don't worry...lock the doors once I get out."

Before she could utter a word of protest, he had slipped out of the car and was moving across the median towards the eastbound lanes.

Once outside of the car, Tim's nerves started kicking in. Hearing his friend in such a dire predicament had spurred him to make a decision, to act. Now that he was out here though, alone, approaching a military barricade that had so many of those things on the other side, his courage began to wane.

"Too late now, Tim," he whispered through clenched teeth.

The plan he came up with in his five-minute walk up to the vehicles, was to creep as close as he could to the barricade in order to look for a weapon. Once he got hold of a weapon, he would then try and see if their car would be able to pick a path through the mess to the on-ramp on the other side. As he approached the barricade, he slowed his gait, creeping forward cautiously, using the bulks of one of the Deuce and a Halfs in the distance and the overturned tractor trailer beyond it to cover him from the shuffling mass beyond. From his current vantage, he could see a pair of legs moving on the other side of the Deuce, it looked like only one; all the same, he gulped down the saliva that flooded his mouth.

Laura watched as Tim closed the door of the car quietly and moved off towards the chaos ahead. She was operating on sheer panic and desperation at this point and more than anything, she wanted to yell at him. Deep down, she knew that he was doing his best to get them all through whatever the hell was happening, but whenever she was as edgy as she currently was, her mind always seemed to drift towards something he did or said to piss her off. He recently accused her of picking arguments with him as a distraction or substitute, providing her with a different set of problems, and ones she could control. That had set her off, mostly because she feared that it was true, but introspection wasn't one of her strongest traits.

She could hear Bjorn talking on the phone in her lap as she leaned forward to lock the door Tim had just exited. She knew she should talk to the man, but couldn't bring herself to pick up the phone in her current state. Instead, she focused on the form of her husband moving off towards the military vehicles. She hated him for leaving her and Luna alone in the car. She knew this made no sense whatsoever, as the alternative was him dragging them along with them, putting them in greater danger. She would never admit it, nor could she help it, but she hated him regardless of the circumstances.

Tim paused about three hundred yards away from the barricades and looked back to the car where his family waited for him. He could see

Laura's fearful face in the rear window. Seeing that they were still safe, he waved to reassure her. He glanced around to make sure he was still alone and shifted off the shoulder of the road into the tall grass that led into the boggy area. Again, taking a moment to make sure that none of those things were about him, he moved slowly, using the drainage culvert as cover, moving steadily towards the Deuce and a Half. Carefully, he scanned the highway for a dropped weapon, even a tire iron would do. He cursed himself for not grabbing one from the car before rushing away from it.

About fifty feet from the Deuce, he could see the turret gunner of the Humvee closest to him slumped over the edge of the turret; he was missing the top of his head. From this vantage point, he could clearly see that there was one of the dead things shambling about in between the Deuce and the overturned trailer in front of it. Feeling a bit more comfortable with the idea that he may only have to deal with one of the things, he moved back onto the pavement. He crouch-walked, moving towards the front of the deuce, his eyes on the winch behind the bumper. *If I can get the winch hook, I might have enough of a weapon to dispose of one*, he thought, trying to feel confident. His legs burned with each crouching step, already tired from the rush back across the walkway; they shook weakly as he moved. Approaching the Deuce, he heard a harsh rasp of feet on loose stone. The thing had heard his feet on the pavement and turned on an intercepting path, making towards the front of the Deuce itself. Tim began to run, covering the final ten feet to the corner of the bumper in a flash. He rounded the bumper to come face to face with the thing from the other side.

*

Will leapt and slid across the hood of a Ford Escort that was stalled in an eternal lane change. He propelled himself off the rear bumper and up to the roof of a Mercedes SUV. His left leg trailed behind momentarily and the fast undead chasing him grabbed his ankle before he was able to pull his leg completely over the lip of the roof. The grasping hand tripped him, stripping the sneaker from his foot, and sending him sprawling atop the car. As he bounced off the metal roof, the revolver jarred free from his hand and dropped off the passenger's side of the vehicle. He twisted and rolled backwards down the front windshield and hood of the SUV and struggled to right himself.

Still sliding on his back, he fell from the front of the vehicle and came to a stop with his back on the pavement. His legs were in the air with the shoelace of his right foot looped around the base of the hood ornament of the vehicle. He scrabbled with his hands trying to pull himself free as the undead came atop the roof of the SUV. It took only a split second for the undead to realize that the pursuit was over; its prey was there for the taking, and it leapt from atop the roof at him. He crossed his arms over his face and closed his eyes, the most primitive defense, curling up in a modified fetal position. The dead thing landed on him, its dead weight knocked the wind from him and spurred him into action. He jerked and thrust and tried desperately to flail and twist free of it before its teeth could sink home. He succeeded at keeping it at bay for a moment when a booted foot crunched into the side of its face, knocking it off of him, sending it sprawling to the street. Quicker than it could recover, the owner of the booted foot was atop it, kicking and stomping and finally driving a crowbar into its head.

Will, still in the grip of panic and terror, continued flailing about and was finally successful in ripping his sneaker free from the hood ornament. He spun to his feet and glanced furtively around seeking the shoe and the gun he'd lost in the fall. He quickly spotted and scrambled around the side of the SUV to recover them before sizing up his unexpected ally. The man was a cop, wearing full riot gear, sans helmet. He was black, around 30 years old, and had a scruffy, tufted beard that wasn't growing in regularly. He held his hands out defensively, and Will realized he was unintentionally aiming his gun at his savior. Sheepishly, Will tucked the gun away and apologized with a nod and his hands held up showing his palms

"What's your name, kid?" asked the cop

"Will."

"I'm Rashid, and just so we're straight, I'm gonna let you know that I ain't no cop. The ones that came in the SWAT van are long gone." Rashid glanced around, taking in their immediate surroundings before continuing. "I wanted some protection and they upped and left all their shit. Now, unless you plan on making friends with more of those fuckin' things, I suggest you follow me."

"Wait…" Will asked and Rashid swung about. "Is there any more of that SWAT armor in the truck?"

Rashid smiled a genuinely delighted smile and replied,

"Yeah, let's get you straight before we go."

A few moments later, both men stood in the back of the SWAT van. Will was struggling to pull on a padded flak vest while Rashid stood in the shadows, watching cautiously out the back of the van. When Will got himself fully geared up, he grabbed a riot shield, fixed it on his left arm, and walked past Rashid. Still checking his gear, he stepped out of the van and he shrieked as one of the dead slammed into the front of the shield, almost spinning him to the ground. He and the thing stood face to face with only a centimeter of Plexiglas separating them. The thing was smearing its face around on the Plexiglas, trying to bite him through it when the crowbar from the side caved its skull in, dropping it heavily to the macadam.

"You're a fuckin' magnet for them things," Rashid pointed out as he slid out of the van and onto the street in the failing light of the day. "My mom got eaten this morning."

Rashid paused as a frog jumped in his throat. He composed himself quickly and finished with, "Fuck this place; I'm leaving the city tonight."

"Yeah, I was headed towards the tunnel myself," replied Will after he was able to wrap his head around Rashid's statement. "Sorry about your mom."

*

Laura watched in panic, still seated in the backseat of the Dodge, as the undead thing came around the corner towards her husband. A weak scream crawled up unbidden from her throat.

"'Kay, Mommy?" Luna asked. Getting no response, she asked again and again and again.

"Yeah, baby, Mommy is okay," Laura finally answered just to silence the child.

Her grip on the headrest in front of her was painful as she watched the struggle between Tim and the undead start to unfold.

Instinctively, Tim grabbed the thing by its throat with both hands and dragged it to the ground; it was strong and resisted. It was wearing gore-soaked military fatigues with a patch indicating that in its previous life its name had been Watkins. Tim did the best he could to pin its arms under his knees as he came down atop the struggling thing. *Now what?* his mind screamed at him as he sat astride it. He had no leverage with which to smash the things head into the ground. He could let go and try to jump clear the thing, but knew that it could easily grab hold of him. Out of options and out of desperation, he placed the heel of his palm under the thing's jaw and pushed back in order to keep its mouth out of play. He then began searching his pockets with his free hand in hopes of finding something to help, coming up empty, he started searching the thing's pockets. Feeling cautiously and tentatively about its many pocketed uniform, he thought he could feel a familiar object in its breast pocket. He smiled victoriously and produced a ballpoint pen from the pocket. Holding it like a dagger, he started frantically stabbing at its left eye. After about five strokes, he abandoned the pen in the socket, oozing gore. He struck the end of the pen twice with the heel of his palm to make sure it drove deep into the brain. He sat astride the corpse for another ten seconds, breathing heavily with his hands shaking, covered in gore. Finally, when he was convinced the thing wasn't getting up, he snatched his hands from under its chin and jumped clear.

Once free of the struggle with the undead, he became acutely aware of how exposed he was with just the body of the truck standing between him and the crowd of moaning dead on the other side. He had no realistic idea exactly how much noise he had made in the struggle with the dead soldier. Crouching low, he scanned as far as he could see under the wheels of the vehicles around him, looking for pursuit. Seeing no more movement in the immediate vicinity, he backtracked to the passenger's side door of the Deuce and stepped up onto the running board. He brought his head up to the window and peered into the dim cab. He breathed a sigh of relief as it was empty, and gently opened the door. He looked back to his family car and gave one more wave back to his wide-eyed wife before slipping inside, onto the bench seat, and gently pulling the door shut behind him. He immediately noticed the keyless ignition that many military vehicles are equipped with, saw there was 4/5 of a tank of fuel, and proceeded to search around in vain for a weapon.

In the family car, Laura watched in panic as Tim fought the thing off. She wanted to get out and scream for him to get back to the car. She clambered over the top of the car seat to sit in the driver's seat and waited to see if she needed to drive up and get him. As she watched, he exited the cab of the big truck and swung around to stand on the hood. He stepped up on the roof of the truck where he crouched and pulled the camouflaged tarp back from the rear of the truck. She watched as he peered in for a few moments. He then stood straight and looked over the wreckage at the barricade.

Standing on the roof of the truck, he tried to piece together what had happened. From what he could figure, the soldiers were channeling people further north, away from the city he suspected. *Evacuating?* Those vehicles that had stopped and piled up in front of the barricade were being prevented from continuing east when, he assumed, the tractor-trailer had attempted to run the barricade on the shoulder. Tim could see the skid marks the truck had left as it careened from the shoulder. By the great many bullet holes in the front of the crashed truck, Tim could guess that the soldiers had opened fire, causing it to swerve and crash which likely had ignited the fire which then swept through the gathered cars. When or where the undead things had come from remained a mystery. Tim could see the movement of more than twenty of the things ambling around, seemingly aimlessly. The nearest of the undead was roughly fifty feet from him.

His interesting, but useless, assessment of the scene complete, he moved on to examine the Humvees straddling the Deuce. His eye was drawn to the dead soldier whose body hung limply in the gunner's turret. Deciding that the corpse of a dead soldier might be his best bet to find a weapon, he quietly stepped down onto the hood, then onto the front bumper and finally to the ground before moving to the side of the Humvee. Peering into the cab of the vehicle he spotted an M4 Carbine in the pass-through between the front seats. He excitedly opened the door, only to get smacked in the face by the rancid smell of congealed blood and vomit. Flies buzzed around his head as he quickly peeked in. He could see the remnants of the gunner's brain sitting in his lap. His stomach recoiled, and he felt the bile rising. He grabbed the rifle and ducked out of the Humvee as quickly as he was able to.

He cast a quick glance about to ensure he hadn't been detected before he moved towards the rear of the Deuce to check the other Humvee. Approaching the rear of the Deuce, he immediately heard the sounds of one of the undead things in the Humvee; it was raging inside, as if it were having a violent fit. It saw him and roared. Tim froze…this wasn't one of the slow ambling things he'd mostly seen up to now. This one was like the thing on the bridge that charged into the opening elevator. Its milky eyes were wide and it wore a mask of rage on its face. Tim skidded to a halt on the roadway and froze, his eyes glued to the spectacle of the thing as it ripped and tore at the door that stood in between he and it.

Laura watched from the car as Tim moved to the rear of the truck, froze in his tracks, and hurriedly shuffled back to the Humvee he had retrieved the gun from. He clambered to the roof and used the stock of the gun he now had to push the soldier back before reaching with his free hand and in rapid succession taking a few clips of ammunition and a pistol from the corpse's vest, dropping them in his cargo pockets. Standing atop the Humvee, he looked at her, and once she acknowledged that she was paying attention with a nod. He pointed to the Deuce then himself, then to her and made a steering motion followed by pointing at her.

"Okay, okay, okay," she said aloud as she strapped her seatbelt on, then mouthed obscenities in silence while she waited for him.

Tim slid off the roof of the Humvee and dashed to the still open door of the Deuce, climbing in and pulling the door shut behind him. Once the cab was secured, he slid across the bench seat behind the steering wheel and buckled the seatbelt. He remembered that the last time he took a hard left-hand corner, at speed, in a car on a bench seat, he had to steer the rest of the turn from the passenger seat. Although before today he had never done it, for the second time in an hour, he said a quick prayer before pressing the clutch to the floor and then turning the ignition. With a loud diesel-fueled roar, the heavy vehicle came to life. Tim popped the shifter in reverse and backed it quickly before cutting the wheel and slamming it into first gear. Hammering the gas, the heavy vehicle roared ahead.

Laura watched as the little smokestack that ran up the side of the cab belched out a puff of black smoke into the crisp fall air and started to move. She maneuvered the shifter into drive, holding still with her foot on the brake. Tim steered the thing into the eastbound lanes until he was parallel with Laura then he swung the big truck across the wide grass median, pulling it alongside the Dodge. She saw him appear in the passenger's window of the truck just above her and roll it down.

"Get Luna and get in here, no car seat... now please," he called down to her.

Unthinking, she turned the car off and reached over the top of the car seat and unbuckled Luna from there. She pulled the child, now fast asleep, over top of the seat along with the diaper bag. She took a minute, burdened with the trappings of parenthood, to look around the vehicle for anything else they would need. She grabbed a pair of water bottles from the center console, throwing them in the diaper bag and jumped out of the car. Tim, having climbed down from the Deuce to help, grabbed the bag and Luna from her and helped her up into the cab. Once Laura was in the cab, he handed Luna up to her and slid the bag in by her feet.

Laura watched her husband run around the front of the truck towards the driver's side door. As he came around the bumper, she saw one of the undead things running like a track star at him. The thing was dressed in military fatigues; its face was streaked with gore, mouth agape and hands splayed in front like ravenous claws.

"Tim!" she screamed and could do nothing more but watch in horror as the thing closed the last thirty feet between them roaring in at him with blinding speed.

Tim noticed the undead as it lunged at him, and he just barely managed to sidestep it, its fingers clutching his shirt briefly. The thing tripped on his trailing foot and was sent tumbling in a thrashing heap between the two vehicles. Tim didn't hesitate for an instant, running as fast as his feet could carry him, he moved around the front of the truck and up into the cab. Door slammed and locked, he reached across to lock Laura's door and hastily put it in gear. As fast as the six-wheeled behemoth would allow, they headed along the right shoulder towards the underpass. Looking in the side-view mirror, he could see the fast undead running alongside them. It was slamming and slapping at the side of the truck; it ripped and tore at anything it could get a grip on. Eventually, as the Deuce got up to speed, the thing faded back into the distance.

He had to slow the truck down in order to push the heavy vehicle past a couple cars, which it had no problem in doing. His concentration was so intense as he steered, picking their way through the mess of abandoned, burnt or broken-down vehicles, that he didn't have a chance to appreciate the scope of the carnage they were passing through. Laura, however, got to witness it all. She saw, among other atrocities, a person burned beyond recognition gnawing on the arm of what couldn't be more than a five-year-old girl with blonde pigtails. The sight of the little girl's limp body being devoured broke her heart. She cried long and hard, her body shuddering and spasming as she fought to remain silent. Tim guided the Deuce onto the eastbound exit which looped almost completely around before merging onto I-86, one step closer to home. The eastbound lanes they merged onto were desolate, barren of any traffic whatsoever. The westbound lanes, coming from I-87, Westchester and the city beyond, were a sea of bumper-to-bumper, stalled traffic. As far as they could see east and west, it was a still river of glass and steel, the only movement coming from the many undead things shuffling and shambling about, both trapped inside and wandering outside the cars. The undead in the westbound lanes heads snapped around upon hearing the sound of the noisy diesel engine of the Deuce. They turned to follow the truck if they were able to; if not, their heads tracked the progress of the truck until it moved out of earshot. It seemed that all life had left the world. If not for Bjorn's phone call, Tim might have thought that he, Laura, and Luna were all that remained. They traveled in silence, each lost in their own grief-riddled wondering. Tim's grief was not so much rooted in what he had lost, but what they had left to lose. Laura's was rooted in the present fear and danger. Both were united in their fear that this was widespread, and they might have difficulty getting to safety. They feared that any mistake they made could endanger each other, and more importantly, their precious daughter.

The undead shuffling about in the westbound lanes was unsettling and loomed menacingly in Tim's thoughts. His grip on the steering wheel was tense, causing his fingers to ache, and he was eager to get away from the heavily trafficked roads. He knew the backroads in this area very well, as he had grown up in nearby Warwick. When they crested a small rise, approaching the town of Goshen exit, three out of the four eastbound lanes were a snarl of wrecked cars, and on the overpass, Tim could see the remains of another barricade. He slowed the Deuce down to see if they could exit the highway, but after a brief examination, he could see that each of the ramps was a snarled pile-up and there was no hope of them being able to navigate it. He opened his mouth to speak to Laura about trying the next Goshen exit, but before he was able to get a word out, the sound of a wet slap startled him.

Tim looked around furtively for the source of the sound before another loud wet slap drew his eye. His face screwed up in disgust as he saw the undead atop the overpass, drawn by the noise of the truck, pushing to the edge of the guardrail and falling to the tarmac below. He hit the gas pedal hard, anxious to be away from those things. He was almost able to put his anxiety aside when he couldn't see the undead. He was almost able, in those moments, to convince himself that it was some kind of horrible nightmarish hallucination.

The next exit, a half-mile further up the highway, was also a no-go; being a hospital exit, it was mobbed and they were barely able to negotiate the highway to move beyond it. They could see large canopy tents set up in the hospital parking lot, innumerable of the things roamed about, feasting on remains. Tim shuddered at the sight and eased the truck through a narrow gap on the left shoulder to continue on towards the town of Chester, where his friend and his family were hiding for their lives. He began to get the idea that there would be barricades and snarled westbound traffic at every exit to the city.

"Laura, do you still have the phone?" Tim asked, remembering he told Bjorn not to hang up.

Without speaking, Laura reached into the diaper bag and produced the phone, thrusting it across to him before returning to stare blankly out the passenger's side window.

"Bjorn…you still there, man?" Tim asked.

The silence that followed was long and Tim began to lose hope.

"Yeah, Tim, sorry, been a bit so I put the phone on speaker and got busy with the kids," finally came a squawked response.

"Getting busy with the kids. That's just sick, man," Tim jested.

"Funny guy," started Bjorn before Tim interrupted.

"Listen, man, we are on 86 now just past Goshen, should be closing in on Chester in a couple minutes. We couldn't get off the highway before now, so keep your fingers crossed that there is a way for us to squeeze through; otherwise, we will have to keep going until we can find an exit and try to double back. We are coming for you guys though; hang in there."

"Thanks, brother, we'll be here," came the reply.

Tim set the phone on the seat next to him as the next overpass came into view ahead. Once again, they could see the barricades set up atop the overpass, but on the near side, it looked as if a tractor-trailer had rammed the barricade. Its burned-out hulk still smoldered in the late morning light. Tim saw no way up the ramp that led to Lowes; it was jammed with cars. As the Deuce drifted down through the gears, Tim decided he would try gong up the exit ramp. He hoped that the soldiers had been successful in keeping cars from headed eastbound. Regardless, Tim swung the truck wide to the left and back hard to the right, bringing the truck in a tight loop. He let off the gas, allowing the engine to brake itself as he cut the wheel, steering the heavy truck onto the ramp.

They could immediately see that there were no vehicles on the ramp as he straightened the wheel back out. At the top of the ramp, however, was the smoldering, hulking mass of a wrecked tractor-trailer. The truck had impaled itself on a concrete partition that had been set up as a barricade. Luckily for them, the force of the heavy truck hitting it had forced the barrier away from the ramp they were headed up. Slowing to a crawl as they approached the top of the ramp, Tim cut the wheel hard to the left, aiming the Deuce between the tractor-trailer and the guardrail on the shoulder. It was too tight, Tim could see that right away.

"Fuck," he muttered hitting the brakes.

They sat for a minute before Tim threw it in reverse and backed the Deuce up as far as the ramp would allow. Before Laura could raise her voice in protest, not that she had any inclination to at the moment, so deep was her reverie, he slammed the truck into first gear and floored it, steering the heavy vehicle towards the narrow gap between the tractor-trailer's rear wheels and the guardrail. Second gear hammered home, followed shortly after by third.

"Hang on," Tim said through clenched teeth, hoping to force the truck through.

He braced himself, as the impact was imminent.

*

Will and Rashid carefully picked their way through the streets of lower Manhattan, moving ever closer to the Lincoln tunnel. With Rashid in the lead, Will fell easily into step behind. He was glad to have someone to follow, having been on his own for numerous blocks, since O'Malley died. With the comfort of having Rashid to follow, Will allowed his mind to wander a bit. He started wondering what they would do once they got out of the city. Were the undead running around isolated and contained to the city? Would they meet roadblocks? Was the city under quarantine? Or, and Will pushed the thought away as it was terrifying, was this everywhere? Where could they find safety? His mind drifted in this vein for a bit before he finally pushed them away, coming to the conclusion that wherever they found safety, it certainly would not be within the confines of a city of 10 million. He held out faith that the National Guard had shut the city off for a reason: to contain it. He only hoped that they would let the living out. A couple times in the next few blocks, people attempted to approach the duo, mistaking them for cops. They were quickly dismissed with a raised crowbar from Rashid or a threat from Will's gun.

"Think we should help these people?" Will asked as a middle-aged man in coveralls scurried back in the shadows from Rashid's threatening stance.

"We don't know them," Rashid started, seeing Will's curious gaze he continued. "They might be infected."

"Wouldn't we be safer though? If there were a bunch of us with weapons?"

"Maybe." Rashid shrugged. "My guess is that these people aren't fighters. If I had to guess, they've been hiding, scared off their asses, and now, the idea that we might be cops is drawing them out. Not one of them has carried a weapon."

"They might act as cannon fodder so to speak," Will posited.

He grasped at straws, trying to get Rashid to see a tactical use for them, his pity and desire to help the people momentarily overcoming his logic.

"You know the saying about bears; you don't have to be the fastest, just so long as you aren't the slowest."

"That's cold, man." Rashid replied, only half-interested in the conversation.

"Colder than leaving them to die?"

Rashid shrugged again and remain silent for a minute before speaking again.

"You think our chances of getting out of the city with a mob of people will be better? What happens when we get to the barricade? Cops just gonna say, 'Oh, sure, all three hundred of you come on out.' I don't know if they'll let you and me out or not, but what happens with a crowd? We gotta turn around and find someplace safe and keep a dozen, fifty, hundreds of people both safe and quiet…"

Will, who had already begun to grasp the situation, listened to the man's logic without response. He knew Rashid was right; the other people had nothing to offer but trouble, but for his small-town upbringing and morality, it was a hard pill to swallow. As much as Will hated leaving others to their fate, he knew that if he had any hope of getting out of the city, it was with Rashid.

As they approached the Port authority garage, where the Lincoln

Tunnel dumps out into Manhattan, Will grabbed Rashid's arm. He heard the sound of loud aircraft coming in low. He had only ever heard that sound once before, when his father had brought him to watch the Blue Devils put on an airshow over Green Bay as a child. His heart sunk; he knew what the noise foretold, and it wasn't an airshow. A few moments later, a set of chest-pounding explosions rocked them. Once the initial blast faded, they could hear a number of other explosions echoing and roaring up the avenues. They ran down the ramp towards the tunnel in time to see water spilling out from the entrance. The initial force of the water subsided and the waterline retreated back a few feet, coming to rest amidst the cars stalled in traffic. The tunnel had been collapsed.

"What...the...fuck..." Rashid said, his jaw sagging in shock.

Will just shook his head in utter disbelief and exasperation.

Looking around them, they could see no lurking undead. After a few moments of stunned silence, they continued moving in the direction of the sunken tunnel. They briefly discussed what Will heard over the police radio back at the Brooklyn Bridge. In short order, they came to the conclusion that the government had probably decided to shut the city off by knocking out all the bridges and tunnels that connect the island of Manhattan to New York State and New Jersey. This inspired a ray of hope into Will; surely they contained it. In his mind, all they would have to do was escape the city and they would be in the clear. He feared the military would be less than willing to allow them out. As they approached the lanes entering and exiting the tunnel, they heard a commotion from inside the tunnel moving toward them. They dove behind the concrete half-wall of the parking garage ramp and watched as a handful of people came running out of the tunnel. Their splashes through the water echoed loudly off the surrounding concrete and stone structures. Will and Rashid quietly watched as the troupe paused to discuss their path.

Completely unsure of their next move, Will and Rashid waited for the fleeing people to pass before they crept out of the shadows. They decided, at length, to spend the night in the back of a box truck that had stalled out and now had its front end submerged in the river water. They waded about fifteen feet out into the new Hudson shoreline before they were able to climb onto the tailgate and pull the roll-top door open. It wasn't the most comfortable of accommodations, but at least it would allow them to keep dry, and hopefully keep any undead at bay. Besides that, if people or the undead did come close, at least they could hear them splashing through the water as they approached the truck. The interior of the truck smelled of machine oil and burned metal. Will shivered in the chilly fall air and had to wrap his shirt around his face to keep the acrid smell from burning in his lungs.

Will could hear Rashid rolling about restlessly for hours before he himself finally drifted into a fitful sleep. A few hours later, they both gave up the ghost of getting any kind of meaningful rest and got themselves geared to move. As the first morning light came up from the east, the two sat dejectedly on the rear tailgate of the truck with their stomachs rumbling. They were both exhausted and both physically and mentally drained. Their morning conversation was terse.

"Ideas?" Rashid said not bothering to look in Will's direction.

"Looks like we either have to move up to the GWB and see if we are right about the quarantine, or we gotta find another way across the river," Will replied.

"My uncle used to work for Carnival cruise lines; they dock up around here," Rashid offered.

Will considered the idea; he was sure that he was right about the bridges and tunnels being destroyed. At least the docks offered hope of a lifeboat or rowboat they could commandeer.

"Sounds good to me, let's get moving and get the fuck out of the city," Will grumbled.

They picked their way quietly and carefully in the dim dawn light, headed a few blocks south to the waterfront. The city was eerily quiet in the early dawn hours. Will watched the traffic lights running off into the distance switching in unison as the dead traffic of the city around them refused to move. The sight sent shivers up his spine, thinking about how many people lost their lives the day prior, and left him wondering blackly, how many more sat barricaded in their apartments waiting for help that would never come. Will knew that they would be waiting, in terror for the undead to break through or to run out of food and water, whichever happened first. The thought of the innumerable undead that were prowling the hallways and lobbies of the buildings throughout Manhattan caused him to shudder. The terror of these thoughts urged him onward, reigniting his resolve to get out of the city. He wanted nothing more than to feel the freezing northern winds sweep down into Benoit, Wisconsin and to hear the dead leaves crunch beneath his feet in the front yard of his parent's house as the clouds drifted past.

Ferries ran both to the south and north of the Lincoln Tunnel; further north of that was where the many cruise ships lay docked. As they moved down towards the waterfront, however, the two lost what little hope they had of using watercraft to cross. The entirety of the docks of Manhattan had been destroyed; cruise ships and ferry alike, sunk into the river. Chunks of the concrete jetties remained with tangled and bent rebar poking out from it. The river was cluttered with debris, and great swaths of it were on fire as diesel continued to burn in the wreckage. Promenades and footpaths lay scorched and smoldering in the morning light. Nothing left to do at the moment, the two continued their walk down to the docks, hoping to find a rowboat or something cast off by the explosions that they could salvage in order to make the crossing.

They searched well into the afternoon before giving up hope of anything but a makeshift raft when Rashid clutched Will by the shoulder. Will spun with fear shooting up his spine, unsure why he was being grabbed, and saw Rashid looking up the ramp into an hourly parking lot.

"Even if we could get one started, the roads are crammed and the tunnels and bridges are shot. Let's keep moving north and see if we can't find something," Will said dejectedly.

Rashid still held him firm for another moment before he finally spoke.

"No, look, man, not the cars...the trailer!"

Sure enough, a low trailer caught Will's eye, and perched on it were two intact Ski-doos. The two raced to the fence, both hitting it at the same time. Will, seeing the barbed wire atop the fence, eyed the padlock for a brief moment, considering trying to smash it off before rejecting the idea due to the noise involved. The barbed wire deterred neither of them for more than a moment. They scaled the fence quickly, both carefully placing their hands on the barbed wire carefully in order to avoid the barbs. Once they were able to safely swing a foot onto the wire, they nimbly went over the top and dropped onto the tarmac below. While Rashid immediately went for the trailer, Will went for the lot booth, where the attendant would be stationed all day, hoping the truck and gate keys may have been left there.

Before trying the door to the booth, Will carefully walked a full lap around it, peering intently in the windows. Finally satisfied that nothing moved either inside or outside the booth, he gripped the knob and turned it, pulling the door wide open and jumping back, pistol at the ready. In any other situation, while not holding a pistol, he would've looked foolish, like a child playing cops and robbers standing in an empty doorway. He was well past the point of insecurities about how he looked; he only cared about not getting ambushed by those things again.

*

The Deuce and a Half bounced off the side of the tractor-trailer, crunching heavily into the guardrail before ricocheting back again. As the avenue narrowed, the Deuce ground itself firmly between the two.

Close to stalling, Tim dropped it into first and floored it, hoping the heavy diesel engine could carry them through the other side. Steel screamed from both sides as the truck grated against both the guardrail and the side of the trailer. The front passenger-side tire of the Deuce blew out as it shredded itself against the tireless wheel of the trailer. Tim's grip on the steering wheel was white-knuckled, and he leaned as far forward as his seatbelt would allow, physically willing the truck to break free. Gradually, the rear of the trailer shifted an inch, then another, and then again. Finally, the trailer shifted enough, releasing its grip on the Deuce, grudgingly allowing the truck to scrape free of the trap he had steered them into. Next to him, he heard Laura sigh audibly as he veered the truck through stalled cars and a narrow gap in traffic, across two lanes and onto the clear shoulder. Lowes lay beyond the guardrail on this side of the road. Tim could tell the truck was on its last legs now, running on a flat tire attached to a bent wheel. The smell of smoke and burning clutch filled the cab as he eased it into the turning lane that led into the store parking lot. He grabbed the phone from the seat next to him and said excitedly:

"We are here, guys. Give me a minute to get Laura and Luna to safety. I've got an idea."

Tim pulled the truck up next to the main entrance, parallel to the building. Without hesitation, he jumped out, and very nimbly for a large man, climbed atop the hood of the truck. He stood atop the hood and turned to his wife.

"Hand Luna to me and get up here, sweetie."

Laura obliged, taking the hand he extended to her to help her up next to him. From here, they stepped atop the cab, and Tim indicated for Laura to climb atop the giant red overhang protruding from the store. Laura, still shell-shocked, didn't have it in her to argue with him about her fear of heights; she simply did as she was told. Tim was extremely grateful; it tore him up to be separated from them in such a dangerous situation. His plan was more dangerous and much less thought-out than he would have liked, but he was desperate and the truck was sputtering. All the same, he left them atop the bright red awning and hopped back in the cab. Safely inside, he grabbed the phone and said:

"I'm going to blow the horn to try and draw all the things out of there. Wait a couple minutes after it starts going to try and come out, okay?"

"No problem, man, ready whenever," Bjorn said.

Tim could hear Lilly's voice in the background start reaching a crescendo of panic, though he couldn't make out the words through the phone.

"Bjorn…Bjorn!" he shouted into the phone, trying to get his attention back from Lilly.

"Yeah, Tim?"

"I need you to grab a ladder and get Laura from the front awning on your way out. Be careful. Get everyone to your car and wait for me if you can. Most of all, move fast, man. Some of these things aren't slow and weak…some are fucking track stars on crack," Tim finished.

The muted sounds of Bjorn arguing with Lilly greeted him in return.

"Good luck, bro," he said, closing the phone at last, absently sliding it into his pocket.

Tim lay his palm in the middle of the steering wheel and took a deep breath as he pressed down. The blaring horn cut through the silence of the late morning, echoing off the concrete building. When the first of the dead ambled out of the structure, he eased the truck into first gear and began to creep away from the building. Turning the wheel, he aimed the truck towards the far corner of the lot. In the rear-view mirrors, he could already see a steady stream of undead things exiting the building and following. As he steered back towards the front of the lot, he could see more of the dead moving down the road from the barricade. *No fast ones yet,* he thought, a sigh of relief escaping his lips involuntarily.

Laura was uncomfortable with the height she and Luna were stranded atop. Although, it was only fifteen feet or so to the ground, with no way to climb down, nor anywhere to traverse to, she felt both exposed and trapped atop the concrete and steel awning. She clutched Luna into her chest, afraid the curious girl would wander off the edge. When she struggled and fussed, Laura pulled her shirt down, fully exposing her chest to the child, who proceeded to nuzzle in and quiet down. Laura nearly jumped out of her skin when Tim laid on the horn of the truck; a shrill scream escaped her lips unbidden. She watched in abject terror as the undead began to spill from the entrance of the store, following after the departing truck. She had to fight to stave off the irrational thoughts that Tim was abandoning them. The undead staggered, limped, and shambled along, the vision of mindless desire. Their breathless moans drifted up to them.

"Wassat noise, Mommy?" Luna asked, looking up at her mother with a sweet round face.

"Nothing, sweetie," Laura responded absently as she watched the gruesome procession across the parking lot. "Just the wind."

As the truck approached the end of the lot, Tim started to get anxious; this was as far as he had thought out his plan. He remembered the car parked a few spots down from them in the parking lot at the walkway and decided to take a chance. He buckled and tightened his seatbelt, picking up some speed to put some distance between him and the mob, then he ran the truck over the curb at the end of the lot. His body heaved and jerked as the truck careened down the steep embankment, coming violently and shuddering to rest in a copse of boggy trees. He dropped the shifter into neutral and unbuckled himself. He first tried to rip the cushion off the bench. Failing at that, he spotted the fire extinguisher under the seat. He grabbed it and propped it between the front edge of the seat and the horn. He threw the diaper bag and M4 over one shoulder and climbed out the passenger side of the truck with a pistol in hand.

Laura had to stifle a scream as the truck careened over the curb and down a steep embankment. She stood, clutching Luna tightly against her. *Did one of those things get in there with him? Did he have a heart attack…a stroke?* She always worried about these things for him since he gained the weight, but now, it just compounded the fear in her heart. The sounds of the horn blaring through the air stuttered and stopped for a moment before cutting the silence once again. Her panicked brain began to overload at the possibilities of the crash. The anxiety subsided slightly when, from her vantage point, she was able to see the door swing open and Tim slide out onto the ground and start moving along the base of the embankment, back towards the store. The panic wouldn't go away, however, as she watched the horde of dead moving in his general direction towards the truck.

Nervously, he looked up the fifteen feet to the top of the embankment. To his relief, nothing appeared yet. He started running back towards the store alongside the lot. It was fairly easy to move quickly along the base of the embankment, and he was able to put nearly a hundred feet behind him before the first of the undead crested the embankment above. Thankfully, the fire extinguisher did its job and the horn kept them occupied with the Deuce. He glanced back, transfixed for a moment as the undead began tumbling down the embankment towards the truck in search of him. He was snapped from the reverie by the sound of Lilly screaming in mindless terror from the lot above. This urged him on faster, half-crawling, half-scrambling up the embankment as he went. Finally, he grabbed the curb and pulled himself to where he could view the lot.

Laying prone on the ground near the top of the embankment, he could see Laura still atop the awning, clutching Luna, looking at him. Even from this distance, he could see her tears. He quickly scanned the lot and could see Bjorn loading his family in their minivan. To the right of that, a few hundred feet distant, moved the main body of the mob of undead, moving inexorably towards the blaring horn of the Deuce. Tim pulled himself atop the curb, gun in hand, and began a cautious jog back towards where Laura was. Tim was cursing Bjorn, thinking the man had abandoned the plan for his family's own safety, but when he cast another quick glance, he could see Bjorn making an intersecting course towards him. Bjorn's scraggly hair whipped out behind him and he smiled broadly at his friend. Tim set his own panic aside for a moment and embraced his friend. They hugged and pounded each other's backs for a moment before withdrawing. Bjorn broke from him and ran into the store, coming out a moment later with an extending twenty-four-foot ladder.

"I spotted this on the way out," he said, guiding the thing's rubberized feet onto the ground.

He lifted the ladder high into the air, extending it at the same time. His years of practice with ladders working construction coming through with smooth precision. Bjorn scaled the ladder like a monkey, coming down seconds later with a red-faced, crying Luna.

"Get her to the car," said Tim. "I'll grab Laura and be right there."

Tim watched Bjorn tear across the lot as he clutched Luna into his chest and felt a bit more comfortable as the little girl was whisked into the safety of the minivan. He eyed the parking lot suspiciously as Laura slowly and cautiously climbed down the ladder. When she was about 5 feet from the bottom, Tim grabbed her around the waist. A small scream erupted from her lips as he swung her free from the ladder, setting her lightly on the ground. He took her hand and the two ran to the waiting van. Lilly was in the driver's seat and looked as if she were out of her mind with terror while Bjorn loaded Luna into the back.

They could hear Lilly screaming for Bjorn to close the door as the two approached. Tim and Laura jumped in the back, and Bjorn slammed the door shut, jumping into the passenger seat. Laura grabbed Luna off the seat, pulling the child protectively into her bosom. The DeMott family, reunited, clutched one another on the rearmost seat as Lilly put the car in gear and took off like a bat out of hell. She was manic, scared to death, and all of them could see in an instant, not fit to drive. Bjorn put his hand on hers and looked at her until she finally looked back.

"Stop the car, Lill," he said calmly to her, not breaking her gaze.

She stopped and he slid the shifter into park and switched seats with her. Lilly climbed in the back with her kids, on the middle bench seat, and broke down, hugging her children into her chest. As she traversed the seats, Tim could see a wad of brown paper towels wrapped around Lilly's bloody left bicep.

Tim kissed Luna on the side of her head, calming now with a boob in mouth, then after kissing Laura on her forehead, he slid around the middle seat, moving to the front of the van to ride shotgun next to Bjorn. They spoke in hushed tones as Bjorn eased the van across the road into the industrial park. Past a park-and-ride, they drove slowly down the desolate roadway straddled by open fields that led into the industrial park proper.

"You hear from your dad?" Tim asked him.

Roger, Bjorn's dad, was a shit-hit-the-fan kind of guy; guns, emergency rations; you name it, he was prepared. Bjorn had always said that meeting up with his father was his best bet in any scenario they discussed.

"No, I tried on Lilly's phone a few times but no dice," he said, glancing at Tim. "Is it *that* kind of bad?"

"From my view of the highway on the way down here, yeah. Bumper-to-bumper traffic, crawling with those things. Looks like they had some kind of evacuation going up 86; you four are the first living people we've seen in over an hour. We need to get somewhere we can think and plan...somewhere we can put the families where they are safe." They exchanged glances and shared an understanding.

In their mid-twenties, Tim and Bjorn had shared a house for a couple years. They were both single and drinkers and had on a few occasions after watching an apocalyptic movie stayed up to the wee hours discussing survival in whatever scenario the movie took place in. The terrifying thing in this reality was, they never anticipated having wives and children to protect and care for. Tim and Laura had a house in a residential neighborhood; a fenced-in yard, but no property to speak of. The fact that it was surrounded by a hundred other houses made him worry that they might find themselves in a dire situation fast if they were to return home.

"My house is probably safer than your apartment...but further away," Tim said

"Yeah, we can fortify your house though, right?"

"I suppose we could, I just worry about the noise we would make hammering and drilling boards up. I think we might find ourselves in a prison of our own making by the time we were done."

"How much gas do we have?"

"Fuck," Bjorn said, looking down at the gauge. "Quarter tank. We were going to hit the Sunoco back in town when we were done at Lowes."

"Your dad's house is off the table then; don't think we would make it to Ridgewood on a quarter tank," Tim said sighing. "It's probably not a good idea to drive into more densely populated areas anyways."

They reached a stop sign with an enormous paper supply warehouse in front of them, standing like a giant white monolith. Bjorn flipped his blinker on to turn left. Catching himself, he grinned sheepishly and shrugged.

"Habit," he said.

A moment later, his face lit up as he came out of the turn.

"WGS," Bjorn stated flatly, satisfied, pointing about half a mile ahead at a beige monstrosity of a cinderblock building with a huge WGS painted in black on it.

"What?" Tim said, looking confused.

"It's a grocer's warehouse. They supply all the supermarkets in the area."

Tim's face softened for a moment before concern washed over his features.

"Stop!" he demanded. "Stop, Bjorn, stop the fucking car!"

Bjorn stopped the car in the middle of the unlined roadway and looked pointedly at Tim with a confused look on his face.

"Quick, pull up there," Tim urged, pointing at a driveway lined with tall shrubbery. "Go, man, don't you hear the shooting?"

The short driveway led to an industrial lubricant warehouse with a sign indicating ILS Industrial Lubricant Solutions above the main entrance. Bjorn pulled up on the side of the building and listened. He could hear the staccato sound of gunshots popping off in the near distance. The lot they pulled into was desolate, only a single car was parked out of the hundred or so parking spots. The car bore the logo of a company called Crystal Globe Security. Tim eased out of the passenger's side door of the van, closing it gently behind him before moving towards the building. He heard the driver's door close behind him and waited for Bjorn to join him.

"Where the fuck are they going?" Lilly called out, her voice panicked as Bjorn slid out from the behind the steering wheel.

Laura didn't respond. Lilly's panicked question echoed her exact thoughts at that moment.

"One of those…things bit me." Lilly said, examining her wound. "You think it will get infected?"

Laura ignored the question, too intent on watching Tim. Her worries controlled her mind, sending it down every path of doom.

Tim handed the pistol to Bjorn and unslung the M4, bringing it to the ready.

*

There was no one in the attendant's booth. Before stepping inside, Will checked his surroundings again, the tension of the moment had broken and he felt the need to ensure his safety. He saw Rashid trying to get in the truck that the jet-ski trailer was attached to with no luck. Once he had made sure there was no one else around, living or dead, he stepped inside the small booth and closed the door tightly behind him, sliding the deadbolt closed. There wasn't much to look at in the booth; it might have been a four-foot by six-foot space without furniture; a stool whose tattered seat had been repaired so many times there was more curled gray duct tape than the original black and orange woolen upholstery on it; a desk area and a mini fridge with a coffee pot atop it sat behind him. He hadn't eaten since the artisanal granola bar he had, the morning prior and was ravenously hungry. He ripped the fridge open, his stomach audibly growling at the mere thought of food, but it only held a black nylon jacket emblazoned with the word 'Attendant' on the back. He then searched the desk for the key box to no avail. Looking under the desk fruitlessly, he finally flipped the stool over in frustration. *Nothing,* he thought. *Whoever owns the lot must take the keys home at night.*

The idea that the attendant went home with the key didn't make sense to him, but he was out of ideas. He stood and turned from the fridge and started towards the door when a worn spot on the paneled wall caught his eye. There was a hole the size of a finger and the faux wood finish had worn off to a grease-stained yellow. In the dim light inside the booth, Will thought he could see the outline of a recessed panel in the wall. He approached, and sure enough, there it was. He popped his finger in the hole, curled it, and pulled. The paneling popped off easy enough and had been covering what looked like a circuit box. His heart sank, but lifted immediately when he opened it. Instead of an array of breaker switches, he found about thirty sets of keys hanging individually from hooks. He snatched all the keys out of the box, piling them into the front of his shirt, and ran out to Rashid. He dumped the keys on the ground outside the driver's side door of the truck, and both men scrambled about the ground, hitting unlock buttons on them until they found the right one.

Ripping open the door of the Cherokee, Rashid set about tearing the contents of the truck out onto the ground looking for the trailer keys. Will grabbed the largest wad of keys in the pile and made his way over to the padlocked gate, hoping to find the one to unlock it; although ramming the gate open with one of the vehicles was an option, he figured that being as quiet as possible would be their best course. It was then, while looking out through the locked gates, that Will realized they had not seen one of the dead things all morning…they also hadn't seen a single living person. He pushed the thought away before he got lost in the significance of it, and within moments, found a key that worked in the gate. Will left the key in the padlock, figuring that they or someone else might need to make a hasty retreat and figured it was good karma to do so. He returned to where Rashid was finishing up unlocking the Ski-doos from the trailer.

Within minutes, the two were struggling to manually drag the laden trailer out of the lot and down to the ramp. Struggling for every foot they moved the thing on its under-inflated tires, they managed finally to get it onto the ramp. Rashid handed him a key that had a piece of foam the size of his fist attached to it, and gave the trailer one final shove.

The trailer rumbled the last 50 feet to the water, the hitch arm bounced noisily off the faux cobblestone finish that was molded into the concrete of the ramp. The din cut through the eerie silence and both men flinched from the sound. When the trailer hit the water, it disappeared from sight, leaving the two brightly colored jet-skis bobbing in the dark, roiling water.

They cast a quick smile at each other and jogged the remaining distance to the water. They discarded their riot shields and waded out to the jet-skis. Will moved to a neon-green and white thing with a blue spatter paint pattern on it. After a brief struggle, he was able to mount and start it up. A few minutes later, they were speeding out across the Hudson River towards New Jersey. Both had huge grins on their faces, their spirits were lifted by the sight of the city behind them as well as the exhilaration of riding on the Ski-doos.

"Let's head upriver once we get to the far shore," Will yelled over the wind and whine of the motors. "The further north we go, the less populated."

Rashid looked at him crookedly; Will understood the unasked question and pointed to the fires and smoke rising from the Weehawken skyline on the Jersey side. Rashid paled when he saw, and focusing his attention, away from the chaos that lay on the shore ahead. The two turned north, moving parallel with the Jersey shoreline. Their pace was slower now, as the recreational craft struggled against the current of the powerful river. After twenty minutes of struggling against the current, Rashid's ski-doo sputtered and ran out of gas. Will noticed him slip behind and picked him up from the stranded watercraft and they continued up the river together on the single Ski-doo. Will was completely focused on keeping the jet-ski within a short swim to the shoreline, but not close enough to risk hitting the rocks in the shallows when Rashid started tapping him insistently on the shoulder. He glanced around and Rashid pointed up in the distance. Will's jaw dropped in surprise, and he crashed the thing onto the rocks, sending them both scrambling up a steep, crushed stone embankment. The two men climbed over a railing onto a promenade. Once they gained the flat concrete at the top of the promenade, they both stood in stunned silence at the sight of the George Washington Bridge, or lack thereof, just ahead.

Both levels of the bridge fell off into nothing just beyond the first support towers that sat at the edge of the water. Cables hung limply into the water. Chunks of steel rose here and there from the cold black water of the Hudson; other than that, the bridge ceased to exist.

*

"Holy shit, man!" Bjorn said, noticing Tim's rifle for the first time. "That's an M4!"

Tim smirked at him, and they moved off along the edge of the building together. Once they reached the corner, they paused, while Tim peered around the front of the building; along the length of it, nothing moved. Once they turned the corner, the two could see that the high bushes blocked their view of most of the industrial park. They could only see the top edge of most of the other buildings that were nearby. Still, the sound of gunshots popping off, continued in the near distance. They couldn't be sure with the echoes coming off concrete walls, but it sounded as if they were coming from the direction of the WGS building. The Chester Police Station lay a mile or so beyond the industrial park, but Tim doubted that the shots were coming from there, they sounded to be much closer than that.

The duo cautiously approached the security car parked in front of the main entrance. They could see a lunch bag sat sitting open on the passenger's seat and a coat draped over the driver's seat. Tim tried the handle, but the door was locked. Just as they were finished examining the car, they heard the sound of chipper whistling coming from the direction of the building. Already on high alert with the undead and the gunshots, they wheeled about, guns aimed at the ready to see an overweight security guard exiting the building. The guard, completely oblivious to their presence, spun and locked the front door with his wad of keys. He dropped the key ring back to his retractable belt-loop and began fishing in his pockets with both hands. His hands came out at the same time, one hand holding the car keys, the other held a roll of mints. Finishing his turn, he lifted his head towards the car and noticed that he was facing down the barrel of two guns. He dropped his keys and mints, clattering on the concrete walkway, and raised his hands.

"Wait a minute, fellas. I'll give you whatever you want," he said. "I got a family."

Bjorn lowered his pistol, but Tim did not lower his rifle; in fact, he advanced on him.

"Get down on your face. Now!" Tim barked.

Bjorn looked at him incredulously.

"Get his keyring off his belt and make sure he doesn't have a weapon, Bjorn," Tim said, quietly to his friend.

Tim knew that they would just be wasting time trying to explain the situation to the guard if he weren't already aware. Especially while their families sat in possible danger around the corner. A moment of hesitation and the reality of the predicament set in to his friend as well. Bjorn moved forward as the security guard lay prone on the ground. He unclipped the key ring from the guard's belt, jogged to the door, and immediately started trying keys in the lock.

"I need you to undo your belt and leave it right there," Tim said to the guard, still fearing he might have pepper spray or a stun gun on him.

The obese guard had to roll a bit to get his hands under him to undo the clasp of the belt. When he was finished pulling the belt off, the man was red in the face, his breath came puffing out in great bursts.

"Now roll away from the belt and sit up," Tim commanded.

This whole scenario felt like an out of body experience. He was pointing a loaded weapon at another human being and ordering him around like a circus animal. What was more shocking to him than that, was that he knew he would use it if necessary. The guard sat up with his eyes squinched shut.

"I didn't see your faces, I swear," he lied.

"Is there anyone else in that building?" Tim demanded.

"No...not until two or three; that's when the cleaner gets here to do the carpets," stammered the urine-soaked guard.

Bjorn, in the background managed to get the door open; he locked eyes with Tim momentarily before he ran off to get their families.

"Take your shirt off," Tim demanded of the guard. "I need to be sure you don't have any weapons."

"I swear, I don't," the guard blurted, his voice on the edge of hysteria as he pulled the shirt out of his waistline and up over his head.

"Now your shoes...slowly," said Tim.

The heavy screeching of tires sounded out from the side of the building, immediately setting panic in him. His immediate thought was that the screeching tires were the cops coming to arrest him. His heart dropped into his stomach, he relaxed as he saw the minivan come whipping around the corner. Lilly pulled it around the front of the building, parking it next to the security car. The families got out in a rush, running to the front door with children in tow.

"Those things are around back!" Laura yelled at him, her voice a panicked shriek, sounding like it did whenever she saw a spider in the house.

The security guard slowly took his shoes off as Bjorn led the five out of the van and into the lobby of the building.

Tim edged over to the security guard's belt and kicked it away. He said quietly to the guard:

"Do you hear that? The gunshots?" He paused for about ten seconds, giving the guard ample opportunity to hear a few shots sound out.

The guard, sobbing at this point, blubbered and nodded as Tim continued.

"The shit has hit the fan, dude. Go home and protect your family if you can." Tim waited not another second and turned his back on the guard, jogging into the building to find his family.

Bjorn waited just inside the entrance and locked the door after him. They waited there in the lobby, most of them watching the guard as he gathered his clothing and gear. They watched him as he got in his car, reversed it, and drove away to an unknown destiny. Only Tim didn't watch; rather, he scanned the lobby the families stood in, not trusting the guard's word.

"Let's clear a room where Lilly, Laura, and the kids can lock themselves in, while we make sure the building is clear," Bjorn said.

Tim nodded and walked to the switch-plate to the right of the main door. He flipped all the switches, and the lights blinked on in response.

"We will need to turn these off before sunset. No need to have anyone coming by to see what's here, but for now, there will be less shadowy corners," Tim said, as much reminding and reassuring himself as he was speaking to the others.

The lobby inside the front doors was a smallish seating area with a pair of couches, two upholstered chairs, a coffee table, and a wall-mounted, flat-screen TV. The sitting area was flanked on the left by a set of elevators and on the right by a glass-walled meeting room. Just beyond the sitting area was the main reception desk with hallways running off to the left and right. Beyond the reception desk was a bullpen area of sorts with a dozen or so desks in one open area, surrounded by glass-walled offices, with another hallway running left to right bisecting that area.

Tim moved to the glass-walled meeting room directly to the right of where they stood; seeing that it could be locked from the inside, he waved everyone inside.

"Lock us out," Bjorn said to Lilly. "We'll come back to check on you guys as often as possible."

Once the women and children filed into the room, the two men moved off. They tried as best as possible trying to look like they were comfortable with sweeping and clearing a building, possibly infested with undead, all while holding weapons they had never fired before. Bjorn had never even shot a real gun before, only air rifles, and Tim had only shot on three prior occasions, and never an assault rifle. They passed down the hall to the right of the main reception desk, moving past three offices, ending up staring into a utility closet filled with office paper and supplies. Thankfully, the offices were glass-walled, so they were able to do a thorough visual inspection before opening and clearing them. They had both held their breath when opening the supply closet, both picturing the worst case beyond the solid panel door.

Tim started making a note of any refrigerators in the offices they came across. He wanted to thoroughly check the fridges and desks for food once they were done clearing the building. They proceeded to the main reception area where they found, around the corner from the elevators, a door labeled as a stairway. Pausing here, Tim dragged a chair from the bullpen area over to barricade the door. He didn't want anything sneaking behind them as they moved further from their families. Moving to the elevators, Bjorn pressed the call button, and Tim stood back with his rifle aimed towards the doors. The one on the left came down and doors slid open. With baited breath, they waited until they could get a full view of the interior of the carriage…empty. He dragged the coffee table into the open door so that it wouldn't close and mashed the elevator call button again.

Tim returned to his ambush position and calmly waited. The second elevator car eventually arrived; it too was empty. After moving another chair in to strand the second elevator, they cautiously explored the remainder of the building, moving slowly, methodically through the second, then third floors until they had opened every door and closet. The only areas they hadn't checked were the doorways that led to the warehouse and the rooftop. Not wanting to be seen during the light of day, they decided to only do a quick scout of the roof and get back downstairs ASAP. They knew it would be best to come back after dark to get a better lay of the land.

Gunshots were still popping off as they stepped out into the light. They took a moment to let their eyes to adjust to the brighter outdoors, then split up, each doing a quick scan around the rooftop before returning to the doorway. The last thing they had to check was the warehouse. The warehouse lay at the end of the back hallway to the left on the first floor, just past the break room the office shared with the warehouse workers.

As the men moved off to scour the building, Laura finally caught sight of Lilly's arm, the paper towels clinging to it by the grip of blood alone.

"Sophie, do you think you and Liam could go play quietly with Luna?" Laura asked the cute little girl.

Sophie nodded soberly, and Laura set Luna down on her feet. The three scurried off to the far corner of the room and began arguing immediately over what game they would be playing.

"Let me see if I can't bandage that a bit better, Lilly," Laura said, moving to the woman's side.

She scoured the room for some things to help her. She found some napkins on a side table next to an empty carafe and a tape dispenser on the table, and set about changing the dressing. When she removed the paper towels, the blood flowed freely from deep puncture marks. Some of the flesh was torn, either the thing was trying to tear a chunk off or Lilly had ripped her own arm free of the thing's mouth causing the terrible wound. Laura had to grit her teeth to keep from passing out. She didn't have an aversion to blood so to speak, but the thought of one of the dead things sinking its teeth into the woman almost sent her reeling. A few minutes later, Laura finished scotch taping the makeshift bandage to the woman's upper arm.

"Do you think I need a tetanus shot?" Lilly asked calmly.

"I don't know that it will help, but it couldn't hurt, could it? I'd try and get some antibiotics and some ointment though. I'm not going to lie, Lilly, it looks nasty."

"Thanks, that's reassuring," Lilly shot back, her voice full of sarcasm with a bit of venom.

"Sorry," Laura cast back. "Just being honest."

Lilly breathed deeply and sighed before responding.

"I know, Laura, I just don't do well in stressful situations."

"Like I do?" Laura shot back, laughing.

"Oh, great! Our anxiety is just going to feed off one another," Lilly replied and joined her in laughter.

It was a terrible feeling being alone with anxiety. The two sat there at the end of the table, both a bit relieved, at that moment, to have each other's company.

Bjorn and Tim stopped on their way back through to make sure everyone was okay. The kids were playing on the floor with toys scavenged from diaper bags while Laura and Lilly held hands in the corner watching them. It reassured both men to see them so; normally, both women were very stand-offish. That they were comforting each other relieved a lot of pressure on them. Sophie followed them to the door and locked it after them, and the men proceeded to the warehouse door.

"Tim, I think if we see something, we should use the pistol to take it out," he said, pointing at the M4 in Tim's hands. "I'm just nervous that that…"

"Will be too loud…yeah, I think you're right about that," Tim responded. "I was thinking about whoever is doing that shooting in the distance. I think that they are just drawing more of those things over to them. Okay then, I'll do the honors of opening doors and you get some practice."

"Or, I can just give you the gun…" Bjorn added.

"Better we both have guns. I'll just save mine unless there's a bunch of them piled up behind that door," Tim said, offering a half-smile to Bjorn as he moved to the door.

Tim gripped the knob and held up three fingers on his other hand then two, then one. He yanked the door open while jumping back himself, in one fluid movement. Bjorn stood with his arm extended straight, gripping the 9mm pistol, his other hand cupping the base of his hand to steady it. He peered into the dark warehouse, squinting to no avail, his eyes couldn't penetrate the gloom inside. At least he wasn't able to hear anything moving within. After a moment's struggle, he was able to force his legs to start moving towards the darkness. Once through the doorway his eyes began to adjust to the gloom. The two men stood on an iron walkway that extended the entirety of the wall it shared with the office area, stairs led down to the warehouse floor ten feet below. The railings and stairs were painted bright yellow, although much of it had chipped off, leaving a mottled grayish-black behind. From behind Bjorn, Tim murmured:

"Let there be light!"

With the click of a switch hammering home, the overhead industrial fluorescent lights leading back into the gloom started powering on, casting an eerie greenish glow that turned into the sickening hazy white that causes migraines for so many office workers. A loud bang at the other end of the warehouse startled them both into high alert. They looked at each other, eyes wide, both immediately wanting to go back and close the door, barricade it and forget all about it. Their nervous glances to one another egged them on to bravery that each man, individually, wouldn't have had. Tim began tapping the stock of the M4 on the metal railing, tentatively at first, but gradually reassured by the sound and his friend standing by his side, at the ready. He started striking it louder and louder. Then there was movement, a flurry of it from the far end of the warehouse. They watched as a small flock of birds flew up into the rafters and began their own racket of chirps, tweets, and other bird sounds. Both men let out audible sighs and started to turn to walk towards the door when a shrill roar issued from the other side of the warehouse. Tim immediately knew what it was, and chills shot up his spine.

"Get ready, man. It's one of the fast ones," he said, taking sight with his rifle.

*

Tar needed to think. He walked to his truck, got in, pulled the door shut behind him, and sat in silence. The notion that his blessed corner of the world was crumbling to pieces around him weighed heavy on his heart. *You already lost everything that matters, why not let the rest fall into nothingness?* an inner voice asked. He started to get angry, reliving the painful memories of the loss of his wife and child years before. Anger had always been his safeguard. It kept him from having to feel any negative emotions, like the ones he was feeling about the world coming unhinged and collapsing. It also was the mechanism that broke his family's spirit; it drove Karl to drugs and ultimately to his death. It indirectly drove Harriet to her grave at forty-eight years old. The only damn good it ever did for him was keeping the tears at bay. He had never fully come to terms with his contributions that led to Karl's death ten years earlier. It was something men of his generation were told not to dwell on. Deep down, he knew that Karl was born a sensitive boy and all the tough love in the world wasn't going to change that; all it served to do was break the boy's trust and his heart. But again, these weren't things Tar dwelt on for more than the briefest of thoughts before the anger flushed them back out.

Karl had started running away at fourteen, begging rides from passersby and stealing ATVs at first. By the time Karl was seventeen, he had graduated to stealing the next-door neighbor Lydia's car. The car was found two weeks after but no sign of Karl. Three years later, Sheriff Daltry came knocking on his front door. Harriet, his wife, never fully recovered from the loss, and when the cancer diagnosis came in, she didn't have the strength, or desire, to fight it.

Tar could feel the black tendrils of depression inexorably grasping him, trying to pull him back to that dark place he stayed in for months after Harriet left him alone. Instead, he held onto that anger. Gritting his teeth against the tears, he swung the door of the truck open and stepped back out into the wind and breathed deeply. Under control once again, he strode towards Daltry who was conversing with Dale in front of the municipal building.

"Daltry!" he called, and when he was in reasonable earshot, he continued. "Tomorrow at noon, get every man that shows up here, every man that's able to swing an ax, over to Elsie's ready to put in some hours."

*

"Welcome to Fort Lee!" Rashid said with a smile, clapping Will heavily on the shoulder. "We made it, man."

The two bumped fists and sat on the railing of the promenade, looking northward to the GWB. They sat there for a few minutes in silence, both relieved at being clear of New York City, but also dreading what might greet them on the streets after dark in New Jersey. The sun had just dipped below the horizon and the gloom of twilight dampened their spirits. The need to know more of their surroundings trumped everything else concerning them at that moment. The two rose in unison and headed for the exit of the riverside park. The promenade led them through a lush arboretum, winding through a park-like forest, the shadows of the trees seemed to amplify the gloom and quiet. When they came clear of the trees, the city that lay before them was shrouded in darkness. The area around them resembled parts of Brooklyn and Queens further out on the island. Corrugated pull-down security gates covered all the storefronts, and the streets were deathly silent.

"The sun just went down; why's it look like its three in the morning?" Will whispered to Rashid. "Where is everyone?"

"Curfew maybe?" Rashid replied, half-asking.

They lingered at the crosswalk outside the riverside park for a moment longer. Rashid shook the idle speculation from his head and shrugged his shoulders before proceeding across the street. Will jogged after the man to keep up. They had just crossed the median of the four-lane roadway when the lights of a vehicle came around the corner a block north of them, illuminating them briefly. The screech of tires was followed shortly after by the bright flash and deafening staccato of a machine gun. Urine dripped down Will's leg, for the second time in as many days, as bullets started skipping off the pavement and concrete around them, sending sparks and stone shrapnel skittering across their path. Rashid let out a quick squeal and the two ran headlong to the far side of the street. Will heard someone call for a ceasefire from the direction of the vehicle.

"Fort Lee is under martial law, get off the streets!" came a voice, amplified through a megaphone a few moments later.

The two heard the command but didn't stop running. As they passed the darkened buildings, they could hear horrific noises coming from within. The terrible moans and growls of the undead mingled with heavy pounding on doors and the screams of terror and pain from the living; urged the two on well past the limits of their endurance. To Will, the worst was the screams of the doomed; they punctuated the night as they moved away from the waterfront into an area heavy with apartment buildings. Finally, Will stopped, unable to keep up the frantic pace. His lungs felt like they were going to burst, the pulse in his head was throbbing to the point that he couldn't hear anything else and his legs burned from the exertion. Rashid continued on for another half block before he noticed Will's absence. Will could just barely see him ahead through the shadowy gloom of unlit city streets, bent over with his hands on his knees. He struggled to his feet as soon as he was able to muster the strength and made his way to Rashid on jellied legs.

"We need to get off the streets," Rashid said quietly, pointing towards a throng of undead moving down a side street as Will ambled up to him.

"Yeah," Will replied, still panting heavily.

"I ain't going in one of these apartment buildings and all the stores look like they're boarded up," Rashid said, cautiously looking around them for headlights or undead.

Will nodded and was able to get the word "Rooftop" out before resuming his panting.

The idea lifted Rashid's spirits a bit, and he began looking for an appropriate building they could climb atop of. They started moving again, slowly now, while both cooled their burning legs down. They proceeded on their current course for two more blocks before they spotted another set of headlights approaching an intersection two blocks ahead. They made it about thirty feet further before Rashid grabbed him and pulled him into a dark alleyway, just as the headlights came into view. They waited, crouched in the darkness, panting and exhausted for a long minute. Will hastily relieved himself against a yellow-lidded dumpster. Blood was pumping in both of their ears, nearly deafening them as they forced themselves to silence. It was so dim that they could only see in gradients of black in the lightless city. The tension of the moment finally broke when the headlights swung in their direction. Rashid pulled Will again, deeper into the alley. A flash of movement came from the far side of a dumpster and collided with Rashid who went down with a yelp in a ball of flailing limbs. Rashid's grip on Will's arm tightened when the undead thing grabbed him and took him to the ground, bringing an unwilling Will down on top of them. Will couldn't see; he could only feel the forms kicking and writhing underneath him. The smell of rancid meat and excrement hit him in the face. He could clearly hear the thing beneath the two of them moaning breathlessly.

*

Bjorn looked terrified but steadied himself and took aim at the distant shape moving at breakneck speed through the gloomy warehouse towards them. *So fast!* he thought as the fear and tension caused his finger to tighten and accidentally discharge a round. The report from the shot was near deafening in the sealed warehouse. The undead ran headlong past pallets filled with barrels stacked two high wrapped in nylon straps and heavy-gauge cellophane. They could only catch quick snippets of movement as the thing hurtled toward them across the warehouse. At last, it came free from the racks and into the main loading area which they stood above. It wore coveralls, stained with oil and blood, its hair ragged and wild. It didn't pause; if anything, it seemed to redouble its speed with them in plain sight. Bjorn shot again, missing it as it took stairs three at a time. In the span of three seconds, it was hurtling up the last set of steps towards Bjorn who pulled the trigger a third time in vain. As it lunged for Bjorn's throat, Tim squeezed the trigger on the rifle. A deafening burst of three shots tore through the air, lifting the barrel of the M4 with a jerk. One of the bullets struck home, blowing out of the back of the undead thing's skull. The corpse thudded to the floor at Bjorn's feet, gore pouring from its ruined head and through the grated walkway, dripping and splashing onto the concrete floor below. Bjorn stood with his mouth agape at the thing before finally uttering:

"Holy shit, holy fucking shit, there is no way those things are that fast, what the fuck?"

Tim scanned the rest of the warehouse for a few more minutes before he decided it was safe enough for the two to do a manual inspection.

"Cover me, man," Tim said as he moved slowly down the stairs with his rifle at the ready.

Bjorn followed, gulping audibly. Slowly and quietly, the two made their way to the other end of the warehouse. Covering each other at every corner, they finally came upon what little remained of a person. The thing must have been feeding on it for some time, the head of what once had been a woman was ripped off, and lay across the aisle from the rest of the corpse. The chest was ripped open and gore was spread across the wide aisle. They did a return sweep up the next aisle. Working in unison, they were able to sweep the remainder of the warehouse in a matter of minutes. Both men were grateful that they found nothing else.

"We gotta get back to them; that machine gun was loud as shit," Bjorn finally said.

"Shit!" Tim responded, totally forgetting the racket that killing the thing had made. Images of a horde of undead crashing through the glass front of the building shot through Tim's mind as they raced back up the warehouse stairs. They hurled the corpse at the top, pausing momentarily to lock the warehouse door, just in case. They crossed the main lobby just in time to hear the screeching of tires as Bjorn and Lilly's minivan tore out of the parking space and sped away.

Tim's head snapped to the meeting room, and he let out an audible sigh of relief that their families were still safely in there, children still at play. Lilly and Laura stood at the meeting room doors, both looking panicked. Although the men were both relieved that their families were safe, the lack of a vehicle left them in a terrifying situation. They had not intended on staying here more than a night, but now it looked as if they had no choice. Without a vehicle to escape in, they were forced to either stay here indefinitely or risk trying to acquire one. Neither of them would even entertain the idea of trying to walk anywhere; not with their wives and children in tow. The logistics of getting a new car meant a person or people venturing on foot out in the open, the thought of which neither of the men relished.

"You left the keys in it?" Tim heard Bjorn say to his wife.

"I don't know. I don't remember," came Lilly's response, her voice edging on hysteria.

"It doesn't matter now," came Tim's measured response. "The building is clear. Let's gather supplies and move to one of the higher floors, out of sight of anyone or…" He trailed off, not knowing what to call them. The word 'Zombie' came to his lips, but it seemed foolish to say aloud, so he kept silent instead.

"Undead?" Bjorn said hesitantly, drawing on the name that categorized all ambulatory dead.

Tim shrugged, accepting the nomenclature for the living dead.

They spent the next few hours gathering and moving food and whatever other supplies they thought might come in useful up to the third floor. Tim and Bjorn stranded the elevators on the third floor and filled the stairwell with all the office chairs they could gather. They set up sleeping quarters in the two offices at the far end of the hall, furthest from, but in sight of the elevators. The office/bedrooms overlooked the road with clear visibility to the WGS building over top of the bushes and trees. They put all the food and toys in a conference room that they set up as a common area. They ate heartily of the lunches left behind in the crew room fridge as well as snacks pilfered from the desks of the office workers and the vending machine in the break room. Tim and Laura had a harder time finding edibles, being vegetarian. It seemed silly in the current scenario to continue their dietary choice, but old habits die hard. After looking through the stash that the kids left behind, Laura found an organic yogurt, two stale, buttered bagels, and a box of raisins that they split among themselves. They made no precautions to ration the food; it didn't occur to them.

Tim and Bjorn spent about two hours on the roof of the building after the sun went down. They passed a bottle of black label between them that they had found in a locked drawer of a desk in a corner office. As they peered at what they could see of their surroundings, the streetlights clicked on outside. They could see the distinct shape of people moving towards the WGS building. The shadows cast by the streetlamps kept them from determining for certain if they were alive or dead, and though they didn't discuss it, they were both confident it was the latter. With the lives of their families at stake, they had to assume the worst. The two talked quietly about their options. They were still about five miles from Bjorn's apartment and three or four more beyond that to Tim and Laura's house. The cheap scotch kept them warm from the frigid fall winds as they talked. They briefly entertained the idea of leaving the women and children here while they tried to fetch Bjorn's work truck at the apartment on foot. Moments into discussing it, each knew the impossibility of leaving their loved ones alone for so long with danger so near.

Eventually, their heads were too light from the scotch, and the cold began to settle into their bones so they retreated back indoors to find some sleep. The scattered gunfire continued long into the night, finally petering off around two in the morning. Tim was still awake and didn't know what was worse: the sound of gunfire that indicated people, danger in and of itself, but living people; or the silence that left too much to the imagination. He had a good imagination, and it was hours before the tension left his aching muscles and he was able to drift off to a fitful sleep.

The sun beating through the windows onto his face is what eventually woke Tim, but seeing that he was alone in the room is what got him upright. Worried about his family, he staggered out into the gray-carpeted hallway to see the three kids playing with cars on the floor. He smiled broadly at his daughter who was busy pushing a red firetruck back and forth, issuing a low growl while she did it. He called it her demon voice, although there was no malice in it; it was strange for such a guttural sound to come out of such a sweet little thing.

Laura and he hadn't planned on children the first five years of marriage; they were perfectly content with their two dogs. A blizzard a few years prior had left them stranded for two frigid weeks in a cabin they had rented on Lake Champlain. The utility lines had been taken out by a falling tree, and the two had nothing but a fireplace, a decent supply of food, and a lot of booze to while the time away. One might assume that Luna was a mistake driven on by poor decision making in that dire situation, but that is not the case. The fifth day into their isolation and the primal nature of their situation set in on Tim. Because of the solitude and quiet, he began to ponder what he would leave behind when he died. He pictured Laura and him at seventy, alone, no one to visit them. Then he pictured Laura alive after he himself passed on, and pitied her abject solitude. He loved her deeply and the thought of this had broken him. A couple days later, he spoke to his wife about his feelings. Laura had always loved kids, but she loved her life with Tim as well, so when he came around on children, it was wonderful for her. They were pregnant before the plow came up the long driveway leading to the lakeside cabin and Luna was born early the following winter.

Now, while Tim stood looking through the glass-walled office at what must be thousands of those monsters surrounding the WGS building, he wished that they had not brought her into this world. He loved her more that life itself, and would willingly give his life so that she could continue on for another minute, but what then? What if he fell? Dread started to settle itself in his heart, and he quickly shifted his focus. His eyes settled on the computer monitor at the desk in the office he was peering through, and he quickly ripped the door open and sat behind it. He opened the cabinet door of the desk, revealing the CPU, and pressed the power button. A couple moments later, the CPU booted up, and to his dismay, a password prompt foiled his attempt to get on the internet. Seeing Bjorn walking towards his family's impromptu quarters, Tim called out to him.

"Bjorn."

"Huh?" Bjorn mumbled, looking around to determine the source of Tim's call, finally seeing him in the dim office.

"Do your phones work?" Tim said. "I mean, to go on the internet?"

He and Laura had downgraded from smartphones about a year ago to reduce their spending and neither had given more than a moment's thought about surfing the web on their circa 2001 flip-phones.

Bjorn's eyes lit for a moment, and he started frisking himself, chest pocket, front pants, rear pants, then down to the side pocket of his painters' pants where he kept his multitool. He looked crestfallen, and at last said, "Fuck. Left it in the van; let me see if Lilly has hers."

With that, he went trotting down the hall, gracefully hurdling the children still at play. Tim left the office and started after him, stopping to pick his daughter up and plant a big kiss on her soft cheek.

"Daddy, stop!" she said, sounding more like "Schtawp" with her squeaky little kid voice.

Tim set her back down to resume playing and carefully stepped through their play area. He found Bjorn, Lilly, and Laura in the elevator lobby at the central bullpen area of the floor plan. This area was nearly identical across all three floors. He could see by the look on their faces that the internet was a no-go. He still spent the better part of the next hour going from computer to computer before finding a laptop that he could access the desktop on, hoping that corded internet might somehow still work. No internet. The television in the lobby, when they got around to it, had the emergency warning being broadcast "Stay tuned for further instructions" came through in a staticky almost robotic tone. After Tim and Bjorn had covered the front doors and windows with cardboard from the warehouse, the families made themselves comfortable on the couches, snacking on chips and soda from the vending machine in the crew room.

After two hours of sitting in front of the television with no further instructions forthcoming, they gave up and Bjorn flicked the display off. They discussed leaving, trying to find a car, the need for food and supplies if they were to stay. Each topic they came to degraded into an argument within minutes. Everyone was scared; the women would not agree to leave, nor to be left and placed in danger unnecessarily, and most assuredly would not bring their children in jeopardy. Tim and Bjorn were trying to be more realistic about it, the reality of weakening, starving, with winter approaching and no supplies, no transportation, no escape route. They tried to emphasize the danger doing nothing put them all in, but the women wouldn't budge.

The decision to act was made later in the day by Bjorn and Tim as they sat alone on the steel walkway in the warehouse with their legs dangling off like kids. They had to make a foray to Lowe's, at least to see if they could scavenge some supplies, maybe lunches from the crew area or loot groceries someone might have left in a parked car. They knew they had to do something.

*

Tar awoke the next morning just as the sun breached the horizon. He took a quiet hour of coffee and cigarettes to consider the course he lay ahead of himself for the day before he stepped out on his front porch, settling his western hat comfortably into position. He knew he had a long and arduous day ahead of him. As he circled around the front of the Silverado, a voice called out from the road, startling him.

"Hold up, Tar. We need to take a ride, you and me," Sheriff Daltry cut in. "Grim business."

His ire raised at getting snuck up on, Tar was ready to yell at the sheriff, but his curiosity stifled the surprise-induced anger.

"What's going on, Daltry?" Tar asked, genuinely intrigued.

"Well..." the sheriff began slowly, brushing his pants off with his hat. He was thoroughly enjoying having the man on a hook.

Daltry wasn't from Donner. He had taken the post of sheriff when his predecessor had retired. He was originally from Fort Collins, though his uncle lived in Donner and he got to know the area well due to the many hunting trips since childhood. Fort Collins wasn't a huge metropolis by any means; Donner was just a world apart from anywhere else Daltry had ever been. The one thing that Daltry could never get used to about the small town was the pace of conversation. Being in law enforcement as well as being a man, Daltry was used to short factual statements. In Donner, it was almost as if people were trying to keep you in suspense as to their point. As pressing as the situation was, he was privately enjoying having Tar on the hook in this way.

"I don't know what you know about the goings-on up at Heartland," he finally continued. Seeing Tar shrug, he continued. "Well, the good doctor has been saving the infected in a few rooms over there. Says she wants to study them."

Tar felt his palms get sweaty with the thought of facing those things willingly. He did his best to hide the anxiety from the sheriff. He didn't want the man to see that the thought had rattled him.

"I've humored her thus far, but too many of us have died already," he stated, matter-of-factly. "It's time to put the dead to rest."

Tar nodded and returned to his truck. He needed a moment to steady his nerves and fidgeted in his glove box for a moment to steady his breathing and slow his heart rate. When he was composed enough, he came out from the truck with his gun belt on and a box of ammo in hand. Daltry waited in his Explorer with the heat blasting to take the chill out of the morning air. The two rode in silence across town, brooding on the inevitable confrontation with Linda and the terror of facing the dead.

"Looks like fortune smiled upon us today," Tar said as he spotted Dr. Henson steering her bicycle into the lot for the municipal building as they drove past.

Linda stared long and hard at the truck as they took off up Route 10 towards Heartland.

*

Over the past thirty-six hours, Linda's attempts to get someone on the phone at both the CDC as well as the CDPHE had grown increasingly frustrating. Her colleagues at the CDPHE, with whom she commiserated with regarding the infection, were literally locked in their offices, unable to even make it to their cars due to the reanimated. Linda was glad she wasn't still with them in Denver; the stories her colleagues told her about the chaos and the scope and scale of the affliction terrified her. They informed her that most of the things were slow, somewhere around 93%. All the conversations and review of her own notes and patient charts left her at a loss. What bothered her most was that she was at her wits end about what could possibly be causing the continued primary infections in people.

They were fairly isolated, nestled up in the mountains. Donner wasn't a cesspool of interbreeding like medical school. These were small town, Christian people, and she doubted that primary infection was due to sexual contact. She suspected that it lay in the food, water, or air, but as she was busy twelve to fourteen hours a day in the clinic and spent most of the remainder of her time trying to get some information from the government, she had precious little time to delve deeper into it. She hated to admit it, but she could already feel that the situation was moving well beyond the point where the "whys" and "hows" mattered.

The phone rang incessantly in her ear, as she tried, once again to hail someone at the CDC, and she finally hung it up. She decided to try to reach someone at the CDPHE one more time before starting her day in the clinic. To her surprise, the phone connected on the second ring.

"Hello?" whispered a familiar voice; it was Walter Tompkins.

Walter had been an adjunct professor for a class in her final year at UCD and her boyfriend for two years after.

"Walter, it's Linda up here in Donner. I'm glad to hear you guys are still at it."

"Linda...I'm sorry—"

"Stop it, Walter," she interrupted. "Have you guys tried that new cocktail you all were talking about last time we spoke?"

"I'm sorry I couldn't keep my dick in my pants, Lin," he continued. She could hear the emotion in his voice. "I just need you to know that, it wasn't you, I..."

"Listen, Walter, I don't care anymore," she barked, irate that he was taking a moment to air their personal drama from years before. "I need to talk to someone about this bug. Please, if you aren't able to talk about it, can you put Jerry on the phone? Or Tara?"

"They're dead, Lin," Walter said, "and I got bit. Those things are everywhere outside—Shit!" Linda heard a roar in the background followed by the shattering of glass.

"Walter?" Linda called. "Walt?"

Linda called for Walter for a few moments but hung up the phone hurriedly when the man's screaming started. She didn't try calling back after that. That conversation was the turning point for her. In her eyes, the disaster was complete; it was time to act. She collected her thoughts for a moment and knew that it was time to update the mayor and sheriff about the situation.

She stood from her desk and walked out of the clinic. The frigid chill that had appeared in the air in the past few days forced her to pull the scarf and gloves from her coat pocket. Once she was appropriately dressed, she mounted her bicycle and rode down the long driveway that led up the Heartland facility. When she hit the main road, she pedaled a mile west and was about to turn into the driveway leading to the Donner Municipal building when she saw Sheriff Daltry's Explorer headed in the opposite direction. There was a man in the passenger seat pointing at her; she recognized Tar immediately. *Why is he pointing at me?* She let the bicycle glide to a rest and stood on the sidewalk with her bicycle between her legs, perplexed. She pondered the sight for a moment before continuing up the drive to see the mayor. She slid the bicycle into the bike rack and approached the main entrance of the building.

About fifteen minutes later, while waiting for the mayor to arrive, she heard the sound of gunshots in the distance. Immediately, it all made sense to her: the sheriff and Tar were on their way to exterminate the infected she was keeping for study.

Linda wanted nothing more than to get back on her bicycle and ride up there to confront Daltry; tell him what a simple, obstructionist moron he was. She wanted to tell him that he destroyed any chance they had at a cure, but deep down, she knew that would be a lie. The truth was that Linda had no idea how to begin addressing the bacteria. It was resistant to antibiotics, steroids quickened its progress, transfusions didn't help, and the only thing she had found so far that killed the bacteria dead was bleach.

She had found out a bit between her research and conversations with the CDPHE and CDC. The bacteria fed on fatty tissues, mainly in the brain. It excreted a protein substance as a byproduct closely related to epinephrine, another similar to glutaraldehyde, and a third substance, propylene glycol. The bacteria would start at the frontal lobe, eating the fats and excreting its protein as it moved back through the brain. The patient's life came to an end when it destroyed the brain stem, stopping breathing. Within minutes or up to twelve hours after death by infection, the subject would reanimate violently. The pseudo-epinephrine seemed to fuel the primitive brain after death, reanimating the body in some cases into a fast, strong, almost rabid version of the former host. In other cases, slower reanimation resulted in a walking corpse in the throes of rigor mortis. Only destroying the primitive brain would stop the creatures at that point. Beyond that, there was nothing. The silence from the CDC and CDPHE indicated that there was no hope for a cure. At this point, she recognized, she was officially on her own. As much as she wanted to decipher the reasons for the continued primary infections, she recognized that it no longer mattered in the grand scheme. What mattered at this point was survival.

She breathed deeply, exhaling loudly, as if exorcising the failures of her research before standing to greet Dale as he sauntered into the mayor's office.

"Morning, Linda," Dale said as she approached the doorway of his office. "What brings you into my life this morning?"

"Knock it off, Dale. I know you sent the sheriff up there to put the infected down," she said, pausing to get an assessment of his reaction.

His hands spread and he gave her a subtle nod.

"Come in, Linda, we need to talk," he said after a moment.

"Why do you think I came down here?" she said curtly

*

About fifteen minutes after they had decided to leave in search of food and a vehicle, Tim and Bjorn peeked warily out from under one of the steel, roll-top loading bay doors at the rear of the warehouse. They hadn't told their wives, knowing their plans would be instantly quashed, as well as being put on house arrest for even considering leaving them. Seeing nothing in the immediate area, Bjorn popped his head out, scanning left to right quickly on his first sweep, and scanning back to the left much slower. He slid nimbly out under the door and down the four feet from the loading dock to the blacktop below. Turning, he held the bay door so Tim could slip out, slightly less gracefully. Together, they lowered the corrugated metal door as quietly as possible until it solidly hit the concrete dock. There was still nothing moving within sight at the rear of the building.

The decorative trees, separating the building from the rest of the industrial park, ended at the rear of the parking lot. Beyond that they could see many acres of tall unkempt hay like grass before another building popped up in the distance. Tim had always had a good sense of direction and, even with the confusion of having navigated the interior of a building, he knew that the Lowes was at their 10 o'clock, probably about a mile off. A tree-topped hill beyond the expanse of fields blocked it from view, however. They took a moment to steady themselves before moving to the corner of the building. Tim leaned his head out, peering around the corner.

"Go to the trees. All clear up to there," he said, waving his right hand to flag Bjorn on.

Bjorn bent down and moved off at a crouch, scurrying quickly to the last tree in the line. There he stopped and peered around the tree at the parking lot and loading area of the Minolta building next door. Finally, he signaled for Tim to come up to him. When the two were together, Bjorn pointed down into the shadows of the loading bay. It took Tim's eyes a moment to see through the alternating shadows and light under the trailers parked there, but he finally spotted one of the things. It was on all fours leaning over the top of the remains of a body, feasting. Tim noticed that Bjorn was staring intently at him. When he caught Tim's eye, Bjorn's extended finger scanned to the front of the Minolta building where Tim could easily see at least a dozen of the things lumbering across the road and parking lot in the direction of the WGS building.

Tim's aversion to getting closer to the initial thing feasting on the corpse was quickly overridden by the sight of that many of them out in the open. He crept around behind the dumpsters, using their bulk to block him from the view of the undead out front before slipping across the open lot and into the shadows of the trailers. Bjorn came right up behind him pressing him further into the shadows under the first trailer in the line. Tim had an idea and shook his finger towards the loading dock. He figured they could sneak past the undead from atop the dock, and if they accidentally drew its attention, they would at least have the advantage of being four or five feet above it.

Silently, they crept along the top of the concrete loading dock, steel roll-top doors on their left punctuating their progress. Tim noticed that Bjorn had stopped behind him, and half-turning, he could see his friend shaking his head 'no.' Tim crept back and shrugged his shoulders. He shot a look at his friend, non-verbally asking him, "What the fuck are you stopping for?" Bjorn leaned over and whispered quietly, "We can't leave that thing between us and them." He gestured with his thumb to the Industrial Lubricant Solutions building they had come from.

Tim saw the logic but a loud bang and a flurry of movement from under the trailer to their right shook both of them before he could acknowledge his agreement. The thing under the trailer had stood up, smashing its head on the underside of the trailer. Tim made sure the safety was on the M4 before jumping down to the pavement below. He landed heavily, underestimating the effects the drop would have on his two-hundred and forty-pound frame. His knees buckled to protect his ankles, and he went forward in a somersault, coming back to his feet like a heavy ninja. He now stood three feet off to the right of the monster. The thing immediately started moving, lurching out from under the trailer towards him. His blood quickened, and fear swept through the fine hairs on his spine being in such close proximity to it. He heard Bjorn jump down from the dock, his work boots sounding heavily on the blacktop behind him. The undead, gore hanging from its open maw and blood streaming down its chin onto its button-down shirt seemed to hesitate, as if unsure which of the two it wanted to pursue before continuing towards Tim, the closer of the two. Tim took the brief hesitation and lashed out with the stock of the rifle he held, smashing the thing heavily in the temple.

The creature staggered back from the blow, striking its head on the side of the trailer noisily, before coming back towards the two men. Tim swung the M4 by its barrel like a baseball bat, trying to stay out of its reach of the thing's grasping hands. He connected with its shoulder, spinning it slightly to face Bjorn. Bjorn held a wooden pallet out in front of him like a giant shield, and the dead thing came lurching towards him. It leapt with surprising speed, throwing its weight against the wooden pallet Bjorn held. The thing fished its hands through the gaps in the pallet and struggled to tear at Bjorn on the other side when Tim struck it down with a massive overhead blow from the M4. The undead finally crumpled into a bloody heap at their feet.

After the fracas was over and the thing lay still, the two men moved out onto the blacktop, away from the docks until they could see the entirety of the building they were behind. They stood in silent anticipation, waiting for more undead to come around the sides of the building. After a span of about thirty heartbeats, drumming in their ears, they moved off into the high grasses behind the building. They talked briefly, taking the opportunity to steady their nerves. Rather than follow the undead-ridden roadway, they decided to move through the high grass in a beeline toward Lowes. The tall grass grew all summer, to almost four feet in height, and was now dead, bent, and brown as the seasons made a turn for the colder.

"It'll be a lot harder to see them coming in here," Bjorn said quietly, only ducking slightly in the tall grass.

"Hopefully, they can't see us either at least. Plus, as long as we stay alert, we should be able to hear them if they do come after us," Tim replied.

"We need some weapons other than guns; not being able to shoot for fear of drawing more of them really sucks ass."

"Yeah." Tim replied absently, thinking of the lawn and garden section in the store they were headed to.

Both of their shins ached from crouch-walking through the brush. After about twenty minutes, the grasses thinned out enough for them to see an embankment climbing up ahead of them. The steep pitch led up to the guardrail and the roadway beyond. As they arrived at the base of the embankment, Bjorn, the slimmer and more agile of the two, crawled like a snake up to the guardrail, peering around the rail supports and through the gaps left between car tires. After what seemed like an eternity, he spun and waved Tim up beside him. Tim bounded up the embankment next to Bjorn, dislodging a couple stones that cascaded noisily down the slope behind him. At the top, he grabbed onto one of the steel supports to keep himself from sliding or tumbling back down the hill. For the tenth time since this chaos had begun, Tim wished that he had stayed in shape and hoped he could survive long enough to slim back down. Once he had steadied himself up top, the two vaulted over the guardrail, quickly hiding next to a Honda Civic in the nearest lane. They peeked into the car, making sure it was unoccupied before settling upright with their backs pressed against it.

Cautiously, the two moved in tandem across four lanes of stalled vehicles. They picked their way through, moving quickly past a car with one of the undead trapped inside. Even though they moved briskly and were being as quiet as possible, the undead had spotted them and started slamming its hands on the glass from the inside, causing a din in the crisp cool day. Suddenly aware of how exposed they were atop the roadway, the men started at a crouching run across the two remaining lanes, pausing only to scan the grass slope and the parking lot beyond. Tim and Bjorn both could see there was only a few straggling undead moving about in the lot below. Most of those visible were the general area where Tim had crashed the Deuce over the curb; but even so, there were only a few. They took this information in stride, using their momentum in running from the occupied car to carry them over the guardrail. They came down and dashed off to the right side of the lot. They could only see one of the undead things on this side of the lot, trapped in a cart-return. They moved swiftly past the trapped undead as it struggled against the lumber cart that had it pinned in, reaching in vain towards them. They continued running even as they made it to the store, dashing straight into the indoor lumberyard entrance.

Thankfully, the lights were still on in the massive store; even still, every shadow in every aisle and shelf held terrifying mystery. The two came to a stop just inside the entrance and looked cautiously around. As the pulse hammering in their ears slowed, returning their full hearing, they moved carefully across the front of the store, taking caution at every aisle they crossed. They crept through the back end of the power-tool section before the main aisle opened up at the cash registers. Heartened by the absolute silence in the store, they started moving faster as they approached the customer service desk, just beyond the web-kiosk of the store rent-a-truck. Tim had rented a truck from here once, to bring a load of sheetrock home in renovating Luna's nursery. Now though, he didn't take the time to try the kiosk, assuming the internet was down. Instead, he leapt over the back of the customer service area. Bjorn stopped in his tracks, keeping a nervous watch of their surroundings while Tim rummaged through drawers filled with receipts and paperwork, hoping to find master keys for the rentals, to no avail.

As he turned away from the drawers, he spotted a large body lying on the floor just inside the main entrance. Even though the corpse was mangled and it was covered by, and surrounded by, gore and entrails, Tim could tell that it was wearing a business suit. For some reason, this struck him as being a bit odd; a man in an expensive looking suit in Lowes. Cautiously, he crept over, taking care to avoid stepping in the congealing blood that pooled around the body. He hovered over the corpse for a minute, suspicious of it, before poking it with the barrel of the M4. With the dead walking, he had no interest in getting mauled while he checked the dead man's pockets. Finally, convinced the corpse was not going to sit up and bite him, he gingerly patted its pockets. Their luck was in. The man's car key came out of his right hip pocket sporting a large three-pointed star logo of a Mercedes-Benz. *That should be easy to spot,* he thought gleefully, thinking about the mostly blue-collar vehicles scattered around the parking lot. Tim spotted Bjorn on the other side of the kiosk and retraced his steps dropping down from the customer service area next to his friend.

"Anything moving?" Tim whispered.

Bjorn shook his head to the negative, not looking at Tim, but rather scanning the store.

"Think I may have gotten us a car, let's hope it's not a two-seater," Tim said quietly dangling the chunky electronic key. "Let's see if we can get some melee weapons."

The two crept slowly down the main aisle leading to the exterior lawn and garden area, making a sharp right in front of the automatic doors that tripped at their passing. The sound of the doors sliding seemed cacophonous in the absolute silence of the store. The two men froze mid-stride, each cringing at the raucous noise. They waited for a dozen heartbeats, listening intently. Hearing nothing, they moved quickly, both men fighting their bladders that screamed at them for release. They scrambled the remaining twenty feet to the rake, hoe, and axe display.

Bjorn cautiously crept ahead to look up the next three aisles, checking for undead, but also looking for a cart. They both realized, at that moment, the impossibility of carrying an armload of ten-pound axes, hatchets, and machetes quietly through the store. Failing at finding a cart close by, Bjorn had an idea and took a few steps down the next aisle. He returned a few moments later with a large wheeled garbage can, the flip-top type that the automated trucks pick up. It was quiet enough at the moment with Bjorn carrying it, but once it was full of a hundred pounds of lawn implements, it wouldn't be so quiet. Tim racked his brain for an alternative solution, but gave up after a fleeting moment. His fear-fueled, adrenaline-pumped body and full bladder made concentrating on one thing for more than a few seconds impossible.

They loaded three full-length axes, one of which was double-bladed, six hatchets, a dozen ax handles, and four machetes carefully into the trashcan, lowering them to the bottom as noiselessly as possible. Tim looked earnestly at him and said:

"We really better make sure we have a vehicle before we wheel this shit-show through the store."

"Grab the handle," Bjorn replied, nodding.

When Tim grabbed the handle, Bjorn grabbed the handle near the bottom of the can and the two carried the ungainly container to the front door of the superstore as quietly as possible. The lawn equipment rattled noisily at first as it settled into place at the bottom, but quieted down after the initial jostling. The front doors were automatic, and the men knew they would cause a bit of noise on the way out but neither wanted to retrace their steps through the length of the store to the open bay lumber area.

"I'll go see if I can get the car. Stay here," Tim said before slipping through the rattling, skipping doors, thinking absently that the store needed to WD-40 them.

Tim worried that the car would beep as soon as he pressed the unlock button on the key and the noise would cause the undead to converge on the vehicle from all directions. All the same, he didn't see any options in the massive lot; so he also didn't make too much of an effort to stay hidden. In fact, he ran to the first car he saw in the lot, and scrambled to the roof of it. Standing upright, he hit the panic button on the key. Nothing. He smashed it again and again and from the far right corner of the lot, where he had run the Deuce off a shiny, very-new-looking Mercedes SUV was honking and flashing lights.

"Fuck!" he barked and took off running towards it, mashing the unlock button as he ran.

He had to veer on two occasions as the undead came out at him from between cars. The first he had seen moving purposely, in its sluggish, limping gait, to intercept him. He easily avoided this one, just by veering then outpacing it. The second undead came out from the far side of a moving van. Tim had to dive awkwardly to the side to avoid its reaching arms, losing his balance in the process. The undead was once a woman with curly blonde hair. It was wearing denim shorts and a flannel over a black tank top. Its maw was agape and crimson-black gore flew from its mouth as it snarled, grabbing and clawing at him. He crab-walked backwards in full flight from the thing, only to collide into another undead that had intercepted him from behind. This one was dressed in weather appropriate attire: Carhartt overalls and a flight jacket over top of it. It had its neck ripped out, its exposed windpipe vibrating hollowly, making an inhuman sound as it bent down towards its prey.

*

Panic overtook Will, laying atop Rashid and the living dead in the pitch-black alleyway. He tugged twice furiously, finally ripping his arm from Rashid's panicked grip. Will rolled clear of the fracas, unsure of how to help the man when he couldn't see where one began and the other ended. He hesitated momentarily and Rashid screamed gutturally. The sound of the pained shout snapped him into action. He put his foot into what he only could assume was the undead's side and shoved with all his strength. A quick flurry of movement followed that Will couldn't hope to track. Rashid was standing a moment later, pulling Will away from the thing and deeper into the gloom of the alley.

The noise of trundling wheels came to them, sounding louder from the mouth of the alley, a moment later, a searchlight shone in towards them from the main road. Will looked back over his shoulder and could see the silhouette of the wretched undead, backlit by the blinding spotlight. When he turned back away, he was truly unable to see anything ahead of him in the alleyway. Rashid dodged to the side, pulling Will behind a dumpster, just as gunfire erupted, the sound tore through the still air of the alley. Bullets whizzed past, skipping off the pavement, pinging off the dumpsters and smashing chunks of brick from the sides of the buildings. The brief but deafening burst of gunfire relented and the alley went quiet for a moment. A burst of movement and crashing sounds came from ahead of them, further in the deep gloom of the alley. Will popped his head out from the safety of the dumpster, and in light from the truck, he could see at least a dozen of the things moving in their direction as they made their way towards the truck. In a matter of seconds, the narrow alley would channel the undead within a few feet of where he and Rashid now cowered. Will tugged at Rashid, who was clutching his own arm and grimacing in pain, and helped him up to his feet. A metallic glint from above the dumpster caught his eye.

Fire escape!

Will swung himself on top of the dumpster, standing on the steel rim at the corner, and was just barely able to get his fingertips on the bottom rung. He hung from it, trying to pull it down with his weight, but the thing wouldn't budge. He assumed it was either locked up with a chain or rusted tight. He used the last of his strength to pull himself up to grip the second rung and get his legs up. Rashid followed after, slowly, having a great deal of difficulty with his injured arm. When he arrived at the top of the ladder, Will could see a length of rusted chain and a padlock holding the ladder in place. That was common in the city, he had learned shortly after arriving. People did it in order to keep burglars, Peeping Toms, or rooftop trespassers away. Will swung his leg over the railing and turned to check on Rashid just as the alleyway exploded with light and noise.

The barrel of the gun mounted atop the truck at the end of the alleyway spit fire, sending bullets tearing through the mob of things that was now gathered around the dumpster just below. He was able to rip his eyes from the dazzling display of the gun, just in time to see Rashid get pulled off of the ladder. One of the undead had him by his ankle and with an injured arm, he couldn't hold on. Will heard the sound of a bone snapping and a terrible moan come from his companion; his heart sunk. Before he could form the idea of climbing down to help him, bullets tore through everything. They pinged and thudded against, and tore right through the dumpster. He watched the bullets tearing through the bodies of the undead that were now bent over around Rashid's body. Will could swear Rashid's eyes met his at that moment, before the things atop him blotted out his view and the hail of bullets tore through it all. The strobe effect the gun had, firing down the dark alley was disorienting, and he had to turn away from the terrible scene, blinking away the light spots in his eyes.

A light came on from inside the apartment that he stood in front of and Will ran from it. Up and around and up and around he went, not stopping until after he'd climbed the final ladder to the rooftop. He collapsed with his back to the edge of the building. He cried then, tears of joy for living, tears of sorrow for the man he had known for barely a day, but mostly tears of loneliness and desperation. He was alone, trapped on a rooftop at night, in a zombie-infested city; a city he had never been in before and was completely unfamiliar with.

When he was done sobbing at his misfortune, he forced himself to his feet to do a quick patrol of the roof, in order to make sure he was safe. The doorway to the building beneath him was locked from the inside, and no other rooftops connected to this one. Most of the buildings around it were much newer, taller apartment buildings. Finally, having walked a complete circuit of the roof, and confident that his immediate surroundings were safe from the things, he collapsed at the edge of the roof near the ladder he had ascended. Buildings loomed above the roof of his building on two sides. A smattering of windows on those buildings was illuminated from within, and occasionally, he would catch a glimpse of movement of a head or elbow from within. He watched these windows intently, searching for signs of humanity. If for no other reason, it distracted him from his loneliness and hunger. Eventually, he drifted off into a stress-induced, nightmare-riddled sleep.

*

"I think I'm going to lay down for a bit, Laura. Would you mind watching the kids?"

"Go ahead, Lilly; they'll get my mind off this mess, whatever it is."

"Thanks. I think there's an extra pack of wipes at the bottom of my diaper bag if you need them."

"Thanks, Lilly. If the bleeding has stopped, you should try and sleep with the bandage off so the wound can start to scab up."

Laura saw Lilly nod weakly as she moved out of the room and down the hall to the office her family had occupied. Laura tried to ignore her superstitions about the bite. Tim had made her watch a couple zombie movies a few years earlier, and now alone with Lilly, she had to fight to keep the superstitions about the things from consuming her with worry and anxiety. She had worked with aggressive developmentally disabled people for a few years and kept reminding herself that biting was common in that population as well as children and animals. She kept telling herself that there was an explanation, that these were not zombies, that Lilly was not going to turn into one.

As hard as she fought to keep the thoughts at bay, they kept insinuating themselves on her, filling her with dread. She took a deep breath to try and clear her brain before moving over to the kids to see if they wanted to play hide and go seek. Before she had a chance to utter the words, she quickly changed her mind to play 'ring-around-the-rosy.' Despite its darker origins, she was less likely to get scared silly. She shuddered at the thought of finding one of the things that the men might have overlooked, hiding in a broom closet while playing with the kids.

Nearly an hour passed at play with Sophie and the two toddlers before Laura began to get concerned about Tim's whereabouts. Moreso, she was tired and wanted a nap herself. Her fears and anxiety, as well as the responsibility of taking care of three children, kept her from going to look for him. At least playing games with the kids had helped distract her from the thoughts of what Lilly's bite might foretell. She tried to call Tim on her cell phone and muttered curses under her breath when the signal failed trying to call him.

After she had started fixating on her husband's location, she made a few meager attempts to engage the kids in play, but her mind was preoccupied. She paced around the room for a few minutes, picturing her husband being eaten in the lobby of the building by a horde of the dead things. She thought that he and Bjorn might have run off together and abandoned them. After all, what contribution were two anxiety-riddled women toting along tantrummy toddlers going to make in this situation?

Finally, she had enough of her fears steering her thoughts and decided to see if Lilly was awake. She decided that she would wake her if not; she couldn't be alone in this anymore. Dread filled her heart as she crept quietly down the hall to check on the woman. *What if she is dead? Or one of those things?* her mind nagged as she approached the office door. Reaching it, Laura found Lilly standing at the windows, looking out across the fields in the distance.

"What is it?" Laura asked as she came up next to the woman, an edge of worry tingeing her voice.

"People," Lilly said flatly, distracted by the distant sighting. "Where are Bjorn and Tim?"

"I don't know, haven't seen them since before you went for a nap."

"Are you fucking serious?" Lilly called, exasperated. "Bjorn you son of a bitch!"

With that, Lilly stormed down the hall towards the elevators.

*

Daltry and Tar strode with purpose into Heartland Healthcare. Betty was seated at the reception desk and looked surprised to see the two together, as it was well known the men had recently nearly come to blows over Tar's shooting of Mabel's boy, Ralphie.

"Tar." She smiled. "Sheriff."

"Betty, where is the doctor keeping those things?" Daltry asked, cutting right through the polite formalities.

"Oh, thank goodness!" Betty gushed. "I was hoping y'all would get around to taking care of this. That doctor—"

"I'm sorry, Betty, where are they?" the sheriff cut her off, anxious to have the business done with before his frayed nerves failed or the doctor returned.

"Yes, well, follow me then," she replied curtly, before spinning on her heel and heading down the hall, moving through the triage area.

They pushed through a set of double doors and turned left where Betty had to swipe a keycard over a reader before entering a code. A shrill buzz sounded, and Betty held the door open for the two men. As soon as they came into the hallway of the lockdown wing, they could hear the violent struggles of the undead within the rooms. The smell hit them both in the face like a hammer, both men hiked their undershirts up out from their collars and pulled them up over their noses. Shivers ran up Tar's spine. He wasn't alone though; he watched as the sheriff unsnapped his pistol with shaking hands. Seeing the sheriff's obvious nerves prodded Tar onto greater courage. He unsheathed his revolver, took a deep, steadying breath, and stepped forward into the short hallway. The lockdown wing consisted of four rooms, two on either side of the hall with a staff area and a common room at the end of the hall.

"How many are we looking at, darling?" he asked Betty, who was already backing towards the doors.

"Seventeen," she said, swallowing past a frog in her throat.

It was clear that Betty was petrified of being in this wing.

"Betty, why don't you go wait by your desk in case someone comes in needing help," Tar asked her, touching her wringing hands with his free hand.

The woman nodded and smiled nervously before stammering out the beginnings of a sentence.

"I do have some paperwork I need to attend to. I should be at my desk in case anyone calls," she blabbered as she scurried away.

The last part of her statement got cut off as the heavy steel lockdown door swung shut, slamming against the jamb.

"Seventeen," Daltry repeated. "Shit."

Thankfully, the doctor was very thorough with restraining them to the beds and gurneys. Some were flipped over due to their thrashing about, but all were still incapacitated. They worked their way through the psychiatric lockdown wing, methodically exterminating the undead in all four rooms. The two winced from the sound of the heavy shots of Tar's revolver echoing off the concrete walls. When they left, the smell of cordite hung in the air mixed with the corruption of dead, rotting flesh and human excrement. They did one final sweep of the area, making sure that nothing moved, before the two silently walked to the exit, tipping their hats at Betty as they passed through the emergency entrance.

When they had settled into the front seats of the Explorer, Daltry finally broke the silence.

"Thank you, Tar. I appreciate the help with that nasty business."

Tar nodded in response, choosing to remain silent. In truth, he was still fighting to keep his coffee down in his stomach, the cloying stench of the psych ward still lingered in his sinuses. As Daltry steered the Explorer back onto Route 10, Tar finally worked up the nerve to open his mouth.

"Just head down to the municipal building, Sheriff. I'm headed down to Elsie's. You remember what I asked you yesterday?"

Daltry looked at him quizzically for a moment and started to speak, but Tar cut him off as soon as his mouth opened.

"As many people as you can muster? Oh, and send Tom with his earthmover. I ain't asking you to agree with me on this Daltry; I'm just asking that you trust me."

Daltry nodded in response as they neared the municipal building. It was the least he could do to return the favor to the man. They pulled into the lot a moment later. Daltry cringed as he saw Linda, still speaking with Dale on the front lawn. His hopes of missing the confrontation were dashed instantly. Daltry pulled his car up to the curb and put it in park, taking a moment to steel himself for the tongue-lashing he was sure he would receive from the woman.

"Good luck, Sheriff," Tar said with a smirk on his mouth as he stepped out of the car.

With that, Tar spun on his heel and started walking across the front lawn on a beeline towards Elsie's

*

Tim found himself on his back in the middle of the parking aisle, sandwiched in between two hungry dead that were reaching down with open mouths, clawing at him. He kicked and flailed out of their grasping hands for a few moments before the blonde female one flopped heavily down atop him, clawing hungrily for his stomach. He put the heel of his palm on its forehead, bending its neck backwards. He was unintentionally screeching as he half-slid and spun, sending it face first onto the pavement. He scrambled forwards, shoving the undead still looming over the top of him sideways into the hood of a car and took off running again. The two undead, once they composed themselves, followed slowly behind, lurching after him.

Tim hurtled blindly across the lot, fleeing from the dead that had nearly mauled him. He was about fifty feet away from the Mercedes-Benz when he realized he was still screaming. He forced his voice to quiet just as the first of the undead crested the embankment, moving from around the rear end of the Deuce. As the undead brought itself erect and started moving towards him, he could see a large number of heads coming up behind it. His heart sank, and he hesitated, unsure if he could make it the remaining distance, or if he should turn and run back to Bjorn in the store. The undead was about ten yards from the SUV and moving slowly, staggering forwards. He remained standing stock-still for a moment before the sounds of shuffling feet closing in behind him spurred him to action.

Go! his internal voice finally screamed. Without a thought more, he started running headlong towards the SUV. He was in full flight, engaged in a footrace that would be, in any other circumstances, a hilarious race between an out-of-shape man approaching middle-age and a withered-looking, elderly undead thing. Tim's heart felt like it was going to burst as his arms pumped. He had always laughed off people who ran as a pastime, stating, "I only run when something is chasing me." Now he cursed his aversion to cardio. He and the gathering horde of undead reached opposite ends of the rear bumper of the Benz at the same time, Tim on the driver's side and the mob rounding from the passenger side. Still mashing the unlock button on the key, Tim grabbed the handle and yanked. The door swung open and he threw himself inside, pulling the door shut behind him and locking it with the key. The moans and growls stopped immediately. Tim was impressed by the soundproof engineering that enabled him to slide the key-nub into the port and turn the ignition without the distraction of the horde of undead outside. Almost silently, the car came to life, and Tim let out an audible sigh. The sound of Michael Bolton singing, "How am I supposed to Live Without You" came belting out of the sound system as he popped it in reverse. Reflexively, he spun the volume dial to zero. He'd rather hear the sounds of the dead slapping at the windows than Michael Bolton.

It took him a couple minutes to guide the thing back out of the parking spot; the Mercedes-Benz had collision-assist and kept engaging the brakes as he tried to barrel through the gathered throng of undead.

Finally, after the third false start, something must have damaged the sensor and he blasted through a dozen of the things. Straightening out the wheel, he took a direct line to the front of the store where Bjorn was doing his best to remain invisible behind the garbage can.

It wasn't until Tim screeched to a halt about fifteen feet from the doors that he realized that Bjorn wasn't hiding; he wasn't even there. He looked nervously around, checking the mob of undead in pursuit in the rearview and drumming his fingers on the receiver of the M4 sitting across his lap, unsure of what to do. He sat behind the wheel, feeling the urge to urinate growing once again. After ten agonizingly long seconds, he finally decided he needed to act. He slammed the shifter into park, cursed under his breath, and jumped from the vehicle. He cast a nervous look about him as he stepped back into the chill air, instantly on high alert. Hesitantly, he approached the sliding doors which parted noisily as he came near. He stepped through the threshold just in time to see Bjorn off to the right running full-speed towards him, a rictus of fear plastered on his face. A roar split the air from deeper in the store. Tim spun without hesitation and hastily ran back to the car, taking a moment to assess the progress the throng had made moving across the lot.

The thirty or so undead were now about halfway to the store and moving steadily towards them. Tim's face dropped as he saw a pair of the fast ones hurtling down the ramp from the main road. They leapt the guardrail and tumbled down the slight hill before turning into the parking lot. As Bjorn rounded the corner, his arms loaded with Power Bars and bottles of Gatorade, the doors slid open again, and Tim could see the silhouette of one of the fast ones barreling down the main aisle towards the doors. Bjorn hurtled forwards the last few feet to the car, arms pinwheeling, and grabbed the trashcan on his way. Tim skidded to a halt at the open driver's door, swung about, and steadied his M4, taking aim. Bjorn dragged the bin around to the rear and unloaded it as quickly as possible into the rear cargo compartment.

The report from the rifle split the air, echoing loudly off the concrete edifice; the fast undead fell. Bjorn poked his head around, his face flushed with exertion, in time to see the undead crumple to the ground, sliding a few feet before starting to rise once again. Tim had missed his head shot, but not the second time. A second report split the air, putting the monster down for good, its head erupting gore from the hole left by the passing of the high-caliber round. By the time Tim got himself situated in the driver's seat, Bjorn was yanking on his seatbelt frantically. Tim watched him for a moment, curiously, before the man realized how he looked. They both took a moment once the doors hermetically sealed them in as the adrenaline let down. Panting, they clapped each other on the shoulder and started laughing.

A screeching roar from behind them split the peace they felt. They both turned to look out of the tailgate window and almost knocked their heads together. In the lot about fifty yards behind, the two sprinters were shoving through the crowd of slow-dead, running headlong towards them.

"Fuck, fuck, fuck, fuck," Tim kept repeating as he cut the wheel and hit the gas.

Once clear of the entrance, Tim hit the gas hard, and they tore down the length of the front of the store, cutting around the outside of the lot to put as much distance as possible between them and those terrible things. He was so panicked by the fast ones that he drove at recklessly high speeds back to the warehouse they had left their families in, Bjorn clutching desperately onto the door handle the entire journey. They tore around back of the warehouse and quickly unloaded the contents of the tailgate onto the concrete dock. Tim made a point to lock the Mercedes and bring the key with them, not wanting a repeat of Bjorn's minivan. When they finally scaled the loading dock and slid under the bay door, their hearts sank; atop the steel walkway stood their wives.

Laura's look was absolutely withering and she stormed back into the office building with Luna as soon as she was sure he'd seen it. Lilly looked pale and weak, but equally as angry. Bjorn started up the steel stairway immediately, not liking the pallor of his wife. Tim made his way past them, intentionally avoiding their conversation. He found Laura and Luna in the office they had adopted as their own.

"How fucking dare you leave us alone, without even telling us?" Laura started, her face a mask of fear and rage. "What if one of those things got in, Tim? Did you think about that?"

"Laura...listen—"

"No, you listen," she barked back.

Tim could see her working herself into a fury and knew that there would be little hope of making her understand the necessity of the trip while she was in that state. He tried to reach for her to sooth her fear and reassure her that everything is okay, but she slapped his hand away.

"It's bad enough that I'm the only one caring for Luna. I have to keep her quiet and content, make sure she doesn't cry or yell," she squinted her eyes, "but you can't even stick around to protect us?"

Tim realized that it was best to sit quietly while she played out her fury. Her fury took a great deal of time, and even after she was done yelling, she kicked him out of the office the family shared.

They had hell to pay for, but the families were safe and now they had an out, the Benz, with nearly three-quarters of a tank. The tongue-lashing they both received was expected and they truly regretted leaving their families behind, but both knew there was no other choice. They knew better than to argue with their wives, but they both knew that they had done what was necessary. Later that evening, they met on the rooftop to share the rest of the scotch.

"Is Lilly okay?" Tim asked.

Bjorn's eyes grew distant and he shrugged.

"She has a nasty infection from the bite. I'm not sure what to do," he said at length.

"I think we should make another trip for supplies," Tim said flatly. "We need food, a nice dose of antibiotics for Lilly, and I'd like to try and get more guns, ammo if we can."

"Laura give you hell?"

"You know she did. How did you fare?"

"Same. She got really weak about halfway through yelling at me and had to lay down. If I'm right, and I know I am, she'll still have plenty to say to me when she gets up."

"Do we tell them we are going out again?" Tim asked after a moment's silence.

Bjorn shrugged again, taking a swig of the scotch and looking off into the distance. Nearly a minute passed before he spoke.

"We kind of have to; we can't leave them unarmed either."

"Yeah..." Tim sighed, softly.

"Think we can make it out of here in the Benz? I mean, leave for good?"

Tim thought a minute about it.

"No," he said "Well, yeah, plenty of gas, but that thing is meant for luxury. If we need to push vehicles out of the way, the engine will seize or the radiator will rupture. We need something bigger," he finished, thinking about the Deuce and a Half.

"What about gas? Three-quarters will get us far, but I wouldn't want to risk us running out on some highway if we do need to bug out."

"I'm hoping we can score some more from the barricade. Some of those Humvees might have gas cans. If they don't, we are gonna have to get a hose and try and siphon from some vehicles on the road."

Bjorn nodded wearily, taking another gulp from the bottle before handing it to Tim.

"The day after tomorrow?" Tim asked.

"They need to understand that we have to go back out," Bjorn stated, staring absently into the distance. "The scattered snacks from the offices, the vending machine, and Lowes are only going to last another day or two. Most of that shit is just junk food anyways."

As they sat atop the roof discussing their course, they noticed the massive horde of dead surrounding the WGS warehouse had started to thin out. They could only guess the implications of that, with the gunfire having petered out the night before; however, it presented an obstacle for them. The warehouse they occupied was in the path of one of only two exits from the industrial park, meaning that large numbers of the things would be moving past them in search of new prey.

Tim, Bjorn, and Laura discussed this in the conference room while Lilly lay feverish under the covers nearby. If she were listening to the conversation, she gave no indication, nor any input. Sophie, Bjorn's seven-year-old daughter, watched the pair of toddlers.

"Well, won't they just walk past us?" queried Laura. "I mean, if we are quiet and stay out of sight, there is no reason for them to come here, right?

Tim and Bjorn just shrugged. They had no clue, really, but Tim chimed in anyways.

"The mob I led out of Lowes was still lurking around the Deuce. Those ones seemed to linger around until something else drew them away. These ones aren't lingering; something has got them dispersing but really, I don't know, maybe they can smell us."

"That's fucking terrifying," Laura said, looking at Tim who shrugged despondently.

"Regardless of any of that, we have five bags of pork rinds, three power bars, and two cans of diet cherry soda left…we will need to get food ASAP," Bjorn said quickly before anyone could latch further onto the 'ifs' of the monsters. "We need to decide who goes for food and to where; obviously the WGS building is out of the question."

"We have Chester on the other side of 86. Either that, or we can start heading towards our homes, but there won't be anywhere to stop for food until we get to your apartment," chimed in Tim. "Or we can head towards Florida and Warwick."

"Lilly is in no shape to travel, especially if we need to abandon the car at some point," Bjorn interjected.

"I don't want to go back out there, Tim," Laura said quietly, her fear-filled eyes looking pleadingly to her husband.

"We got a car, although I'd like to try to get another Deuce and a Half. That means making our way back to the highway." Tim paused, trying to gauge Laura's reaction to the suggestion.

He already knew that the only way he would allow Laura and Luna out of the building was when it was time to leave for good. Laura still looked shell-shocked, but did not balk at his suggestion. Either she was too petrified to actually digest what he suggested, or she finally recognized the necessity of preparing and gathering supplies. He guessed the former.

"I suggest Bjorn and myself going towards Chester, seeing about a truck, more weapons, and if the coast is clear, antibiotics from the CVS. Maybe, and just maybe, if the fates align, we can see about getting some food from ShopRite."

"That seems a bit unnecessarily risky," Bjorn replied. "That strip mall is huge, probably hundreds of those things about."

"We won't know unless we look," Tim said with a shrug.

The room was quiet for a few minutes as Bjorn and Tim waited for their wives to digest what was needed and make a decision on what they were willing to tolerate from their husbands. Finally, Lilly broke the silence, shifting around under her blanket she reached up. Taking Bjorn's hand in her own, she spoke quietly to him. Even though she was quiet, the rest could hear what she said, although they did their best to give the appearance that it was a private moment.

"You'll come back to me?" she asked hopefully.

"You can't get rid of me that easily," Bjorn responded, and she was kind enough to smile weakly at his attempt at levity.

The following day, the two families saw little of each other. They stayed in their offices most of the day, whiling the hours away playing with the kids. In the evening, they shared a meal consisting of the remaining snacks scavenged as well as a packet of Ramen noodles they found in a briefcase. The mood was fairly light, although conversation was scarce. They were all very hungry, and the weight of the task at hand the following day weighed heavily on all their minds.

*

Bang

Thoom

Thud

The sounds woke Will. He came to his senses nearly immediately, recognizing the rooftop. He spun to a crouch, fully alert. The fear and anxiety of the day before came flooding back into his head.

Boom

Was something coming through the door?

Thud

Off to his right that time, Will scanned over towards the sound just in time to see a body dropping past the building he was on a moment later.

Thud

He stood erect and collected his wits, looking upwards in the early morning light at the buildings he fell asleep watching.

Smash

A window broke out as Will watched. One of the dead, that seemed to be looking right at him, climbed through the opening. The thing fell like a sack of wheat a moment later.

Thud

It hit the street below. Will turned back to the building ahead of him, the one that shared a wall with his building. It was a plain brown brick wall for three stories above the rooftop he was on; after that, windows rose for the twenty stories that the building stood above it. Almost one after the other windows were breaking all around him as the undead locked in apartments went after the first meal they could see. *Go ahead, assholes. Do me a favor, kill yourselves off.* Will laughed briefly until they started landing on the rooftop he was on.

Smash

He looked back down the fire escape and could see the movement of one of the undead further down the alley. Directly beneath the ladder, he could see an assortment of corpses scattered about. His fears blazed anew when one of the building jumpers that hit his rooftop survived the fall and started crawling towards him. This spurred him to action. He spun and immediately started climbing back down the fire escape as quickly as his feet would carry him. Windows smashed just behind him on two occasions as he fled downwards, descending six stories to the bottom of the fire escape. He didn't hesitate for a moment once he reached the chained drop down ladder. He threw himself over the railing and propelled himself downwards towards the dumpster and pile of bodies below. As he descended, he spotted Rashid amid the pile of dead, staring up at him through dead eyes, undead milky white eyes, his arms reached upward for Will with his mouth working. Will paused on the bottom rung, unsure now how to proceed. A flash of movement on the fire escape above broke his reverie. He took a quick glance and could tell the thing above him was definitely not human, or at least a living one. He hooked an arm inside the rungs of the ladder, bracing himself and pulled the pistol out of his belt. He flipped the safety, took a deep breath to steady himself, and aimed carefully, just past Rashid's reaching hands. He squeezed his finger and fired a single shot. Rashid crumpled to the ground below. The alleyway amplified the sound of the shot; Will could hear it echoing off the brick buildings in the silent city for a few heartbeats. He jumped down into the dumpster and came out nimbly, his legs still aching from the exertion of the prior day. He heard the distinctive scrape of shuffling feet on the ground from far behind as he turned towards the street.

Will ran to the street without looking back, slipping and nearly falling on a pile of brass bullet casings at the end of the alley. Keeping the New York skyline at his back, he jogged down the double yellow line to avoid the falling undead that continuously thudded and crashed out of the windows, onto the sidewalk and the occasional car roof. His stomach rumbled uncontrollably, and he realized he hadn't eaten in two days. As he ran, he could hear the undead things throwing themselves at locked doors and barred windows to either side of him. Other dead filed out of unsecured doors and windows, following after him.

As he turned northward, keeping the river on his right, he was gathering a sizable following, one that grew larger with every block he passed. By the time he came to the retaining wall that doubled as a sound barrier which separated the city from the I-95 bridge traffic, he had hundreds of the things following behind him. He trotted along the wall, doing his best to maintain a steady jog. He wanted to outpace the things, hoping they would lose interest once they could no longer see him. He was moving westward, away from the river now, hoping that the wall or the highway would decrease in height at some point, allowing him to climb it and get away from his fan club and the city for good. Block after block went by with the wall staying constant twenty-five feet tall. The undead crowding the streets behind him urged him ever onward as their numbers steadily increased. After jogging about ten more blocks, he spotted the ribbon-like roadway of an off-ramp curling away from the other side of the wall. It cut across the air above the street he was running on and appeared to come down two or three blocks over. Spurred on by a clear avenue of progress, if not escape, he turned left onto a cross street as soon as the opportunity presented itself, without looking.

He came face to face with a squad of soldiers in camouflage contamination suits. The surprised look on the lead soldier's face indicated to Will that they were just as shocked as he. Wide-eyed, he nearly collided with the man, who swung his M4 around to bear. Will slid to the ground underneath the barrel.

"Wait, wait, wait!" he yelled. "I'm human, not one of them!"

He slid on his knees, coming to rest surrounded by them, all with their guns trained on him. The soldiers hesitated, staring emotionlessly through the circular lenses built into the suits they wore.

"What do we do about this?" he heard a muffled voice ask from within one of the suits.

"Orders. The Captain said we head to the address and see if the occupants are alive, evac if they are. That's our mission," said another muffled voice with authority. The one that just spoke moved closer to examine Will before finishing his directive.

"Check him for weapons then leave him for the stiffs."

*

The next morning, Tim and Bjorn were awake before dawn, their nervousness about the day kept them up half of the night, and when they slept, it was restless. They had been running over different ideas as to what was needed, and how to acquire it as quickly as possible while drawing as little attention as possible. The two met in the lobby and brewed a pot of foodservice coffee in a Bunn machine in the staff break room. Only after both had prepared their coffees did Tim finally break the silence.

"Still drinking that nasty, flavored shit?"

Bjorn shrugged with a halfhearted smile as the two moved into the warehouse. They sat on the walkway in silence for a few minutes, drinking their coffee and sorting their thoughts and feelings.

"I think we need to leave the Benz at the intersection before Lowes," Bjorn finally spoke, breaking the silence that had once again settled in. "We will be quieter, more cautious moving on foot."

Tim thought about it for a moment before replying.

"The overpass is mostly blocked anyways; I don't think the car would do much good anyhow. There is only one lane we made with the Deuce that would get us on 86 eastbound; other than that, log jammed,"

Tim said at length, nodding in agreement.

Another few minutes passed as they sipped on their molten-hot coffee.

"Lilly any better this morning?"

"She was still sleeping when I got up," he replied. "Sophie was watching cartoons downstairs in the lobby. I told her to go back upstairs to keep an eye on her mother and brother and to get him out of the bedroom when he starts getting fussy, so she can rest."

"She's a good kid."

"Yeah, she was going to bring her mom some water after I said goodbye, all on her own."

Before heading out, they grabbed a roll of garbage bags from the dock, figuring they would help carry stuff better than the odd briefcase or gym bag that they found lying around the office. The sun was fully up in the sky as they crept as quietly as possible into their respective office-bedrooms to say goodbye to their wives while the toddlers still slept. Each man held onto their corner of the universe for a long embrace before breaking free to start their mission.

"Remember to call the elevator back up to you after we leave," Tim said to Laura. "And block the doors open. Keep an eye out so you'll see us returning to unblock it, but I want you guys safely closed in up here."

Laura nodded and followed them to the elevator. On their way to the bay doors, Bjorn tugged on Tim's sleeve and nodded to an oxy-acetylene rig strapped to the wall next to the doors. Tim looked oddly at Bjorn before opening the bay door wide enough for the two to walk out side by side.

"Keep your eyes peeled for a plow blade or something we can use like one," Bjorn said.

"What for?" Tim replied.

Bjorn began to detail out plans for reinforcements he considered welding onto a vehicle. He had worked as a welder for nearly a decade before settling in his career as a carpenter.

"I've been thinking about stuff we can do to fortify a vehicle since we talked last night, but thought it wouldn't amount to anything since we needed to locate both a torch and a truck. Looks like we just need a truck now."

They rolled the gate down behind them, slowly as to make less noise. They then took a minute to let their eyes adjust to the bright morning light. The wind was whipping in from the north and had a wicked early-winter chill to it. They could see a handful of the undead scattered about the field behind the building, as well as a great many along the road to their right. One of the dead noticed them as they hopped off the dock and moved towards the SUV. It moaned softly and nakedly veered towards them, its intestines hanging from a gaping wound on its stomach. They got situated, Bjorn behind the wheel and Tim riding shotgun, holding the M4 across his lap.

"Make sure that one follows us out of here. We don't need to leave him lurking around the loading area," Tim said.

Bjorn waited till the body of the thing slammed against Tim's window before dropping the Mercedes into gear, grinning when Tim yelled, "Fuck, man, move it!"

As the SUV crept away, the dead thing left a bloody smear on the window as it rolled clear. Keeping the walking corpse close in the rearview mirror, they rounded the corner of the building and aimed the car towards the main road. There were a great many creatures across their path, in the process of migrating away from the grocery warehouse. Bjorn looked nervously at Tim who visibly tensed at the sight.

"When we hit the road, hit the horn a couple times; let's try to draw them away from here," Tim said as his hand moved to the handgrip of the rifle on his lap.

Once the undead behind rounded the corner, Bjorn hit the gas, weaving around a couple undead as they bounced down onto the main road. Bjorn had to make some evasive maneuvers, as the road was crowded. Tim's mind got lost in the sight of so many of the dead ambling about. Hundreds were scattered across the roadway, the parking lots of other buildings, and the fields that lay in-between. In that moment, the gravity of the cataclysm started to settle in on him. From the safety of the SUV, for the first time, they could see the grander picture of the undead-ridden world around them, their vision not clouded by the immediacy of danger. Bjorn laid on the horn, startling Tim from his somber thoughts as well as drawing the attention of a great many of the dead. They bumped their way through a small gathering of the things, even running over a couple of the less mobile undead before the SUV broke into a clearing.

"Floor it, man," Tim said tensely and unnecessarily as the engine roared, propelling them down the roadway.

Bjorn swerved around a few more dead as they turned down the final stretch of road leading to the intersection. They slowed to a halt about thirty feet from the intersection, and Bjorn quietly slid the shifter into park. They both nervously looked behind at the numerous undead that now bee-lined their way across the open field towards them. They were all slow and would take some time to close the half-mile gap, but still, that was much more attention than either of them had expected.

"What do you think, man?" Bjorn asked.

"I don't like it," Tim replied quietly. He paused, digesting the scenario. After a moment, he continued, "But, if we went back now, they would just surround the warehouse."

Bjorn saw the logic, but couldn't fathom what they were going to do out here with an army of undead monsters advancing on them.

"Bjorn, leave the keys under the seat, please," Tim said as he swung his door open and swung out of the car.

"What for?" Bjorn asked as he swung his legs out of the car, having turned off the engine.

"Well, we may get separated at some point, and I don't want either of us to get stranded out in the open," he replied as diplomatically as possible, leaving the implications of the statement hanging.

Bjorn nodded soberly at the sense of the statement and left the key under the driver's seat as he slid out. He quickly moved around the front of the vehicle to join Tim at the edge of the road. The two moved on the outside of the guardrail, keeping as low as possible to minimize their visibility. They made their way up to the burned-out tractor-trailer that Tim had sideswiped on their way off the highway. Tim quietly moved over top of the guardrail to the passenger's side running board of the truck, hoisting himself up to the window to peer around them. The barricade was a couple hundred feet ahead, and Tim could already see the shifting and shuffling forms gathered all around the Humvees parked there. He looked down at Bjorn and shook his head at him.

"A lot?" Bjorn half-mouthed, half-spoke.

Tim nodded in assent.

Bjorn pointed back the way they had come, and Tim turned to see the crowd of undead had just reached the SUV.

"Fuck," Tim muttered and swung himself up on top of the fender of the Peterbilt truck. Tim stepped onto the hood to get a better vantage of the mob ahead, and Bjorn nimbly climbed up next to him.

"Rock and a hard place, huh?" Bjorn asked rhetorically, holding his pistol down in front of him with both hands.

"Well…I'm guessing we're gonna need to do some shooting here in a minute," Tim said absently, intent on the Humvees ahead. "Humvee on the left has the roof hatch open; let's make for that and hope none of those things are inside it."

Tim hopped loudly from the bumper of the truck to the roof of the Subaru Outback ahead of it, nearly falling off when a pair of hands shot out of the sunroof grabbing for his ankles, the dead driver and passenger were still buckled into their seats within. Bjorn leapt onto the hood of the car next to it to avoid the grabbing hands. The two moved their way ahead slowly, weapons at the ready. The things in the Subaru were joined by others, equally trapped in vehicles, slapping and pounding on windows, moaning and growling. The raucous noise built until some of the undead roaming about ahead finally took notice, spinning to face to two men.

In the span of a few heartbeats, Tim and Bjorn were running as fast as they could, jumping from rooftop to rooftop, shifting and swerving to avoid grasping hands as the roaming dead surrounded the vehicles in pursuit. Finally, they both ended up together, on top of a huge Tahoe SUV. The vehicle was so massive the things couldn't get more than a hand on top of the roof. The Tahoe was the final car in the line; ahead lay a deadman's land of forty feet before the makeshift barricades and military vehicles. The roadblock consisted of yellow and black diagonally striped sawhorses behind which sat the two Humvees. The forty feet, however, might as well be forty miles with the sea of undead that lay in front and around them. If they used their guns, they would have the potential to attract innumerable more undead from the village ahead and the highway below, not to mention the horde in the Lowes' parking lot and the mass of undead already headed up towards them from the industrial park. Tim couldn't come up with any other options, however, and the growing noise of moans and growls wasn't conducive to thinking clearly.

"We gotta move fast; the longer we wait, the more will come," Bjorn said over the assembled horde's growls and hisses and hands scraping the paint and windows.

They both looked frantically for a spot to jump clear of the herd, but nowhere was better than anywhere else. They were completely encircled atop the black steel island, sitting in a growing sea of arms and teeth.

*

The soldier nearest to Will pushed him down on his face and crouched over top of him. The soldier placed his knee on the back of Will's neck before proceeding to pat him down. One thought vaulted to the front of Will's mind, even more pressing than the prospect of being disarmed and left for dead by the soldiers: the thought of the herd of dead that followed just a hundred yards behind him. Before he could think about saying anything, the man frisking him, shouted out, "Gun, we got a gun!" the soldier yelled excitedly.

Will let out an involuntary grunt as the man's knee ground deeper into the back of his neck, stones from the blacktop digging painfully into his cheek. The soldier's hand worked its way to the grip of the pistol poking out from his waistband. He could tell, even from his limited vantage, beneath the knee of the one, that the rest of the soldiers instantly tensed with weapons trained on him for a kill shot. As the gun was jerked out of his waistband, the soldier slid it along the ground, scraping and bouncing on the blacktop towards the rest of his squad before finishing the pat-down. One of the other soldiers picked up the revolver, opened the cylinder, and dumped the bullets from it. The bullets tinkled and bounced on the ground, almost musically before the soldier swept his foot across, sending them towards the sewer drain near the curb. He then threw the handgun like a baseball over the wall Will had been running beside just moments before. Will's heart sunk into his stomach.

"You guys got a good supply of ammo?" Will grunted out from the ground with the knee still pressed onto his neck.

The soldier in charge looked at him, eyes squinting suspiciously before answering.

"Enough. Certainly more than you, why?" He finished his sentence with a smug, wry grin.

"Just making sure you got enough for that," Will said pointing at the corner of the building near the retaining wall. The soldier looked up just as the first few undead came staggering around the corner, instantly recognizing a fresh meal standing in front of them.

For a moment, all that you could hear was the sound of a couple hundred shuffling feet, and the moaning of the dead, then the sound of a machine gun roared through the air, splitting the relative silence. First one, then a handful of the dead appeared, followed by the main body of the herd came around the corner. The soldier atop Will shifted off of him into a firing stance as all of the soldiers began firing their weapons into the approaching mass of undead.

*

Bjorn got shaken from his thoughts of doom and despair by the blast of the M4, roaring on full automatic, next to him. He looked over, and Tim was firing down into the throng. The undead were slowly piling into the gaps the heavy weapon created, as Tim sent the entire clip ripping through them.

"Try and cover me," Tim said as he slid another clip he had looted from the dead soldier into the receiver.

Having created a hole about five feet from the front of the Tahoe, he ran down the hood and jumped for it. He leapt over the top of the first few rows of dead and disappeared for a moment as the mass of undead swarmed around him. He hit the pavement hard, dropping into a forward roll. Bjorn fired at two of the things he saw reaching downward for Tim, taking one out and spinning the other away. That was all the help Tim needed. He regained his feet and was firing point-blank into the faces of the ones that stood in front of him. He switched the rifle to burst and cleared a path in front of him. He gained in speed as he moved away from Bjorn, with countless hands grabbing and scratching at him as he moved. The momentum he was able to gain was enough for him to vault over the sawhorse and scramble just out of the reach of three undead that were converging on him. He scrambled up onto the roof of the Humvee with undead hands grabbing and clawing at his feet and ankles as he swung up top. A fingernail hooked into his ankle, scraping deeply and painfully as he again reloaded the M4. As soon as the new clip clicked home, Tim threw himself headfirst into the top hatch. Not wanting to have his legs mauled by anything that might be inside, he came to a stop, face down inside the Humvee.

His senses were assaulted on all sides by the massive amount of undead smashing against the side of the vehicle and windows. He was still trying to get his bearings with all the confusing sensory input. Before he was able to make sense of his surroundings and recognize the wretched smell inside the vehicle, a pair of hands grabbed the sides of his head, fingernails digging deeply and painfully into his flesh. The stench of rotting meat and excrement assailed him as the hands started dragging him further into the open interior. The hands clutching the sides of his head smelled wretched, and oozed cold viscous liquid onto his face. His own hands dropped the M4, clattering to the floor of the vehicle below, and his hands scrambled across the things chest before settling on its throat. Thrashing about and trying to wriggle free, he finally got a look at the thing that held him. It was wearing a camouflage contamination suit and was trying desperately to bite through the face shield at the hands clutching its throat. Tim struggled and wriggled until he got the rest of his body down the hatch. He steered his weight down on top of the undead, pinning it, and was able to pry its gloveless fingers off his face.

Tim looked for his rifle, but his eyes came across the soldier's pistol first, sitting in its holster, belted around the rubberized suit. He snatched the 9mm pistol out and held it under the dead thing's chin and pulled the trigger. Nothing but a click as the hammer struck home; the gun was empty. *Fuck!* he screamed internally, his mind on the verge of overload from the panic and struggle. His eyes, glancing furtively around the cab, spotted the M4 underneath the undead soldier's foot. Wrenching the rifle free, he spun it to bear on the dead thing's head and pulled the trigger. It barely registered in his mind as a hail of bullets tore through its head, showering the driver's side door with brain matter and congealing blood.

The only thing he knew was the report from the M4, as gunfire exploded in his own head, deafening him painfully in the process. The sound of the rifle reverberated heavily in the armored vehicle. He was in such excruciating pain that it took nearly a full minute for him to regain his senses.

Finally, his head cleared a bit, just as a hand came down from the hatch above and grabbed him by the hair. Gore poured down onto his face as he looked up into the face of a rabid creature. Its mouth roared, but Tim couldn't hear; he could only see the gray face, streaked with black and crimson blood as it slid down at him, pulling his head towards its open mouth. Unthinking, Tim shoved the barrel of the rifle up into its gaping maw. He used the rifle to push the head away from him even as it viciously ripped hair from his scalp. He clenched his eyes and again pulled the trigger, the discharge of the gun caused his ears to painfully pop in the enclosed vehicle. Gore showered down on him from the corpse, covering him from the knees up. He gathered the base of his shirt with his left hand and wiped his face with the inside of it before opening his eyes again. The ruined skull hung down the hatch above his head. He had to close his eyes to avoid the gore that poured down from it as he got his feet under him, and standing, shoved it up and out of the Humvee.

Tim emerged from the interior covered in blood and gore to see Bjorn still atop the Tahoe, which was now being shaken by the huge assembly of undead gathered around it. Tim nervously looked around for more of the fast undead, but no more appeared to him. He set about trying to figure the mechanisms that operate the SAW machine gun mounted to the roof of the vehicle. He could see the belt fed bullets and knew it was loaded, so he aimed it at the mob ahead of him, making sure to start low so as not to hit Bjorn. Pressing the trigger, he fought to keep the muzzle down as the SAW set to work cutting down the creatures.

The undead fell as a scythe cuts through wheat, the gun cutting legs out from under the undead, spinning them to the ground or ruining their skulls, putting them down for good. He was still deaf and, although he couldn't hear the gun, he could feel the sound concussions coming from the SAW hitting him in the chest as his bloody hands struggled to keep the gun in control. To him, the silent way to the weapon mowed the things down provided an amazing almost cathartic relief to the adrenaline-fueled encounter he had just gone through. Having cleared a large swatch of roadway of the undead, he yelled silently to Bjorn for him to run. Bjorn jumped down from the hood of the Tahoe and Tim raised his M4, preferring its accuracy over the barely controllable SAW. He provided cover for Bjorn the entire way up to the barricade. Once Bjorn reached it, he nimbly stepped on the sawhorse and launched himself over the last few things to the hood of the Humvee. Tim extended a blood-soaked hand to help him get up top and gain his balance.

"Holy shit, man. You look like something straight out of a fucking horror movie," Bjorn said, wiping the gore off his hand onto the roof of the Humvee.

Tim just saw lips moving; his lip-reading skills were extremely limited and usually depended on an expected response. He just shook his head and pointed at his ears trying to indicate that he couldn't hear. Bjorn seemed to get it. They both dropped down into the Humvee, feet-first this time, pulling the hatch closed behind them and sealing it. They then wrestled the dead soldier's body to the rear of the vehicle. Bjorn settled into the driver's seat, gingerly, not too eager about sitting on the blood and gore-soaked seat which earned him an exaggerated eye-roll from Tim. Tim would have liked to drive the vehicle he had commandeered, but his inability to hear made that a less than desirable choice.

By the time both were situated in their respective seats, the horde that had crowded around the Humvee was at least ten deep. The mob was rocking the heavy vehicle gently. Tim was struck by the pleasant feel of the gentle, ocean-like movement. That coupled with his inability to hear the groans, moans, and growls of the things allowed his mind to drift off to a memory of fishing with his grandfather. He leaned his head against the window, thinking of the fond memory he had forgotten about until just now. His right ear suddenly popped, loudly and painfully. He winced, involuntarily curling up on his seat and clutching his ear in agony. Moments later, once the initial pain subsided, he noticed the sound of a loud ringing, similar to the emergency broadcast announcement they had been monitoring regularly for the past thirty-six hours. The sounds of the world gradually faded into the tone so he could somewhat hear once again, even though he was still painfully bothered by the pressure in his left ear. Oblivious to the surroundings while dealing with the pain, Tim didn't even notice as Bjorn guided the Humvee onto the eastbound lanes of I-86. About ten minutes later, Tim's left ear finally released, the pressure causing another few minutes of agonizing pain and joining the other ear in the constant ringing.

"Where are we going?" Tim unintentionally yelled at Bjorn, trying to hear his own voice over the ringing in his ears.

Tim struggled to hear Bjorn's response of, "I don't know, I just needed to get out of there. I was worried that we wouldn't be able to push through the crowd of them."

Tim nodded absently before yelling back.

"We need to get supplies and get back."

His narrow brush with death made him desperate to hug his Laura and Luna. Bjorn's hands went up in exasperation.

"Yeah, from where though?" and turning to Tim, he added, "Those things are everywhere."

Tim sat quietly considering the options. The ShopRite and the WGS were already off the table as realistic options. There were a few restaurants in Chester they could probably get a supply of food from, but most were along the busy main avenues, in and around the ShopRite plaza, or on the main street in town. Finally, Tim spoke.

"Do you think we could kill all those things we just ran from?"

The question lingered heavily in the air for a minute, with both men considering the benefit of killing all or most of the undead in the immediate area around their family, the weapons they could gather from the barricade as well as having a semi-secure area in which to gather supplies. Without realizing it, Bjorn had let off the gas, and the Humvee coasted to a halt in the middle lane of the desolate eastbound lanes of the highway.

They looked at each other in silence as if measuring each other's resolve, then Tim turned and jumped into the back, ripping into the ammo cans in the rear.

"Two more cans of bullets for the mounted gun and three of M4 rounds," he yelled back up to Bjorn, "and three grenades; turn this fucker around!"

"On it," Bjorn replied, smiling as he swung the heavy vehicle about.

The two discussed the strategies they could think of on the short ride back to the exit. Bjorn and Tim were great at brainstorming; they had on numerous occasions got together to bounce ideas off one another only to have hours long brainstorming sessions, be it on ideas for building houses that they often daydreamed of or ideas for shit-hits-the-fan preparation. This time, they had ten minutes to devise a tactic for killing hundreds of undead.

The Humvee drifted to a halt at the bottom of the ramp, nearly blocking off the roadway. Bjorn leaned on the horn while Tim dragged the two ammo cans up top and prepped the SAW with a fresh feed of bullets. Tim set aside the used canister as it was not empty, but nearly so. After thirty seconds or so of honking the horn, Bjorn stepped out of the Humvee and scaled the roof with the M4 and a can of ammo. They waited in silence as the bodies of dozens, then hundreds of the things swelled up against the side of the Humvee.

*

Laura followed Tim and Bjorn down the hallway to the elevator. She waited, listening as the elevator car slid down into the distance below her before pressing the button to recall it. While she waited, she dragged the small table near the door. When the doors slid open, Laura squealed in fear as Sophie came skipping out of the elevator, frightening her. Sophie jumped back at the scream and started giggling with Laura on the floor. Laura pushed the table into the doorway, triggering the safety to keep it open.

"I had no idea you were down there, Soph; I almost locked you out!"

"I was watching the SpongeBob movie."

"Oh, that sounds like fun, what are you doing now?"

"I'm going to get mommy some water and make sure Liam is okay in there."

"Mind if I tag along?"

Sophie smiled at her and shrugged her shoulders. Laura had always enjoyed Sophie; she was an imaginative, cute little thing, but they had never spent much time together before everything fell apart. They walked to the bathroom together and filled a wax-coated Dixie cup with water for the girl's mother. Laura asked Sophie to wait a minute for her. Laura's bladder hadn't been the same since Luna was born and she needed to clean up a bit after Sophie scared her. Once she was ready, she took Sophie by the hand, and the two left the bathroom and started down the hall towards the office Sophie's family shared. The sound of glass shattering jolted through Laura's body, causing another scream to rush from her lips. She was skittish by nature, and often found herself punching Tim, whether or not he intentionally scared her. Tim wasn't around now, and Laura could only picture the worst case down the hall. In her mind, one of the monsters from outside had somehow gotten into the building and was upstairs feasting on Lilly.

She shuddered at the thought and hesitated, bringing Sophie to a halt. *Where's Luna?* her mind screamed at her, her motherly instincts kicking in even at a perceived, imaginary danger. Laura calmed herself with a breath and she forced herself to continue down the hallway.

"Mommy!" she heard Luna call from the office their family had occupied since moving in here, across the hall from Lilly's. *She must have just woken,* Laura thought, hearing the child's usual morning call for comfort. They neared the conference room, Sophie skipping merrily at her side, about fifteen feet from the living quarters they adopted. Laura peered eagerly at the glass of the door looking for Luna's sweet face.

The glass shattered outward from Sophie's family's room, spraying bloody shards out into the hallway. Laura froze and yanked Sophie back behind her. A screeching roar came from the office, sending chills down Laura's spine. A commotion came from the door, and Laura shoved Sophie into the conference room as Lilly erupted into the hallway, violently wrestling herself free from the door.

"Mommy!" came Luna's yell again, this time filled with fear.

The Lilly-thing screeched and lunged for the door.

"No!" Laura screamed at it.

The thing that was once Lilly turned slowly, its milky white eyes settling on Laura at last. Laura peed a little as she looked at Lilly's ashen face. The face had a bluish tinge to it, but for that and the eyes, she looked the same. Her face was contorted in rage, and roared once more and charged down the hall toward Laura. Laura staggered a bit as she turned to run. Collecting herself quickly, she ran straight down the hall, the Lilly-creature coming quickly up behind her. She thought she felt a hand touch her hair, sending chills up her spine as she leapt over the table into the elevator, turning quickly to mash the buttons. She didn't have time to think about where she was going; she just needed to get away from the terrible thing. *The table!* her brain screamed at her. *Shit!* She kicked at the table to push it out from the door. The table slid into the Lilly-thing's path, tripping it and sending the undead thing sliding on its face into the elevator at Laura's feet.

Laura's eyes widened in panic and she started screaming in terror as its hand lashed out, trying to grab her ankle. She jumped over it and out the door as they slid shut behind her. She could hear the monster inside hammering on the door as the elevator slid downward. She collapsed onto her knees, crying. A moment later, Sophie laid her hand on Laura's shoulder, evoking another shrill scream. They laughed for a moment, breaking the spell of terror that gripped Laura, before the thought of Luna snapped her back into the moment. She got up and ran to the door where Luna stood with tears running down her cheeks. Laura sighed as she opened the door, scooping up the sobbing toddler and holding her tight against her.

"Laura?"

"Yeah, Soph?"

"Something is wrong with my brother. He got hurt."

*

As the soldier kneeling on Will's neck moved clear of him to assume a firing position, he crawled quickly away from both the firing guns and the approaching dead, mostly though, he was eager to be away from the soldiers altogether. Once he was clear of the fire, he stood, tentatively at first, wishing desperately for the meager security his revolver had provided him. He briefly considered finding someplace to hide so he could scavenge the soldier's corpses when the undead were finished feasting. His thoughts of that were dashed when the buildings all around them exploded with activity as the gunfire tore through the silent city. He backpedaled from them, slowly at first, breaking into a run when he saw the first soldier get pulled down under the weight of the dead. The soldiers were covering each other as they retreated up the street towards Will's fleeing form, but the roar of machine guns attracted more from every direction. Will stopped paying attention to the firefight as the empty street ahead of him became increasingly active with the undead. As he ran, the undead on the streets grew thicker and thicker as they streamed from buildings, alleyways, and cars for as far south as he could see.

A few of the undead made lunging swipes at him as he weaved around them, but as a whole, they seemed intent on the source of the noise than in his lone fleeing form. He pitied the soldiers, but was reassured in abandoning them to their fate by their unwillingness to help him, and now, because of them, he now ran weaponless. *Fuck, fuck, fuck, fuck,* his mind repeated like a mantra as the streets in front, and around him filled with the dead, weaving and running on the roofs of cars when necessary. He made his way to the end of the block. To the right was a public park that seemed to be fairly sparse with the things, and he aimed for it at a jog. He veered through the wrought iron archway heading down the path towards the playground ahead. Glancing to the right, he could see a baseball field with a couple miniature, uniformed zombies milling about in their pinstripes and cleats. Spotting something in front of one of the dugouts, he veered quickly towards it. The children wore helmets with full face cages to protect them from wild pitches and the like, their bodies sporting grievous wounds wherever their protective attire hadn't covered them. Will had his eyes set on a duffel bag near the visitors' dugout. The bag spilled youth-sized aluminum bats out onto the ground as Will shook it out. The undead children moaned and growled, moving to converge on his spot. He grabbed two of the light three-quarters-sized bats and ran off to the west side of the park, quickly outpacing the shambling children. The sound of gunfire petered off far behind him, and he slowed to a jog. He knew now that the distraction of the guns was over that he would now be the primary target of everything he came across that was still moving in the city.

At the west end of the park, Will paused at the curb to get his bearings. Smoke rose from buildings in the distance all around him, the silence punctuated by the high-pitched warble of an occasional car alarm. On all of the streets encircling the park, he could see the subtle movement of the undead, shuffling about, searching for a victim. He spotted a sign for Interstate 95 with an arrow indicating the on-ramp lay ahead. Starting off towards the intersection, he turned west once he arrived. From here, he could see the on-ramp was just a single block down; the traffic, though, was snarled. Cars packed the streets from curb to curb, and the undead lurked in great numbers both in and around the stalled traffic. He hesitated, trying to assess how best to navigate the street, considering briefly trying to go around the block but deciding at length that he'd rather not risk going three blocks when he could most likely navigate this one, even if he had to run. Besides, every other street he had seen was crawling with the things as well. He also thought that there were bound to be more soldiers and didn't want another chance encounter; the next squad might not be as kind to him.

He wanted out of the city as quickly as possible. Before stepping off the curb, he glanced around once more, just to be sure he wasn't in imminent danger. As his head swung back around, his eyes came to rest on a red Honda scooter leaning against a utility pole in front of a business. A sign announced the shop as being The Fort Lee Beanery and café, and a great many undead patrons milled about both inside as well as outside of the building. He immediately dismissed the scooter as an option with so many undead so close. He changed his mind though when he saw the feet of a corpse poking out from behind its rear tire. He moved across the street to the north to flank the corpse. His eyes continued to scan the body until its entirety came into view, seeing that it wore a helmet. He immediately recognized the potential for mobility through a gridlocked city. I-95 would most likely be just as crowded with disabled vehicles as the surface roads and he knew his chances of escaping most encounters would be greatly increased if he were riding a scooter.

His feet ached as he approached the far side of the street in front of the building next to the cafe. He tried to quiet his footfalls so as not to draw the attention of the numerous things milling about on the street or within the cafe. He made a wide berth to avoid the windows of the cafe, sliding in between two parked cars in front of a storefront monogrammed as being "Haney & Smith Insurance." He paused with his arms resting on the bumpers of the cars he squatted between before stepping onto the sidewalk. Looking both ways, he discerned that he was in the clear for the immediate future. He trained his eyes on the mutilated corpse lying next to the scooter. Blood and entrails surrounded the body in a wide circle, dark crimson footprints led away from it in all directions. Aside from the helmet, there was nothing obvious about the corpse that cemented his idea that it was the scooter's owner, but Will was committed at this point. Most of the undead outside were further up the street, milling about in front of a walk-up counter. He waited patiently to be sure that he wouldn't immediately draw their attention when he moved. The pains coming from the soles of his feet urged him forwards, eager to be on a set of wheels with a motor. With another fast glance about him, he stepped on the sidewalk and started crouch-walking towards the scooter.

Will hesitated a moment and tried to gather his wits in front of a door with trapezoidal, pressed tin letters arranged to indicate that it was the home of 2114-A, B, C, and D. He was certain the door led to apartments above the insurance company. He also knew that one more step would bring him in front of the cafe's windows and that it would only be a matter of seconds before the dead assembled within would be tripping over themselves to get out the door and devour him. His eyes were drawn back to the gore on the sidewalk, and he assessed the corpse once again, hoping to catch a glint of metal from the scooter's key. Nothing shone aside from the dim sun glinting off the half-congealed blood that surrounded the body. The corpse wore a heavy chain over its shoulder and although its fist was balled and seemed to be clenching something, he couldn't be sure. He sucked in a deep breath, steadying himself, and exhaling slowly and loudly. Something slammed heavily into the door behind him, rattling its hinges, followed by the sound of heavy fists hammering on the door. *Fuck, one of the fast ones!* Will thought. As he turned and backed away from the door, the sound of a flurry of movement came from inside the cafe and he started to panic.

"Fuck," he yelled.

He struggled to keep himself composed as he ran over to the corpse, dropping his aluminum bats, clattering on the ground and grabbing at its blood-slick, closed fist. He slipped and nearly fell in the pool of blood as he grabbed the hand and worked the clenched fingers open, only to discover that the hand was empty. The door behind him burst open, striking the brick half-wall below the plate glass windows violently. Seeing the first zombie come ambling through the door barely ten feet away, he started to rush. His panicked hands and knees slipped around in the pooled gore as he flipped the carcass to see if the key might have fallen under it, finding nothing. As he stood and moved to the curb to check if the key had fallen off onto the road, he slipped on the blood pooled underfoot. He came down heavily on his ass in the blood and had to put his palm down in the gore to get back up. One of the undead roared, sending a jolt of fear shooting up his spine. He looked back as the first of a great many undead piling out of the doors of the café closed the last few feet.

*

Undead from atop the overpass tumbled over the railing, their brains either too ruined or just incapable of understanding the consequences of such a fall. They simply saw Tim and Bjorn or heard the insistent blaring of the horn and moved in the most direct fashion towards them. Their heads ruptured on the pavement below, twenty feet in front of the Humvee. A few of the undead slipped around the rear of the vehicle, and Bjorn busied himself with the M4, trying to keep the bulk of the horde on the near side, facing the ramp. Eventually, when nearly all the dead in the vicinity were either on the hundred-meter-long ramp or otherwise moving towards them, Tim braced his forearms and pressed the trigger of the SAW. Great swaths of undead fell as he swept the heavy mounted weapon across the field of dead. Slowly, he became confident with the heavy gun, though his arms shook to the point of losing sensation.

The undead that had only been wounded by the first pass of the heavy gun regained their feet and were taken out, either by the next pass of the SAW or by well-placed shots with the M4. Bjorn pivoted the weapon back and forth from the ramp to the roadway, where undead were making their way across the guardrail from the westbound traffic. After a few minutes, as they had discussed, Tim slid down into the driver's seat and Bjorn slipped into the gunner's turret. As Bjorn reloaded the SAW, Tim reversed the vehicle about a hundred feet, leaning on the horn the entire time. They regained their previous positions and waited as the remaining undead gathered. A handful of stragglers could still be seen coming down the ramp towards them, and even more could be seen coming down the westbound ramp, making their way through the stalled traffic and over the guardrail. The undead that staggered towards them, with an occasional runner, didn't build up in significant numbers so using the SAW would have been wasteful. Tim busied himself reloading M4 clips from the ammo cans while Bjorn worked on his marksmanship, his attention to detail in his day job helping a great deal with his assessment of shots, though the recoil of the weapon took some getting used to. They sat in the middle of the highway for nearly an hour, taking turns with the M4. Finally, the undead petered out, leaving the two men waiting increasingly long periods of time for the straggling undead to approach, until at last, no more came.

"Ready to go scavenge?" Bjorn asked.

"You bet. Let's hit the barricade first; try and get some more ammo and fuel."

Tim drove the Humvee to the top of the overpass, tires skipping and slipping on blood and bodies stacked three high in places. He steered the heavy vehicle into the open area in the center of the bridge, directly between the two Humvees barricading the westbound traffic and the one remaining Humvee barricading the eastbound lanes.

"Only fire if you need to now," Tim said softly to Bjorn as the two climbed out the top of the armored vehicle. "We don't want to draw more over from the Chester side."

After nearly an hour of constant gunfire, the quiet atop the overpass was tense and palpable. Aside from a couple stragglers they spotted on the Chester side of the highway, everything appeared placid from their vantage atop the overpass. The two men crept slowly towards the Humvees on Chester-side barricade with Tim following closely behind Bjorn, relying on the other man's senses as his ears still rang. Bjorn climbed atop the Humvee on the right and scanned the area down the barrel of the M4. Tim prowled around the Humvees checking out the interiors, making sure they were clear before joining his friend.

From atop the Humvee, Tim was able to spot another M4 laying on the roadway ahead of them. With another thorough glance around, he scrambled down off the Humvee and retrieved it, noticing only after grabbing the strap that the gun was coated in partially congealed blood. Wiping the blood from the gun and his hands onto his pants, he returned to Bjorn's side. They loaded four fuel cans from the other Humvees into the one they had been driving. Tim offloaded the corpse of the undead in the contamination suit out of the Humvee and onto the roadway. Hunger panged at the two. Tim, of larger girth than Bjorn more so, especially after the work of hauling and loading. Even though their hands were weak and shook from the use of the weapons, they now had confidence in their killing ability, as well as an ample supply of fuel and ammo.

"What do you think?" Tim asked, looking across the ramp at the gas station convenience store.

"I'm worried about the family, to be honest," replied Bjorn, his low voice nearly lost in the wind with the ringing in Tim's ears.

"Yeah, me too," he replied. "But if we don't get food now, we'll have to come out again tomorrow after going hungry tonight."

Bjorn sighed heavily, knowing that Tim was right. He was eager to be back in the safety of the office building with his wife and children and had a bad feeling. He usually trusted his feelings when he got them, but chose to ignore it this time to get the job done. Without another word, Bjorn started off, heading towards the guardrail and the gas station beyond.

Even if they weren't fearful of attracting more undead, the stalled traffic would've prevented them from driving, so they set off on foot. Armed to the teeth and carrying the roll of garbage bags, they made their way over the guardrail just beyond the westbound barricade. Cautiously, they moved through waist-high dead weeds, down the embankment. They leapt over a pool of murky scum-coated water that had collected from highway runoff and climbed the opposite embankment. They scrambled the last five feet up the dirt berm, pulling themselves atop the blacktop pad at the rear of the convenience store.

Cautiously, they circled around the back of the 'On the Run' store, aware that many undead still lurked about, and many more would have been brought closer by the sounds of gunfire. Tim, crouching down against the wall, could see a multitude of things moving across the front parking lot and down the roadway in the direction of the intersection. Upon that sight, he knew that they wouldn't be making it to a pharmacy to get an antibiotic for Lilly. There were simply too many undead. He cast a sidelong look to Bjorn, to see if the man saw the futility of it. Even though Lilly looked terrible, the risk would be too great. Beyond the road and parking lot, he saw many more dead atop the hill that the CVS sat on, staggering about seeming aimless. The area was choked with them. Tim guessed that they lost direction or purpose when the gunfire subsided and now were waiting for some other stimulus to urge them on.

Bjorn, who looked longingly up the hill at the pharmacy, didn't mention trying for it. The greater supply of foods, as well as medications and first aid supplies within the pharmacy, would have helped them greatly, but all that was needed was one of the things to notice them and they would be set upon by hundreds of the things. Neither of them would entertain the idea of fending off that many undead off especially with the knowledge that this time, they would be doing it without an armored vehicle to guarantee their safety. The two men lingered on for a few minutes, staring at the roaming dead on the streets while mourning their luck.

After they had finished scoping out the surroundings, the two men crept back around to the rear of the store. Bjorn followed behind, dejected. His fears of the undead battled with his fear of failing his family as Tim approached the rear door. He fully expected it to be locked, and was caught off balance when the heavy steel security door swung outward freely in his hand. Once he regained his balance and ensured there was no immediate threat, he warily located a large rock and wedged the door open. The two exchanged uncertain glances as they peered into the darkened doorway that led into the rear of the store. Tim coughed intentionally, hoping that any of the things within would be drawn out to them by the noise, or at least stirred so they could hear the movement. After waiting for a long, tense moment, Tim gulped down his fear and nervously stepped into the doorway, pausing for a moment inside to allow his eyes to get adjusted to the dim interior. He quickly scanned to make sure there was no movement before searching out the other exits from the storeroom. His eyes eventually settled on a light switch. He switched on all the toggles on the panel as Bjorn joined him inside. The overhead fluorescents flickered on, casting their sickly glow on the assortment of boxes of food and cleaning supplies that were piled in the center of the room as well as along the walls. There were boxes labeled with meat, cheese, and snack food names.

"Truck day," Bjorn said just at the same time that Tim thought it.

"Lucky us," Tim said, meaning to sound sincere, but his voice rang hollow.

He stepped fully into the lit room, dropping the garbage bags and pulling boxes off the stack.

"Too bad we can't drive the hummer up here," Bjorn said, looking hopefully at Tim.

"No fucking chance of that," Tim responded to the implied question. "Leave the meat and cheese, it's probably bad by now. Let's drag the rest we can use outside so we don't have to come in and out."

In all, they dragged ten cartons of assorted foods and four cases of beer outside before securing the door behind them. They decided rather than making numerous trips to the Humvee that they would move all the boxes in steps, first moving the entire pile to the embankment, then to the bottom by the murk-water, then across, then up the embankment. This way, they could keep a better eye on their immediate surroundings. By the time they had loaded up all the supplies they had gathered into the Humvee, the sun was getting low on the horizon. The slate gray of the sky was darkening, casting a depressing pall over everything. They quickly discussed and decided to leave the Mercedes-Benz parked at the intersection where they'd left it, where it could act as an emergency escape vehicle. Tim drove the Humvee through the remnants of the barricade back towards the industrial park, stopping briefly to retrieve the key from the Benz before resuming on their course. Finally, they arrived back at the industrial lubricant warehouse where they drove to the loading bay. Tim slid the Humvee into park, and they sat in silence for a minute.

*

Will grabbed the utility pole to help propel himself away from the horde pouring towards him from inside and around the coffee shop when a flash of light reflecting off metal caught his eye. In mid-swing, he looked down, catching sight of the key still in the scooter's ignition. *Idiot!* he scolded himself as he came down to his feet and grabbed the scooter by the seat, starting his escape. He dragged the scooter, clattering backwards between two parked cars to the street. At least two dozen of the things were on the sidewalk at this point, with many more spilling out from the cafe. The horde made an incredible amount of noise as it forced its way through the coffee shop, pushing furniture across linoleum floors, dislodging porcelain cups and metal spoons to crash noisily. That noise drew the attention of more dead on the streets. All around him, the sounds of the breathless moans and scuffling feet started drowning out all other noise, with one exception.

The sounds of the fists hammering the door seemed to intensify as the throng of undead growled and moaned its way towards him. Will flicked the key and hit the ignition, and as the scooter purred quietly to life, he cast a glance at the roadway ahead for a clear path. Eyeing the opposite sidewalk, he twisted the throttle, the scooter buzzing away from the gathering mob, across two lanes of roadway and up onto the walkway. He felt the gentle purring of the motor more than heard it as he weaved around broken glass and swerved quickly to avoid a toppled garbage can, hurtling down the sidewalk. When one of the undead shambled across his path, he saw the stupidity of any two-wheeled vehicle in this scenario. He couldn't ram his way through it, and if it got a hand on him, it could rip him off the scooter or clothesline him off it. Instead of risking a fall, he stopped the scooter, dropping it unceremoniously onto its side, and ran up to the undead creature, kicking it squarely in the chest. The zombie bounced off the sole of his foot, crashing sidelong through a bank of garbage cans before coming to rest on the street. Without following up on the results of his kick, he jumped back on the scooter and was off again, just ahead of a new crowd that was gathering, as undead streamed out of the buildings on this side of the street. The tiny motor revved noisily in first gear as Will weaved cautiously through the blocked intersection, finally, heading up the off-ramp from I-95. He knew that the highway would aim him away from the city, though, even if it were against traffic he didn't figure he would hear the objections of many motorists. The assembling crowd of undead lost interest as it lost sight of him, and the sound of the scooter was taken by the wind of the brisk fall morning.

Finally, after having worked his way through all the snarled-up toll lanes and splits that the highway forced him through, he was on his way westward, away from the city. He was correct in his initial assessment that the highway wasn't any better than the city streets. Cars lay disabled across all eight lanes including both shoulders.. He moved slowly, swerving around side view mirrors and cars that were stuck in eternal lane-changes. Undead, trapped inside the cars, slapped at the windows and smeared their bloody decaying faces across the glass as he moved past. Some of the creatures were able to exit the vehicles, and did, joining a growing crowd of shuffling cadavers that followed after him. The westbound lanes appeared to be much clearer with the bridge destroyed so he made his way across to the center divider and lifted the scooter over top of the concrete partition. He was able to travel at a decent speed for a few miles. It wasn't until he saw signs for Hackensack that the cars began to pile up once again, slowing him down to walking speed. He rode on the shoulder, hugging the guardrail for a while, swerving around vehicles blocking the path when necessary. The undead in the cars were an endless source of unease for him as he traveled. Anytime he slowed to maneuver around a car, one or more of the things would start pounding on the windows, or worse, exiting from a vehicle in pursuit. This kept a steadily burning pit of fear churning in his stomach.

The view of the Hackensack cityscape below the highway was unnerving. There was no sound but the breeze blowing, bringing the occasional sound of a car alarm or a window smashing, as it whipped through the trees. Fires burned unchecked in many different areas of the city below. No vehicles moved, although there was a decent amount of foot traffic. Will shuddered at the thought of all the undead roaming the streets. His soft heart pitied the thousands he was sure were still hiding behind barricaded doors, waiting for help to come as their food and water dwindled. The thought caused him greater panic than traveling out in the open did. The smoke that billowed from a great many places in the city below joined with the steel gray of the sky, giving the appearance of a heavy mist that encroached and enveloped most of the world around him. All along the horizon, he could see pillars of black smoke drifting upwards, obscuring the meager fall sunlight even further.

The world seemed dead; at least what he was able to see of it. He thought a great deal about Wisconsin as he traveled, thinking of the endless farmland and rolling hills. He wondered how widespread this catastrophe was. One thing he spent a great deal of time speculating on was wondering how all the people trapped in these urban areas would get food, even if order was miraculously restored. How would they ever clear all the undead from the buildings and subways, sewer systems, and basements? How would they even begin to clear the traffic from the streets to resume food shipments? How many would die of thirst, starvation, or archaic diseases like dysentery while waiting for help? He was grateful to be on the road, grateful for the choices made that moved him from the barricade on the Brooklyn Bridge and got him clear of the city. The thought of being trapped in some building evoked feelings of suffocating claustrophobia in him.

Lost in his thoughts, a flash of white light barely registered in his periphery as he swerved around a work van that was pinned against the guardrail. He was thrown suddenly and violently from the scooter and landed heavily on his side. The impact of the landing blew the wind from his chest, and he slid painfully along the roadway, ripping his flesh in numerous places. He had no idea what had just happened, but when an undead in a Porsche next to him started slapping at the window next to his face, he pulled himself quickly back to his feet. He picked up the scooter and twisted the key...nothing; no crank, no clicking, nothing. He tried again and again before strangeness in the dim autumn sunlight caught his eye. He looked back towards New York City to see a mushroom cloud blossoming from over the top of a rise behind him. He stood there in the midst of a line of dead cars, some with dead people flailing about inside them, transfixed on the sight behind him, his mouth agape in horror. He could feel the tears welling up inside him when a little voice screamed desperately at him, *Go! Go now, you ass! Run!*

*

Daltry slowly stepped out into the frigid mountain air and moved clear of his truck. Linda could see he was actively avoiding looking over at where she sat with the mayor. The two were seated outside at a picnic table so Dale could smoke his cigarettes. Linda stood off a few feet to his right to keep clear of his smoke. She watched Tar get out of the Explorer and walk across the yard without even a glance in their direction. A moment later, the sheriff tipped his hat quickly at the two and started to walk purposely towards the sheriff's office.

"Daltry," Dale called as Linda opened her own mouth. "Linda here has some things she shared with me that you need to be aware of."

The sheriff stopped, silently cursing Dale for forcing the confrontation he dreaded. He dropped his head down to his chin and stood stock-still for a moment before shirking off the burden of caring and approaching the table. When he caught Linda's eyes, he removed his hat.

"Ma'am," he said nodding to her.

"Don't you fucking patronize me, Daltry," she snapped at him

"Don't think for a minute that I don't know what you and your buddy did up there."

"Dr. Henson, please," Dale interrupted. "Save the bickering, and tell him, please."

Linda took a breath to compose herself before looking the man in the eyes and was about to start when a beat-up old ford ranger pulled up to the fire lane in front of the building. Linda let out her breath without speaking, as both Dale and the sheriff turned away from her to watch the truck. A young man exited from it and walked over without closing the door behind him. Linda had never seen the man before. A moment later, Tar, having seen the truck pull up, rejoined them.

"Bobcat?" Dale asked as the young man approached. "You on leave?"

"No, Mayor Thomas, I'm AWOL," the boy stated matter-of-factly.

Daltry shifted a bit uncomfortably from his seat atop the picnic table at that as Bobcat continued.

"Listen, Sheriff, Mayor…can we talk in private?" he said, looking suspiciously at Linda, a woman he had never seen before.

"Bobcat, this is Linda Henson. She is the doctor here now that Henry passed on." Dale looked at Linda. "Linda, this is Charlie Hendrikson's boy, back from the Air Force in Colorado Springs. Just spit it out, Bobcat; with all the chaos been going on, the doc probably needs to know it anyways."

Susan, the police dispatcher, and her sister Elenor, the town clerk, who were seated on the bench next to Dale's office, crept closer to listen in. Bobcat nodded and gulped before starting.

"You gotta understand, stuff was really getting crazy on the base these last week or so. Half the base was either sick or had turned." He paused, licking his lips nervously.

"We know all about that, Bobcat, happening up here as well," Daltry interjected, seeing the boy's uncertainty.

Bobcat's shoulders slumped a little, upset at hearing that his hometown was affected by the sickness.

"My folks?" he asked, his voice both nervous and full of concern.

"They're alright, Bobcat, please continue," Daltry urged.

"Rumors were flying all over the base. Some saying it was a chemical attack, terrorism, the Russians, you name it and people were spreading it. Absolute silence came down from the Brass above though; that's what clued me in that it was something serious. Usually when the rank and file get in a tizzy about this or that, the Brass won't address it directly. They usually will spread something downwards, a rumor or scrap of information to defuse the rumor-mill. When the big-wigs all took off in helicopters this morning, well, that's when I knew it was big-time. That's when I decided that I was going AWOL. As soon as I saw them go, I knew nothing good was going to come of it."

"Where to? Where'd they go?" Daltry asked, for no other reason than to ask.

Bobcat shrugged and continued.

"I was on overnight duty, refueling the helos as they came in."

"I'm sorry," Linda interjected "Helos?"

"Jargon for Helicopters, Lin," Daltry said, nodding back to Bobcat.

"I caught the ear of one of the drivers. He was stationed with the Pacific fleet before he got assigned to chauffeur the Brass back stateside. He told me that we bombed most of the bridges and roadways in and out of Los Angeles yesterday morning. They were making a last ditch effort to quarantine the city. It didn't work." Bobcat licked his lips nervously before he spoke again. "He said that we dropped a nuke on LA last night. When the brass took off, I took off. Drove here straight from Colorado Springs."

Daltry scratched his chin and looked at the sky for a minute before shaking his head in exasperation and spitting in the dirt.

"Shit," was all Tar could manage. He sat heavily on the bench and let the ramifications of the news settle.

He was stunned. His mouth hung open like he was about to say something, but the reality of the United States nuking its own people was something he wasn't prepared to wrap his mind around. Susan and Elenor both stood to the side in stunned silence, the ashes on their cigarettes growing longer as the moments ticked by.

"What about Denver?" Tar asked at length. "You had to drive through or at least hear something unless you took to the mountains."

"I took to the mountains," Bobcat absently replied, then added hesitantly "There was a lot of smoke coming from the direction of Denver and Boulder; didn't try to get close, though. There were too many of those…things roaming around on the roads."

The last statement hung in the air for a minute.

"As good a time as any to mention it," Daltry interrupted. "I haven't been able to get anyone in nearby law enforcement on the phone all day, not Steamboat, not Fort Collins. Hell, we haven't talked to anyone outside the town since yesterday morning. Susie over here had been trying nonstop most of the morning."

Daltry spat off to the side again and stroked his face, continuing after a moment.

"I hate to say it, but I'm starting to think Linda is onto something."

"Well, if the military is bombing civilian targets, population centers, why haven't we heard anything on the emergency bands from the Feds or state government?" Tar asked, refusing, just for the moment, to let the conversation die.

Daltry paced off thoughtfully for a moment before turning to ask another question.

"You said half the base was sick, Bobcat?"

"Toxic-Taco-Tuesday they called it," Bobcat said, nodding.

"So that's it?" Tar asked, a bit angrily. "We're on our own then?"

Daltry shrugged helplessly.

*

Will tore his eyes from the blossoming mushroom cloud and ran as hard as he was able to. He finally slowed his pace to a jog after a quarter mile to conserve energy. The mob of undead that managed to extricate themselves from vehicles was growing larger with every few vehicles he passed, and were managing to keep within sight of him, now that he was on foot. He was able to outpace them, and thankfully, none of the fast ones approached yet, but he knew that he would have to rest eventually, and the dead moved tirelessly. The sun had started to creep low on the horizon when he decided he should get off the highway. He figured he could probably climb atop a truck and be safe, but fears of getting surrounded while he slept kept him moving forward. The temperature had dropped overnight and he doubted he would be able to sleep outside, exposed on another chilly October night. The course he decided on was to try and scavenge a coat from one of the cars then get atop a building like he had in Fort Lee. Even if the dead lingered below a fire escape, he could enter the building if needed and exit from elsewhere, though the thought of moving through the darkened halls of a strange building sent chills up his spine. He began to scan the contents of the disabled vehicles as he moved, not daring to take more than a passing glance however, as the crowd behind moved closer with every pause.

He saw an exit ahead for Route 17 north ahead and started running. He wanted to put as much space between himself and the horde that followed as possible, hoping that he could get off the highway without them becoming aware of it. On the ramp, he stayed to the far left, moving alongside the guardrail. He crouch-waked and crawled, keeping the stalled traffic between him and the horde behind him in an attempt to stay out of sight.

Will spotted a police cruiser on the roadway ahead, where the exit ramp merged onto Route 17, and crept up to the driver's side door. It was empty, and peering through the glass, he could see there was a shotgun locked upright against the dashboard. The door was locked, and he paused to consider his options briefly, his hand absently moving to rub his sore feet. At length, he finally decided against smashing the window to get the gun. He figured he would only worsen his position by the noise it would make, possibly drawing a horde on to him, for a rifle that he may not be able to break free, or may not have any shells even if he could get it. Even in the best case scenario; he gets a loaded shotgun that he then must use to get rid of the crowd the initial noise lured over, bringing even more to him. No, he cemented his decision, better to leave it and hope the cop is dead or undead nearby so he could strip it off his pistol and keys. Just as he was getting ready to move again, he heard the sound of hundreds of low, whispering moans and many shuffling footsteps behind him. His eyes widened in panic, and he slipped as quickly as possible around to the front of the car. He crouched down low enough so that he could still peer over the hood and see the mob that had been following him moving past, still on I-95. His immediate panic subsided, replaced by relief that they weren't pursuing him down the ramp.

Nervous that in his flight from the horde of dead, that he hadn't gotten a good lay of his surroundings, he started scanning the ground and immediate area for anything he could use as a weapon if the need arose. He shifted around the passenger side of the police car to put the body of the cruiser between him and the undead moving past on the highway above. He was still nervous that they would spot him or he would make some noise that would cause them to descend upon him once again. As he came around the front bumper, he came face to face with a legless zombie. The thing scrambled on its chest and arms the last few feet and lunged mouth first at him. Will let out a terrified gasp and lashed out with both hands instinctively, nearly getting his thumb bitten, as he grabbed it by the sides of the head. He gritted his teeth and slammed it face first into the pavement, again and again, its face and skull thudding against the blacktop until the thing's arms stopped reaching and clawing for him. Once the dead thing had finally ceased its struggles, he scrambled off the ramp onto Route 17. He was too petrified to look back over his shoulder, afraid that the horde from the highway had resumed pursuit.

His lungs and feet burned from the flight, and after a minute, he settled into a trot, eventually evening his pace into a slow jog. The blisters that appeared on his feet caused sharp pains that stabbed like daggers into the backs of his feet with every footfall. After a couple minutes of jogging, he could no longer resist the suspense and whipped his head around to see if the mob of undead was once again in pursuit.

He was encouraged that he could no longer see them, and slowed his pace, looking down at his gore-covered hands. He cringed and smeared the half-congealed black and crimson slime onto the blood-soaked knees of his jeans. He dropped to his knees and took a quick self-inventory. His feet were covered in blisters and a singularly painful scratch from one of the dead. He was nearly covered, from head to toe, in blood and gore in various states of drying. His muscles ached and cramped like never before, and his stomach seemed in constant complaint as he hadn't eaten or drank anything in more than two and a half days. The realization that he was most likely suffering from severe dehydration got him up and moving with new purpose.

The sun crept ever closer to the horizon, and he started jogging again, despite the pain. He crossed from a town called Rochelle into another town called Rochelle Park, peering inside every unoccupied car he passed for a bottle of water or juice. He had no idea where he was going, only having ever been in Jersey once before when a friend was the guest DJ at a club in Hoboken. All he knew was he was headed north, away from the city. *Away from what was once the city,* popped through his head, his thoughts turning dark, pondering what he'd witnessed earlier. The thought of how many people had been exterminated with that one bomb haunted him. Ten million lived in the city, but how many were there to visit or to work? He had to put a great deal of effort to shake the soul-wrenching thoughts from his head. *You can protest later asshole; you've got to survive now,* his inner voice scolded.

Lights flickered on ahead, startling Will as they illuminated the sky. A few moments later, the street lamps on either side of the four-lane highway flickered on, lighting the road he was on. He slowed his pace, both to catch his breath, as well as to try and gauge whatever was going on up ahead. He walked up the middle of the highway, keeping the center divider just to his left. As he came around a gentle bend in the road, he could see clearly that he was approaching a shopping mall, the parking lot lights illuminated seemingly endless acres of cars. He could also see that a few tents had been set up in the lot. They looked military, which both scared and excited him. His recent encounter with the soldiers in Fort Lee made his stomach knot up in fear. Knowing that he looked a wreck, being covered in blood like he was, he was also very nervous that they might just open fire on him, thinking he was undead. *It could be salvation though,* he argued with himself. The adrenaline and thoughts that raced through his head were swept away as a loud sound started thudding through the air. What kind of salvation could he expect from the same people that dropped a nuclear bomb on New York City? It was safer to steer clear of authority at this point he decided, but the well-illuminated lot offered many other possibilities.

A shopping mall!

Will remembered a movie where people had barricaded themselves inside one, but he couldn't remember the end. He was struck by hope for the first time in days though, and decided to approach the mall from the other side of the lot, far from the tents. Ignoring what was obviously a military compound, his eyes settled on the sea of glass and steel; viewing all the parked, empty cars in the lot as a potential lifesaver; if only he had the ability to loot them without drawing unwanted attention, be it from undead or from soldiers.

The loud whooping sound grew steadily louder as he walked across a grassy knoll that ran around the edge of the huge lot. At first the sound was just rattling windows of the cars that he passed until finally he was forced to cover his ears from the noise. He ducked down between cars as the form of a huge Chinook helicopter lifted sluggishly into the air. Hope and despair swept through him as the heavy two-propeller monster gained in altitude then leaned into the west and drifted slowly into the distance, leaving silence in its absence. Once the warbling sound of the helicopter faded into the west, he turned his attention back to his immediate surroundings.

He eyed the tents warily, noticing that the little compound of a few tents was ringed by chain-link fencing. Rows of razor wire glinted across the ground in front of the fence and held numerous bodies, trapped within its coils. He saw no movement from within the area and decided to creep closer for a better look. Moving quickly through the rows of cars, he was reassured momentarily, seeing for the first time in two days an area that seemed free of the undead. Car windows were smashed and the dead that once flailed within had been put down. They sat at eternal rest, still seat-belted inside their steel coffins. His eyes took this in, though they barely strayed from the military area. The anticipation grew as he came closer to the compound, with each step the anxiety that he would need to dive and roll from gunfire grew. Every second out in the open lot, he anticipated a crowd of undead to come from between parked vehicles. But none came.

*

"Bobcat, I'd really appreciate if you could stick around for the meeting we are going to call. It'd go a long way to convincing some of the townsfolk, especially the ranchers and homesteaders," the Mayor asked.

"We'll see, Dale, I wanted to let you all know what's going on before I head home. Time is wasting, and I'm thinking hard about just getting my parents and heading north."

"What's north?" Daltry asked.

"Open country, less people." Bobcat shrugged as he turned to leave. "Hopefully less of those things."

"Wait, why didn't the military do more at the start?" Linda asked at the man's back.

"No time." Bobcat shrugged, turning back around. "Everything was fine one day; the next day, half the barracks was dead, or whatever they are."

"That quickly?" Daltry cast out.

"I came back from leave time on Wednesday morning, half the base was sick from the night before. That night was when the shit started to hit the fan. Two days later the helos evacuated anyone of importance. We are only talking about twenty-four...thirty-six hours, tops."

"Should've been enough time to do something," Tar trailed off.

"That's military bureaucracy, Tar. Too many bosses to call, especially in the middle of the night. No one wants to wake the boss up; not to mention that the boss never answers his phone after hours. I'd guess by the time the relevant info made its way to the shot-callers that it was already too late. Guessing they knew it, too. That's when the order was given to evac the Brass." Bobcat shrugged again dismissively. "Now, gentlemen...and ma'am, I've got to go see my folks."

With that, Bobcat walked to his idling pickup, hopped into the open door, and buzzed out of the municipal parking lot, heading west on Route 10. Linda, after a few moments of silence, proceeded to fill them in with all the details specific to the bacteria that she had as well as the news about her last call to the CDPHE.

"Gentlemen," Linda said, standing and starting to pace around the table, looking pointedly at Daltry, where she expected to find the most resistance. "I fear that this infection, this microbe, has grown to catastrophic proportions."

"What exactly does that mean, Linda?" Daltry queried, casting a suspicious eye on her.

"As you know, I've lost contact with the CDC and now my colleagues at the CDPHE." She gulped, thinking of the earlier conversation that was violently interrupted. "Those factors, coupled with the news that Bobcat brought...well, we need to start considering the very real possibility that we are in the midst of a biotic crisis."

"A biotic who?" Dale said, shaking the word out of his head.

"A potential extinction event, Dale. Now, while the lack of external communication rules out our ability for us to verify this, I did receive confirmation from the CDC that the infection was reported on every land mass with the exception of Antarctica." Linda trailed off as Dale stood up, throwing his arms in the air and stormed back to his office.

Linda turned her palms up and looked pleadingly to the sheriff.

"Linda, that's a big pill to swallow," he said, intentionally not looking her way.

"Sheriff, dammit, I'd be a liar if I said that there wasn't a possibility that I could be wrong about this, but I don't think so." Linda felt her blood begin to rise and her emotions started building towards anger. "Take it however you want to, Daltry, but everyone in this town's lives are at stake, and you're the fucking sheriff!"

She walked back to her bicycle with her fists clenched in fury. She wondered if her recommendations would have been better received if she were a man, and suspected so. She was frustrated and infuriated at her inability to impress on them how dangerous this bug was, on a macro scale, not just in individual cases. *Fucking men!* she thought as she straddled her bicycle and pedaled furiously back to Heartland. She hoped that Betty had left for the evening, as she was certain that the mess she knew she would find there would likely push her over the edge.

*

The compound in the parking lot of the mall was barren. Whoever had occupied this place previously left on the Chinook and took a big chunk of Will's hope with them, leaving the despair and discomfort of a chilly autumn night in a undead-infested city behind. Tent flaps fluttered in the chill evening wind as he circled the chain link and concertina wire enclosure, looking for the point of entry. There were small towers at each corner that looked prefabricated. They were surrounded by sandbags and seemed to be bolted to the pavement.

Coming around the second corner about two hundred yards from the compound, he saw a backhoe and a smoldering mound of bodies piled two-stories high. Illuminated by the parking lot lights, his gaze lingered on the greasy black smoke that drifted up from the pile, barely fifty feet from the Macy's entrance. When he forced his focus back to his immediate surroundings, he noticed that the entrance to the compound was fifteen feet to his left. The front gate, the only gate, was piled six feet high with sandbags on either side of a padlocked chain link gate. Only the gate was free of the wicked concertina wire that ringed the entire compound.

Will stood there for a few minutes, staring blankly into the empty camp, as if he were willing someone to come greet him. The only sound was the tent flaps whipping about in the wind. Finally, the spell broke and he limped weakly back to the car lot, peering through the windows of each vehicle as he proceeded down the aisle. He finally found what he was looking for inside a Con Edison truck. He pulled the handle, and thankfully, the door swung open. He reached in and pulled a winter parka off the seat. He pulled the coat on and immediately shoved his hands deep in the pockets, opening and closing his fists, trying to help work warmth back into them.

Thinking about the supplies and luxuries within, Will approached the shopping mall doors but to his great disappointment, they were welded shut. Peering in through the dark doors, he tried to wait for his eyes to adjust to the darkness within to no avail. He was a little confused as he thought the lights were always on at shopping malls. He was thinking about the food court in the mall back home. He loved being able to pick and choose his meal from anywhere he wanted. Thoughts of his previous meals on his shriveled, empty stomach filled his consciousness and he immediately moved to find a rock with which to smash the glass doors. Having found a fist-sized rock in the shrubbery near the trashcan, he turned back to the mall and spotted light coming from the glass above the doors. Perplexed, he started approaching the doors again only to have the confusion clear. The mall wasn't dark; on the other side of the doors were wall-to-wall undead, pressed so tightly against the glass by the ones in back that the ones in front weren't able to move. Looking closely, he could see that only their eyes and mouths moved. He had just spent a good few minutes with only a centimeter of safety glass separating him from hundreds of the things. His whole body shuddered violently thinking about this. He turned and scurried away out of their sight, doing his best to put them out of his own mind. He stepped down from the curb, wishing desperately for a cigarette as he moved back into the parking lot.

He spotted a case of water in the rear compartment of a station wagon and smashed the window without hesitation. He drank two bottles immediately and spent the next five minutes bent over, retching the fluid back onto the roadway. He sipped from a third one and spent the next two hours scavenging and looting the cars in the parking lot, breaking windows with his rock to pop trunks. On a few occasions, he had set off car alarms, forcing him to hurriedly unhook the battery of the car to silence them. He learned quickly to avoid the high-end vehicles. He gathered his scavenged hoard in book bags he'd found in cars and threw them over the front gate of the military compound, waiting and watching warily for any movement from within. After a minute of tense waiting, he finally moved forward to the fence and climbed the gate.

Once he dropped down inside the compound, he collected his loot and dragged it into a tent. In all, he'd managed to collect: a case and a half of water, four bags of groceries which he dug into immediately, two blankets, and an aluminum baseball bat he had found laying in the bed of a pickup truck. He found a pair of clean socks and running shoes that fit him in a gym bag, driving gloves, an emergency window hammer/seatbelt cutter that had helped him get in most of the cars, an assortment of pocket knives, and a machete in a shopping bag labeled Campmor. He spent about an hour surrounding himself with his loot, securing as much of it as possible in an aluminum frame climbing pack and gym duffel bag. He was very aware as he packed that he needed to be fleet of foot so he packed the backpack with the necessities, putting much of the food, water, and extra weapons he had found in the gym bag for easy disposal if he needed to lighten his load.

He tenderly took off his slip-on loafers and cringed at the blood-soaked socks that were revealed. His feet had been aching him since Fort Lee, but the need to keep moving had kept him from attending to it. Now, he had the time and means to care for his bloody feet. The sweat, blood, and moisture in his shoes kept the wounds from drying out, allowing him to pull the socks off with minimal tearing. Blisters had formed and then ripped open, leaving open sores on the pads of both feet as well as behind his ankle. In the crooks of all his toes, athlete's foot sores had painfully crept in. He washed the wounds as best as he could, scrubbing gently with a clean shirt and letting them dry out before putting his new socks and shoes on. He ate and drank heavily, knowing he'd either be forced to leave much of the provisions behind or carry a heavy burden.

His thoughts turned again back to New York, the image of the mushroom cloud burned into his memory. He cried for a while sitting on the cold blacktop inside the tent, for his friends he'd left in New York, for the millions of strangers, but mostly for himself. He had never faced such hardship, not even close. Besides all the pain and fear, the thing that was the hardest for him to bear was the absolute loneliness. He thought about his mother and father and his brother Jim back home, and he cried for them and whatever fate they met. Eventually, emotionally drained, he drifted off to unconsciousness. He slept long, dreamless, and sound.

He awoke just before sunrise, a rime of frost covering the ground around him. Shivering violently in his parka, he sat up and pulled the blankets close around him, rubbing his hands together for warmth, his body left an outline of his sleeping form on the ground behind. He got to his feet slowly, his muscles were cramping and sore like he had never felt before. He figured that since he was up and moving to get warm, he might as well scour the little compound for goods. Mainly, he was hoping they'd left a gun behind for him. When he came out of the tent he slept in, he was confronted by a corpse on the ground just inside the tent flap of a neighboring tent. It was bespectacled and wore a lab coat. What was once a woman now was covered in frost and had a bullet wound in the middle of its forehead. He had seen enough death recently that he stepped over the body, unfazed, into the gloom of the dark tent beyond. This seemed to be a barracks; cots lined the walls of the tent and clothing of all sort littered the area. He was able to locate some thermal underwear he stowed in the pocket of the parka before moving onto the last tent in the compound. As he neared the entrance of the tent, he caught a glimpse through the gap between tents and the chain-link fence beyond, of a handful of undead that were moving across the parking lot outside. They seemed without purpose, but all the same, the fences surrounding him started to feel more like a prison than a haven. He wanted to be on the move quickly. He poked his head inside the final tent and the smell of death hit him in the face like a hammer. He winced back from it, and his eyes started watering. He poked his head back in, quickly assessing that it was a medical tent. Half a dozen bodies clad in camouflage lay in various states of wholeness on examination tables. All were missing at least one limb, and all were shot in the head.

Will took this all in a cursory glance, before the stench overwhelmed him. He moved back to the tent he had slept in and tore his clothes off, quickly donning the thermal underwear. He felt the urge and urinated in the corner of the tent, before pulling the rest of his clothing and gear on. Once he was fully dressed, he dragged his packs over to the gate. He prepared and unceremoniously shoved two peanut butter sandwiches into his mouth in huge bites. Something caught his eye to the right. He looked, realizing that he was so intent on the contents of the tents that he hadn't checked any of the guard towers. He ran a quick circuit of the little base, checking them to no avail. They had left a heavy machine gun mounted in one, but one of the bolts was stripped, preventing him from removing it. Beside that point, the thing looked like it weighed a ton, and the ammo case its bullets laid in was both heavy and noisy. He moved away after briefly trying to get it loose, recognizing the futility of it.

He was moving his gear to the gate for departure when a loud inhuman screech tore through the crisp morning air, coming from the direction of the piled, smoldering bodies. Will's head snapped around to see one of the fast things hurtling towards the base at breakneck speed. His heart dropped in his stomach seeing it closing the distance with its head thrown back like a sprinter. Three more of the damned things came tearing around the other side of the corpse-pile, roaring and charging towards him.

*

Tar walked the half-mile to his house to grab his gloves, chainsaw, and his thermos before stepping back out into the wind. He pulled his truck into the diagonal spots in front of Elsie's and strode inside. He walked past the few that had already gathered and were gossiping noisily just to the left of the door. As he marched past, he tore the map of Donner off the wall in the foyer and strode to his usual seat at the counter. He set his thermos on the counter.

"Fill that would you, Darla?" he said, winking at her as she moved from her book of crosswords.

He walked to the wall next to the kitchen window and scotch-taped the map onto the fading floral wallpaper, using tape from a dispenser kept next to the specials board. Within ten minutes, a dozen men were waiting at the map, drinking coffee and waiting to hear what Tar was so vehement about that he had the sheriff acting as his errand boy. Finally, Tom stepped in the door, and Tar nodded at the assembly and addressed the room.

"Tom, we need you and a couple with strong backs over to Denkin's Pass. Get started with the earthmover blocking the roadway; we will worry about prettying it up later."

"Whoa there, Tar," cut in Dale, the mayor. "Just what the hell do you think you're trying to do here? You don't have the authority or any reason to damage a state road,"

"Dale—" Tar started.

"We got emergency vehicles that may need that road. The military or who knows could need to get up here." Dale was working himself up as he continued.

"Dale!" Tar repeated as he felt the blood rushing up his leathery neck.

"I'm the goldarned mayor here anyways. I'd like to know where you get off coming in here with this cockamamie nonsense."

Tar was maroon with anger. He looked right through Dale with bloodshot, glassy eyes. Taking his revolver out of the holster, Tar placed it on the table in front of him, eyes boring holes through the mayor.

"I think you might need to wait over in your office, Dale," he said, composing himself enough not to throttle the man. "You heard what Dr. Henson told us yesterday, on top of what Bobcat came in talking about. Besides, with everything else that's been going on around here lately, who gives a shit about some roads? What's it gonna take for you to understand the situation we are likely about to find ourselves in. Not only are you standing in the way of progress here, Dale, you just stepped on my last fucking nerve."

Dale paled at the sight of the gun and the implied threat. He usually got his way by talking the loudest. When that didn't work, he had little else to fall back on. He fell silent and moved away from the group toward the door, though still within earshot. Tar took a few breaths to even out his demeanor as Darla brought his thermos over, setting it on the table in front of him.

"Now, Stan, you still have that old backhoe?" Tar asked the man.

"Yeah, runs like a beaut," Stan replied.

"Great, we need you to get over to where Route 10 enters Roosevelt National Forest. You're gonna want to rip a trench across the road from forest to forest about five or six feet deep and two or three feet wide."

"What for, Tar?" Stan sheepishly asked. "I got no problem doing it, just wondering what the point is."

"You all know me. I'm not one to panic, you all know that. So please, trust me when I tell you that we need to start acting here before it's too late. The hour is upon us. Harold," Tar called, seeing the vet walk through the door. "Go home and fetch your M16 and go with Stan to protect him. Same goes for the guys going with Tom. Same goes for everyone. No one walks around without a weapon from this point forward. Spread the word."

"Daltry gonna take issue with that, Tar," ventured Dale from the counter.

"Trust me, Daltry is coming around. He knows what we need to do; it's just a matter of time before he recognizes this situation for what it is. As for the rest of us, time is not a luxury we have if we want to protect our friends and family."

Tar waited a minute for his statement to settle before looking continuing.

"That leaves us 125 north of town and Route 14 to worry about. Any of you know the Stevens' and Taylors' well?"

"I know them well enough," Ty said, looking away from the map for the first time.

"Well, unless any of you have any better ideas, we're gonna need you to get their permission to use their barns as part of a barricade across 14."

The Stevens' and Taylors' barns sat on opposite sides of the road about three miles out of town. The farms sat just east of a bridge crossing the Illinois River and was the only spot for twenty miles where structures sat opposite one another on the road. High prairie extended for miles on either side of the river.

"Why not just take out the bridge, Tar? Would be easier?" Harold asked from the doorway.

"In three weeks, the river is going to freeze solid. Anything that wants to cross, living or dead, won't have any problems. The barns are the only real defensible way, especially since the stockade fence ties into it on the one side."

Harold nodded and moved out into the steel gray morning.

"I'll see what I can do," Ty replied

"We need to see if we can't get Randy's wrecker busy collecting everyone's broken-down vehicles and dragging them up 125 to block the road," Tar said, referring to the old farmer's habit of keeping broken-down vehicles on his property for parts or storage, or just because it was his. "About five miles up where the North Platte pinches in against the road, gonna need the cars stacked three high and four deep angled towards the river in case someone tries to ram it."

"I'll go talk to old Randy. I know him fair enough; we used to skip class to drink back in school," Ernest said with his thick drawl. "He is a stubborn old git. Gonna need something more than 'cuz Tar says so'."

"You can tell that old buzzard that I'm calling in my debt," Tar said, referring to an incident that happened years before.

Tar had seen some fires burning high up in the hills behind his house. The season had been unusually dry on that summer night, and so Tar decided to investigate, to make sure it wasn't a wildfire. It happened to be a bonfire, and Randy's seriously inebriated teenage daughter was alone with a handful of boys. Tar didn't like the way the boys were looking at her, and despite the protests of the young men, he took her home to her father.

"Any of you that haven't heard yet, the US government nuked Los Angeles." He paused for effect using the moment to nod acknowledgment to Bobcat, who having seen to his parents, had returned and was sitting quietly among them. "Whatever this illness is, we are not safe from it, or from our government, that much is clear. That leaves the burden of responsibility for our community now resting squarely on our shoulders."

Tar stepped away from the map he had been sketching his perimeter on.

"We'll worry about the gaps once we have the town shut down to traffic. Bobcat, take the rest of the men out to the outlying ranches and homesteaders and try to convince them to bring their families, food, cattle and weapons inside the perimeter we are creating."

"You got it," came Bobcat's response

"You know better than of any of us what the outside cities are facing right now. Do your best to convey the urgency of this," Tar said, making towards the door. "I'll be over at the municipal building talking to the sheriff if anyone needs me."

By the time Tar got clear of all the questions and caught up with the sheriff, Daltry was standing outside the municipal building having just finished meeting with a few of the townspeople that had come in with questions about Bobcat's warnings. Dale scurried away quickly into the building that housed his office as Tar approached. Daltry held his hands out towards Tar.

"Now just wait a minute there, Tar. Dale is right; you can't go destroying a state road," Daltry said. "I know that some funky stuff is going on, but I really don't like the idea of isolating us up here."

"Dammit, Daltry, enough of Dale's bureaucratic nonsense. It's time for us to circle our wagons here. No one is coming to help us. Not the government, not the state police, no one. At this point, we can assume that anyone that shows up is a threat."

"You can't just go and destroy the roads, man. What are we gonna do when people drive up? Send them back towards the heavily infected areas? Boulder and Denver? Fort Collins?"

"Damn right we are," Tar replied matter of flatly. "Listen here, Aaron; we have the luxury of isolation up here. We've been hurt a bit; twenty or thirty deaths is no small matter to us. But what are we going to do when thousands of people come up through here, hungry and desperate? You think your law is going to prevent someone from robbing and killing to feed their children? You think that pea-shooter on your hip is gonna be enough to stop them all?"

"You'd turn 'em back and let them starve then?" Daltry responded, eyes narrowing at being called by his first name. "Send them back to die on the road?"

"If there is a choice, us or them, it's always going to be us, Daltry," Tar snapped at him, getting angry. "And I'm not dead-set on turning people away. I'm just talking about having some measure of control over who comes in here and who doesn't."

Tar ran his hand over his mustache, a habit he formed while he gathered his thoughts.

"Aside from desperate people, what happens when those other things, the dead, run out of people to eat? How many people are there in Boulder and Denver? Close to a million if you count the areas around it? Another two-hundred thousand east in Fort Collins. Even if one in a hundred comes this way, we'd be overrun without any issue." Tar stopped his tirade, seeing that sense had found its way into Daltry's head, then finished with, "Come on, Sheriff, we need you to head over to the National Guard armory and get us some heavier equipment than we have. Shotguns and revolvers aren't going to cut it if those things come through here in force."

"I really don't like the idea of having a bunch of Category Five weapons floating around, Tar."

"Then keep them locked in the police station. Better to have them and not need them than get overrun when we are able to prevent it."

"I can leave first thing in the morning," Daltry said. "I've got to talk to Dr. Henson still and try to unruffle some feathers."

"Afraid morning may be too late, Sheriff. With Boulder and Denver burning, I sent the work crews out armed, just in case." Tar was interrupted by the sound of a distant gunshot. Daltry started off, and Tar stopped him with a hand on the chest.

"Go get weapons, I'll handle this…and, Sheriff, stockpile for the apocalypse because this just might be it," Tar finished.

*

Thinking quickly, Will ran back to the tower that held the machine gun and spun the heavy weapon to bear on the gate. One of the tents stood in between, blocking his vision, but he heard the first of the undead collide with the chain-link and the sounds of it shaking violently. He pressed the trigger and the machine gun roared to life. Lead screamed through the tent towards the gate beyond. A few flocks of birds took to the air in the distance. He let go of the trigger after a moment, allowing the muzzle to drop back down. He had never fired an automatic weapon before and found it both terrifying and exhilarating. The fabric at the peak of the bullet-riddled tent pulled back, sliding down the steel supports, allowing him to see the gate through the gap.

Even with a clear vantage, he couldn't see anything, either moving or incapacitated. Just as he tried to wrap his head around the implications of that fact, the other three hit the gate in stride, bending it inward, but blessedly holding them back. Will took aim and pressed the trigger again. The machine gun again roared through the early morning air, his hands ached as he fought to keep the muzzle down and aimed in the direction of the undead. Their bodies shook violently as the bullets tore through them, falling one after another as random chance sent a bullet ripping through their heads.

Will jumped back, screaming as a hand grabbed the top of his sneaker. In front of him, one of the fast undead was pulling itself up towards him. He lashed out, kicking it in the face three times in rapid succession before dislodging the thing from him. It took his new shoe with it as it fell. *The bastard thing must've climbed the gate,* he thought as he tried to train the muzzle of the gun down at an angle to shoot it while it scrambled back to its feet. It howled in rage and threw itself back at the stout tower. The damn gun-mount wouldn't let the muzzle drop far enough. He glanced at the machete hanging from his bag, on the ground below, right next to where the undead stood. After a brief struggle with the gun, he looked up to see the monster's head and arm surface above the platform again. Its hand was scrabbling around trying to get a grip on him. Without a thought, Will grabbed the ammo can and swung it with all his might. The chain of bullets, still connected to the SAW, ripped out as he swung it and connected with its head. The dead thing dropped down out of sight again, Will hoped desperately that the thing was down for good. Another screech from below sent chills down his spine, dashing the hopeful thoughts from him. He latched the ammo can hurriedly and waited. Again, the head and arm came up; this time, Will was ready, his sphincter clenched as he stomped down on the thing's wrist, pinning it down. He then brought the ammo can to bear, smashing the thing repeatedly in the top of the head. Well after it had ceased its movement, he continued swinging the can at it. Finally, a moan and some wretched metal scraping sounds from behind him broke him free of his rage. He snapped his head around to see one of the slow zombies wrapped in concertina wire, struggling its way towards him. Behind it, a number of other undead moved with purpose towards him, making their way across the parking lot.

Will jumped off the tower, rolling as he hit the ground. He grabbed his bags on the fly and hurled them over the gate as he approached, finally launching himself up and over as well. He saw numerous undead now on the edges of the parking lot, making their way towards the noise and movement. He cursed himself for using the machine gun, though he wasn't able to come up with any alternatives for how he handled the fast dead. Still, the noise probably had every dead within a mile headed in his direction.

Will angled back towards Route 17, making a wide berth around any of the undead that ventured near to him. He was barely out of the lot when he slowed to a halt, the added weight of the packs weighed him down and he had a belly full of food that was now insisting it be released. He grabbed two fistfuls of fallen autumn leaves from the grassy knoll and ran towards the intersection ahead. He came to a stop, casting off his pack and bag where Route 4 meets 17, in the middle of a wide area clear of undead and cars.

He hated the idea of what he was about to do, but his only choice otherwise was to soil himself and spend the day in filth and discomfort, which he considered briefly before dropping his trousers. He wiped with handfuls of crunchy fall leaves after quickly squeezing the contents of his bowels out on the sidewalk. He giggled uncontrollably despite the ever-increasing presence of the undead that was converging on him. Not fully clean, but relieved, he yanked his drawers up and, grabbed his packs, and moved out of range just as the nearest thing lurched toward him. He uncomfortably walked north on the highway, eventually finding a cast-off T-shirt laying on the seat of an open convertible. He finished cleaning himself with it and continued on. Smiling in comfort and relief, he walked briskly up the median. He thought of the helicopter taking off the night before and assumed they had been out of range of the EMP, unless the thing was shielded somehow. He worried momentarily about radiation sickness, but pushed the thoughts away, as his immediate dangers were much more pressing. Traffic clogged both sides of the highway so he made no attempt to try and start any of the cars. A couple miles up the road, he spotted a black Nissan Xterra with a pair of mountain bikes dangling from a rack mounted on the rear tailgate.

A couple solid kicks later, and Will was riding north on a new-ish looking Specialized mountain bike. It was a woman's bike, but he didn't think anyone would be left to mock him for it; besides, dismounting in an emergency would be much easier with the lowered top tube. The smells of burning buildings and tires and the sound of gunfire was ever-present as he moved that day, usually distant, occasionally close by. Once, he was sure someone took a shot at him as a bullet pinged into a car trunk a couple feet to his right. He hurriedly ducked into traffic at that point, weaving through cars until he moved over the crest of a rise. As before, a crowd of undead was forming behind him, but he easily outpaced them on the bicycle.

As he rode the bicycle northwards on 17, the Garden State Parkway came into view, elevated, to the left. It, too, was packed with vehicles. Many of the cars that he could see were burned-out hulks steaming in the early morning condensation. Ahead, where the Parkway once had crossed over the top of Route 17, was now a pile of twisted steel and concrete, the bridge having collapsed onto the roadway below. The rubble field blocked all four lanes of the roadway on which he traveled. He had to pick his way across, carrying the bike over the top of fallen heavy chunks of concrete, bent rebar, tarmac, and other vehicles. One car, laying on its side atop the rubble, held two undead things that thrashed and flailed at the shattered windshield to get at him as he edged past. Will was still struggling to cope with the devastation of New York. He assumed they were trying to contain the spread of the things when they blew up the tunnels and bridges. They must have given up hope on New York in order to nuke it, but Will couldn't comprehend why, when all of the areas outside the city were just as devastated. It didn't make sense to him. He could only assume the person pushing the button was not getting accurate, up-to-date information. He pushed these dark thoughts aside as he ducked underneath a toppled box truck that had fallen from the roadway above and created a tunnel as it landed, leaning against the concrete bridge support.

When he came back out to the light, he spotted a speck in the sky near the horizon that he did a double take to be sure of. A helicopter was approaching from the west. It was a Blackhawk; he immediately recognized it from a movie he'd seen a few weeks earlier. The helicopter moved off to the east, the propellers whooping loudly as it passed overhead at speed. In the distance, he briefly as it opened fire, its guns flashing brightly even at this distance. He forced his eyes away from the image, knowing that the helicopter whatever its mission, was no help to him, nor could he follow it. Instead of lingering to watch the spectacle, he dragged the bike out from under the truck and continued north. The sight of the black helicopter provided him some hope that order would be restored, although he didn't dare be seen by the soldiers inside for fear of being mistaken as one of the dead.

Will sheltered that night inside the cab of a Peterbilt truck near a town called Ridgewood. Fires raged behind the concrete sound barriers on either side of the highway for miles. With the sun low in the sky and the smoke from the inferno around him burning his eyes and lungs, he had no choice but to seek cover. Locked in the safety of the cab of the truck, he drifted to sleep almost immediately, his body rebelling against the incredible amount of stress he had been putting it through the past few days. His body hadn't felt this drained since he first moved to New York. It had taken a few months adjustment before his body caught up with the pace and the sheer amount of walking that was required while living in the city.

He woke with a start in the middle of the night. The heavy truck he rested in was rocking gently, and he could hear a great deal of commotion coming from outside. His heart nearly jumped through his chest in fear as he wiped the condensation from the inside of the window. It took a moment for his eyes to adjust to the smoky dark sky outside, and even when he could see, he disbelieved his eyes at first. He had to shake his head to clear the last vestiges of sleep from it. Refocusing, he could clearly see a vast army of dead streaming past the truck, crowding the entire highway around him for as far as he could see. His heart sunk and he clenched his fists, fearing that they would stop around the truck;

that they somehow would sense him inside. If they did, he knew that he would die here. They didn't stop, however. The army of corpses shambled past, bouncing off the truck and cars around it, limping along the highway, channeled northwards by the concrete partitions on either side. Will watched in horror for many minutes after the last of the stragglers had passed. Had they been following him? The thought kept him awake and worrying for a few hours before the exhaustion in his bones took him back to the oblivion of sleep.

*

Without waiting to see Daltry's reaction to being told what to do, Tar trotted over to his truck, started it, and steered it out towards 125 south. Crossing over the North Platte River, he began to develop some plans for retreat if the first defenses they were starting construction on were to be overrun. Taking out the bridges that crossed the rivers and many tributaries, in and and around the tiny town, was the first thing that came to mind. He promised to look into rigging the bridges at a later date. Unlike the branch of the Illinois River that ran through the Stevens' and Taylors' properties out west, this branch of the Platte wouldn't freeze over until late in the winter; it ran swift and deep. He wheeled the truck through the traffic light onto 125 and accelerated. He was certain that was where the shot had rung out from. Another shot split the air ahead of him, and he floored the accelerator.

Work hadn't even started on the southern barrier yet. Tom, Sean, and Dave Jr. all stood atop the caterpillar right where they were supposed to be fortifying the pass. Tar struggled to see which of the young men had been shooting, and at what, when he pulled up behind the Caterpillar. He stepped out onto the narrow, two-lane road, carved out of the rock, taking his 30.06 from behind the seat.

"Hey, Tar. A couple of them slow things came out of the woods at us, as soon as we were about to get started," Tom called down, adding proudly. "Davey and me took care of them."

Tar lowered his weapon, relaxing and breathing freely. With all the stress and tension he had been feeling lately, he was anticipating disaster at every turn.

"Okay, boys, let's get to work. The longer the road is open. The more of those things are going to slip into town." He indicated to Dave and Sean. "Those things might make for easy target practice, but I got a feeling we are gonna be seeing some real desperate and dangerous people coming through here shortly, not to mention the faster ones."

Tar slid his rifle back behind his seat, thinking twice before calling to them again.

"Make sure you guys keep a lookout. If they come armed, it's better we see them first than the other way around, if you catch my drift. I'll try to hunt down some two-way radios for y'all. That way we can talk without panicking everyone every time we hear a shot."

Dave Jr. tipped his hat and jumped down from the earthmover.

"Alright, Tar. We'll get to it," Tom called, slipping behind the wheel and cranking it.

Tar hopped into his Silverado and drove off to get some dinner at Elsie's.

Darla had a cup of coffee waiting for him by the time he made it to the counter.

"Tough day, I take it?" she said.

"Gonna get tougher soon enough," Tar grumbled. "Heard from your daughter?"

Darla's daughter Missy was attending college in Topeka.

"Not yet, you know how kids are though..." Darla trailed off realizing who she was talking to.

"Yup, always too busy," Tar interjected before the silence could become uncomfortable.

"Liver and onions?" Darla queried, hoping to move the conversation back to lighter territories.

"You know it, extra bacon." Tar grinned.

"Butcher said no pigs came in this week, so all out of bacon...still want the liver?"

"In that case, just a burger and potato salad will do. Thanks, Darla," he said. "Oh, and Dar?"

"Yeah, Tar?"

"Do me a favor, and leave the diner open from now on...I mean to say, go home and sleep and all, but keep the lights on and the door unlocked."

"Okaaayyy..." She replied, clearly confused

"Look, you heard what we were on about earlier; Elsie's is the obvious meeting place. I'll cover all the expenses If Stan gets uptight about it. This is important."

"I'll pass it along to Stan; he left for the night, though," she replied, putting his order up for Danny to cook.

*

Will woke the next morning, his heart was as heavy as the smoke filled sky outside the cab of the truck. He forced himself upright and cracked the window using the hand crank. The combination of his body heat and the hazy sun coming in through the glass made it uncomfortably humid in the cab. The chill air coming in through the open window was refreshing; he closed his eyes and breathed deeply of it, smoke and all. He mechanically ate peanut butter sandwiches while the rest of his senses awoke. He wanted a cup of coffee desperately, or a cigarette, or a beer. His mind gradually drifted to consider his options for the day, weighing the very real possibility of stumbling upon the horde that had passed in the night.

The aches and pains of his body eventually convinced him the best option was to spend the day in the truck. Here, he had a safe, relatively warm, and comfortable place to rest for a bit. He had food to eat and water to drink. Every hour he spent gave the horde time to move further away from him. He emptied his morning bladder into a plastic 7-11 Big Gulp cup the trucker had left behind then fell fitfully back to sleep for a couple more hours. He finally woke for the day in the hazy light of late morning. The smoke in the air was beginning to thin out, although black plumes continued to blot the sky in the distance. He spent the morning perusing the contents of the glove box, mainly the large spiral-bound atlas which he studied at length. Later, in the mid-afternoon, he got restless and decided to make a foray out of the truck, to scout the surrounding cars for anything useful.

Stepping down from the truck, he emptied his portable toilet on the ground and set it back on the floor of the cab before moving away. He stretched mightily, willing away the anguish his muscles were in. Now that he'd had some time to rest, his aches were amplified. He carried his machete in one hand and the glass hammer in the other. After scanning the endless rows of vehicles, his eyes settled on a pickup truck in the southbound lanes. It looked like the sort of thing the good ole boys back home drove. The idea of that piqued his curiosity.

Moving closer, he could see the vehicle was not empty; one of the undead sat in the driver's seat, buckled in place by its seatbelt. When he got to within fifteen feet of the truck, the creature spotted him and began thrashing about violently. He could see that his estimation of the truck was correct. Two rifles sat across a rack mounted across the back window inside. His anxiety level and the thrashing zombie's rage matched each other in intensity as he crept closer to the truck. As he closed the last few feet to the driver's side door, the thing inside redoubled its efforts, violently slamming its hands and face against the glass. Will looked nervously around, carefully gauging his surroundings before approaching the driver's side door. The noise the undead was making rattled his nerves more than anything; the last thing he wanted was to get ambushed or surrounded by the undead. The thing in the pickup truck smashed face first into the window, its bloodied, ruined face working its jaws up and down as if trying to bite him through the glass.

Will's heartbeat drummed in his chest as he steadied himself, drawing a deep breath. He yanked the door handle and jumped back as the door was shoved outwards by the weight of the corpse inside crashing against it. Will lashed out quickly with the machete, cleaving deeply into the top of the thing's head as it lunged, within the constraints of the seatbelt, to get at him. He hacked twice more just to satisfy his own revulsion and paranoia, pausing to ensure it was dead before hacking at the seatbelt. It took five solid swings, first across the shoulder strap and then across the lap belt where it clipped into the receiver, but finally, the body fell free from the truck onto the pavement at his feet.

Still suffering from the heebie-jeebies, Will hit the thing in the head again just to be sure, his skin was shuddering and crawling. He took a moment to center himself, peering around the roadway for movement or noise before ducking into the truck. He pulled the door shut behind him and locked it, too paranoid to relax otherwise. He took the guns down from the rack. One was a .22 caliber version of an AR-15 and the other was an air rifle; this one he replaced on the rack. The AR wasn't loaded, so he started methodically searching the cab for ammo. Opening the glove box, he found a loaded 9mm pistol as well as a box of fifty Winchester bullets for it. Behind the seat, he found a half-empty box of .22 caliber bullets. Elated with his stroke of luck, he loaded and slung the rifle from his shoulder. He held the pistol in his right hand with the machete dangling by its strap from his left. He shoved the glass hammer and the two boxes of ammo into his pockets before pivoting his attention back to the roadway outside the pickup truck.

He calmed his excitement and took a long minute, examining his surroundings before stepping back out onto the empty roadway. Excitedly, he ran back towards the Peterbilt, freezing in mid-stride at the concrete median divider when he saw a form moving inside the cab of the truck. He ducked behind the median and watched the figure as it rifled through his pack. He settled in uncomfortably, using the concrete divider to steady his aim with the pistol, waiting for the person to come down from the truck. Knowing he wasn't alone sent his paranoia through the roof. There was no doubt in his mind that the person had been watching him and had waited for the opportunity to rob him.

*

A gentle knock on Tar's front door snapped his mind back to the world. He had been lost in years gone by, reminiscing about his wife and son over a few cups of bourbon. He answered the door with a bottle in hand to see Linda standing on his porch.

"Linda," he said, with only the slightest trace of a slur.

He reached up to touch the hat he wasn't wearing at the moment and then looked confused briefly. Linda's shrill laugh cut through his confusion and he smiled genuinely at the young woman.

"I'd love a drink, Tar. Why don't you fetch us some glasses and we can have a sip together on the porch."

Tar smiled and moved off to do as she bade.

A moment later, the two sat at the bistro table, looking through the boughs of the birch in his front yard. The chilly fall weather had almost entirely stripped it clean of leaves. Those same leaves rustled in the wind as the two warmed themselves with a glass of liquor.

"Tar, I'm not really up on this kind of thing," she started bracingly, hesitant.

"What is it, Linda? Spit it out; no need for mincing words with me."

"You think it's true about them using a nuclear weapon on Los Angeles?"

Tar lit a cigarette and started tapping his Zippo on the table in front of him as he tried gathering his own thoughts on the subject.

"I believe it," he said at length.

"Why?" she responded, her voice barely more than a whisper.

Tar stroked his mustache and took a deep drag from the cigarette.

"Strategy? Mercy? Who knows. But for certain, I believe that they would do it, if it served some goal they felt needed to be reached."

Linda sat in silence, trying to digest what kind of sociopaths would be capable of giving that directive, of choosing to snuff out the lives of so many. The thought wounded her to her soul.

"So, if they did it to LA, where else?"

This time, Tar sat thoughtfully, smoking and drinking in the cold, windless evening air. At length, he turned to the young doctor.

"It gives me a small spark of hope though, Linda. It means…what I hope it means, is that they are trying to fight this. Things just may be that grim that nuking cities is the only way, but at least there still is someone who can push the button."

"That gives you hope? The idea of that scares me more than anything," came her measured response.

The two chatted for another hour before Linda bade him goodnight and took off on her bicycle, leaving Tar to his morose thoughts.

Not wanting to be alone in the house that bore so many sad memories, Tar made his way down to Elsie's where he polished off the remainder of the bottle before passing out.

The next morning, he woke confused, having slept a fitful few hours on one of the restaurant booths. He swung his legs clear of the table and rubbed his eyes.

"Morning," Darla called with a cheerful smile from across the room as she tied her waist apron on. "Sheriff Daltry came back through about an hour ago, said for me to tell you that he got what you asked him to."

Tar clapped and said, "Hot damn, that's good news, Darla. Coffee if you would?"

"It's brewing now, sweetie," came her response.

Thirty minutes later, Tar walked out of Elsie's into the early morning gloom, stretching his back and wincing as a series of cracks rippled up his spine, sounding like dry sticks breaking.

"How's she looking, Tom?" Tar called as the man climbed down off the bulldozer and walked wearily towards the diner.

"She ain't pretty, but she's about 15 feet tall and runs from cliff to cliff," came the man's groggy response.

"Morning keeps getting better and better. Hey, you mind if I run the bulldozer today while you get some rest?" Tar asked. He could see that the man wanted to decline so added, "I wouldn't ask, but time is of the essence, my friend."

"I guess so," Tom replied, hesitantly. "She needs diesel, though; you know how to run one?"

"Haven't done it in years, but it'll come back to me." Tar smiled, pulling himself up to the cab of the sun-bleached yellow of the earthmover.

Tom hopped back on and the two rode into Henry's filling station across the street while he filled Tar in on the specific temperament of his machine. Once through his lecture, Tom stepped down, tossing the keys to Tar and wandered off towards Elsie's. While filling the tank, Tar considered where might need the most help fortifying, eventually settling on the east side of town. Although the west was potentially weaker, Fort Collins was a much larger city than the distant Steamboat Springs. The east was where protection would be more needed in his eyes, and his plan to form a wall of timbers was much more ambitious and labor intensive than the barrier to the west. He stalled the tractor three times as he pulled out of the station before finally catching the gear and heading east to meet up with Stan and Harold.

A few miles down the road, from atop a slight rise, he could see the backhoe in the distance. Adjusting his vision for the sun, low on the horizon, in his eyes, he could clearly see a figure running towards him down the middle of the road. The figure was about a hundred yards ahead. Tar let off the accelerator, letting the weight of the earthmover drag itself to a halt before he turned the machine off. He swung the cab door open and brought his rifle to bear, trying to will his eyes to see through the early morning glare through the scope.

He could clearly see that it was Stan running towards him. A gunshot split the air a moment after he watched Stan's knee explode in a mist of blood, the sound coming a bit late as it traveled the distance to Tar. Stan dropped face first onto the tarmac. Tar dropped down and moved behind the front tire of the earthmover. Using its bulk as a shield, he steadied himself and looked through the scope of the 30.06. Focusing his gaze, he scanned the area, eventually coming to rest on a man walking out of the forest wearing camouflage. *Smoky Branch,* Tar thought, recognizing the pattern. The man had a cigarette in his mouth and held a rifle. He was moving purposely towards Stan's fallen figure, roughly fifty yards further away. Tar could hear more voices from the left and right. He scanned the gun across the roadway, immediately spotting a Black Chevy Suburban stopped on the other side of the trench Stan and Harold had been digging, and at least one other person near it.

*

Will moved south along the concrete partition at first until he was past the rear of the truck's trailer, nervously scanning the area for more people. Seeing no one, he moved north well past the front of the truck, again seeing no one. Finally, he was content that he and his robber were the only two people present and he settled in, watching the open door of the truck. A few moments later, the person climbed backwards out of the cab, dragging his bags down after her. It clearly was a woman by the hip-hugger jeans she wore.

"Freeze! Don't you fucking move!" he snarled at her as he strode ahead, pistol extended.

She dropped the bags to the blacktop below and spun towards his voice, hands raised. Clearly, she was terrified.

"Come down from there," he called, getting within fifteen feet of her before stopping, gun aimed at her chest.

"Please, don't shoot," she shrieked in panic, flinching from the sight of the gun. "I saw you leave. I haven't eaten in three days," she added, pleadingly.

"Lift your shirt and spin around," he called to her. When she hesitated, he added, "I need to know that you don't have a gun."

Sheepishly, she obliged.

"Are you alone?" he asked

"Yes, my brother and I were evacuating."

"Your brother?" He looked at her nervously, ducking down a bit and scanning the area. "Evacuating?"

"Yeah, there was a mandatory evacuation order from the governor issued three days ago for the northern end of the state. We ran out of gas waiting in traffic." She broke down at this point and started crying in great heaving sobs. "My brother went for gas two days ago and never came back," she gasped through sobs.

Will blushed, realizing that he had fully terrorized an already traumatized, helpless woman, a helpless, beautiful woman no less. He lowered the gun to the pavement and approached her. She scrambled away from him so he stopped, squatting in front of her.

"I'm sorry. Really, I am," he said softly to her. "I'm sorry for all you've been through, and I'm sorry for scaring you."

Will looked at her evenly, and when she began to settle, he continued, "When I saw you in the truck going through my stuff, I just saw someone robbing me. After the past few days of running scared, starving, and cold, I reacted poorly."

She composed herself quickly, embarrassed at crying in front of a stranger.

"Where are you going?" she asked

"I don't really know. I've just been running away from the city. I guess I've been headed in the general direction of home though. Where were you and your brother heading?"

"I don't know," she replied, wiping her tears away with the corner of her sleeve. "The military was directing everyone northwards. We tried to get off for gas a few exits ago, but they blocked all the exits off."

Will squatted in silence for a minute, having an internal debate on what to do with her. He thought briefly about leaving her here. She would probably slow him down, especially if they encountered the fast undead. He shook those thoughts from his head, however, unable to reconcile the idea of abandoning her. There also was his undeniable attraction for her.

"I don't expect you to, after the way I scared you and everything, but you are welcome to come with me. I plan on heading out again in the morning," Will said. "I want to give that horde that passed through last night sometime to move ahead, and hopefully off the highway."

She looked him up and down with a hopeful expression on her face, trying to gauge him as a person at a glance. He instantly became self-conscious, having wiped his ass with a T-shirt a few hours ago and most of his clothing covered in blood and bits of gore; he didn't feel that he looked very welcoming.

"What's back that way?" she asked nodding southward.

He shook his head. "Just death, and a lot of it." He looked at her with all the sincerity he could muster and continued. "They nuked Manhattan yesterday. They took out the tunnels and bridges with bombs or missiles as we were trying to get across. Then they nuked the fucking city."

His voice trailed off at the end, and the two sat in silence on the roadway for a few minutes. She finally broke the silence they shared.

"We?" the girl asked.

"I was traveling with a guy. He died in Fort Lee two nights ago," Will said somberly.

"I'm Jen," she said, hand extended.

He smirked and shook her hand.

"Will," he replied.

"I can handle myself," she said.

He nodded and replied:

"Me too, or at least I'm beginning to know how."

"That's not what I mean. I mean don't try anything, okay?"

"Oh, yeah, I…okay, no problem," he stammered in response, standing up embarrassed and brushing the imaginary dirt off his bloodstained pants.

"I didn't mean you would…I just don't know you," she said. Seeing his discomfort, she added meekly, "Sorry."

"No, don't be." He paused. "You need to worry about you. Don't apologize for the way that makes others feel. Let's get in the truck, I…we shouldn't linger in the open any more than we need to."

Will grabbed his bags off the ground and followed her up into the cab, cautiously admiring her form as she climbed.

They got settled; Jen ate ravenously and immediately fell asleep. Will flipped through an issue of Rod and Reel he found behind the seat. He flipped the pages, his mind spacing out at the pictures. He was trying his best not to dwell on the terror of the past few days. He hoped Jen wouldn't lose her mind when confronted by the things. He hoped more that she didn't always eat as much as she just did. After a couple hours, she woke with a start. She recovered quickly and the two spent the rest of the afternoon getting to know one another. It was awkward at first. For Will, it felt like a blind date, but the ordeal they had both been put through helped ease them through the initial strangeness of the conversation.

"So….Wisconsin, huh?" Jen asked, snacking on a can of honey-roasted peanuts he had scavenged from a car in the mall parking lot.

"Yeah," Will replied absently, with his thoughts planted on what he would find if he made it home.

"What's there?" Jen said, followed by, "I've never been."

"Where I'm from...nothing. Absolutely nothing." He paused, adding, "I've been kinda hoping that means none of those things too." He gestured outside the truck. "What about you? What's your story?"

"Jersey girl, born and raised." She pursed her lips and nodded proudly. "I was born in Hackensack, but grew up in Garfield."

"How old are you?" Will asked, getting uncomfortable asking the question to someone he was attracted to.

"Twenty-two, why?"

"Just curious, I'm twenty-four," he added then turned away, looking at the magazine in his lap, hoping that he wasn't blushing. "What do you do?"

"Do?" she asked. "I go out with my friends, I go to school, I work, I shower, I brush my hair and teeth..."

She continued on like this for a while before Will started laughing and she joined him. Aside from a quick excursion to Jen's car to collect her belongings, which included a hatchet, the two stayed in the truck the rest of the day. Over the next few hours, he found out that she really liked talking. He heard about how she had finished her associate's degree at Bergen County Community College the year prior. She was enrolled in her second year of the nursing program there. Her on-again, off-again boyfriend, Dave, was at Rutgers studying business, but 'mainly partying' she informed him with an eye roll. They were currently in an 'off' moment, as he couldn't handle the rigors of partying, classes, and a girlfriend, she informed him.

Will was relieved that she was single, though, in their present circumstances, making an advance on her would lead to some really uncomfortable situations if it weren't reciprocated. Besides, although he was certain that Dave was dead like everyone else, he doubted that she accepted that truth yet. Even though he was covered in drying blood and the filth of days of physical exertion with no bathing coupled with the pressures of basic survival he couldn't stop thinking about kissing her. He wouldn't, of course, but that made him want to more. She was pretty, smart, and best of all, she was nice. In all the time he'd spent in the city, he had met very few nice people, and most of the ones he had met just wanted something. Most couldn't be bothered even looking at you, and those that did acted off-put if you tried to strike up a conversation. Will was a decent looking guy; he just grew up differently, in small town Wisconsin where everyone was nice, or at least acted like it.

"Sooo, if you're from Wisconsin, why are you headed north?" she asked.

"Well," he said, pulling the spiral-bound atlas out of the glovebox with a flourish and a smile, "if I want to make it home alive, I'll avoid populated areas." He grinned. "Really though, my original plan was to take 80 as far west as I could go. But once I hit 17, I had a big crowd of them following me, so I just decided to keep going. Been tossing the idea of Canada around, at least to avoid the cluster-fuck of cities we'd have to get through if we stay in the states."

Jen nodded knowingly. Then broke into laughter.

"I have no clue what you are talking about," she managed to get out in between bursts of manic laughter.

Will smiled, appreciating her silliness, even when it was directed towards him. The two whiled away the rest of the day swapping stories and playing some driving games Jen knew. A few times through the course of the day, they had to hush their voices as the undead came by. Luckily for them, they were alerted to the presence from behind when the things banged into the big empty trailer behind them. The ones coming from the north, ahead of them, were easy enough to spot. Gradually, the shadows lengthened and the gloom of evening put a pall on their moods. They ran out of things to talk about and instead, sat in silence, each left to their own thoughts. The two sat staring gloomily out through the windows, admiring the smoldering rubble heap that had once been Ridgewood, New Jersey. Will heard the gentle, steady breathing of Jen sleeping next to him on the bench seat. He moved his blankets to the floor of the cab and drifted off, thinking pleasant thoughts for the first time in days; the smell of her hair, the way her skin felt when they touched hands accidentally, the mischievous glint in her eyes when she was making a joke at his expense. Nothing woke them that night.

*

Tar swung the scope of his rifle back to the man who was advancing on Stan from the edge of the forest. He steadied himself and slid the trigger back towards him. The stock bit into his shoulder, rocking him back slightly. It took a moment to train the scope back to his target and did so in time to see the man's head spray gore out from the back as he crumpled down into the tall grasses. Satisfied that the closest target was no longer a threat, he scanned back to the roadway and found a second target, a head poking out from behind the suburban. Tar waited to make sure it was a hostile; seeing a glint off what he assumed was a scope, he pressed the trigger again. By the time Tar got the scope trained back on the target, he could clearly see the person's head laying on the pavement.

Having fired two shots from the same location, Tar decided it was time to move. He crouched and scrambled around to the rear of the bulldozer, his body painfully reminding him that he was no longer a spry young man. Using the rear passenger side tire as his cover, he scanned the other side of the road for targets.

A shot rang out followed immediately by a ping a few feet to his left, as the bullet bounced off the body of the earthmover. That shot was followed quickly by a second. Tar drew a bead on a new target running back to the cover of the forest. He hurriedly took a shot before the man made it to cover and saw a chunk of bark blow off the bole of a pine tree a few feet to the man's left. He readjusted, steadying himself, and squeezed off another shot, just as the man passed into the gloom of the forest. He wasn't able to see if he hit his target. By the time he got his head back and the scope sighted, the man was out of sight. Tar knew he had no time to dwell on it, so he scanned the area again slowly, cautiously sweeping from left to right and back again. Seeing nothing move, he shifted his cover again, moving around to the front passenger side of the Caterpillar. His bones creaked and his joints complained as he tried to stay compact while moving. As he came out from cover, the sound of an automatic weapon firing sent gooseflesh down his spine, so fearsome was its sound in the cool morning air.

"Shit," Tar mumbled flatly as he dove for cover.

Tar landed heavily on his side between the front and rear tires of the tractor, his left elbow, pinned underneath him, knocked the breath from his lungs. Bullets whizzed past from the field off to the right of the Caterpillar, some skipping off the tarmac, others pinging off the steel frame of the tractor. Ignoring the pain from the dive, he crawled under the front axle of the heavy machine, using the tires to his left and right and the scoop in front of him for cover as he checked his limbs and rifle for damage. How many shots had he fired out of the ten in the clip? *Four,* he thought, *six left.* He hoped there weren't many of these bastards left to kill. *Maybe they'll get spooked and run,* he thought optimistically. *Nah, they woulda run at first sign of resistance* his brain continued to ramble on as he looked through the scope for a new target. *Whatever they are running from is scarier than a single armed man...what happened to Harold? He was supposed to be protecting Stan?* His thoughts started to take him away from the situation at hand when Stan's voice cut the tension.

"Tar, machine gunner in the woods to your right. Two more of them flanking to the left," he yelled, prompting a burst of fire from the direction Tar's feet pointed as he lay there.

Tar swiveled as nimbly as his fifty-eight-year-old body would let him, laying prone with the rifle poking out around the front of the tire. He quickly located the two men, both in hunter's camouflage, firing at Stan. One was standing firing a pistol, the other on one knee steadying himself as he aimed a rifle. As quickly as he was able to, he scoped in on the one standing and aimed at the center of his chest. The man fired off one more round before Tar squeezed the trigger. The bullet tore through the man's chest just inside his left nipple, the force of the bullet spinning him down to the ground. Tar readjusted quickly, drawing a bead on the kneeling one. He exhaled, watching as the barrel of his new target's rifle lifted when the man's head spun around to watch his companion twist his way down to the ground. Tar pulled the trigger again, hitting the man square in the sternum. He scrambled out from under the Caterpillar towards his most recent victims, eyeing them for movement as he positioned the entirety of the tractor between he and the machine gunner.

"Stan, you alright?" he called, examining the body lying in the roadway, looking for movement.

"Stan?" he repeated after a minute of silence.

As if in reply, the buzzing sound of the machine gun tore through the air and Stan's limp form got hit with a handful of shots from the barrage. Tar winced as he watched, knowing the man he had known for thirty years, was now dead. He gritted his teeth and swung his rifle atop the scoop of the tractor, trying to get a bead on where the gunner was. A moment later, the machine gun fired again, forcing him to duck down to avoid the burst that pinged off the heavy, yellow-painted steel of the scoop. As soon as the machine gun went quiet, Tar swung up again and returned a shot directed where he remembered the gunner being. He waited a moment and had to drop to his knees, grunting in pain, to avoid the next volley. He decided to move positions to force the gunner to readjust so he hobbled on his pained knees to the rear tire of the Cat.

As he moved, he could see a vehicle approaching from town. The vehicle came further down the road, passing the Stelman's farm shed, he could see it was Daltry's Police issue Ford Explorer. He made a big sweeping movement with his arm, trying to flag the vehicle to the driver's side of the Cat, but couldn't be sure if Daltry saw. Tar assumed the best bet would be to lay down some suppression fire so Daltry didn't get a face full of lead. He swung the rifle around the rear of the tractor, drawing a bead on where he thought the gunner was, and fired. He waited two seconds and fired again; two more seconds then another shot; two seconds then click. *Fuck, out of ammo,* he thought as he ducked back behind the tire. The police cruiser pulled up next to him as he was sliding his revolver out of its holster. Daltry slammed the shifter in park and rolled out of the driver's side door, coming around the front of the truck to join Tar.

"Just one shooter?" he asked.

"Only one shooting at me at the moment. Can't say that's all of them," came Tar's even response. "He's let off four or five bursts; would like to think he is low on ammo, his friends, at least the ones I saw, are dead. If he is alone, I'd expect him to try and make for SUV parked over there any time now."

With that, Daltry poked his head around the back of the Caterpillar and duck back just as fast as another burst split the air, sending lead skittering and zipping past.

"Stan's dead on the road up there; no idea where Harold is," Tar continued.

"Cover me," Daltry said and took off running towards the black Suburban.

Tar was dumbfounded for a second before he recognized what was happening. He popped up on the step of the Cat, swinging around the front of the cab to shoot. He fired his first shot at the same time as the muzzle flare from the machine gun revealed the shooter. Tar steadied himself, sure that Daltry was the target and fired again and a third, then a fourth, fifth, and sixth time in rapid succession. He emptied the revolver, knowing that his aim wasn't nearly as good with the pistol as with the rifle, figuring maybe he'd get lucky with one of the shots; at the very least, he was hoping to throw off the gunner's aim and keep him from hitting the sheriff. Tar holstered his gun as he slid off the tractor, moving to the side of the scoop to watch Daltry's progress.

Daltry was still running, crouched low, but no more fire came from the machine gun. Finally, the sheriff leapt over the trench that Stan and Harold had worked overnight on. Daltry rolled, coming out of the jump, and ended at rest crouched behind the passenger's side of the Suburban.

"You get him?" Daltry yelled back to him.

"No idea; doubt it from this distance, but at least he ain't shooting," Tar yelled back before seeing a flash of movement at the edge of the woods on the other side of the Suburban.

A man staggered out of the brush, holding a pistol and bleeding profusely.

"Shooter on the driver's side," Tar yelled.

Daltry spun raising his service pistol to bear as the man lifted his own pistol. The two fired simultaneously. To Tar, it looked like the two were dueling, both arms extended and smoke coming from them both. Both men fell to the ground, and Tar watched helplessly as two undead came shambling out from the forest from where the man had emerged a moment earlier.

Tar ran around to the driver's side of the Explorer, hoping that the sheriff had left the keys in his hasty exit.

"Yes!" he said through gritted teeth as he twisted the ignition, popping it in drive and immediately flooring the accelerator.

The old truck roared down the road, past the body of Stan Simons, screeching to a halt a few feet from the trench. Tar stepped out onto the blacktop to see the undead tear into the body of the man who shot Daltry. A third undead came ambling out of the woods, stark naked, with a tattoo of Bob's Big-Boy on his chest. This one was paying attention to the police cruiser rather than the body on the ground. The undead started ambling towards the trench, moaning softly. Tar's heart thumped in his chest as he ran towards the unmoving form of Daltry. The body of the sheriff was blocked from the view of the first two undead by the body of the Suburban, but the newest one, the one moving towards Tar, was coming across the front bumper.

Tar hesitated, measuring the jump. Damn his years. As a younger man, he would've jumped the trench in stride; now nearly sixty, he was worried he'd break something. He nodded his head and jumped the three-foot gap, coming down painfully on one knee as he landed. The undead growled, opening its mouth as it moved in, its quarry nearly within grasp. It lurched forward attempting to close the last six feet and get its hands on Tar. He scrambled on his hands and knees over to the prone form of Daltry and pried the 9mm pistol from the man's unconscious hand just as the thing hungrily leapt at him.

*

Laura's heart broke at that moment, knowing instantly what had happened to the little boy. She grabbed Sophie by the hand and pulled her away from the scene, before her little mind could absorb and start to understand what she was seeing.

"Can you help him?" Sophie asked, her pleading voice was on the verge of tears.

Laura couldn't find the words to speak so she just cried and held Sophie into her chest. Luna was trying to push the little girl away from her mommy while she soothed the child with a breast, but Laura held them both tightly. After a few moments had passed, Laura felt the panic creep back in as her thoughts turned to the undead version of Lilly that she had sent downstairs. *What if it managed to hit the floor button to bring it back up? What happens when the men get back? Lilly will attack them!* These thoughts haunted her until she finally decided to act. She gathered the kids up and dragged them back down the hallway and hurriedly dressed them up in their coats. She collected whatever food she could find from the boardroom and dragged everyone up to the roof. She returned downstairs for a moment to drag the coffee table from in front of the elevator to the roof. She used the table to barricade the door and hoped the monster wouldn't find them. Gunfire sounded in the distance from the general area of the highway. Laura assumed it was the men and hoped they'd return soon.

Nearly two hours passed on the rooftop with Sophie helping Laura keep Luna entertained. The cold had long ago stopped bothering them, their hands numb from the bitter cold and their noses running freely. The gunfire had petered out about thirty minutes prior after what sounded like a hellacious gunfight. Laura had spent the time trying to keep her focus on the girls, though her mind was trying to drag her down into despair. Suddenly, something heavy slammed into the metal rooftop door. Laura had wedged the table against it and it held for the moment. She stood up, panic welling, unsure whether to scoop the kids and run *to where?* She thought about running to the door to try to hold it, but her fear paralyzed her, refusing to allow her to move closer. Gradually, she pushed aside the terror and worked up the nerve; hesitantly, she approached the door. The Lilly-thing had managed to push the door open about an inch and had its fingers wrapped around the door. It roared as Laura came within its range of vision and threw its weight into the door again and again. Laura let out a little scream and jumped as the little table's legs bent under the stress of the attacks. She pressed her back against the door, using her legs to brace her. She gained some satisfaction as the monster withdrew its fingers before continuing the barrage. The minutes went by like hours. Laura used all her strength to keep the monster from pummeling its way through the door, away from the children. As the sun crept lower and lower on the horizon, she began to cry. At least when the guns were firing, she knew that her husband was alive. It had been at least an hour since the last shot had rung out. *He is dead,* her mind told her, tormenting her. *Or worse, one of those things.* She squinted her eyes and hit herself in the head with the heel of her palm a few times to try and knock the terrible thoughts out.

"There is a car coming this way, Laura," Sophie called from around the corner where she was playing with Luna.

"Please, keep Luna away from the edge, Sophie."

"Is it my daddy?" the little girl asked as she took Luna by the hand, her eyes shining with hope.

"I don't know sweetie, maybe, I need you to yell down to them if it is, okay?"

"Okay, I will."

"Soph, can you bring Luna to me, please?"

Laura had to turn back around as if hearing her voice had caused the undead Lilly to redouble its efforts to break down the door. A moment later, Sophie came around the corner, carrying Luna awkwardly like a sack of laundry.

"Mommy!" Luna said sweetly with a big smile on her face. Laura hugged the little girl tightly, terrified for her.

"The car turned in here!" Sophie called excitedly.

*

Tar whipped around with Daltry's pistol in his hand and put a bullet through the thing's forehead, its collapsing body tumbled heavily into his legs, nearly spilling him onto the ground. He walked purposefully around the front of the giant SUV, firing into the side of the head of one of the other undead as it came into view, feasting on the fallen shooter's corpse. Tar's lip curled unconsciously, as he swung the pistol to the left, firing a shot into the temple of the final undead.

He ripped the doors of the Suburban open and walked around the rear of it, making sure that no other enemies lingered before returning to Daltry's body. He'd been shot in the chest, under the armpit where his vest didn't protect him, but was still breathing. He dragged Daltry's unconscious body over to the trench then climbed down in the five-foot deep hole to transfer the body to the other side. He struggled and was just barely able to pull himself up and out on the other side. His old muscles ached with the effort and his joints screamed at him. Finally out of the trench, Tar cracked his knuckles and tried to shake the early arthritic pains away. He grabbed Daltry unceremoniously by one foot and dragged him to the rear of the Explorer.

Fifteen minutes later, the Explorer roared up the driveway to Heartland Healthcare. The main entrance doors slid open as he ran in.

"Betty, get a gurney, Daltry's shot," Tar yelled.

She looked at him blankly, trying to digest the words she wasn't expecting. Finally, the spell was broken, and she scurried around the desk and ran through the double doors that led to the triage area. The triage that, prior to a week ago, only ever held more than one patient a handful of occasions. More recently, the hospital was the scene of insanity, a multitude of dying people came through its doors every day and a good portion of them ended up turning into those things. Betty was shell-shocked to say the least. A moment later, she came out running with a gurney. The two ran to the tailgate of the Ford and loaded the sheriff onto it. Tar walked with Betty back to the double doors then excused himself.

"He got shot by a pistol, Betty. I don't know if you need to know that, but I gotta run." With that, he stepped back out into the morning light.

He was seething with anger and was bound and determined to find out where Harold was. If he was at home in bed, Tar wasn't sure he would let the man continue breathing, so foul was his mood. He cursed as he saw Harold coming out of Elsie's with a pair of coffees and a greasy bag. The borrowed police Explorer screeched to a halt in the middle of the street and Tar got out slowly. In his younger years, he probably would've knocked Harold's teeth out without saying a word. Even though he was much older now, he had to fight hard not to do so now.

"Hey, Tar, I just popped home to take a shit, headed back now with breakfast and coffees. Stan's got the trench done across the road. We were just gonna get start…"

"Stan's dead, Harold," Tar said coldly. "You left to get a fucking cheeseburger, and a bunch of assholes ambushed him."

Harold's entire face sagged in shock and disbelief as he heard the news.

"I—" He started to talk before Tar interrupted.

"They were probably lying in wait, talking about what to do when the only guy with a gun hopped in his car and drove away. I want you to think about that, Harry; I want you to think real hard on that. All you had to do was pick up your damn walkie-talkie and any number of people would've run some food out to you guys." Tar paused, suddenly remembering that he'd left his rifle leaning against the Caterpillar. "I need you to go get Cyrus, and you two bring his timber truck over there," he finished, indicating the east barricade with his extended finger

Tar walked over to his truck that he'd left at Elsie's earlier, reached behind the seat, and grabbed two boxes of ammunition. Returning back to the Explorer, he drove back to the site of the gunfight. He'd already decided that he was going to send Harold back with Stan's body in the cruiser. He couldn't stand to see the man at the moment. He was so full of anger and adrenaline that he wanted a day of backbreaking labor to clear his head and help him figure out what to do.

An hour later, the tractor-trailer Cyrus owned pulled up alongside Tom's earthmover. Cyrus, fat and bearded, hopped down from the driver's seat and Harold from the passenger's side. Tar ignored Cyrus and said immediately to Harold, "Load Stan up in the Explorer and head over to the hospital with the body. Send Terry and Roy over here to help out." Tar finished and started walking over to Cyrus but stopped to look at Harold again when he saw him lingering. "Harold?"

"Yeah, Tar?"

"Leave your M16, coffees, and food here," he finished, taking Cyrus over to the side of the road to discuss the plan for the day. After looting the guns and other supplies from the Suburban, they set to work.

By the time they'd wrapped up for the day, with the help of Terry Hauser and Roy Campbell, Cyrus and Tar had managed to fell fifty trees, strip them of branches, and with the help of the timber truck, stood them upright in the trench. They back-filled the trench with the Caterpillar all while Roy drove vehicles from Randy's salvage yard to use both to brace the wall as well as strengthen the wall to protect it from ramming. The sun had gotten low on the horizon, so it was time to quit.

By the time he stepped through his front door, Tar was so exhausted that after he had fed his dog, Captain, he collapsed on the couch without even taking his boots off. He hadn't slept in the bed that he and Harriet shared since her death; in fact, he only ever went upstairs to use the bathroom, always averting his gaze so as not to have to see Karl's bedroom when he did.

Tar was sure to let the other three know that they would be finishing the job without him the next morning. He knew the limits of his body and doubted he'd be able to get up the next day, nevermind put in more hours. Just as he lay down on the couch, a knock sounded from the front door. Tar briefly considered yelling at whoever it was to go away, wanting nothing more than to sleep. His new sense of purpose and responsibility eventually overcame his exhaustion, especially in light of the tragic events of the day. He struggled to his feet and limped, painfully over to the front door, seeing Dr. Henson standing on his porch.

*

The two awoke to another chilly morning and packed their bags in silence. Will felt self-conscious and spent the time together in the cab of the truck wishing that he had procured a toothbrush in his travels. Finally, with coats on and bags packed, he wiped the condensation off the driver's side window to get an idea of the day ahead. A light snow blew sideways in a bitter wind as the two stepped down from the cab of the truck. He wished they could stay a day or two more, knowing their next rest might not be so comfortable, especially if the weather was taking a turn for the worse. His overwhelming desire not to spend any more time than necessary in densely populated northeast New Jersey is what motivated him to step outside the truck. Jen was just happy to have a stomach full of food and, for the first time in three days, not to be alone. Will pulled the hood of the parka up enough that it kept the wind off his neck, kicked the kickstand of the bike, and the two set off northwards on foot.

Will's destroyed feet had started to scab over in the two nights he'd spent in the truck, and within minutes, he felt them crack open and fresh pus and blood ooze from the wounds. The pain caused him to hobble a bit, but after the first few painful minutes, it didn't slow him down too much. Although they picked their way through the stalled cars moving fairly quickly, they stopped more often than he liked. Jen was not used to walking so much and with her having a shorter stride than he, added to the frequent pauses as she struggled to keep up with his limping pace. She did her best to bite back her complaints though, as did he. He tried convincing her numerous times to ride the bike to no avail. 'If he walked, she walked,' she said as they approached a town called Waldwick. It was late morning, and they hadn't any luck locating a second bicycle; Will was looking around them intently for one. He wanted to get off his aching feet badly, but wouldn't ride while she walked. Besides that, he was really anxious to be clear of New Jersey and riding bicycles could double or triple their pace.

The wind-driven snow stung their faces, and they hunched as low as they could into their coats to escape the chill. All around them the wind whipped; the eerie sound of the wind whistling occasionally brought with it the sounds of gunshots and moaning, punctuated with an occasional human scream. It took just over three hours before they had a handful of undead lurching along behind them. Will assumed most of the dead on the highway had joined up with the mass of bodies that poured through two nights before. Jen was extremely unnerved by their presence, and he had to keep reassuring her that it was okay. He filled her in on what he knew about avoiding, killing and otherwise surviving in this devastated shadow of the world. He was a bit worried that she would have issues with toileting out in the open, but she took it in stride and he made sure not to look.

In the distance, Will heard the sound of gunfire erupt. He heard random shots fired throughout the morning, but this was different; it was steady shooting rather than the staccato sound of isolated shots.

"Is that—?" Jen asked.

"Yeah, let's be careful," he interrupted.

The shots seemed to be coming from ahead of them, but neither could be sure. The concrete noise barriers that ran the length of the roadway on both sides played with sounds, the echoes confusing what direction they might be coming from.

They continued on as they had been for another forty-five minutes with gunfire continually splitting the air; multiple small arms from the sounds of it. It reminded Will of opening day of deer season back home. Everyone over the age of three was out in the woods going to their favorite spot before dawn. When the sun crept high enough to illuminate the gloom, everyone had a belly full of hot coffee and was already set up; that's when the shooting began. By ten o'clock that morning, anyone that was getting a deer, already had one dressed and on the top of their truck; everyone else was usually too drunk to care, most taking pot-shots at anything that moved.

"Could be that herd from two nights ago," Jen offered.

Will hoped not; that was a herd of hundreds, if not thousands, of dead and unless it was the military up ahead, he doubted a handful of people with pistols and hunting rifles was going to take out that mob. By the lack of automatic weapon fire, he doubted it was the military. More than likely, they would run into the remains of an undead feast in the next couple hours, though he didn't feel it necessary to share those thoughts with Jen. They continued on. The wind lightened up a bit as the morning wound towards mid-day, carrying the smell of smoke, excrement, and decaying flesh with it. They both pulled their T-shirts up over their noses in an attempt to filter out the nauseating aroma.

A sign on the right side of the roadway indicated they were approaching the Town of Saddle River. Towns in New Jersey looked like one big town to Will, where he was from, there was twenty minutes of farmland or forest between every town.

Coming around a gentle bend in the road, the source of the gunfire unfolded before them. A quarter-mile ahead there was a massive mob of undead gathered around a Quick Chek station that sat to the right of the highway. Will stuck his arm out to block Jen from going further and ended up touching her breast. He uncomfortably snatched his hand away and crouched down between cars. She had just joined him when an undead thing trapped in the sedan behind them started thrashing against the window, scaring a fart out of him. She squealed and then giggled, putting a hand over her mouth as he blushed. They both moved back a couple car lengths to get out of sight of that thing. Will crouch-walked until he could get a decent view of the scene before them. He could see a few people standing atop an RV parked at a gas pump, firing weapons into the massive horde. The mob seemed to be surrounding all sides of the RV, rocking it heavily to and fro.

"What do we do?" Jen said quietly to him.

"Try and sneak around," Will said flatly; there was no other way.

If they tried to help the people, the horde would just turn on them. Hundreds if not thousands of the things were taking up the entire parking lot as well as most of the northbound lanes.

"We can't just leave them, they're trapped," Jen hissed at him.

"You tell me what we can do then, Jen," he replied, sensing that an argument was brewing.

"I don't know, we just can't leave them though," she said, getting angry.

Will threw his hands up at this point, exasperated. *Women,* he thought. He racked his brain for a few minutes, debating what to do before speaking again.

"Okay, we do it your way," he said. "I hope you're ready to run, or ride the goddamn bike."

Will moved to the concrete divider and slid over it with Jen following closely behind. He pulled the bike over and the two weaved their way through the cars as far as they could get from the northbound lanes. Will led them up the far breakdown lane where they hit a clear spot of road. They moved briskly, passing on the opposite side of the highway where the Quick Chek was. Jen tugged at his shirt as they continued northward.

"What?" he said, half-spinning to address her.

"Are we going to help them?" she shot back.

"Yes, just keep moving for now," he said, resuming movement.

"Don't roll your eyes at me; Dave used to do that," she finished as she followed.

They got about two hundred feet north of the mob when their path ahead was blocked by a massive pile-up, forcing them to cross back into the northbound lanes. After a couple hundred more feet, Will moved ahead to a tractor-trailer. He stopped at the driver's door and handed the bike to her.

"Get on and start going," he said quietly to her.

She started to protest, but he was already climbing to the top of the cab, then transitioning from cab to trailer. He looked down at her as he unslung the AR-15 from his shoulder.

"Go! Now!" he said sternly to her as he lay down on the top of the trailer taking aim. "Unless you don't want to help them?"

As she turned away, pedaling on the bicycle, Will took aim at the exposed gas tank of a tractor-trailer in the center lane, just north of the gas station and fired. He missed. He wasn't even sure if a .22 bullet would penetrate the steel at this distance, but as long as the people on the RV stopped firing their own weapons, he thought that the noise of the shots should be enough.

Pop. Pop. Pop.

He started squeezing off shots, one after another, coming to one knee when he realized that he wasn't going to hit the tank without a scope and a larger-caliber rifle. After his fifth or sixth shot, he took a moment to see how his plan was progressing. He could see the northern edge of the horde had shifted its attention and was now moving towards him; the people atop the RV had stopped firing and were looking right at him. Will waved and continued firing into the throng of undead. A few more shots, and Will could see the bulk of the horde turn and start moving. He stood up, dusting himself off, and cupped his hands over his mouth yelling back to them.

"Good luck! Bon voyage!" he shouted, smiling as he slung the rifle back over his shoulder and clambered down to the road as quickly as he could.

He hit the ground running, and already he could hear at least two of the fast bastards roaring behind him. The foot race was on. Will slid the pistol out of his waistband and flipped the safety off. His feet screamed for mercy, his legs burned and his lungs begged for air, and he could see Jen ahead, picking her way through the cars on the bicycle. He was gaining on her. *Shit, move it, lady,* he thought.

Jen turned to look when she heard many footsteps behind her. Will saw her eyes widen in fear. He hit a clear lane for a couple car lengths and hazarded a glance behind. There were at least ten of the things. Despair swept over him, but the adrenaline still pumped.

"Faster, dammit!" he snarled at Jen.

He knew immediately that it was futile, catching up to her about twenty steps later. He grabbed her, pulling her off the bike. The two ran together, Will had to slow down a bit to stay with her as he scanned the vehicles for something that offered hope, something defensible. Glancing behind, he knew that he had to act fast; the speed they were moving at was allowing the things to gain on them.

"Keep going," he said, skidding to a halt.

Spinning, he brought the pistol to bear, firing as soon as he drew a bead on one; it dropped like a sack of cement. The two following immediately behind it tripped over its tumbling form, coming down heavily. Will took advantage of the tangled mass of undead limbs and the narrow paths between the cars, continuing to fire at head level at the line of undead. His sphincter clenched as the stream of roaring undead, their faces contorted in rage, closed in on him. He continued firing, trying to remain calm as the bodies falling got closer and closer. Finally, there was only one, a mustachioed, obese thing in stained white brief underpants and a filthy tank top. It roared one last time as it closed the final few feet, diving at Will as he pulled the trigger one final time.

Click.

Fuck, was all Will was able to think. The next thing he knew, he was on his back with the massive thing atop him. His head had bounced violently off of the blacktop beneath him, the meager padding in the hood of his parka was the only thing that kept him from losing consciousness. He held the obese raging creature at bay by its throat, needing to use both hands as it leaned down into him with its considerable bulk. The thing tore at him with its fingernails, alternating between tearing at his face and the arms that kept it from its meal. The thing punched, slapped, and clawed at him furiously. He tried squirming out from under the thing, but its massive gut held him pinned in place. He started to release one hand to try to reach his gun, in order to bludgeon the thing with it, but as soon as he loosened his grip, the ghoul redoubled its efforts. It roared inches from his face through a mouth that drooled gore and ichor.

Will struggled desperately under the weight of the enraged thing. Before a minute had passed, he could feel his strength waning. The will to fight was still there, his body was just failing him. Inch by inch, the hot acrid stench that emanated from its mouth came closer to his face, its hands flailed around his face and neck, pinching, grabbing, and scratching. Will swung his head violently back and forth, trying desperately to keep the thing from him. He knew it was just a matter of seconds now. His arms were shaking with exertion, and a hard knot of despair tightened in his gut. A tear trickled out of the corner of his eye.

*

"I don't know why everyone is turning to that son-of-a-bitch, I'm the Mayor here. Errol Morrisson is building the damn barricades. Goddamn, son-of-a-bitch threatened my life yesterday," Dale finished, voice filled with righteous indignation.

"Who?" she said, having no recollection of ever hearing the name before

"Oh, yeah, I mean Tar," Dale corrected, calling Tar by his given name.

"Errol?" she said

"Yeah, Tar is just a nickname he got for falling, drop-dead drunk, into a tar-pit as a teenager." Dale smirked at the memory despite his apparent anger. "Don't you tell him I told you, though. He is on his high horse, bossing everyone around the past couple days. He even sent the sheriff on some errands yesterday. Town's going to hell in a hand-basket if you ask me, no one respects the hierarchy of command anymore."

The sad, middle-aged man seemed a shell of the person who handily dismissed her the day prior. As Dale indicated, Linda guessed that the title of 'Mayor' meant nothing anymore now that there was little need for a pencil pusher. The ineffectual petit-tyrant that carried the title so proudly over the past few years had now been cast aside as inconsequential. Linda felt bad for the frail ego of the man for a brief moment. The moment vanished when the mayor opened his mouth a moment later.

"Elenor, dammit, I asked you to bring me a cup of coffee!"

"Yes, this is a terrifying moment in history," Linda said absently, making a subtle jest about the mayor's priorities.

Thoughts of her parents came unbidden into her mind. She had left them in a nursing home in Pueblo, and felt a sudden pang of incredible guilt thinking about them. She could've had them transferred to Heartland, but was always too busy, or making convenient excuses like 'they are doing fine there, they have friends' or 'I don't want to turn their lives upside down.' The truth was, it was easier on her to have someone else care for them. Now they were probably dead, and if not, there was no realistic possibility that she would ever see them again. She felt the need to talk to her father at that moment, to kiss him and thank him for everything. She needed to apologize for abandoning them in the elder care home that she never visited, and rarely called. She wanted her daddy to kiss her on the forehead and tell her that it would be alright. The tears welled up way too fast. She quickly excused herself and left Dale behind with his coffee problems to go cry in a bathroom stall. No need to give the little man an excuse to call her emotional or unstable.

Having lost her cool and not wanting to see Dale again, she made her way out of the municipal building and headed down the road to Elsie's. Someone in there would surely know where Tar was. She also wanted to drown her sorrows in a hearty bowl of chili. She ended up in a lengthy conversation with Darla about Daltry's condition. Linda was uncharacteristically forthcoming with information, HIPAA be damned. She figured, at this point in the disaster, that the truth was the best way to communicate with the community, now that everyone needed each other. She recognized the needs of the town; though she was often too busy with the clinic to address it, the safety and integrity of the town itself weighed heavily on her mind.

She had read a dissertation a few years earlier about the sociological effects of high-mortality diseases in isolated communities. The study focused on indigenous tribes in rural Africa, but she figured most of the data applied here in Donner as well. The study showed how lifelong neighbors and friends turned on each other, fear, suspicion, and superstition ripped communities asunder. She already could see the tensions rising, the fistfights, alphas muscling past one another to be the 'big-boner,' as she liked to call it. The whole thing broke her heart. Even though she was a transplant here, she had fallen in love with the idyllic views and small town way of life in Donner. Seeing it start to fray at the edges was terrible for her. All she could do was focus on spreading positivity and hope that it would be more infectious than the undead. Finally, with her bowl of chili and cup of tea long gone, she asked for her check.

"On the house, doc," Darla said with a wink. "Besides, money isn't worth much of anything these days."

This lifted Linda's spirits; these moments when she could see the close-knit community grasping some important concepts in the catastrophe, that need superseded recompense. She felt hopeful, seeing that these people were starting to place decency and values over greed and materialism. There was no truer statement to Linda than that the true value of a society should be measured by how the most wretched are treated. Having sublimated her sadness and given her some hope, she turned towards the door.

"Thanks, Darla. It was nice talking to you."

"You as well, doc. Good luck with Tar; he is bound to be ornery," she said flashing a sincere smile, before turning to bring the dirty dishes to the back.

*

Hot liquid exploded all over Will's chest and face. *Did it vomit on me?* his confused mind asked, incredulously. His eyes were squinted shut in the struggle and had no idea what happened as the thing above him stopped fighting and fell limp on him with gore spewing from its ruined skull and neck. He struggled to crawl backwards and free himself from the dead weight of the huge corpse. Finally free of its weight, he rolled, ripping his Parka off and wiping as much of the foul-smelling fluid off of his face as he could. He saw a maggot squirming in the shirt and couldn't contain it any longer. He retched, holding the back bumper of a car as he did. He could see Jen standing next to him, holding a bloody hatchet in her hands. He blacked out, collapsing back to the ground. An interminable amount of time later, he was snapped to his senses with her yelling at him and smacking his cheek.

"Get up, Will! We have to go now!" she was screaming and tugging on his arm with a surprisingly strong grip.

Her voice lightened the darkness of his consciousness before it started slipping away again.

"Will!" she screamed at him, again slapping him.

The sharp pain brought him back to awareness. He shook his head to clear it. The first thing that registered was the sounds of many, many dead very close by, moaning and shuffling. As his eyes came into focus, he couldn't miss the massive wave of undead moving towards them, barely twenty feet away. He grabbed his guns and pack from the ground and was off without a word. About fifty feet up the road, Will regained his senses and balance and the two settled into an even jog. They moved just fast enough to increase the distance from the horde but slow enough so that their pace didn't tire them too much. Suddenly very cold without the parka, he scoured the pack he carried, coming up with a handful of shirts. He pulled them on, one at a time. Feeling a bit warmer, he reloaded the guns as they jogged.

"What the fuck was that about?" Jen yelled, punching him in the bicep.

"You insisted that we had to help them," Will laughed, the fear, tension, and revulsion leaving him as he slowed in a deep belly laugh. "It was the only way I could think of. Don't worry though, the people all seemed very happy as a thousand undead things walked away from them."

"Asshole!" she said, swatting at him. "You could've gotten us killed you know…in fact, you would be dead if I'd have listened to you; that fat fucker would be eating your face right now."

Will laughed long and hard, the relief of making it out of that jam alive overwhelmed him. As they moved down the highway, she shot a withering gaze at him. He just smiled broadly at her and said earnestly, "Thank you…really, thank you for coming back."

Her eyes narrowed suspiciously at him, but she let it go after a minute.

"Just don't do anything stupid like that again," she added.

"I'll remember that the next time you insist we endanger ourselves for strangers," he said, just loudly enough for her to hear.

She punched him again, three more times. The next time they stopped for a break, Will spotted a murky pool of stagnant water off the side of the highway. He walked up to it and smelled it; it reeked like metal and asphalt, but nothing fouler. Despite the freezing temperature and the incessant wind, he took a minute to wash his face and hands off in it, shuddering as he scrubbed the last of the gore off his face and out of his hair. When he was done, he looked back and saw Jen squatting a couple lanes over. He stood and made sure they were still alone while she finished toileting. He thrust his hands inside his pants to warm them while she finished her business.

"Do we need to keep going so fast?" she asked, coming around the car to face Will, looking strangely at him with his hands down his pants.

"It's freezing," he replied. "And yes, we either need to keep up this pace, or we have to go straight through the night."

"Or," she said after a minute, "we can leave the highway and take our chances at finding a house to sleep in."

Her smile indicated all he needed to know; that they would be sleeping under a roof that night. He wanted to argue, having had such terrifying experiences in populated areas. The thought of moving through the cars on the highway in absolute darkness with a huge herd following behind made him bite back his argument before it could fully form.

"Let's walk on till mid-afternoon then; a couple more hours at this pace, and we look for someplace while it's still light out," he said resignedly.

Will pushed the pace hard for the next couple hours, wanting to make sure they were well ahead of the mob following them. After an hour, the massive crowd was nowhere in sight, just a small band that was forming as they moved through the traffic followed behind. The sound barrier wall fell away on both sides as rows and rows of stores encroached on the highway. The parking lots and stores crawled with the living dead on both sides, and he was worried that they would need to use the guns again before long. He really wanted to avoid it, knowing that a huge number of the things could be on them in minutes in the overcrowded shopping district they were passing through. Just as he was getting ready to steer them off the main road, he noticed a small building standing on its own across the highway. The sign outside advertised it as the Ramsey Outdoor. He grabbed Jen by the arm and veered directly towards it.

When they got to the front door, it was locked. Will banged furiously on the door, both hoping and fearing that someone had holed up inside. He was worried if they broke in, they would get shot. Unfortunately, his frantic banging had caught the attention of a small handful of undead milling about in front of a bagel shop next door. They waited at the door as long as they dared, hearing no sounds coming from inside. Jen followed him around the back of the building just as the undead came clear of the trees separating the two parking lots. They had done almost a full circuit of the stout cinderblock building when Will noticed some pipes and conduit running up from the ground on the front corner of the building. He grabbed and tried to shake them, reassured that they were steel and not flimsy PVC. He quickly started to scale the corner of the building, pulling himself up, hand over hand by the conduit. Jen tried to follow but didn't have the upper body strength to shimmy up.

"Stay out of sight. I'll let you in as soon as I can get to the front door," Will quietly called down from the roof.

He moved quickly from the edge so as not to have to argue with her. Towards the rear of the building, he spotted the roof access hatch. He tried to pull up the hatch, but it was clearly locked from the inside. He moved back to the edge where he'd left Jen.

"Jen," he called.

"What?" she called back, a bit sharply.

"I need your hatchet," he said.

"It's the only weapon I have," she replied, her voice still dripping venom.

A moment later, the AR-15 clattered to the ground to her right. As she bent to pick it up, the four undead that had been stalking them came around the corner, finally spotting their quarry.

"Jen, run!" Will called sharply to the oblivious girl.

Jen's head snapped up in time to see the gaggle of dead lurching towards her from the right. She let out an involuntary scream as she jumped back holding the rifle. She scurried away around the next corner of the building, taking a wide berth so as not to risk ending up face to face with an another one. Will walked around, following her progress from above. When she had placed some distance between herself and the undead, he called to her again.

"Throw up the ax, Jen," he said a little panicky. "The sooner I get inside, the sooner I can let you in!" He hesitated a moment before adding, "And please don't shoot unless you need to; there are way too many undead around here."

Will had to duck as the ax came soaring past his head. He moved across the roof and started hacking at the rooftop, above where the front door was. He hacked and hacked at the thickly tarred roofing paper and the sheathing beneath it until his arms ached. Many minutes passed, and he had sweat pouring down his back, but finally he had made a hole wide enough for him to squeeze through. He flung his backpack down through the hole, crashing through a ceiling tile as it dropped. He took a long look at the gloomy store, ensuring there were no sounds and no movement before sliding down, feet-first on his stomach. He hung from the lip of the hole he'd created. Even hanging down from the edge, he was looking at a ten-foot drop to the floor below. He hung there, considering his best course of action for long enough that he no longer had the strength to pull himself back up when he tried. Finally, his worries about Jen, coupled with the exhaustion in his muscles won over and he just let go. Cursing aloud and hoping for the best, he landed with his knees bent and rolled out of the fall.

His knees hit his chest hard, knocking the wind out of him momentarily. He had to take a moment when he finally got his breath back to make sure nothing was broken or sprained before he ran to the door. Jen's terrified scream from outside greeted him as he reached the steel-rimmed glass door.

*

"Come in, doc," Tar said, pushing the screen door out for her.

"Can we talk out here, Tar?" she asked, preferring the outdoors despite the cold.

"Yeah, no problem, doc," Tar said, grabbing his coat from the coat tree beside the door and stepping out onto the wide front porch.

The two sat down at the bistro table, Tar grimacing through the agony of his aching joints.

"How is Daltry doing?" he asked once seated.

"Touch and go," she replied. "Whether he lives or not is up to him at this point."

"Or God," Tar responded

"Or that, yeah," Linda responded, uncomfortable with the deific reference.

"Listen, Tar, I spoke with Dale earlier," she began. "He told me that you'd been the tip of the spear as far as getting the town buttoned up."

Tar nodded.

"I think we need to be clear with each other on what we are trying to accomplish by shutting down the roads in and out of town," Linda said.

"Well, what exactly do you think we are accomplishing then?" Tar said gruffly, a little irritated that he was forced to engage in an existential discussion when his aching bones were longing for some rest.

"Well, frankly, Tar, we are potentially talking about the continuity of the species."

Tar sat in silence for a minute before getting up without a word and walking back into the house. He returned a moment later with a bottle of Bulleit bourbon and two glasses. Setting the glasses down, he poured two fingers in each before sitting back down.

He downed his glass in one gulp, filling it again as he spoke.

"I've given some thought to that possibility, Linda. Though, I'm sure there are plenty of pockets of people that will survive. We aren't the only mountain community, nor are we the most isolated."

"How many will have the ability or the foresight to shut off their communities and act in the best interest of each other? I'd guess most will do as our culture trains us; worry about our families and leave everyone else to worry about theirs. Despite our isolation, we are still getting infected. I'm hoping that shutting the town off entirely will stop new cases, but I think the only reason we see fewer cases, is that most of the elderly and young are already dead."

Tar nodded slowly sipping on his glass.

"Oh, and can you spread the word to all the testosterone-driven brutes around here to stop punching the undead."

Tar laughed a little at the statement, unintentionally; it just tickled him.

"I'm not kidding, Tar. We've had six people die already by punching those things in the face; all it takes is a skinned knuckle or a good punch to the mouth and a tooth punctures the hand, then they're infected."

"Alright, Linda, I'll spread the word. It's gonna be hard for some of these cow-punchers though; the fist is second nature to most of them."

Another drag and pull from his glass and cigarette and Tar continued.

"Back on topic though, we don't know about Europe, Asia, or anywhere else for that matter. It might be a bit premature to—"

"Europe is the same as us. While I can't speak about how widespread it is, a doctor in the CDC I spoke with a week ago indicated infections in or around nearly every city with an international airport. The human race is dying, Tar."

"Fuck," Tar said quietly, tapping his fingers on the sides of his tumbler. He looked at her, sadness showing on his hardened features. "I just hoped that it was somewhat localized."

Linda shook her head grimly.

"Sorry to bring the bad news, Tar," she said softly, "but as the only one with the foresight to start protecting the town, I feel it's important for you to know what the stakes are."

*

Jen came running up the safety-glass door a moment later with a terrified look on her face. She smacked the door rapidly with the heel of her hand. He hurriedly flipped the bolt to unlock it, and she pushed her way in as soon as it was open.

"Goddamn it, Will, it took you long enough!" she said diving through the door, throwing herself onto the floor.

She was out of breath from running in circles around the building to keep clear of the undead. Will locked the door quickly behind her, and as soon as she was able, he led her back into the gloom of the store, away from the wall of windows at the front of the store. They watched from behind the cash register counter, as the four undead shambled up to the doorway. Two moved off around the building immediately, and the other rotting things lingered for a moment before they too moved off, as if on some other errand.

Aisle by aisle, Will and Jen moved, scanning for both undead and human alike, ending their sweep at the entrance to the rear stockroom. Entering the stockroom, they were confronted by a pitch-black room, no windows or ambient light penetrated the gloom. Will felt around, finally locating a light switch after a few tense moments in the dark. He flipped the toggle; no power. They retreated back to the camping aisle and returned a few moments later, each armed with a flashlight.

Their hearts were drumming in their chests as they entered the dark room. Shadows appeared menacingly all around them, created by the beams of the flashlights. For a few terrible moments, Will thought there was something moving off to the left, but Jen had just bumped a hammock, sending it swinging in the gloom. There was no one in there, dead or alive. Once they determined it was clear, Will hung heavy tarps over the front doors and windows, allowing them to light battery powered lanterns and see without drawing unwanted attention from outside. They transformed the dim gloom of the store into a fairy wonderland, torches and candles blazed randomly throughout the store, atop shelves, counters and suspended from the ceiling. For the first time since this nightmare began, the two of them were able to move freely at night. In the relative safety of the store, they laughed and feasted on the rest of their perishable foods and whiled the afternoon and evening away in good spirits. Will dumped a five-gallon bucket of arrows on the floor, carrying it into the stockroom with a lantern and a roll of composting toilet paper. For the first time in five days, the two were able to use the toilet properly and privately. For Will, all too conscious of his breath around Jen, he was most excited to be able to brush his teeth, having found tubes of Toms of Maine and travel brushes to brush with.

Sometime after the sun went down, Jen interrupted a lively game of charades when she heard the shuffling of many hundreds of feet noisily moving their way on the roadway outside. The two pushed the edges of the tarp aside and watched in silence for nearly thirty minutes as the horde shambled past. The sight killed their joy as quickly as a bucket of water snuffs out a campfire. They toileted and made their beds in silence, drifting off to sleep a short time later.

They spoke briefly in the morning and decided to stay at least one more day in the safety of the store. They spent the better part of the morning rummaging for supplies, collecting a tent, stocking up on MREs and camp-ready meals, a second aluminum frame pack, sleeping bags, thermal underwear, and a healthy supply of paracord and rope. A row of rifles on the wall behind the register allowed Will to add a scoped Remington R-25 GII to his gun collection, as well as a Desert Eagle handgun. He took the heavy pistol mainly because he always thought it was a bad-ass gun. He provided Jen with a pair of 9mm Glock pistols, figuring that they would be ideal for her due to their low weight and recoil. Jen picked a scoped bolt-action 30.06 rifle for herself, stating flatly that she wanted to learn how to shoot one.

They gathered all the pertinent ammunition atop the counter to stow in their packs while Will tried to steer Jen to a rifle with a cartridge. She refused to budge, stating the rifle she picked was 'pretty.' They loaded the packs to about 35 pounds each, figuring that was the most they could carry over a long distance and still run if they needed to. Will packed a 3-wheeled camp cart with the rest of the ammunition, food and cold-weather gear they were bringing. It took the remainder of the day to pack up.

As their preparations came to a close, the afternoon was lengthening and the sun started creeping downwards towards the horizon, they settled in for another evening of games and chatter. Neither of them relished the idea of leaving their sanctuary the next day, and after a very short discussion, they decided to stay at least one more day. Will figured he could school Jen on the basics of shooting so staying an additional day wouldn't be a total waste.

Early the next morning he took a pry bar he found in the stockroom and was able to pry the padlock off the roof hatch. The two spent most of the morning aiming and dry-firing weapons at random objects so Jen could get a feel for the new weapons. Will started to get anxious after eating lunch; the store he had dropped into that was so safe and held such promise to him, now felt claustrophobic. The urge to get moving was becoming overwhelming. That evening, over a game of travel checkers, he finally broached the subject with Jen.

"I'd like to leave in the morning, Jen."

"What's the rush?" she said. "We are safe, warm, and dry."

"I don't know," he replied, falling into silence.

They each took another turn while Will sorted out his feelings, finally speaking.

"I guess seeing the bomb hit New York fucked me up; I just want to keep moving." He paused. "I don't like New Jersey. This place is fucking terrible; nothing but dead and undead here."

"Fuck you, asshole!" she said reflexively.

Like most Jerseyites, she was fiercely defensive about her home state, especially from outsiders.

"That's not what I mean, Jen. It's just so populated, especially with the undead." Will paused and finally was able to express his real fears. "I feel like the military has probably quarantined the populated areas, and I'm nervous that they'll drop another nuke while we linger around because we are comfortable."

Silence hung in the air for a bit before Jen finally spoke.

"King me," she said, moving her checker, fully satisfied with herself.

Will struggled to get the little magnet checker to stick to the other one.

"Okay," she said. "We will hit the road again; just give me one more day, okay?"

"Deal." He surrendered to her smile.

Will kissed her that night. He didn't even think about it as his head drifted in and their lips touched. For a moment, all seemed right in the world, then she pulled away.

"I'm sorry," he said, embarrassed.

His heart went from soaring to forlorn in the span of a heartbeat.

"No, don't be," she replied. "I...I just—"

She started sobbing lightly, turning from him. The silence hung between the two for the span of a few heartbeats before she spoke again.

"I guess Dave is dead, I guess I know he is. But it's too weird right now, we always got back together, even though he is a shit. I don't know that I can come to terms with it at all just yet."

Will left it at that, there was nothing else to say. They both went to sleep with a weight on their hearts. Will thought he heard her sobbing at one point, but was too lost in his own misery at the moment to do more than put a comforting hand on her shoulder.

By the time he woke in the morning, Jen was up and dressed.

"Come on, sleepy, you're the one who wanted to leave," she said, smiling.

"I thought you wanted to stay another day?" he replied.

"Nah, lets hit the road," she said pulling her boots on. "We can make it to New York State, today, easy."

Will shrugged and went to the stockroom to relieve himself and brush his teeth. When he came out, she had gathered everything by the front door and was waiting for him. He pulled on his thermals, then his clothes, leaving his bloody jeans behind in favor of gaudily colored hiking pants. Finally, he pulled on a two-tone, down-hooded coat.

"You look like a 90's aerobics instructor," Jen said, laughing hysterically at his outfit.

"It'll all be covered in dirt and blood soon enough." He shrugged off her mockery.

"Someone is moody today," she replied.

Will shrugged again, pulling his pack on and clipping the straps across his chest and stomach before helping her with hers. Jen yanked the tarp down that had hung over the door and the two scanned the parking lot and highway. There were a few undead scattered about the road, but nothing they weren't used to seeing. A thought struck Will and he turned to Jen.

"I'm going out the back. I'll make sure it's clear around the building and meet you around front," Will said locking the door behind Jen and running to the back of the store.

He grabbed a can of safety orange spray paint on his way to the store-room. A minute later, Jen watched as he came around the front of the building carrying a sixteen-foot extendable ladder that had been stored in the back room. She looked at him quizzically, but he rushed past her standing by the front door.

She watched, amused as Will set about spray painting, *Safe inside, use roof* in three-foot high letters on the front of the building. He left the ladder leaning against the wall.

"Wasn't that thoughtful of you," she said, smiling at him.

Will shrugged sheepishly and took up the handles of the cart. They both looked back for a moment at the shop before stepping back on the road to resume their journey northward.

Not even an hour into their travels, Jen put her arm on his bicep, stopping him in his tracks.

"What?" Will said, scanning their surroundings nervously.

After she didn't respond, he looked at her. She was pointing at a truck impaled on the stone railing of the bridge they were about to cross. He looked at her, confused.

"Huh?" he bumbled out, not understanding.

"The train tracks, Will; we can walk the tracks north," she said, clapping him on the shoulder and rushing to the edge of the overpass they were on.

"Oh, shit!" Will said, realizing they could make it well into New York, only needing to be careful at railroad stations and railroad crossings.

*

Tar took a deep breath, steadying himself as he downed his second glass of bourbon before sliding it away from him.

"That's a heavy mantle to lie on my shoulders, Linda; I'm not a young man anymore," Tar said, trying to digest the scope and scale of their predicament. "What more can we do? Should we start inviting people in?"

"I don't know," Linda said honestly. "It's dangerous to trust people, but we might be dooming ourselves if we don't. On the other hand, if we let the wrong people in, we are screwed."

Tar looked at the growing ash of his cigarette and remain silent. Linda continued.

"Do you think we would be able to turn back a large number of desperate people without getting overrun or incurring heavy casualties? What happens if a large enough mob of infected come through? Are there enough bullets in the state for what might come up from Denver?"

They sat in silence for many minutes, Linda finally sipping on her bourbon. Tar finally spoke, feeling the need to give voice to the concerns he had.

"If we turn them away, we risk them attacking us; if we accept them in, we risk them attacking and or robbing us. I hesitate to turn good people away, but how can we tell who is who?" Tar said. "Is there some head-shrink test you can give them?"

"Nothing that couldn't be see through and deceived if they wanted to," Linda said. "Although I feel that people traveling with women and children are probably a safer bet than groups that consist only of men."

Tar lit another cigarette off the butt of his last and nodded appreciatively.

"You're making a lot of sense there. I'd say a lot of it depends on how the women are treated in the group. I'm sure there are a lot of rapists out there, either taking by force or demanding in return for protection," he stated, seeing the simplicity of that as he refilled Linda's glass. "I guess we'd need to speak to the women alone to get a better idea. Although, a group of rapists and murderers would refuse to allow that, and a group of honest people wouldn't entrust us with someone they are legitimately protecting...a Catch-22."

"Yeah, seems so." Linda paused, out of ideas and feeling a bit light headed from the half-glass of bourbon. "We would need to check everyone for bites, most likely hold them in quarantine for a period before even considering letting them in. During the process of checking for bites, we can look for bruises and such, but it still begs to question how we are sure we are getting accurate, not coerced information?"

"Well, I guess we can chew on those questions for the time being." Tar replied as he stood and yawned, stretching broadly as he did. "I appreciate the conversation, Linda, but the days have been long lately, and right now, I need sleep,"

Tar turned and abruptly walked inside the house without another word.

Linda poured herself another glass of the bourbon and sat on the porch for a few more minutes. She was glad she had made the trip out to talk with Tar. Their conversations always provided food for thought. A gunshot sounded in the distance, a common occurrence these days. Tar had started assigning guard duty to some of the townspeople. Even with the roadblocks well underway, the dead still roamed through the forests and mountains, eventually finding their way into town, attracted by light or noise. Tar had even created a few designated safe spots in town, where anyone who needed help could come and someone would always be there, armed and ready. Elsie's was one, the Roosevelt Motel lobby the second, and Heartland was the third.

Linda shuddered at the thought of the dead roaming the darkened streets, and didn't relish her bicycle ride back to Heartland. At last, she steeled her nerve and stood up walking to her bicycle. She hopped on and started pedaling down the middle of the street back to Heartland as the first snows of winter began to fall.

*

Will rushed after Jen towards the railroad station, catching up to her at the edge of the overpass. The street entrance to the train terminal was just beyond the small bridge. Both stood looking for a way to descend to the tracks from the outside rather than risking whatever terrors might lay within the terminal. They paced about a hundred feet in either direction before they agreed on the best path of descent.

Will tied a rope around the handle of the camp cart, and the two hoisted it up over the wrought iron fencing. Both of them clung to the rope, easing the cart slowly downwards, hand over hand until it came to rest on the concrete thirty feet below them. Will tied the rope to a concrete support at the end of the bridge, jerking it sharply to make sure there was no give in the knot. He then helped Jen over the fence, following behind her once she had successfully descended to the platform below. Will cut as much of the rope as he could salvage, leaving a bit over twenty feet of it dangling from the bridge above.

They hopped off the concrete train platform down to the tracks below, dragging the cart behind them and started off northwards. The buildings and bridges quickly gave way to woods and brush as they moved. Traveling on the railroad tracks was slow and annoying at best; the distance between ties was the perfect amount of space to make for awkward stutter-stepping every other stride. Dragging the cart behind made it nearly intolerable. Will pushed the cart on the grass or even the crushed stone that lay beneath and on the sides of the tracks wherever possible. All the same, it made for a nuisance. He debated abandoning the thing, but the memories of those first few days of starving and cold kept him persevering.

By noon, they reached the next station. A placard hung above the benches on the platform, indicating they were in Suffern, New York. They stopped for a short meal break atop a short railroad bridge that carried the tracks over a series of roads. They plopped down onto the ties and let their aching, tired feet dangle off the edge. Will began to take his shoes off, but the bright color of blood on his socks made him change his mind. He knew that if he took them off, he'd have a hell of a time trying to get them back on. Instead, he dug out the atlas he had taken from the truck, tracing the unmarked gray line of the railroad tracks running parallel to I-87. Following their course, he determined that I-86 intersected with the tracks just north of Harriman. I-86 would be the next leg of the journey, bringing them halfway across New York State.

"Around every corner we round, I expect to see a concrete wall or military barricade," Will said, absently shoving a bag of turkey jerky into his mouth.

"Yeah, every time I hear guns, I get hopeful that we are close to rescue. Where do you think they are?" Jen asked.

Will just shrugged, chewing intently and washing his snack down with a bottle of water.

"I dunno," he said quietly at length. "The entire eastern seaboard from Boston down to D.C. is just one big overpopulated stretch of cities. If they quarantined the cities, I guess they are west of here."

Jen nodded and sat quietly for a few minutes.

"Do you think we can recover from this?" she asked, looking pointedly at him. "I mean, how are they going to clear all those things out of all the buildings?"

"The fact that we have seen so little in the way of the military makes me worry that things might be beyond that point, or maybe they've just given up on anyone still living out here." A moment later, he added, "Let's just take it one mile at a time, okay?"

She nodded in response and the two sat in silence as they finished their meager meal.

A short while later, when they had finished eating, but were not yet ready to start moving again, one of the undead below spotted them atop their perch. It started flapping its arms slowly and moaning loudly. The two watched for a few minutes to see what would happen. Over the course of a few minutes, a handful of other undead started to gather. These new arrivals eventually also noticed them up high. One by one, they added their own moaning complaints to the din.

"Do you think they are communicating with one another, or are they just reacting to the noise that first one was making?" Will asked, watching the spectacle below.

"They seem so stupid," Jen said, watching the way they stood below flailing their arms upward at them. "I can't imagine they are communicating."

"Yeah, they don't seem to have much in the way of problem solving either, do they?" he responded.

"Why don't people just, y'know, lead them into a pit or the ocean or something?" Jen asked. Will paused to think about it for a minute before replying.

"Maybe everyone that is left is just like us, and that group atop the RV. Scared, hungry, and running for their lives. Maybe, if there is a large enough group somewhere, they could start working on their strategy, but we are so hopelessly outnumbered. I guess that any larger groups like that will be in the rural areas…" Will trailed off, worrying about groups of men getting together and how they might respond to a pretty young woman. "It's terrifying how quickly it all happened, and even more terrifying to think how many are trapped in their houses, waiting for help that will never arrive."

A wailing shriek from a short distance away got them up and moving again; the last thing they wanted was to deal with more of the fast ones. The bridge carried them a few hundred more feet before ducking below a raised roadway. The tracks crossed and then ran parallel to a wide stream a few miles down, leading them through a deserted train station in a town called Sloatsburg by mid-afternoon. They stayed cautiously close to the tree line on the opposite side of the tracks until the station, its parking lot, and the intersecting roads nearby were long behind them.

As the afternoon started bleeding into the early evening, they discussed what they would do for the night. Although they had equipped themselves with a tent, they hadn't really considered until now how terrifying it would be to sleep in a tent out in the open. They discounted using it as soon as the conversation began. They both kept an eye out for something promising as the sun crept lower on the horizon.

A short while later, they passed through a burned-out village with a train station indicating that it was Tuxedo, New York. Off in the distance, gunshots could be heard. The duo moved quickly through, not wanting to draw any attention from living or dead upon them. A couple miles past Tuxedo, they came upon a restaurant on the opposite side of the road. Will steered them towards it. Across four lanes of roadway, they scurried, stopping at the edge of the parking lot to see if they dislodged any undead from their hiding spots. The sign advertised it as the Duck Cedar Inn, but it looked as if it hadn't been operating for quite a few years.

"Do we go in?" Jen asked.

"The place is huge," Will stated, admiring the size of the structure. "I don't really like the idea of wandering around in the dark to make sure it's clear."

"So what then?" she asked.

Will knelt there at the edge of the stretch of empty roadway, looking uncertainly at the building before an idea struck him.

"The porch roof looks flat enough to sleep on," he answered at length.

He moved across the open lot and onto the front steps. From there, he climbed the railing and swung up to the rooftop at an inside corner.

"Toss the rope up and I'll haul our gear and help you up," he said quietly from up top.

*

The next morning, Tar was seated on his usual stool at the counter of Elsie's, enjoying his usual breakfast of steak and eggs. The door swung open and men filed in, nearly twenty in all coming to rest in a semi-circle around Tar.

"Most of us were out tending our herds or harvesting squash, and others…well truth be told our wives lit into us for not helping," John Stanley said with a smirk on his face. The same face turned grim a moment later when he continued. "We heard about Daltry."

Tar nodded in acknowledgment, waiting for them to get to the meat of it.

"We know what you're trying to do, protecting the town and all. If you'll have us, we'd like to help out and do our part."

"Sit down, boys; let me finish my breakfast and then we'll talk about what needs doing." Tar smiled broadly at the men.

A group of refugees came up the long hill of the pass the next day. They were a desperate and terrified group of people, looking for no more than a clear road to take them away from Boulder. After the conversation between Linda and Tar the night before, they had come to an agreement that any people wishing for no more than a way through would be given a chance to pass, with an armed escort, to the other side of town. The group of five, two men, two women, and a child came forward to the beginning of the 'kill-zone,' the name Harold had given to the one-hundred-yard clearing leading up to the wall of dirt that formed the barricade.

"We've got company at the southern barricade," Harold called through his walkie.

"Roger that," Tar's voice came back through the receiver. "I'll be right on over."

"Halt right there," Harold called down to them. "Our...well, Tar is coming," he finally stammered out, not knowing what to call him by.

Tar climbed the logs staggered into the backside of the earth, forming a staircase of sorts, to the top of the berm. He looked to Harold for any information, who, in turn, just pointed at the group. Tar smiled in spite of himself, turned to the group, and addressed them.

"What brings you to our doorstep?" He said, touching the brim of his hat.

"We are just traveling the backroads into Wyoming. We don't want any trouble, just want to keep moving," a haggard-looking man stepped forward and spoke. His grizzly beard and filthy, bloodstained clothing told the tale of much hardship in the recent days.

"Although any food you could spare would be welcome as well," he added, seeing the clean, well-fed men and women atop the barricade.

"You have guns, ammo, or gear...anything to trade for it?" Harold called back.

The man's brow furrowed as he considered. He looked back to the others who stared back with pleading looks on their faces.

"No," he called back flatly. "Never happened across any guns; been using baseball bats to get by."

"Tell you what. You tell us your story, and we'll give you a meal," Tar called down to them. "But, you need to be as specific about the areas you've traveled through as possible," Tar added, as a precaution. "The only way we are gonna let you pass through here, however, is as naked as the day you were born. We aren't taking any chances with people these days."

"Get a bag with a couple days of food together for them," Tar called quietly to Roy.

"Deal, mister…for the food at least," the man said, coming forward.

The small group gathered about ten feet from the base of the wall. The defenders, safely behind the packed earth mound and sandbags, listened to their tale. They were from Aurora. Originally, nine of them had been stuck and surrounded in a batting cage for the first few days of mayhem. When the vending machines ran empty, they starved for a couple days before deciding that they had to move. They lost the other four in the immediate chaos of running from there. They had been on the road for five days and hadn't eaten in two before coming up the pass. Boulder was on fire and Denver was 'Hell on Earth' as they called it. They'd been shot at, robbed, and fended off the abduction of the women on two occasions in that time.

Tar tossed them the food as soon as the tale began. The two men alternated telling the story as they ate ravenously. His heart ached for the people, especially the boy, who couldn't be older than twelve. The boy who looked so much like his own son at that age. He thought hard about the conversation he'd had with Linda the night prior and wished that they could've come up with something solid to test people. He thought they could trust this group, but not enough to risk the community.

Once the story was over, Tar made up his mind.

"Listen, we can't invite you in. As you are well aware, there are murderers, rapists, and opportunists everywhere. Until we come up with a way to screen people…if we do, we are not letting anyone into town who can't be vouched for by someone that already lives here."

"Yeah, we understand that. We appreciate the food, though; it'll get us through another day at least, and that we thank you for," the grizzled man, named Donald, said.

"What we can offer you, if you accept our terms, is to tend a homestead outside our walls." Tar called.

Harold was looking at him incredulously.

"We don't know them, Tar! What the fuck are you doing? You gonna have them livin' on our doorstep?" he hissed at the side of Tar's head.

"You would not be allowed in the town, but we would trade you food for a bounty," Tar continued.

"A bounty?" the man called back.

"Yeah," replied Tar, racking his brain for an answer. Finally adding, "You would be welcome to hunt and forage the areas outside the walls, and we would offer a day's worth of food for every twenty ears you bring in."

He felt unnecessarily bad for them; in theory, it all made sense, logically, to turn them away. But when faced with the choice to turn people, including women and children, away to face certain death, he wavered. He only hoped that his softness would not bring harm to his community.

"Ears? Like off men?" the grizzled man called back.

"Right ears," added Tar, quickly. "Off the undead. We would also need you to report any people you came across to us."

"So you want us to live among the dead, hunt them, and be your eyes and ears; for food?" the man asked.

Tar nodded before adding, "I know it probably ain't the best job offer you've had, but it's the best we can do, for now."

The group conferred with each other quietly, the conversation growing heated briefly as the one man grew angry at the idea, before he was calmed by one of the women.

"What the fuck are you thinking, Tar?" Harold asked, red-faced and wide-eyed.

"Look, Harold, I want to protect everyone of the people that live in this community, I think I've made that obvious. That being said, I can't, in good conscience, turn that boy or them women away."

Harold was flabbergasted. He couldn't argue the point, but it still scared the shit out of him to have a potential threat living at their doorstep.

The group was escorted, naked, with blankets wrapped around them, to the western barricade. Tar and a group of five other armed men he'd pulled from the barricade walked them to the O'Connor farm. The O'Connor's had abandoned the place in lieu of the safety the town proper after a large group of undead slaughtered their livestock and surrounded their house one night while they cowered inside.

"Make yourselves at home. Please respect that this is someone's home and that you are only occupying it temporarily. The O'Connor's have farmed this land for a hundred and twenty years. They're good people."

The group nodded soberly.

"I don't like leaving you all out here unprotected; all the same, we don't know each other...yet," he ended hopefully.

Tar gave the group their clothes and gear back.

"Once we figure a way out to safely bring people into the community, we will get you all in there, so long as you keep to our arrangement and don't give us cause not to," Tar reasoned. "I'll leave a pistol and a box of ammo on the bridge before the wall to help you in case things get grim. Though, I'd advise you continuing to use the bats or maybe an ax. The noise from a gun will only draw more of those things from miles around."

The men, Donald and Billy, came forward and shook Tar's hand.

"Thank you," said one of the women, coming up and hugging Tar unexpectedly. "We haven't seen a lick of kindness since this mess started, so, thank you for giving us a chance."

Tar nodded, pushing himself away from the woman. He tipped his hat to the rest of the group and departed, leaving the new occupants of the farmstead to settle in.

*

Once everything was on the porch of the restaurant, they set up the two-pole tent and climbed inside. They ate in the dying light sitting on top of their sleeping bags and fell asleep shortly after their cold, meager rations were finished. It was a restless sleep, even though the roof was fairly level. To a sleeping form, it felt as if they were going to slide or roll off every time they shifted. Both were awake and sitting in the tent, clutching themselves and shivering, long before the sun climbed over the trees to the east. Exhausted and cranky, they both ate jam sandwiches on stale bread and packed their belongings in silence. They climbed down from the roof and walked away, leaving the Duck Cedar Inn behind them. They walked sluggishly across the road and stumbled through the thick brush to the railroad tracks as the early dawn light brought the world slowly back into focus, the pre-dawn grays slowly separating into distinct objects.

They walked slowly, dispirited by the poor night's rest and for Will, Jen's rejection still stung him. He understood her position, but the rejection still wounded him, despite it. The expression 'not if you were the last guy on earth' popped in his head and he gave a sardonic laugh.

"What?" Jen asked

"Nothing," Will shot back a bit harshly.

Jen looked at him weirdly for a moment, then uncharacteristically let it drop. She had been thinking about Dave most of the morning. How many times he had cheated on her and she took him back. She had the ability to see the good in everyone and was able to forgive without regret. Although thinking back to the relationship with Dave, she had lost a lot of friends due to her choice to stay with him. They loved each other; Jen just knew that Dave was too young to understand how to act in a relationship, especially when alcohol and temptation were involved. She had forgiven him time and again, and always he came back, crying later on, to confess what he had done. The last couple years hadn't been fulfilling or even particularly happy for her, but at least she didn't have to be alone. Even in their 'off times,' Jen knew he would always come back. But now, she was starting to come to terms with the fact that she would never see him again. Jen was surprised at just how much this fact didn't matter to her. It left a hollow pit in her, sure, but that was just the vacuum he left, the loss of a feeling. She guessed that whatever part of her truly loved him had died somewhere along the line leaving only the part that needed him. She looked at Will, wondering about him, how he would be, if they could love one another. *He sure is cute.* She smiled in spite of their situation. She was sorry that she had pushed him away those nights ago, but she hadn't really confronted the idea that the world was over, at least the world she knew. *Fuck Dave*, she thought finally, startled from her thoughts as a gunshot sounded in the distance.

Will grabbed her roughly by the arm and dragged her and their pull-cart off the side of the tracks, down the embankment of crushed stone.

"Who's shooting?" Jen hissed as they tromped towards the thick brush

"No idea, but I think that they are shooting at us," Will said as he started crouch-walking farther down the rail line.

Jen froze for a moment, terrified at the prospect of being shot, before noticing Will far ahead and following after.

"How do you know? They could've been shooting at anything," Jen asked as she came up to his side.

"The grass to the side of the tracks rustled a moment before I heard the gunshot," Will said, casting a look back at her. "Could've been coincidence, but I'm not willing to give them another shot though, if it wasn't."

Will saw a confused look on her face and, understanding the confusion, continued.

"Bullets travel faster than sound."

They traveled another thousand feet, crouch-walking alongside the tracks, before Will yanked her painfully into the thorn bushes to the side of the tracks. Jen opened her mouth to yell about the thorns scraping and pricking her all over, but Will clamped a hand over her mouth. He held a finger up to his lips and she saw his eyes were wide with panic. She swiped his filthy hand away from her mouth, not seeing the flash of hurt come across his face. The two had their pistols drawn and waited in silence near the edge of the woods as two men in camouflage hunting jackets and blue jeans walked down the tracks talking quietly among themselves.

They were so focused on the two men walking on the tracks that they didn't notice the dog until it was too late. A beagle started barking about ten feet from them. The men unslung their rifles and had them trained by the time Will snapped his head back from the dog. Will stood with his hands raised.

"Woah, woah, I'm just passing through, I'm not one of those things," he said purposefully moving his body to block their sight of Jen.

"Get on out here, boy!" the man with a potbelly and white beard said. "Topper! Get over here, boy, and shut it!"

The beagle came running through the underbrush and came to a stop standing next to the man. It continued its incessant barking until the man nudged it with his leg. Will slowly picked his way through the brush hoping Jen was retreating back into the woods as he did.

"Throw that pistol over here, kid, and that rifle on your back as well," said the really skinny one with a packet of chew in his lip. "Where's that little piece of ass we saw you with?"

The words had no sooner left his mouth than a gunshot rang out from behind Will. A surprised look came over the skinny man's face, and he looked down to see a hole in his chest. The fat man looked confused momentarily at the sound of the shot; he was watching the kid the whole time and couldn't understand how he'd gotten the shot off. Will dove to the side trying to get out of the sights of the rifle the pot-bellied man held. The man took a shot just as he was coming out of a roll, the leaves just behind him whipping. Will heard two more shots before he was able to get his body behind a tree big enough to give him cover. As he peeked around the tree, Topper came around the base and started ripping at his pant leg. He kicked the thing sharply, sending it skittering away, yelping.

"Will?" he heard Jen call out.

"Yeah, Jen, I'm here," he called back to her, trying to get a peek at the railroad tracks where the men were. "You okay?"

"I killed them, Will." He could hear the raw emotion in her voice.

Will glanced out to make sure both men were down before he came out to take the scene in fully. The two men were laying, unmoving, on the tracks with the dog nosing around the fat one. Will collected his weapons and ran back to where Jen was vomiting through her tears.

"Jen, it's okay," he comforted her, putting his arm around her shoulders.

The roars of the fast ones in the distance sent chills up his spine.

"We gotta go Jen, now!" He grabbed her roughly and started pulling her through the weeds back towards the tracks.

When they got onto the tracks, Jen was moving, and Will let go of her and started running full-out, the cart bouncing along behind him as he tugged and yanked it along. He was checking behind every few seconds to make sure she was still moving. However, he needn't have worried. Her grief and horror at killing two men evaporated as the roars of the undead in the distance wiped everything but fear away. Both tumbled and fell at least three times, tripping over the awkwardly spaced ties. They pulled each other up and grimaced through the pain of splinters and jagged stone ripping into them each time.

*

"Daddy!" came Sophie's voice from somewhere outside, immediately eliciting panic in him.

Tim and Bjorn looked at each other, confirming that their ears were not playing tricks on them. They scanned the area around the dock. Bjorn's heart was in his throat at the thought of his daughter out in the open.

"Daddy, up here," came Sophie's voice.

"Soph, get away from the edge, sweetie. Who are you up there with?" Bjorn called, seeing her atop the roof.

"Tim!" screamed Laura from somewhere above, out of sight. Her voice was full of panic. "Help!"

Without thinking, Tim ripped up the bay door and ran through the warehouse towards his wife. He had to wait on the elevator for a minute and Bjorn caught up to him. Bjorn was pale.

"What?" Tim asked

Bjorn made no indication he'd heard the question, just stared ahead at the doors with a grim look on his face. Finally, the doors slid open and the duo stepped in with Bjorn mashing the third-floor button. When the doors slid back open ten seconds later, they immediately heard the sounds of trouble. From the stairwell, they could hear the sound of heavy rapid banging and Laura continuing her shouts for help. Tim took off running through the door, hurtling up the stairs towards the sound. Bjorn lingered behind, making his way slowly down the hall towards the room he and his family resided in. When Tim reached the last flight of steps leading to the roof door, he could clearly see one of the fast undead, that clearly had once Lilly, thrashing and raging against the door. He pulled up short, unsure of how to handle the situation.

"Open the door, Laura," he shouted, finally deciding on a course.

The Lilly-creature snapped its head around at the sound of his yell, and lunged at him, mouth open and hands reaching.

"Tim?" Laura yelled, her voice full of hope and residual panic.

He managed to sidestep the attack, barely, and yelled back at Laura.

"I need you to open the door now, Laura!" He screamed, panic welling as he was trapped in close quarters with the undead.

The door swung open and Laura stood there holding Luna with little Sophie by her side, her mouth an 'O' of terror as he ran onto the roof with the Lilly-thing right behind him. Worried that the thing would alternate to his wife and kid, Tim ducked and spun his leg, tripping the undead version of his friend's wife, sending her sprawling across the tar and gravel of the rooftop. He ushered Laura and the children through the open doorway and onto the stairs, pulling the door shut just as the Lilly-monster hit it with full force. Tim slid the bolt home, locking it.

Tim put his arm around Laura and pulled her into him as they walked slowly down the stairs to the third floor. Upon exiting the stairwell, they found Bjorn holding the unmoving body of his son in his arms. Bjorn was weeping, his tears dripping onto the toddler's face, mixing with the blood that marred Liam's angelic features. There were no words to say in that moment; Bjorn's grief overcame them all. They all hugged each other, tears of loss, relief, heartbreak, and elation all mixing together. They stay that way for nearly an hour, before Laura finally broke free to go lay Luna down.

Tim stripped down to his skin in a bathroom and bathed in the sink as best as he was able, washing the gore and filth of the day off. It had been a triumphant and terrible day; he couldn't shake the exultant feeling of mowing down the multitude of dead that came at them earlier. It mingled strangely with the grief he felt for his friend's loss. He approached Bjorn once he was done with his impromptu shower. Liam's body was nowhere to be seen, to Tim's great relief.

"Why don't you and Sophie stay with us tonight?"

"I'd appreciate if you guys could keep an eye on Soph," he said, staring blankly ahead. "I doubt I'll sleep tonight."

Tim sat with his friend for a while, silently, before the strain and stress of the day hit him. Wearily, he stood up, setting his hand on Bjorn's shoulder.

"I love you, man. I know you're broken right now, but remember that Sophie needs you...we all need you." Without waiting for a response, he staggered down the hallway into the office his wife and child, and Sophie were in.

The kids were asleep, and Laura was sitting up under the covers looking like she wanted to talk. She looked at him as he came into the office, locking the door behind him.

"You will not leave me alone again," she said flatly.

"Never," he responded collapsing on the floor, nestling into her.

He wasn't awake long enough to hear if she had anything else to say.

Tim slept through the night and was awakened in the morning by sun baking in through the windows. The dry heat that built in the office wreaked havoc with his sinuses, and again he awoke with a headache from it. Once again, he was the last to rise. His muscles ached from the exertion of the previous day as he pulled on his shoes and groggily made his way carefully down the glass-strewn hallway, past the conference room that held the remains of three days of snack-meals. He finally came to the bathroom next to the elevator and brushed his teeth while relieving himself in the urinal next to the sinks. He saw no one in any of the offices on the third floor and began to get concerned. Fetching himself a cup of coffee in a Styrofoam cup, he made his way back to the elevator. Once inside, he punched the second-floor button followed by the 'G' button. He let the doors open to the second floor, glancing around quickly before continuing down to the first floor.

Laura and the kids were gathered in the lobby, sprawled out on the couches and floor watching Finding Dory on the LCD mounted above them.

"Where's Bjorn?" Tim asked.

"Think he went to the loading dock, said something about welding," Laura responded without taking her eyes from the TV.

Tim grunted in response and went off to find his friend. When he arrived at the loading dock, the bay door was open and he could see Bjorn tinkering about on the Humvee outside. He glanced nervously around, worried that something might have slipped inside through the open bay door. Once he was satisfied that nothing had, he closed the door to the office area tightly, descended the stairs, and joined Bjorn outside.

"Hey, bud," he said.

"Hey hey," Bjorn responded, sounding weirdly upbeat. "We need a sheet of half-inch steel or something I can weld on."

"For…?" Tim added.

"Trying to rig a cow-catcher of sorts on the front of the Humvee."

Tim nodded appreciatively at the suggestion and proceeded to examine the bracket Bjorn had welded to the Humvee.

"You okay, man?" he said at length.

Bjorn looked at him coldly, the stress, strain and lack of sleep apparent in his eyes.

"Of course I'm not fucking okay. But I need to keep moving, for Sophie. So, if you please, let's keep it light. I don't want to dwell."

Tim nodded, keeping quiet for a moment for his brain to settle on the topic at hand, rather than the one he wanted to discuss.

"What about the rear bumpers of the trailers next door?" Tim asked. "Couldn't we cut them off with the torch and weld them to the bumper, angled away from the middle?"

Bjorn thought about it for a minute, not liking it as much as his plow design. Without a word, Bjorn ran around the side of the building, disappearing out of Tim's sight. He started to follow slowly after, then stopped, refusing to move out of sight of the bay door. When he reached the corner, he could see Bjorn running out across the road and out of sight. *What the fuck is he doing?* Tim thought. About five minutes later, Bjorn came barreling through the bushes on the side of the building, scaring the wits out of Tim, who sat quietly on the loading dock, lost in this thoughts.

"Help me get the welding rig loaded on the Hummer," he panted, out of breath from his impromptu jog. Tim helped load the rig. It took both of them to hoist the tanks. They slid the bay door noisily closed, and Bjorn slid behind the wheel. Sixty seconds later, he pulled up behind the paper goods warehouse down the road where a wide V-shaped snow plow was sitting.

"We gotta make this as fast as we can, man; if Laura finds out I left again, she will kill me," Tim said with an honest amount of nervousness in his voice.

They used the winch pulley setup on the Humvee to hoist the plow up while Tim manually shifted it into place to be welded. Bjorn tacked it in place with the torch so they could drive back to finish it in the relative comfort of their own loading dock, before Laura noticed they were gone. It was mid-afternoon by the time they were finished with the plow; the blade sat about a foot off the ground, enough that it hopefully wouldn't get hooked on the ground, but low enough that it didn't interfere too much with the driver's view of the road ahead.

When they finally came inside, Laura was staring absently at the DVD menu screen while both of the kids slept. They had passed out on the couch cuddling together. Tim and Bjorn sat down in the room as Laura started to speak.

"We could get some potting soil from Lowes and turn the entire rooftop into a garden, you know."

Tim's eyes widened at the possibility he had never considered.

"That's too smart!" Bjorn responded before a shadow crossed his face, and he lowered his head thinking about his dead child and undead wife.

Tim appreciated that the rooftop was currently the prison holding the Lilly-thing from killing them all.

"That is an amazing idea, Laur, but I think we may be leaving here sooner rather than later."

"Where would we go?" Laura asked, a bit annoyed that her plan would go unfulfilled.

With his eyes, Tim tried to explain the need to get Bjorn away from here for his mental health. To Laura, it looked like he was having a fit with his face. She started giggling at him.

"I don't know where to," he eventually said. "Away from here."

Bjorn got up at this point and walked away, going to the elevator. Tim sat with Laura downstairs eventually the two drifted off to sleep. When they awoke a couple hours later, Sophie was awake. The little girl was happy as a lark playing with her dolls while the movie played again on the television. Tim worried for her, as well as Luna...especially sweet little Luna. What a terrible mess the world had become; how terrible it would be for children not to be able to play outdoors. He did his best to hold out hope that the military would sweep through and take back control, though, a deep seed of doubt gnawed at him. His mind whispered darkly to him, telling him that this was the world now. There would be no return to normalcy, that this was the new norm. He didn't have the hope or any certainty to push those dark thoughts away, so he sat in glum silence.

Luna stirred and woke as he pondered the new meaning of life in the undead world. Clearing his head, he stood and fetched a big marker from the conference room behind them. After five minutes of intense drawing on the floor, he stepped back and admired his work. They played hopscotch with the girls for a bit before Tim decided to go upstairs and check on Bjorn.

Coming off the elevator, he instantly knew something was wrong. He heard loud banging of fists banging slowly on steel and gentle sobbing coming from around the corner.

*

Over the coming days, the barricades they worked feverishly to construct came under attack on multiple occasions. The majority of the attacks came from the south, the direction of Boulder and Denver. At first, it was humans, and small groups of undead that roamed up to the defenses. Other groups, primarily large groups of men, required a show of force to steer away. The town had suffered a handful of casualties from these groups, each time strengthening the defenses in anticipation of the next attack. Tar recognized that these men were predators and allowing them to roam freely, even while they were safe behind the walls, endangered a great many other people. He was merciless with the groups of men. He referred to them as 'bastards not worthy of another breath', and he sent men out in pursuit after they had been driven off, allowing no survivors, whenever possible.

The bitter cold that had set in after the first snow, and the requirements to keep the barricades comfortable for the men and women who manned them complicated things. He tried to rotate people out after four hours in the cold. The smoke from the fires they needed to keep warm at their stations pinpointed out their locations to any enemy looking, drawing some in who might not have otherwise have come.

In the east, they had strung concertina wire from the edges of the wall they'd erected through the forest in either direction. They fashioned pillboxes on either side of the log-wall out of prefab concrete sewer sections. These pillboxes were manned by two men each, a spotter and a sniper. They were covered by machine gun nests fashioned out of crushed cars a hundred yards behind the wall. A sniper position was set up as a rear-guard at the farm shed. The idea was to allow the men in front to withdraw in stages while suppressing an enemy advance.

In the west, a pair of shipping containers sat end to end between the two barns with steel plates from road construction welded on to protect those atop the containers. Snipers and machine gunners were stationed in the barn's lofts. A six-foot deep, eight-foot wide trench led off from either side of the barns, meeting up with stockade fence from the existing farms. The stockade fence was reinforced up with more concertina wire. Tar knew that the west barricade was the weakest, but as all of the attacks from humans and most from the dead had come from the east and south, it was largely neglected.

"I feel a change in my bones," Tar said to the others gathered at the south berm on the third morning after the first big snow. He assumed it could be his arthritis getting funky with the change of weather, but heaviness on his heart made him feel otherwise. "Something about the stillness of the air."

*

A road swung up from the east to run parallel with the railroad tracks, and Will caught sight of one of the fast undead pacing them on it. As he watched, it spotted him and roared, veering through the brush. It hit a barbed wire fence at speed and flipped over, tangling its arm and leg at the same time. Will didn't need much of a distraction to trip on the ties and he fell, smashing his face into the rail of the track. He willed himself back to his feet after a blow that should've knocked him out, never taking his eyes off the enraged zombie that struggled mightily to pull free of the wire. A second fast one came into view, roaring up from the west side, splashing through a narrow stream and stumbling up the side of the crushed stone before Jen put a bullet in its head. The two ran on for ten minutes as fast as they were able to stop the staggering railroad ties. Finally, Will staggered to a halt, blood running down his face in rivulets. Jen came up a moment later, panting. She was hunched over, hands on her knees, trying to muster up a breath with which to speak.

"Holy shit!" she gasped out, gathered another breath before continuing, "We gotta keep moving."

Will fished out a shirt from his pack, and Jen helped tie it around his head to stop the bleeding. They set off again at a brisk walk, and once they got their wind back, they stepped the pace up to a jog. They continued for a few miles until they spotted an overpass ahead. *Just a country road, passing over*, Will thought as he led Jen off through the brush. They skirted around the embankment and took a nervous break atop the roadway, with a clear view for over a mile in both directions down the tracks. They sat in silence while Will struggled to re-tie the shirt around the wound on his head, a three-inch gash from his temple to jawbone. Jen finally came over and splashed him unceremoniously in the side of the face with rubbing alcohol from the cart and set about properly bandaging it with a gauze pad and bandages from the first-aid kit in the camp-cart. Will winced as some of the alcohol got in the corner of his eye. Blinking away the sting of the alcohol, he admired the musky, earthy smell of her armpits as she worked on his face.

"You're a crack shot with that thing," Will stated, voice full of admiration, thinking of the fast undead she had taken out in mid-stride.

The compliment made her think back to the men she had killed. The first one was an accident; hearing him refer to her as a 'piece of ass' caused her to flinch in revulsion, pulling the trigger. The second one she meant to kill as he was shooting at Will. Nothing in her life had prepared her for taking a human life. The idea of it had never even crossed her mind, and now here she was, having killed two men in a matter of a minute.

Will could see the curious mix of emotion sweep across her face.

"You did the right thing, Jen. You most likely saved my life back there. What do you think they were going to do to me after they took my weapons?" She looked at him wanting to believe what he said before he continued, "What do you think they would've done to you?"

He said this last statement soberly and let the thought hang in the air while he finished eating a peanut butter sandwich. Chewing on his last bite, he unslung his rifle and peered back down the tracks through the scope, scanning up and down the tracks and moving left to right. Seeing nothing, he moved to the north side of the bridge to examine the next leg of their journey. The tracks continued for another mile or so before they angled off, out of sight, behind some forest. Satisfied that they weren't being followed, nor walking into a horde of the things, he slung his rifle and walked over to the cart, examining the flat tire it had acquired during the recent mad-dash from the fast things. He resolved to leave it behind the next time they needed to run from something; his shoulder ached from the jarring tug of pulling it along over the ties.

They continued up the tracks, keeping a nervous eye on the highway that now ran closely to their right, alongside the tracks. There were plenty of trees, though without summer's heavy foliage to block sight of it, they had a clear view of the lines of endless cars, many of which had forms moving about within. The proximity to the cluttered roadway made them both nervous. Though they had traveled a great many miles along similar roads, now that they were on the relative solitude of the tracks, they had no desire to be back near the danger of the highway. They walked on, tensely, as the cart clattered along on the tracks, the flat tire hitting the ties heavily, continually jarring the handle in Will's hand. On the left side of the track, a massive parking lot came into view, followed by another train station, this one was quite large. They walked down the far side of the piled crushed stone, again keeping the tracks in between themselves and the platform. A few undead moved around the lot in the distance but nothing moved atop the platform.

Harriman

The name rang a bell in Will's head and he tossed his pack on the ground, stopping abruptly to rip out the atlas. Once he got it flipped open to the correct page, he saw that they would hit I-86 by the early evening. A wide smile crossed his face.

"What?" Jen whispered, too aware of the undead in the distance

"We are close to getting off the tracks," he said, both excited and nervous about the next leg of their journey. "We are only a few miles away from 86. We should start looking for a place to spend the night soon."

He hefted his pack back on and the two set off, returning to the top of the tracks once the station and parking lot were out of sight behind them.

An hour and a half later, they passed through the beginnings of an industrial park, with warehouses appearing off on the left side of the tracks. A short distance beyond, the ground around the tracks dropped away, revealing a vast expanse of roadway all around them. Ribbons of tarmac passed over and under the tracks ahead in at least two spots. Off to the right what looked like the remnants of a massive battle that had occurred at a toll plaza. Thousands, of undead milled about the burned-out remains of hundreds of vehicles, scattered nearly a dozen lanes of the highway. More than twenty military vehicles were scattered about the area though the inhabitants were nowhere to be seen, aside from the occasional olive-clad undead staggering about. The two watched in silence for many minutes, hunkered down behind the cart, keeping its bulk between them and the scene ahead. They briefly discussed their options for the remainder of the day, eventually concluding that moving forwards would almost assuredly bring the dead upon them. Running from or engaging in a fight with hundreds of dead things ahead did not play into their plans for the evening.

They spent that night in the cab of a tractor-trailer parked in the rear of a building labeled Takasago Corporation. They had spotted the building from the tracks at a distance and returned to it after turning back from the devastation at the toll plaza. The truck had its driver's side door ajar, and although a large circle of blood and gore sat just below, there was nobody and the cabin was clean and clear. They settled comfortably into the rear compartment of the sleeper cabin. Once they had eaten and pored over the atlas for a bit, they both drifted off early, the stress of the day and the poor sleep the night prior had taken its toll.

They following morning they awoke well rested just after sunrise. The morning sun baked through the windows making the cab uncomfortably warm. They ate a quick morning meal while Will referred to the atlas one more time before they got their packs on and the cart ready for travel.

"Okay, since we're going to move through the surface roads of the area rather than risk the horde at the toll plaza, we need to make sure our weapons are loaded and ready to use. I don't think we'll have the fortune of walking alone today." Will said as they stepped down to the open lot around the truck.

"Aye aye, Captain!" Jen said with a silly salute and a stunning smile.

Her smile stoked a fire in his heart; he longed for her. His heart ached as they prepped their weapons and started the day's journey. The two walked a quarter-mile up the road that the Takasago warehouse sat on before they cut behind a nondescript concrete building with the union symbol of the IBEW mounted on the front. They spent the next half-hour picking their way through the woods behind the building, moving towards the roadway beyond. Will waved for her to wait as he moved to the edge of the woods.

Route 6 lay ahead, scattered with traffic. Looking intently at the vehicles, Will could see a number of undead moving about randomly. Though not nearly as crowded as the parkway or 87, he knew that if they were going to stay on 6 until it met with 86, they would gather quite a large following very quickly. A half-mile or so down the road, an overpass carried Route 17 overhead, meeting up with 86 a mile or so further. If they were to go that route, he thought they could avoid the scattered undead piling up behind them, but face the unknown immediately, as their visibility of what lay on 17 was blocked entirely by its altitude relative to them. Jen grabbed him roughly by the backpack, nearly toppling him as she pulled him down onto the asphalt. Will looked back after his initial surprise to see a dozen of the undead shambling towards them through the trees. The decision was made, and the two ran headlong up Route 6, towards the exit ramp leading to Route 17.

Once they reached the top of the exit ramp, the scene unfolded before them. Traffic was stalled just as it was everywhere else, aimed northbound and gridlocked bumper-to-bumper. The shopping center to the right of the road was mobbed with undead, dozens roaming about the parked cars and open space in between the Pizzeria UNO and the Kohls. Will was thankful that all the undead they were able to see on the roadway around them appeared to be locked in their vehicles. They thrashed at the windows and ripped at the seatbelts that restrained them as the two passed quickly by. The two cut across traffic and moved into the southbound lanes as soon as they were able to. For some reason, the southbound lanes were eerily clear of any vehicle traffic, though a few undead staggered about. They moved at a quiet jog, trying to avoid detection by any of the undead while they swiftly moved out of range of those that followed them from the woods below. They crossed two intersections that were blocked by police barricades set up to keep vehicles in the northbound lanes.

Finally, the roadway to either side of the highway fell away, and I-86 stretched out in either direction from under the overpass. To the east sat another toll plaza, this one devastated by a massive pileup of vehicles, blocking all the westbound lanes. West of the overpass, the westbound lanes were gridlocked for as far as the eye could see. The eastbound lanes were absolutely barren. Seeing this, Will led Jen down the exit ramp to move westward.

He felt good about their decision for all of five minutes. They had left the mob from the woods behind, and the few on the roadway above were left behind as well. The undead in and around the cars jammed on the westbound lanes, however, quickly amassed behind them. The undead that followed behind fell over the concrete divider and drifted across the grassy median in pursuit. An onslaught of a handful of fast undead and the ensuing gunfire needed to dispatch them didn't help matters for them.

By the time half an hour had passed, as they were moving under an overpass just beyond a state police barracks, they had nearly a thousand undead following, across all six lanes of the roadway. There were so many undead in the westbound lanes, their combined moaning drowned out everything but their shuffling footfalls, drawing more and more dead upon them. Will and Jen couldn't take a break for more than a couple minutes without being converged on. It was during one of these short breaks that Will, looking at the atlas, came up with a plan to elude the mob later in the day. The village of Goshen further down the highway cut across the town at two points. His plan was to lead the mob off the highway, lose them on the village side streets, and join back up with I-86 after a night's rest on a rooftop or tractor-trailer cab. Until they got to that point, they would just have to do their best to stay ahead of, and ignore, the moaning mass behind them.

The fast ones came out frequently. There was no concrete sound barrier on this highway to keep the undead from the surrounding houses and streets away. Will guessed that the combined noise of a thousand moaning, shuffling undead was drawing them to the anticipated meal. He was thus prepared when another fast undead hurdled over top of the guardrail, sprinting headlong at him with its mouth wide and hands splayed out. As he pulled the trigger, the thing tripped on a rock, sending the bullet well over its head. Will readjusted his aim quickly, and fired just as the thing closed the final few feet, hitting it between the eyes as it dove towards him. The body of the dead thing collided with Will just below the knee. A loud pop sounded.

Will tried to stand up; he had no idea how he got on the ground in the first place. He refused to accept that the agony in his knee was serious, crawling to his feet. When he tried to put weight on it, however, he swooned from the pain and fell back to the pavement. A low, pained moan slipped unbidden from his lips. His heart sank as the undead closed in on them.

*

Moving cautiously around the corner, Tim could see Bjorn on his knees, holding the handle to the stairwell door, bracing it shut. As he came fully into the open, he could see the man was sobbing softly as he held it closed.

"Lilly got out?" he said incredulously.

Bjorn didn't react or respond in any way; he just knelt there and cried.

"Hold that door tight, man. I'll be right back," Tim yelled, turning to run down the hall.

He made it to the office his family used and started packing all their belongings into a bag as quickly as possible. He heard the door clatter open and a ruckus ensue. Grabbing a machete from atop the desk, he ran back down the hall. He slowed to a stop, the seething determination to kill ebbed from his bones as he saw Bjorn holding Liam's little undead body at bay. Tears streamed down Bjorn's face as he stared pleadingly at the little thing that was once his son. Tim stood, slack-jawed at the scene, his own heart breaking for the man and the little boy that the monster had once been.

"Bjorn..." Tim said softly, approaching.

Bjorn's head snapped around, eyes fixing on the machete he held.

"Don't you fucking come near him with that thing!" Bjorn shouted.

Tim, realizing he was still holding the blade, dropped it immediately.

"Okay, Bjorn, what are we doing here?"

"I don't know," he sobbed out as the little thing clawed weakly at the hands holding him under the armpits. "I don't know."

The elevator doors dinged as they began to open, and Tim backed up so he could see who it was.

"Sophie, go get Laura, quick please!" he said turning his attention back to Bjorn. "Do you think we can lock him in one of the offices, Bjorn?"

Bjorn just continued looking into the eyes of the furious little creature in his arms, trying to see if some part of his son was left in there, behind those milky eyes. Tears and snot continued to run freely from his face as he replied, "No one touches him!"

"No one will, I promise," Tim said softly, backing out into the elevator lobby, giving Bjorn plenty of room to move past with the tiny zombie.

As Bjorn crossed in front of the elevator with undead-Liam, the door dinged again, doors sliding open. Sophie and Laura screamed from within, startling Bjorn who then dropped the little monster on the floor. The little thing grabbed onto Bjorn's pants and sunk his teeth in, just above his ankle. Screams sounded anew from the elevator. Tim swung his head around the corner, looking in on his wife.

"Get everyone in the Humvee now," Tim yelled and slid the bag into the elevator.

Laura had a panicked, frightened look on her face, and she

screamed mindlessly at him in response. The doors of the elevator slid closed, and Tim turned to Bjorn who had regained control of the undead child. Seeing that, he hazarded a glance at the man's leg where the thing had bitten him, apparently not hard enough to get through heavy Carhartt pants he wore. Bjorn moved down to the conference room they had been using as their dining hall. He squatted down, grasping the thing by the sides of its face, even as it clawed at him. Tim watched heartbroken as the father bent over the top of the little monster and kissed it softly and lovingly on its forehead. A tear ran down Tim's cheek as he thought of having to do that to his own child, and he turned away before he started breaking down.

"You okay?" Tim eventually awkwardly asked as the elevator slid downwards.

"No," Bjorn said flatly, shooting an incredulous look at his friend.

"I…that's not what I meant. I'm sorry, man."

Laura and the kids stood huddled in the lobby, waiting. Tim looked around as if saying goodbye to his lifelong home before they all moved quickly towards the loading dock. Tim grabbed the bag of toys Laura had gathered from the floor, seeing that she was struggling with it as she carried Luna and the bag he had tossed her. Before sixty seconds had passed, all that remained of the two families were crammed into the Humvee with all their worldly possessions, which amounted to a bag of blocks and dolls, some clothes, and a few cases of food and ammo. The lengthening gloom of the evening seemed even darker than usual as Tim twisted the ignition.

Bjorn curled up in a ball with Sophie on the back seat, consoling his terrified daughter while tears streamed down his own face. Laura held Luna on her lap in the passenger's seat while Tim put the armored vehicle in gear and started out of the parking lot as the last light of day slipped down below the horizon. A loud thump sounded from behind them broke the silence and Tim, looking in the rear-view mirror, saw the form of Lilly, face down on the pavement behind them. He watched in silent horror as her form struggled to rise on shattered legs before pulling itself along using her hands and elbows to follow the Humvee. Tim accelerated, leaving the ghastly thing behind before anyone else caught sight of it.

Tim snaked the Humvee through the traffic of the industrial park and down the on-ramp to the highway, putting it in park at the bottom of the ramp. They sat in silence for a minute before Tim felt the need to break it.

"Where the fuck are we going to go now?" he queried, getting no response but the rumble of the engine.

After five minutes of silence, Tim locked the doors and turned the ignition off. The efforts of the past few days crashed home, and Tim had neither the energy nor the will to move any further.

"Okay, we will decide in the morning, I guess," he said flatly while struggling to move the bloodstained seat into a position more conducive to comfortable sleep.

No complaints came from anyone, other than Luna, who fussed a bit but was silenced shortly after by the breast thrust into her mouth.

*

"Get on the cart!" Jen yelled at him.

Hope lit in Will. Jen might not be able to carry him, but surely she might be able to outpace the horde pushing him on the cart. He crawled over to the thing, swiping the bungee cords that held the bags on top in place. He threw the bag full of cans of Sterno and the fish-flavored MREs, which neither of them could stand the taste of, out of the cart, dumping its contents across the road. Having cleared a spot for himself, he struggled upright and collapsed heavily on the cart, nearly toppling the rickety thing. Jen shoved the cart roughly from behind, just barely avoiding the first of the undead creeping across the roadway. With a great effort, she was able to get the cart moving fast enough to start jogging, eventually gaining some distance from the dead. Will struggled to get his pack off and across his lap, with his gun at the ready.

The cart's wheels wobbled as they turned. Will had been rough with the thing the entire journey and it was now paying the price. He wondered how much further it would carry him before a wheel fell off. Jen panted and puffed as she struggled up a rise to keep them ahead of the horde, while Will took out any that strayed too close. The wheel that was flat was digging down into the asphalt when they were going straight and sliding out when they turned, making every step difficult.

They had passed a huge housing development off to the right of the highway and hundreds more undead flowed from that direction, joining the slow-motion chase. Thankfully, after they passed the community, the houses and buildings fell away, leaving only fields, woods, and marshland on either side of the road. The gathering behind them only grew in small increments from the undead in the westbound lanes. Jen was able to keep up a steady, fifty-foot cushion between them and the assemblage, but Will could see her strength was waning after only twenty minutes. Her 120-pound frame struggled to push his hundred and seventy on a broken cart loaded with supplies. Will tried hard to think of a possible way out, not knowing which would give out first the cart or Jen, only knowing that one was going to, and soon.

"Hang in there Jen, we can do this," he said, trying to sound confident.

The only response was her ragged harsh breathing. He wished she could produce a larger gap so they could look in the cars headed westbound for crutches or a wheelchair. They were able to gain some additional ground coming down a large hill; however, those gains were lost in climbing the hill that followed immediately after.

The day dragged on long past the point where Will thought they would be forced to stop. Failing to come up with any other feasible way out, he started jettisoning their belongings from the cart to lighten the load. There was a very real possibility that this might be their last day on earth. After a couple minutes, Will, his guns and ammo, and a handful of sandwiches were all that was left in the cart. He even cut the straps on Jen's pack as she struggled behind the cart. He was amazed at her tenacity; a man would've left him miles back. He loved her that moment the way a child loves their mother. He knew eventually she might have to abandon him. He decided that when that happened, he would make her run and do his best to give her a good start against the mob.

They crept along at a snail's pace, Jen was openly weeping at the effort, her pants showed signs that her bladder had failed her, and still she kept moving, just barely keeping them ahead of the mob. The sky started to darken, and the wind started to whip a terrible cold rain across the highway, making their horrific plight even more miserable. Night fell upon them like a smothering blanket, taking the last of the light and what remained of their hope along with it. Will struggled to make out forms around them, knowing that his ability to kill the fast ones was severely limited in the moonless night. He thought he was going mad at first when he saw the headlights of a vehicle on the on-ramp ahead. The wheezing gasp from Jen behind, gave credence to the visage. It was the first sound he'd heard from Jen in hours, aside from the hoarse sounds of her breathing.

The headlights flicked off and both wondered if they were ever there to begin with. Again, they were in the dark of night. A roar from the side snapped Will harshly back into the reality of their current state. One of the fast undead roared in from the left side of the road. He couldn't get the barrel of the rifle around quick enough, so he smashed the stock into the things gaping maw, knocking it to the pavement. Jen paused long enough to stick her gun against the things head and pull the trigger before continuing to push the rickety cart. Ahead on the ramp, they could just make out the outline of a vehicle.

Urged on by the sight of the vehicle ahead, Jen tapped deeper into unknown reserves and ran again, her breaths came in great heaving gulps and wheezing blasts. After five long strides, the cart finally gave out, dumping Will onto the pavement. Jen, too exhausted and sluggish to respond, tripped and collapsed atop both he and the cart. The burst of pain from his knee overwhelmed him, making him swoon and groan uncontrollably. Ammo skittered and rolled across the roadway, and Will comically thought of all the undead slipping and falling on the bullets behind them. He laughed despite the situation as he struggled up to one foot.

They had lost everything except the guns they carried in the tumble. Will leaned heavily on Jen's shoulder as she walked and he hopped towards the truck. They could see the darkened military vehicle now, and hope lit inside both of them. *The military!* their inner voices screamed exuberantly. The Humvee was barely a hundred feet ahead of them. The undead pushed ever closer to them as Jen half-carried Will. Three falls and forty seconds later, and the two slammed into the passenger's side of the vehicle. Their fists and hands battered the windows.

"Please help us!" Jen wailed. "Let us in, please!"

*

All five of them jumped at the sound of the bodies hitting the passenger door. Luna and Laura screamed and the child started crying in her mother's lap. Tim readied his pistol, thinking to go out and dispatch the undead so he could get back to trying to sleep.

"Wait!" Laura called. "They aren't dead."

Before Tim could protest, Laura reached behind her and opened the rear passenger's side door. With the door open, Tim could hear the people outside yelling for help and saw Bjorn pushing Sophie behind him and raising his pistol towards the dark outside. A girl jumped in followed by a boy dragging his leg behind him. He didn't need to close the door behind him as a body hit it, slamming it shut. The whole vehicle rocked as the mass of undead swarmed around the Humvee.

"Thank you, thank you, thank you, thank you," Jen gasped through her tears, her chest heaving in great sobs. Will lost consciousness while forcing his knee to bend in order to fit in the back seat. He lay slumped over on Jen's shoulder.

"Holy shit!" Tim muttered. "You guys okay?"

"Will hurt his knee," she said, finally starting to gain composure. "This morning. They've been following us all day."

Tim wished Laura hadn't opened the door, and had he the

opportunity to, he would have stopped her, but the two seemed harmless enough. He guessed that anyone traveling with a woman who wasn't a victim was probably okay. All the same, with his family's lives at stake, he knew better than to trust them. The paranoid, overprotective part of him nagged at him, insisting they could be part of a larger group, preying on survivors, it warned him about how they could be infected, reminding him of Lilly and Liam.

"Listen, we are willing to help you guys, but I need you to drop those guns," Tim said to her flatly.

Jen looked at him, eyes narrowed, remembering their encounter on the tracks the day before. She made no move to drop her pistol.

"Look, we don't know you…and I don't want you holding that pistol near my wife, near our children until we do. I don't think that is too much to ask; we let you in the fucking car after all."

Finally, Jen blew out her breath and dropped the pistol onto the floor of the Humvee. She wriggled the rifle slung over her shoulder off her back, sliding it into the rear of the vehicle before she broke down and started crying. Once the immediate threat of weapons was handled, Tim was able to relax, just the slightest bit.

"Where are you two from and where are you going?" Tim said.

"Will is from New York City, I'm from Garfield," Jen replied. "We are heading towards Wisconsin through Canada."

"What's in Wisconsin?" Laura asked, hoping for a positive response.

"Don't know. That's where Will is from, originally. He picked me up on the highway down by Ridgewood," she stammered out, realizing for the first time that she was just along for the ride. "I guess I've got nowhere else to go, so I'm just going along hoping for the best."

"Is he bit?" Bjorn asked flatly, speaking for the first time since he got in the vehicle.

"No, his knee just blew out when one of the fast ones collided with him," Jen replied.

The line of questioning made her suddenly very nervous for Will, not knowing that these people were any better than the ones on the tracks. If they wanted, they could just push him out of the vehicle and there would be nothing she could so about it. She studied the woman and baby in the front seat and the little girl the man next to her shielded.

"Where are you all headed?" she finally ventured.

"We don't know yet," Tim said, having seen her nervous glances around the vehicle, he added, "I'm Tim. This is my wife, Laura and our daughter, Luna. That's Bjorn and his daughter, Sophie. We are good people, but we won't hesitate to put a bullet in you and leave you for the undead if you fuck with us."

He let that statement hang in the chill air of the dark cab of the Humvee for a moment before continuing.

"That being said, you have nothing to fear from us if you are decent and honest and helpful."

Jen nodded in response as the mob of undead outside continued battering on the heavy vehicle. The adrenaline and exhaustion finally took over and she passed out. After a moment, Bjorn put a hand in front of her mouth and nose to make sure she was breathing before attending to Sophie in the rear compartment of the Humvee.

"Thank you for letting us in," Will said quietly. He had awoken shortly after passing out but figured he would play possum to see how things played out. "You saved our lives."

"Sandwich?" Tim said.

"Please," Will said, casting a longing and loving glance at the unconscious form of the woman who, despite the risk to herself, had seen him through to safety.

They sat in relative silence mechanically eating sandwiches that Laura passed around. Tim and Bjorn looked strangely comfortable even with the vehicle being surrounded by the things. Everyone else averted their eyes and seemed tense. Jen and Will shifted uncomfortably around in the back seat with Bjorn; Luna was fussing in the front seat. Having eaten, they settled in for a long restless night with the incessant sounds of the undead moaning outside while rocking and banging on the Humvee.

"Were you guys military?" Will said, for the first time appreciating the Humvee as well as the weapons and ammo stockpiled in the rear.

"Nah, just came across some luck scavenging the past few days," Tim said. "Jen says you're headed to Wisconsin?"

"Yeah, I grew up out there, in Benoit," Will said, looking around briefly and not seeing recognition he added, "About four and a half hours from Green Bay, in the middle of nowhere."

"What was in New York?" Tim asked, guessing the middle of nowhere was the reason the kid ended up in New York City.

"College mainly," Will replied, "A change of scenery."

After thinking about it for a moment, he added, "New York is gone, you know."

Laura spun around, and Tim too, and she looked at him with a puzzled expression.

"A nuke went off a few days back," Will said flatly and peered out the window, looking for the sky above the clawing hands and decaying faces, hoping to see the stars.

They all sat in silence for a good while after that.

*

Late in the morning, a nervous, bespectacled man came stumbling up the road towards the southern barricade. With Daltry still recovering in the hospital, Tar had broken out the heavy weapons the sheriff had brought back from the National Guard armory. What began as a fifteen-foot-tall mound of earth was now reinforced with machine gun nests, manned round the clock on each end. A sniper and machine gunner were also placed atop the cliffs on either side of the road. The lessons of the first few costly encounters with hostile groups had taught them much. In the spring, they planned to reinforce the front of the mound with cinderblock, to create a wall. Tar wished they had done it from the start, but with the freeze already upon them, they had to wait for the warm weather or the mortar would fail.

The skittish man made his way nervously towards the barricade, glancing behind him frequently. He moved hesitantly through the labyrinth of disabled cars before stopping at the final car in the row. The Labyrinth was more of a ramshackle arrangement designed to halt any vehicles from approaching, as well as not allow any organized unit to advance in great numbers; it also allowed the gunners atop the cliffs to attack their flanks. Ahead of the nervous man was the kill zone, a gap of three hundred feet with no cover except a dozen barrels filled with fuel-soaked firewood. The man visibly gulped and looked back again before steeling his nerve and coming into the clear of the kill zone.

"You can stop right there," Tar called down from atop the mounded earth.

He'd been summoned about twenty minutes earlier when the man first appeared further down the road. The stranger stopped in his tracks, his gaze coming up to meet Tar's. The man flinched.

"Spit out what you've come to tell us; it's pretty obvious you are on some errand here."

The man gulped and steadied himself, mouth ajar. He hesitated briefly with a confused look on his face before starting.

"Grayson says you got to take down this wall, leave your weapons where they are, and head out of town north, towards Wyoming." The man gulped nervously and added, "He says to tell you that it's the only way any of you get out of this alive."

Having finished his errand, the man started running back towards the relative safety of the automobile labyrinth.

"Should I take him out?" Harold asked, lying out prone with his .50

caliber rifle trained on the man.

"No, that man is no threat; couldn't even say words without pissing himself," Tar said while he chewed on his lip. "I'd guess whoever this Grayson fellow is will do the job for you anyway. Might as well save the bullet."

"Well shit," Harold replied spitting out sideways.

"Everybody keep vigilant. We just had a messenger make a direct threat against all of us," Tar said sternly through his walkie-talkie. "Every warm body with a gun get to the south barricade, now!"

Within five minutes, two dozen men and women arrived. One by one, Tar ordered them into position. Anyone with hunting rifles, he sent atop the cliffs to bolster their sharpshooters. He sent runners to the north, east, and west to make sure everyone was apprised on the situation and ready just in case. The runners returned within twenty minutes, reporting that all was quiet at the other barricades. Then they waited; they waited for hours. Tar was left to think one of three things: either they were being bluffed, carefully flanked, or the attack would come under cover of night. As the hours ticked past, he was left to assume it was the last.

"Okay, if they're gonna hit us, they'll probably do it at night. I want two experienced hunters to patrol the mountains around the pass in case they've got people moving in position to flank us. Every second man can try and rest up where you are; we need everyone alert and ready come nightfall."

Harold and a man named Jethro offered their scouting services. Jethro was a trapper who came in from the wilderness to the northwest of Donner after his family was attacked and killed by the undead. Many of the outlying farmers, hunters, trappers, and homesteaders had either moved into the confines of the walls or had met their end in the unprotected areas outside the barricades. One of the advantages of a small town was that everybody pretty much knew everybody, and those coming in from the farms were all set up in homes of good Samaritans that had freely offered the space.

Harold and Jethro were sent out with binoculars, night vision headsets, scoped rifles, and flare guns. Their instructions were to kill any groups of up to four people in size they encountered, and to use the flare gun and run if they encountered any force larger than that. Tar felt better about their safety with the scouts out there. Harold was a bit of an asshole, but the man was top-notch with a rifle and he knew the terrain. Jethro survived off the land year-round, so there was no doubt about his abilities.

With the orders given out, Tar moved to the tents they had set up at the base of the earthen mound. They were the kind of tents set up for outdoor receptions and were now being used to warm the men. They had dragged in two wood burning stoves and piped out the exhaust. Styrofoam coffee cups littered the area around a table, and a trio of kettles sat atop the far burner. A handful of cots were spaced around the heaters, allowing the weary to get some shut-eye. Tar had initially meant to grab a cup of coffee, but knowing the night they may have in front of them, he chose a cot instead.

He awoke and rose slowly, easing his stiff body into wakefulness. He sat up on the cot, both giving his body a chance to wake as well as listening carefully to anything alarming from outside the tent. After a moment, he stood, arching his back which provoked a series of crackles and pops from his spine. He stretched and twisted to loosen his joints before walking to the tent flap to reveal the dying light of day. He groggily fetched a cup of coffee from the kettle. Boxes of foil-wrapped sandwiches sat on and under the table, bringing a wonderful aroma to his senses. *Bless you, Darla,* he thought as he checked the boxes. Choosing a burger and fries, he sat back down on a cot and ate in peace while sipping his coffee. With a full belly and warmed up from the stoves and coffee, he lit a cigarette as he came out of the tent. He felt mentally ready for whatever the evening had in store for him, even as his stomach flopped about uneasily.

Two hours later, the sky was black and moonless; the stars blotted out by heavy clouds that hung low over the town. A stiff breeze blew in from behind them, whistling in their ears. Still no sign of an attack.

"Maybe it was all bullshit," Bobcat said, sidling up next to him, his collar pulled high to protect his neck from the cold. He held a rifle at the ready.

Tar shrugged in response. It was possible, he thought, but the look on that man's face gave him no doubt that whoever this Grayson fellow was, he was dangerous. For him, it wasn't a matter of if, but it was just when and where they would attack. For the third time in twenty minutes, he peered intently down the road, having heard what he was sure was movement. *Just the wind*, he thought for the third time.

About five minutes later, the wind settled down and the moans of a great many undead came drifting up the road towards them.

"Get some burn barrels going out in the kill zone," he called to Bobcat before grumbling, "Can't see a fucking thing out here."

Bobcat ran into the tent and came out a moment later with a burning log he held with fireplace tongs. He ran to the top of the wall and slid down the steep embankment to the road beyond. Except he didn't hit the road, he slid into a person. The log rolled free of the tongs and disappeared quickly behind numerous shuffling legs. Bobcat was confused for a second until teeth ripped through his jeans and into the flesh of his calf. He screamed in agony and tried to rip his leg free of the bite. Hands grabbed at him from every direction, pulling him down to the ground beneath them as their teeth ripped at his flesh. Renewed agony shot through him as one of the undead bit his thumb off. Bobcat tried flailing free, but there were too many of the things tearing at him. Light from above shone down on in his face. He instinctively flinched from the brightness, and the sound of a rifle report ended his agony.

Atop the wall, the scene before them unfolded; the undead were gathered in the kill zone by the hundreds. The sounds of their moans and shuffling of feet were masked by the wind. Tar shone his flashlight over top of the assembled horde as they began moving up the embankment

"Ho-lee shit," Harold whistled out to the left of Tar.

"Is this a coincidence or...?" Tar asked no one in particular before screaming. "We need some fucking light up here!"

Two teenagers popped up a minute later, one carrying a torch, the other a pair of red plastic gas cans. Tar recognized them as Randy Sickler's boys. The boys poured the contents of the cans down the frozen embankment, filling the air with the acrid smell of gas. Before they had a chance to light it themselves, the fuel hit the smoldering log that Bobcat had dropped. Bluish flames burst forth, tracing in and around the feet shuffling about below as well as the undead climbing up the embankment. The defenders watched in silent horror as dozens of the dead things shuffled amidst the flames, one after another catching fire themselves. The undead were silhouetted by the fire and what remained of their fat burned greasily, adding to the stench of death and excrement in the air. The dead that had been edged out of gorging on Bobcat's entrails moved past the feast, making their way up the burning embankment towards the defenders. Gunshots started ringing out as the men and women defending shook off the initial terror and panic. The burning dead allowed them to see well enough to target.

Next to Tar, atop the mound, Tim Starik flew from his feet, rolling back down the berm towards the tent and vehicles, coming to rest in a terrible mess of limbs. Before he could grasp what had happened, Harvey Tilmore on the other side of him dropped to the ground, rolling backwards to the same fate. Tar whipped his head around furiously trying to decipher this new mystery when a tracer round whizzed past his left arm. His eyes widened in fear as he looked further down the roadway beyond the sea of dead, to see the distinctive muzzle flash of a heavy machine gun. As Tar watched, the occasional tracer round lit through the air as it cut its way across the open terrain towards the barricade.

"Get down! Get the fuck down!" Tar yelled at those around him, hitting the dirt himself.

The machine gun nests tore furiously into the undead as they ascended the embankment, but for everyone mowed down, there seemed to be two to take its place. The flaming undead were inexorably moving up the ramp towards them. As Tar crawled backwards down the ramp, he could see the heads of the first dead appearing over the top the crest of the mound.

It was only luck that a gap in gunshots, Tar was able to hear the squawking of the walkie on his hip. He scrambled down the slope towards the tent with it pressed into his ear, trying desperately to hear what was being said. Finally inside the meager shelter the tent offered, he heard it.

"—east, need reinforcements," screamed through. "I repeat, taking heavy gunfire at the east, need reinforcements."

Fin

CHECK OUT OTHER GREAT ZOMBIE NOVELS

DEAD ASCENT
by Jason McPhearson

The dead have risen and they are hungry...

Grizzled war veteran turned game warden, Brayden James and a small group of survivors, fight their way through the rugged wilderness of southern Appalachia to an isolated cabin in the hope of finding sanctuary. Every terrifying step they make they are stalked by a growing mass of staggering corpses, and a raging forest fire, set by the government in hopes of containing the virus.

As all logical routes off the mountain are cut off from them, they seek the higher ground, but they soon realize there is little hope of escape when the dead walk and the world burns.

CHAOS THEORY
by Rich Restucci

The world has fallen to a relentless enemy beyond reason or mercy. With no remorse they rend the planet with tooth and nail.

One man stands against the scourge of death that consumes all.

Teamed with a genius survivalist and a teenage girl, he must flee the teeming dead, the evils of humans left unchecked, and those that would seek to use him. His best weapon to stave off the horrors of this new world? His wit.

CHECK OUT OTHER GREAT ZOMBIE NOVELS

RUN
by Rich Restucci

The dead have risen, and they are hungry.

Slow and plodding, they are Legion. The undead hunt the living. Stop and they will catch you. Hide and they will find you. If you have a heartbeat you do the only thing you can: You run.

Survivors escape to an island stronghold: A cop and his daughter, a computer nerd, a garbage man with a piece of rebar, and an escapee from a mental hospital with a life-saving secret. After reaching Alcatraz, the ever expanding group of survivors realize that the infected are not the only threat.

Caught between the viciousness of the undead, and the heartlessness of the living, what choice is there? Run.

THE DEAD WALK THE EARTH
by Luke Duffy

As the flames of war threaten to engulf the globe, a new threat emerges.

A 'deadly flu', the like of which no one has ever seen or imagined, relentlessly spreads, gripping the world by the throat and slowly squeezing the life from humanity.

Eight soldiers, accustomed to operating below the radar, carrying out the dirty work of a modern democracy, become trapped within the carnage of a new and terrifying world.

Deniable and completely expendable. That is how their government considers them, and as the dead begin to walk, Stan and his men must fight to survive.